Sittin' On A Goldmine Productions, L.L.C.

info@sittinonagoldmine.co

www.sittinonagoldmine.co

ISBN: 978-1-952739-59-0

MITZY MOON MYSTERIES BOOKS 10-12

PARANORMAL COZY MYSTERY

Lies & Pumpkin Pies

TRIXIE SILVERTALE

CHAPTER 1

THERE'S NO REJECTION more poignant than that of a vending machine from the late 80s spitting out your money with brutality. If the temperature inside this fieldhouse ice rink wasn't subzero, I wouldn't be so desperate for hot chocolate. I catch my bill as it drops and carefully straighten each corner, taking special care to smooth out all the undesirable wrinkles and make my one-dollar bill as irresistible as possible.

Holding my breath, I gingerly feed it into the temperamental machine—for the third time.

Success!

The ancient contraption makes several questionable clicks and groans before expelling a paper cup which teeters on the metal grate landing pad.

I hastily steady it as molten cocoa sprays into the receptacle with surprising force.

Who knew getting a steamy beverage at the broomball arena could qualify as an extreme sport?

The dangerous transaction ends and I retrieve my drink. The rich chocolate aroma lifts my spirits and the heat against my mittens instantly warms me.

The rowdy pregame warm-up is well underway by the time I exit the extravagantly named "snack bar," which consists of three vending machines: sweets, savories, and hot chocolate.

Twiggy waves with uncharacteristic enthusiasm as I cautiously climb the wooden bleachers.

"Sit down. Sit down. You're gonna miss the face-off."

As a film-school dropout, I should warn you that no one will ever be able to utter the words *Face/Off* in my presence and not evoke an instant image of John Travolta and Nicolas Cage.

"So, what am I looking at here?" I gesture toward the aggressive display on the ice.

Twiggy was my grandmother's best friend in life, and is my sole employee at the Bell, Book & Candle Bookshop, which I inherited when Grams passed. I use the term employee loosely, since she technically works for free. She allows me to compensate her with entertainment, which usually features my natural clumsiness getting the best of me, or other forms of public humiliation. The fact that I successfully climbed the grandstand without slipping and spilling my hot chocolate seems to have displeased her.

She kicks one of her biker-boot-clad feet up onto the opposite knee and rubs her mittened hands on her dungarees as she exhales loudly. "Look, kid, it's a lot like hockey, but without skates."

Shrugging helplessly, I'm forced to remind her of a couple things. "Spoiler alert, I used to live in Arizona. Remember? Not a lot of hockey."

Twiggy shakes her head, and her severe grey pixie cut barely moves. "Yeah, I keep forgetting how much of life passed you by. Listen up, I'm only gonna explain this once. Ice rink. Two teams. Five guys and a goalie on each team. This is National League play, so, obviously, they're allowed to wear broomball shoes. The sticks are a modern version of the originals, which were actual brooms with the broomcorn bound tightly with cloth or, later, duct tape. The goal is to get that ball into the opposing team's net. Like hockey."

I scrunch up my face. "Doesn't hockey have a puck?"

"Geez, kid, the point was—object goes in net. Did that hot chocolate cook your brain, or are you always this dense?"

It's not clear how to answer that question without incriminating myself. So, ignoring her question, I return to my favorite pastime: watching Sheriff Too-Hot-To-Handle run around on the ice. If I'm lucky, maybe he'll take off his helmet and I can drool over his tousled blond hair as it falls into his eyes.

That's right, my sort-of-boyfriend is the team captain for the Pin Cherry Harbor Abominables.

A foghorn blasts, and the teams clear the ice.

The overly enthused voice of the announcer crackles from the speakers. "Ladies and gentlemen, and all you little Whisk Leaguers, welcome to the National Broomball Alliance National Championship!"

Something about that title feels as though it was approved by the Department of Redundancy Department. The sport doesn't strike me as one with a big PR team. I almost ask Twiggy about the Whisk League, but when an inordinate number of kids in numbered jerseys start banging on the plexiglass with wild abandon, I go with the obvious.

The announcer continues, "Tonight's match between the Pin Cherry Harbor Abominables and the Koochiching Arctic Arrows will decide the best team in the country!"

The crowd—and, surprisingly, there is an enormous one—roars and stomps their feet against the wooden planks.

"The winner of tonight's match will go on to represent the United States of America in an exhibition match against the Canadian champions!"

The crowd cheers, "USA! USA!"

"That's right, ladies and gentlemen, our boys are going to show those Canucks how it's done! The exhibition match will be played in Montréal in front of the Winter Olympics selection committee. Our fellas are going to take broomball to the Olympics!" The crowd is on their feet. The obsession with this strange sport has deep and thunderous roots.

The players on the visiting team are announced first, and then comes the home team. Apparently, there's a song and everything.

However, I have to admit, when they announce team captain Erick Harper, I stomp my feet right along with the rest of the broom bunnies. If I'd ever learned that cool trick of sticking your fingers in your mouth and whistling loud enough to deafen most humans, I'd certainly be doing it.

The players take their positions on the ice, and the referee holds the ball in the air between the two players who are facing off.

Despite Twiggy's insistence that she wouldn't offer any additional explanation, she happens to mention that these two men are the centers.

The ball drops and the brooms fly!

The play is exceptionally invigorating. Our boys are running down the ice, passing the ball back and forth, when a moose-size man from the Arrows checks our forward into the boards so hard his helmet comes off.

Erick, number 10, races across the ice and checks the Moose, knocking him backward with a shocking crash.

The referee's whistle blows, but the crowd is screaming for blood and the adrenaline on the ice is ready to deliver.

The two assistant referees join the fray and pull the men apart. Whistles screech and penalties are awarded.

Erick and Moose are sent to their respective penalty boxes.

Play continues with each team down a man.

The first half ends without further incident, and with the Abominables in the lead. Play during the second half becomes desperate, and two more fights break out.

"Why is Erick getting involved in so many fights?"

Twiggy beams with pride. "He's the muscle."

I have no complaints about his muscles but don't understand what they have to do with the fighting. I say none of this to Twiggy; however, the look on my face must show my confusion.

"He takes care of his team. If the other team pushes his guys around, he pushes back, harder." Her bloodthirsty grin is unnerving.

"Oh, he's like the mother hen."

She snickers and slaps her leg. "Yeah, you be sure to say that to him, kid."

The game ends, and the Abominables take the title. Fans storm the rink to congratulate the players. The smell of victory is in the air, and there's a huge celebration on the ice.

I scan the sea of puffy jackets and stocking caps, but when my eyes land on number 10, there's no rejoicing.

Erick and Moose, helmets off, are having angry words and Moose has a handful of Erick's jersey.

Just when I think things couldn't get worse, short

and squat Deputy Paulsen toddles out onto the ice, in uniform, to break up the fight. With her tendency to draw her gun at a stiff breeze, I sincerely hope she doesn't shoot Erick.

"I gotta get down there, Twiggy. You don't need to wait. I'm sure Erick can drive me home. Thanks for introducing me to broomball." I raise my hands and make little explosion gestures next to my head. "Mind blown."

She shakes her head and clomps down the bleachers to join the festivities.

My foray into ice-based celebrations begins with a stream of polite "excuse mes," but quickly devolves into a snowplow and shove strategy. When I finally break through the crowd, the view is less than desirable.

Deputy Paulsen is threatening to arrest everyone, and Moose and Erick are in an intense shoving match. Moose temporarily gets the upper hand, and Erick goes down hard.

"And stay down, Harper." Moose spits on the ice. "Out here, you're nothing but a punk. Your badge is useless in the rink." A trickle of angry spittle clings to Moose's thick black beard.

Testosterone and adrenaline swirl together to create a dangerous concoction.

The sheriff fires up off the ice, and a left hook lands hard on Moose's face.

Moose teeters backward and crashes down with a thud of finality.

Erick leans over the mountain of a man and shouts, "I don't need a badge to take you out. Nobody takes cheap shots at my team. You better remember that on and off the ice—if you know what's good for ya."

My eyes widen. I've never seen Erick so angry, but his instinct to protect his teammates is no surprise.

Paulsen grabs his arm and drags him toward an exit. "You're drawing quite a crowd, Sheriff. You better quit while you're ahead."

The heat of the moment fades and his shoulders sag. It's clear that he's not proud of what happened, but when his young teammate with a broken nose, courtesy of Moose, slides over and pats Erick appreciatively on the back, I can hardly blame him for taking care of his guys.

Outside the tight throng of spectators, the ice is far more slippery than it looks. Apparently, those broomball shoes have some serious mojo. Within seconds of my renewed attempts to reach Erick, my feet are circling like those of a cartoon character, and I land abruptly on my backside. Lucky for me, I've built up enough padding back there to avoid any serious injury.

The commotion catches Erick's attention, and he wrenches his arm free from Paulsen's grasp. "Moon, are you okay? What are you doing out on the ice? A fragile desert flower like you shouldn't be mixing it up with these broomball hooligans." The tenderness in his blue-grey eyes reminds me of the gentleman lurking inside the Abominables' enforcer.

He carefully scoops me from the ice, and I reach up to push his blond hair back from his sweaty face. "Congratulations. Moose will think twice before he comes after any of your teammates again."

Erick scrunches up his face and shakes his head. "Moose?"

"Oh, that's the nickname I gave the big guy you were fighting with."

"We weren't fighting. It's part of the sport."

"Whatever you say, Sheriff." I bend to retrieve my dislodged stocking cap, eager to cover my haystack of snow-white hair, and the slipping starts anew.

Erick steadies me. "Let me get that for you." He grabs the hat and places it on my head like a caring parent.

"Can you also give me a ride home, kind sir?"

He chuckles and pulls me close. "It'll cost you." His words are accompanied by a mischievous wink.

My tummy tingles. "I can pay. I'm a rich heiress, remember?"

He leans down and whispers warmly next to my cheek, "Money can't save you, Moon."

I struggle to get air in my lungs as my face turns a dangerous shade of crimson.

He points toward the entrance. "You can hang out in the snack bar. I'll come find you as soon as I get changed."

"Copy that."

His broad shoulders shake with laughter as he heads into the locker room.

What can I say? The phrase is one of the few things that "stuck" from my months of on-set experience in the fast-paced world of filmmaking. As a production assistant it was my job to do whatever was needed as quickly as possible, and "copy that" was the way to let the powers that be, on the other end of the walkie talkie, know that I was on top of things. If it ain't broke, don't fix it.

Erick is unusually quiet on the drive from the fieldhouse to my bookstore, and my natural snoopiness fails to see the benefit of patience. "What's up? Aren't you happy your team won the championship?"

He nods and taps his thumb rhythmically on the steering wheel of his squad car. "Yeah. The guys worked really hard this season, and they deserved the title. But, now that the thrill of the win has faded, I'm feeling a little foolish for letting Klang get the best of me."

"Who's Klang?"

A soft grin spreads across Erick's face. "The guy you called Moose."

"Oh, that guy." I want to mention how shocking it was to see him in a fistfight, but clearly his own conscience is already berating him enough. "Is he gonna be all right? I mean, he'll definitely have a black eye. But other than that, he's not seriously injured, right?"

Erick shrugs. "He's a big boy. I'm sure he'll be fine." His tone carries less bravado than his words.

He turns down the alley and stops by the heavy metal side door leading into the Bell, Book & Candle. "Breakfast tomorrow morning? At Myrtle's Diner?"

I twist in my seat and stare. "Always, but don't you want to come in or something?" There's honestly not much I can offer him in my mini-fridge and microwave-equipped back room, and I'm not feeling brave enough to directly invite him up to my swanky apartment.

"Nah. Thanks, though."

My disappointment must be more obvious than I intend.

He reaches over and clasps my hand. "It's not that I wouldn't enjoy a nightcap, Moon. I've got a lot on my mind. I'm gonna head out to the icehouse on the lake and fish a little before I call it a night. I'll see you at breakfast." He leans over the center console and gives me a quick peck on the cheek.

"Yeah, sure. It was a big night. I'll see you in the morning." I jump out of the cruiser before I can say or do anything to embarrass myself.

He politely waits while I fish my keys out of my coat pocket and fumble with the lock. Once I'm inside and the door has closed behind me, the sound of his engine fades as he backs down the alley and drives away.

Note to self: work on flirt game.

"Oh, I'm sure it's not you, dear."

"Grams! The rules! If these lips aren't moving, you don't get to comment. Stay out of my head, woman!" Maybe I'm overreacting, but my heart is racing and my bladder is quaking.

The late Myrtle Isadora smooths her silk-and-tulle Marchesa gown with one bejeweled hand, while she checks her manicure and ignores my reminder.

To be clear, my recently deceased grandmother didn't actually cross over. Her ghost is permanently tethered to this bookshop that she left me in her will.

"All rules aside, dear. You know how Erick feels about you. I'm sure there's some other reason he couldn't come in for a nightcap." Her ethereal hand rubs my back, and I find a strange otherworldly comfort in the gesture.

Arching an eyebrow teasingly, I offer my hypothesis. "One reason might be that I can't offer him an actual 'nightcap' since you won't allow me to store booze on the premises."

"Alcoholism is no joke, Mizithra." She clutches one of her strands of pearls and scowls.

"I know, Grams. One day at a time . . . and all that. I respect your struggle, but now that you're a ghost, shouldn't I be allowed to have a bottle of wine or two on standby?" I bat my eyelashes and my big grey eyes beg for leniency.

In true diva fashion, she ignores my question. "How was broomball?"

I bring her up to speed on the crowds, the cocoa, and the fights. "I better hit the hay. I have to be up, and functional, at an unmentionable hour to meet Erick for breakfast. I should've offered to bring him midmorning donuts instead."

"Sweet dreams, dear." She snickers as she fades through the wall into the printing museum.

She doesn't need to read my mind to know what I'm hoping to find in dreamland . . .

CHAPTER 2

THE STIFF BLACK hairs of my semi-wild caracal's tufted ears tickle my nose. "Really, Pyewacket? Was it absolutely necessary for you to wake me up five minutes before my alarm?"

"RE-ow." Feed me.

"Yes, Mr. Cuddlekins, your *command* is my command." I dig myself out from under the luxurious down comforter and search for my slippers. Reindeer onesie pajamas are all fine and good, but I won't last long with bare feet in this weather. An Arizona girl like me is used to high temperatures and dry air, and the brutal winters in almost-Canada are still a bit beyond my comfort zone.

Stumbling toward the plaster medallion that opens the secret door from my apartment, I trip over my fiendish feline, and narrowly escape a fall. "Pye, if you want me to serve up your Fruity Puffs, then at least clear a path for me to make it downstairs in one piece."

He calmly ceases his twisting around my legs and waits patiently while the door slides open. His understanding of the English language is impressive, and my grasp of the subtleties of *caracal* continues to improve.

The early morning light lacks the strength to penetrate the depths of the bookstore. Shadows linger in the curves and corners. As I trudge across the Rare Books Loft, a strange unease settles on my shoulders. Stopping halfway to the wrought-iron spiral staircase, I slowly turn and survey the neat rows of oak reading tables. None of the green-glass lampshades are aglow, and when I reach out with my extra senses, I don't feel anything suspicious.

"Maybe I still have one foot in dreamland, Pyewacket. You'd let me know if there was an intruder, right?"

"Reow." Can confirm.

I'm still figuring out what it means to be a psychic, and I don't always interpret the messages correctly. The magicked mood ring my grandmother left me is somehow responsible for triggering my latent abilities. However, as mood rings go, it's exceptionally cantankerous. The swirling mists within the black cabochon can be quite helpful, but only when they choose to be.

At the bottom of the winding staircase, I risk stepping over the "No Admittance" chain. Thankfully, the universe is smiling down on me today, and I manage to make it to the other side without tripping and falling.

Once I've squared away Pyewacket with a generous portion of his favorite sugary cereal, I brew myself some wake-up juice. As the welcome scent of java fills the back room, I reflect on my new book-filled world.

One thing I don't miss about my life below the poverty line in the Southwest is working as a barista. Don't get me wrong, I love coffee. I can't imagine starting my day without a proper cup of black gold, but I prefer to order it at the diner, which is named after my grandmother and run by her first ex-husband. This little sip of go-go juice is designed to keep me from climbing back into bed and skipping my breakfast appointment with Erick.

I trudge upstairs with my cup of coffee and dress with my eyes half closed. Ghost-ma's absence is surprising, but I've barely got enough time to run down the block to the diner as it is. I'll search for her in the adjacent printing museum when I return.

The lessons I learned the hard way during my first winter, on the shores of the great lake that graces this region, have served me well. I've layered my clothing, tucked my scarf inside my jacket, and pulled my stocking hat down over my ears. My thick mittens make it impossible to send Erick a text, so I jog to stave off hypothermia and hope to arrive before I'm officially late.

I push open the door of Myrtle's Diner, and the smell of breakfast embraces me as I stomp my feet back to life and wave to my surrogate grandfather.

He peeks through the red-Formica-trimmed orders-up window and gives me his usual spatula salute.

Walking toward the corner booth, I'm surprised to see it empty. I slide onto the far bench so I can see the door and wave to Erick when he comes in. Although it hardly seems necessary, since the sole occupants of the restaurant are two locals at the counter and me.

My favorite waitress, Tally, slides a steaming mug of java onto the table along with a small melamine bowl of individual creamers. "Mornin', Mitzy. Did you hear about the storm?"

Since moving as far north as I have ever ventured in my life, I've learned that the hot topic of conversation in the winter is always the next storm. "I hear it might be worse than the blizzard in '84."

Tally puts a hand to her aproned chest and gasps. "You don't say? Well, I better run to the Piggly Wiggly after work and stock up on canned goods."

I nod and smile. I don't have the heart to tell her I was joking and actually have no knowledge of the legendary snowstorm of 1984.

After several satisfying sips of my coffee, my girlfriend senses and my extrasensory perceptions join forces. Something is definitely not right. First of all,

Erick is never late. However, if he was going to be unavoidably late, he would absolutely text me.

Fishing my phone out of the large pocket of my puffy coat, I double check to make sure I didn't miss a message.

Nothing.

Odell strides out of the kitchen and places my breakfast in front of me. "Somethin' wrong?"

I drag my eyes away from the phone and stare at him for a moment. The grey utilitarian buzz cut speaks of practicality, and the deep lines of his face hold a lifetime of stories.

"I was supposed to meet Erick. It's not like him to be late."

He nods. "Not like him at all. You get started on your breakfast. I'm sure he'll walk through that door before you finish."

Our eyes meet, and I grin. "Um, have you met me?"

His coarse laughter warms my heart. "Ya got a point." Odell raps his knuckles twice on the silver-flecked table and returns to the kitchen.

Halfway through my scrambled eggs and chorizo, the mood ring on my left hand shudders with an icy warning.

Gazing down, the face of Deputy Paulsen stares back from the swirling cabochon.

Now, that's one way to ruin my appetite. I pick at the perfect, sacred home fries, which would normally be scarfed down without hesitation, and push my plate away.

Taking a last, desperate glug of coffee, I collect my dishes and tuck them in the bus bin behind the counter. Old habits die hard.

Waving goodbye to Odell and Tally, I slip my mittens back on and continue down Main Street to the sheriff's station.

Deputy Baird is manning the desk and, true to form, she's deeply involved in a game on her phone.

She barely looks up when I walk in, but nods her head anyway.

That is the official signal, which allows me unescorted access to Erick's office.

I push through the crooked wooden gate, inhale the scent of burned coffee, and walk across the empty bullpen. As I approach the sheriff's office, a knot of resentment forms in my stomach. Based on Furious Monkeys' head nod, Erick is sitting at his desk. Why didn't he text me?

I'm working up a wronged-girlfriend speech as I turn the corner into his office. Imagine my surprise, and immense disappointment, when I discover Deputy Paulsen occupying his chair.

Caught off guard by her unwelcome presence, I blurt the first thing that pops into my head. "Erick isn't in here."

The portly deputy makes a show of searching under several stacks of papers on the desk and inside her coffee mug. "Nope. Not in here."

I shake off her reply. "Obviously. Let me rephrase my question, Deputy. Where is Sheriff Harper?"

She leans back in Erick's chair and fixes me with a self-satisfied grin as she jerks a thumb over her left shoulder. "Back in the holding cells."

I openly roll my eyes as I offer an insincere thanks and head down the narrow hallway. You may wonder how I know my way to the holding cells? Let's say that I've been there before, not as a visitor, and leave it at that.

Why was Paulsen looking so smug? She's probably soaking up the glory of sitting in the sheriff's chair. Ever since he defeated her in the last election, I've questioned her loyalties. Erick is always the first to say what a good cop she is, but one has to wonder. I push through the metal door at the end of the hallway and search the small passageway.

Maybe she was gleeful about sending me on a fool's errand. I definitely don't see Erick standing outside any of the cells. Maybe he's checking on a prisoner. "Sheriff Harper? Sheriff, are you back here?"

The hairs on the back of my neck lift in warning and I swear there's a soft groan.

Sounds like someone in pain. What if he's hurt?

Racing down the short drab corridor, I skitter to a stop in front of the middle holding cell. "Erick? What are you doing in there?"

My normally freshly scrubbed and shaved boyfriend is camped on the cold metal bench, head in hands, with a hint of stubble peppering his jaw. "I wish I could say I was glad to see you, Moon. I'm sorry I didn't call to cancel breakfast—they took my phone."

I grip the grey steel bars with both hands and pull my face close to the cell. "Who took your phone? What's going on? You're not making any sense."

He leans back against the cinderblock wall, and that's when I notice that there's no badge pinned on his uniform. The two empty eyelets shout a deadly warning.

My extrasensory perception offers a single clairaudient clue. "Murder." Suddenly, this morning's flash of uneasiness makes perfect sense. "Who was murdered?"

Erick's weary blue-grey eyes snap to attention. "Did Paulsen fill you in?"

I throw my arms up in the air. "No! No one is filling me in, including you. Would someone please tell me what's going on?"

"Gerhardt Klang's body was discovered outside the service entrance behind the ice rink this morning. The Zamboni driver comes in early to prepare the ice before the figure-skating lessons. He didn't recognize the victim. But when Paulsen and I arrived on the scene, and I realized who it was, I had to take myself off the case." His monotone voice belies the storm brewing beneath the surface.

"All right. You recused yourself. That kind of makes sense, but why are you sitting in a jail cell without your badge?"

"A lot of people saw the two of us fighting last night. They also heard me threaten the victim." Erick runs a hand through his hair and attempts to scrape the long bangs from his eyes. "Once Paulsen confirmed the ID of the victim and the deputies found my bloody jersey in the laundry bin, she asked me to surrender my badge and gun. She's holding me for questioning until she gets the ME's report."

I kick the bars with the toe of my snow boot and grimace at the unexpected pain. "Classic Paulsen, always overreacting and eager to arrest everyone. You're the sheriff. Can't you pardon yourself or something?"

Erick sighs heavily and slowly gets to his feet. He walks to the bars and reaches one hand through.

I slide my hand in his and get an immediate clairsentient dose of his uncertainty. "Hey, we both know you didn't do this. You're not a murderer. I'll look into things. You said it before, my hunches can be surprisingly accurate. I'll figure out who actually murdered Klang, and you'll be out of here in no time."

He squeezes my hand. "Thanks for believing in me. I don't think Paulsen honestly suspects me, but the evidence isn't in my favor right now. It's not a good idea for me to be seen poking around this case. I don't want any rumors of impropriety. It's probably for the best if I stay in here until someone clears me."

"Don't worry, *someone* will do exactly that. Mitzy

Moon is on the case." At least my grandstanding brings a weak smile to his lips.

I pull him closer and kiss him through the bars. "I'll bring you some lunch."

He stares at me with admiration. "Thanks, Moon."

CHAPTER 3

DURING THE BRISK walk back to the bookshop, I risk removing a mitten to place a call to my attorney, who also happens to be a powerful alchemist. I put the call on speaker and get my glove back on before frost-bite claims a digit. “Good morning, Mr. Willoughby.”

His sigh offers no indication of whether I’ve met his standards of etiquette. “Good morning, Mizithra. What is it you require?”

Busted. Although, I can’t imagine why it offends him that my calls tend to coincide with when I need something. He should feel proud that I trust him so completely that it never occurs to me that he might not be able to help. However, his tone indicates he doesn’t see it that way. “Silas, I’m sorry to bother you, but Erick is somehow in jail for the murder of some broomball player named Gerhardt Klang. Paulsen is having a field day holding him for questioning, but you and I both know there’s no way he did this.”

"Certainly not." Silas harrumphs. "Gerhardt Klang is an archeologist of considerable notoriety and a tenured professor in the anthropology department at the local community college. I was not aware he played sport. What evidence places your sheriff under suspicion?"

"All circumstantial. Erick got in a fight with the guy at the broomball game last night, and, in the heat of the moment, he kind of made some threatening statements." I swallow and add an afterthought. "Oh, and there was blood on Erick's game jersey, but that had to be from the fight."

Silas grumbles on the other end of the phone.

"What is it? That didn't sound like a good grumble."

"A powerful motive carries a degree of heft. I assume you'll be wanting a copy of the medical examiner's report."

"You couldn't be more correct, Mr. Willoughby."

"Very well. I will officially offer my services to Mr. Harper, and, acting on his behalf, obtain a copy of the ME's report as soon as it becomes available. Is that satisfactory?"

"That's completely awesome. I'll dig into this case and see what else I can find out. Any idea why Klang would play for Koochiching county's broomball team even though he was a professor at Birch County Community College?"

"I am afraid I do not follow the ins and outs of the Great White North's broomball league. I believe your best resource on that subject will be Twiggy."

"Copy that. Keep me posted, Silas."

"Indeed."

Ending the call with my mentor, I take a quick detour into the cul-de-sac on Main Street, beside the bookstore. The cold came early, but the snow is late. This combination allows for the formation of impossible ice walls and waves along the shore of our great lake.

Some of the fins and swirls are almost transparent, while others hold the whites of glacial milk. My desert-based childhood never prepared me for such a deep attraction to the cycles of water—the beauty of floes. It would've been amazing to visit this place with my mother. The tragedy of losing her when I was eleven hurts as freshly as if it were yesterday.

Wandering down memory lane causes me to lose track of time. Only the chill threatening to nip off my nose ends my reverie and turns me away from the harbor.

The thick wooden door at the front of my bookshop, with its intricate carvings of magical vignettes, is unlocked.

Twiggy is in the house.

Hurrying to the back room, I find her hunched over the keyboard of our ancient computer.

"Are you working on the weekly order?"

Her fingers abruptly stop and the chair sweeps around to reveal the irritated face of my volunteer employee. "Is that your idea of a joke, Your Highness?"

Oops. Time to do some serious backpedaling. "Not at all. I was legitimately asking. If it's not too much trouble, I need another skein of green yarn for the murder wall. You know we can't have red, because it reminds Grams of blood and gives her a fright. I don't want to be accused of scaring any ghosts."

This jab at my grandmother brings a chuckle, and Twiggy nods her head appreciatively. "I wish I could see her, you know. You and Silas are lucky. You got the gift, and he's got those transmuted spectacles he's always bragging about. You say her ghost looks about thirty-five, eh? She was in her sixties when she passed, and, of course, she'd been sick for a couple years . . . Sure would be nice to see her looking young and full of life."

This unusually verbose speech from Twiggy catches me off guard and I nearly forget what I came for. "Yeah, I wish you could see her too. She looks great in that fancy dress, with all her rings and strands of pearls."

Twiggy shakes off her brief foray into emotions like a dog drying his coat after a dash into the lake. "Anyway, you musta wanted something before I went on a trot down flashback drive. What can I do ya for?"

Her folksy twist brings a smile despite my agitated state. "Gerhardt Klang was murdered last night. I'm—"

"Boy, oh boy! Good thing Harper's got a badge. If not, he'd be my number one suspect." Twiggy cackles and slaps her thigh.

The color drains from my face and I struggle to find the right words.

Her eyes widen. "You can't be serious? That devil of a deputy! How could she think for one minute—?"

"Well, she does. Erick is sitting in a holding cell right now waiting for a time-of-death ruling from the medical examiner. I need to dig into this, Twiggy. Everyone's always saying that Paulsen is a good cop, but we both know she's had her eyes on the sheriff's chair for quite a while."

"I'm your gal. Erick's the best lawman this town has had in decades. What do you need?"

"I probably need to know more about the victim. If I can understand him, hopefully I can figure out who else had a motive. I mean, who has *the* motive."

Twiggy leans back in the cracked, brown-leather office chair and crosses her arms. "Shoot."

"All right, first off, why did Klang play for the Koochiching Arctic Arrows if he was a professor at BCCC?"

Twiggy lets out a low whistle. "That is not a short story, doll."

Pulling out a weather-beaten wooden chair from

under the small table, I take a seat and match her pose. "I've got nothing but time."

By the time Twiggy finishes breaking down the finer points of the various rivalries and secret alliances amongst the teams, I'm shocked to still be awake.

"So, to shorthand it, Klang is an arrogant so-and-so, and only wanted to play for a team that he could captain?"

She nods curtly. "That's the gist of it."

"What do you know about his day job?"

Twiggy sniffs and shrugs. "Not a thing."

"Great. How am I going to find out why a bigwig professor, in the prime of his life, is teaching at a community college in almost-Canada?"

Twiggy shivers uncontrollably. "Isadora? Is that you?"

Grams pops into the visible spectrum with a mischievous grin. "Tell Twiggy it's me, and everything's fine, and then—I have an idea!"

Tilting my head toward Twiggy, I confirm her suspicions. "What's your idea, Grams?"

She rubs her ethereal hands together gleefully. "You could go undercover at the community college!" She shrieks with glee, throws her hands in the air, and spins like a dervish.

"Grams thinks I should go undercover as a BCCC student."

Twiggy groans and shakes her head. "Let's agree

amongst ourselves to call it 'the college.' It's the only one around; not like there'll be a lot of confusion."

"Understood. What do you think about her plan?"

"Might as well. I'll work my contacts in the broomball league and you can make nice with some students."

My shoulders droop and I flop forward, banging my forehead on the table. "The things we do for love. I didn't enjoy college the first time around. Hooray for second chances."

Grams swirls around the room, spouting off addendums to her astonishing plan. "I'm sure you can use the same name you used before, Darcy something. Technically, you never went to the college even though you were posing as a college student . . . but that was at the high school. Never mind. The name's fine. I'll start working on wardrobe. You'll have to get Silas to mockup some identity papers. You're starting right before Thanksgiving break, and you'll need to have transfer paperwork or something."

"*Mamma Mia!*, Grams. Simmer down. I'm pretty sure this is one of those situations that can be easily handled by a large donation. And, if it happens to go to the anthropology or archaeology department, it seems like that might make the perfect *in*."

Twiggy stands and rakes a hand through her short grey hair. "They'll need a temporary professor."

"Silas!" The three of us shout in unison.

Grams works on wardrobe and backstory, while I

make a quick phone call to Mr. Willoughby to confirm that he has the necessary background to teach the archaeology classes while the community college searches for a replacement for Professor Klang. Was there ever any doubt? He also has an idea how to grease the wheels for my late-semester enrollment.

I reach up to pull the candle sconce lever, which activates the sliding bookcase door to my secret apartment, and smile. If anyone had grabbed this heartbroken kid as she was bouncing from one foster home to another and told her what the future would be like, she probably would've punched him in the nose and called him a dirty liar.

I stride across the thick Persian carpets in my beautiful apartment toward the walk-in home for a collection of vintage clothing—a place I like to call wall-to-wall *Sex and the City* meets *Confessions of a Shopaholic*—and whisper, "Progress looks good on me."

"What's that, dear?"

"Nothing. Wondering what you plan on forcing me to wear, and whether or not we can negotiate a heel in the two-inch range?"

Grams giggles mercilessly. "If you want access to the best gossip, you gotta have something other people want. And everybody wants designer handbags and Jimmy Choos."

"I'm sorry I asked."

"Nonsense. Let's go with the blonde-to-russet ombré wig, the distressed designer jeans, with Jimmy

Choo boots and this Mark Jacobs satchel. You can pretend it's a book bag."

"Yes, Mistress."

Her ability to affect matter at will is nonstop now. She's grabbing clothes and shoes from their resting places, tossing them wildly onto the padded mahogany bench in the center of the walk-in closet.

I wiggle my toes into the carpet, dreading a full day in high heels. "Can't I be the cool geeky kid who wears skinny jeans, high-tops, and ironic snarky T-shirts that say things like 'Wanted: Dead & Alive—Schrödinger's Cat'?"

Grams freeze frames and her image flickers like an old VHS tape.

"Grams? What is it?"

"Mizithra Achelois Moon, I did not break my promise to your father, and spend the last months of my life filling this closet for you, to have you simply toss it all aside for *skinny jeans*."

"Sorry, Grams." However, her comment gets me thinking. "I'm going to run across the alley and check on Dad. He was supposed to get back from the railroad convention in New York two days ago, but I haven't heard from him." I slowly back out of the closet.

"You'll be trying all of this on as soon as you get back, sweetie."

"Yes, Mistress."

Her tinkling laughter echoes off the tin-plated ceiling as I make a hasty retreat.

CHAPTER 4

THE DUNCAN RESTORATIVE JUSTICE FOUNDATION is open for business and the kind young woman seated in the reception area is either guessing, based on the bone-white hair my father and I share, or she has a reference photo of me next to her computer.

I'm sure I've never met her before, but as I stride across the terrazzo floor, temporarily distracted by the life-size bronze of my grandfather, Cal Duncan, she calls out a greeting.

"Hello, Mitzy. Your father is in the penthouse. Would you like me to announce you?"

"Sure. Also, I forgot my passkey."

She smiles politely, but her eyes are flecked with suspicion.

Definitely as sharp as she looks. I don't actually have a passkey. It's not that I asked for one and my father refused; it never occurred to me to ask.

"No problem, Miss Moon. I'll program the elevator to take you to the penthouse floor."

"Wow! Hi-tech. Thanks."

I enter the marble-clad hallway and step into the plush elevator. Everything is so shiny and new, even the buttons have a posh glow.

The melodic ding of the bell precedes the door sliding open to reveal the towering figure of my father. "Mitzy! I've been so busy since I got back. Sorry I didn't call."

"No problem."

He wraps his powerful arms around me and kisses the top of my head, as I close my eyes and grin from ear to ear. I'm still getting used to the idea of having a dad. So far, I like it.

Amaryllis walks out of the back room with her hair in a haphazard bun, wearing a thick bathrobe and fuzzy unicorn slippers. A hint of camphor and eucalyptus wafts down the hall. "Don't come any closer. I caught a nasty cold while we were in New York and I definitely don't want you to get it. So, I'll say hello and goodbye from a distance and let you and your dad catch up."

"Thanks for the warning. And I love your slippers."

She chuckles, which causes her to launch into a coughing fit, waves goodbye and shuffles back into the bedroom.

Dad and I walk into the kitchen and he motions

for me to grab a seat at the breakfast bar while he brews us some coffee.

"So things must be pretty great with you and Amaryllis if she's comfortable being sick around you?"

Jacob's broad shoulders shake with laughter. "Yeah, things are wonderful. She was a real trooper in New York. She loaded up on decongestants and coffee to get through our meetings, but by the time our plane touched down in Pin Cherry, she was ready to collapse. I've been catching up on emails and playing nursemaid for the last couple days, but she deserves it."

He sets my coffee on the polished black granite counter and places one hand on his refrigerator door. "Cream alone, right?"

"You know me so well."

We share a chuckle, and he nods. "I'm getting better. I remember our first lunch, when I attempted to share your french fries."

"Rookie mistake, Duncan."

He laughs and passes me the creamer. "So, what's new in Pin Cherry?"

Pouring a little milky goodness into my java, I watch it swirl. "Unfortunately, Erick is sitting in a jail cell suspected of murder."

"What? Sheriff Harper is a suspect?" My father tilts his head in disbelief.

I quickly explain the details of the situation and the unfortunate broomball fight.

Jacob's expression turns serious. "Broomball is no joke around here. The rivalries are brutal."

"Did you play?"

He nods and takes a deep breath. "I played intramural in college, but I preferred the speed and violence of hockey when I was a kid."

I arch one eyebrow. "Well, good news. Broomball has significantly upped its violence quotient."

"So what's your angle on this case?"

"Hmmm? What makes you think I have a case?"

His head drops and lolls from side to side. "Come on, Mitzy. I may be new to this dad thing, but I know enough to be certain you've got a plan to clear Erick's name."

"All right. Ya got me. I'm going undercover as an archaeology student at the college. Silas will be the temporary replacement professor, so between the two of us, we should be able to uncover some additional suspects."

"Sounds like a pretty good plan. Let me know if there's anything I can do."

"Thanks, Dad. I will. However, I have to get back. Grams—" My eyes widen and I lower my voice to a whisper. "Does she know about Grams?" I point meaningfully to the bedroom. "And me seeing ghosts and stuff?"

My father shakes his head. "It doesn't come up naturally, you know?"

My thoughts immediately turn to Erick. "I know

better than you think. Anyway, I have to get back and endure a wardrobe session with, *you know who.*"

His smile is everything. "Trust me, I have many reasons to be happy that I was born a *son* and not a daughter."

I chuckle knowingly as I step into the elevator.

"Oh, Mitzy, do you have plans for Thanksgiving?"

I've never actually had plans for Thanksgiving in my entire life. I shrug, and as the doors slide closed, I reply, "I don't think so."

My stomach tingles as the elevator drops. Plans for Thanksgiving? I never imagined myself thinking about something so domestic. I certainly won't be hosting anything at the bookshop. A mini-fridge and a microwave don't scream gourmet kitchen. Maybe I should ask around?

Passing through the lobby, I give a friendly wave to the receptionist.

In an effort to postpone my appointment with fashion destiny . . . I believe this community college student needs to do some back-to-school shopping!

The phrase ignites a series of sweet childhood memories. Before my mother was killed, and I became a perpetual foster child, August was our traditional spree. Cora Moon was a fiercely independent single mother, forsaken by her family, but determined to raise her daughter with every advantage. She would save whatever she could from the two or three jobs she was juggling, and we would spend a whole evening planning out our route.

At the time, I had no idea that shopping at second-hand stores could be frowned upon by certain segments of society. I felt like a princess. On one glorious Saturday in August, we would make our way to anywhere from five to ten second-hand stores and thrift shops in our search for clothes, shoes, and the occasional amazing backpack. I always felt so special. I had a mountain of new clothes and an entire day of my mother's time, which was the best part. I didn't understand how precious it truly was.

Once I entered the foster system, school shopping became a distant memory. I had my handful of well-worn items, and, possibly, if I had severely outgrown them, I would be allowed to purchase something new. Generally, I received hand-me-downs from the biological children or older foster children in the same home.

Cut to—

Grams severely over-indulging my clothing needs with a designer dream closet.

A quick trip over to Rex's Drugs for a notebook or two seems to be in order. I wave through the window of the diner as I hurry past, coat zipped tightly against the weather.

The bell dings when I enter the drugstore, and an elderly woman with a beautiful mountain of snow-white hair piled atop her head offers a friendly wave. "Welcome to Rex's. I'm the missus. Rex passed away several years ago." Her warm smile continues to beam, and she pats her carefully pinned beehive. "You and I have the same stylist." She laughs and slaps her hand on the counter.

My time in this small, friendly town has changed me. A year ago, I would've thrown a fake smile her way and dove between the aisles without a word. However, I've grown accustomed to this slower pace of life and learned firsthand the benefit of friends. "Were you born a snow princess like me, or did you have to earn it?" This comment brings uproarious laughter from Mrs. "Rex."

"Oh my, you are as sharp as everyone says. Of course, you must be Mitzy Moon. Not a lot of folks with that hair and those hips in this town."

My smile wavers as I consider the "hips" comment. Backhanded compliment or folksy banter? Not that it matters. I'm not operating under the mistaken impression that I resemble a string bean. "That's me. I'm actually here for some stationery supplies. Where are your pens and notebooks?"

She points with her left hand. "You'll find all that stuff in aisle three. And if you don't mind a seasonal theme, there are some sheets of spring-flower paper on sale."

"Thank you kindly." I meander down aisle three and peruse the selection. Since I'm not an actual student, I don't actually need *anything*. But she's sweet, and I'm sure Twiggy will figure out what to do with whatever I buy. I grab three notebooks, two packs of ink pens, a roll of tape, and a handful of spring-themed sheets. On my way to the counter, I notice a little rack of books. Maybe Erick would like some reading material. The fact that I own a three-story bookshop, bursting at the seams with volumes, does not prevent me from buying the latest best-selling mystery novel for my incarcerated boyfriend.

"I'm glad to see you picked up some of the spring paper. It's a great price and you really can use it year 'round." She rings up the sheets and slips them into a bag. "Well, these pens are very nice. Blue and black. That's such a good idea. You know they're erasable?" She slips the pens into the bag.

"Oh, they're erasable. That's good." I suppress an eye roll.

"You know, I think this tape is buy one, get one at fifty percent off, if you want to grab another roll."

I don't feel like I have the option to say no. "Oh, great. I'll go grab another one right now."

She waits patiently for me to return with the second roll of tape. She doesn't ring up a single thing in my absence.

"So that's one full price and a second roll at fifty percent off." She taps in the price of the two rolls of tape—longhand—and adds them to the bag. "You'll love these notebooks. The pages tear out smooth, so you don't have all those little fidgety bits all over your nice carpet."

I nod and smile.

"Oh, I've heard good things about this book. You

must read a lot of mysteries, with all the sleuthing that you do."

Dear Lord baby Jesus! Does this woman know everything there is to know about me? And is she going to finish this transaction anytime this century? "It's for a friend."

She leans across the counter and lowers her voice to a conspiratorial whisper. "I heard about Sheriff Harper being in the clink. I tell you what, I've known that boy since he was knee-high to a grasshopper, and he wouldn't hurt a fly! The thought." She shakes her head in dismay.

I clench my teeth and double-down on the smile. At long last, the purchase process comes to a close. I hand her my cash, because cash is king in Pin Cherry. Almost no one takes credit or debit cards. I've learned that the hard way.

"Well, you let Erick know we're all pulling for him, sweetie."

"I sure will. Thank you so much."

The frosty air waiting for me outside is a welcome cool down. Clearer heads and all.

I'm suddenly struck by the urgent need to visit Erick and update him on my plans. Plus, I promised him some lunch. I better run and place my order before the rush hits.

When I pop into Myrtle's Diner, Odell already has an order of meatloaf and mashed potatoes packaged to go.

"Thanks, mind reader."

He smiles briefly. "Anytime." His expression hardens and he shakes his head. "You let him know, we're all pullin' for him."

Nodding, I beat a silent retreat.

No one questions my return to the station, so I head to the cells without hesitation. The color of the walls seems as though it was chosen specifically to drain one's will to live.

Erick's stubble is a little scruffier and his mood has definitely soured.

"Hey, I thought I'd stop by with your lunch and give you an update."

He nods. "There isn't one."

I maneuver his takeout through the bars and set the trade paperback on top.

He doesn't budge.

"It's meatloaf from the diner, and I got you some reading material. Also, I'm supposed to let you know they're all pulling for you." I withdraw my hand and offer a weak smile. "There might not technically be an update on the autopsy, but Silas has agreed to represent you and I'm going undercover at the community college to see if I can find any additional suspects."

Erick is too exhausted to muster appreciation.

I happen to know firsthand how frustrating it is to be accused of a crime you didn't commit, but I'm a little surprised he's so depressed. "Erick, why are you letting this get to you? You're the sheriff. You're on the right side of the law. You know how this works. We get the medical examiner's report, we confirm the time of death, and your alibi takes you off the list. You're in the clear, and Paulsen will be forced to do some actual investigating and find another suspect."

He leans against the bland beige bricks and the muscles in his jaw flex with tension. "It's not gonna be that easy, Moon."

"Why not? Of course it will be that easy."

"I don't have an alibi."

"What? I'm sure your mom heard you come home last night, right?"

His silence is unsettling.

Quick side note: he bought his mom a house when he got back from his second tour in Afghanistan to repay her for all her years of hard work as a single parent, making sacrifices to raise him right. Now he lives with her and takes care of her. It's extremely sweet and seems like a built-in alibi. I'm confused by his lack of faith in his mother's hearing. "Erick, what aren't you telling me? You dropped me off, and then what?"

"I went out to the icehouse to fish. I was upset about the fight with Klang, and knew I wouldn't be able to sleep. I lost track of time. There was a bottle of bourbon in the ice chest. Long story short, I didn't think I should drive home."

"You slept in the icehouse?"

"I slept in the icehouse. I had barely pulled into the driveway this morning when I got the call about a body at the rink. I ran inside the house, changed into my uniform, and wound up in this cell. So—"

"So, no matter what time Klang was murdered, you'll still be a suspect." I grip the bars and let my head rest against the cool metal tubing. "I can be your alibi."

He looks at me as though the distance across that small cell is a vast ocean. His eyes are a mix of gratitude and disappointment. "I would never ask you to lie for me, Moon. I appreciate the offer. I do. But I didn't kill him, and there's gotta be another way to prove that."

"Silas and I will find something. You know me. I never give up."

At least my words bring the hint of a smile to his strong jaw. "Yeah, I know. I'm also curious to see your disguise."

For the first time since he landed in the cell, there's a tiny spark of life in his eyes.

"No problem, Sheriff. Darcy Brown starts school tomorrow. If you're still in here, I'm sure she can bring you some dinner." My efforts finally pay off and he enjoys a hearty laugh at my expense.

"Looking forward to it." He locates the motivation to take two strides and retrieve his meal.

My heart hurts for him.

He picks up the sack and leans to meet me through the bars. "Thanks, Moon."

Our lips meet in a forlorn excuse for a kiss.

"You know, I always did like a bad boy, Harper."

My lame attempt at humor barely rates a half grin. The flash of levity vanishes and the weight of his situation once again settles over him.

Deflated, I turn to leave. "See ya tomorrow, Sheriff."

The crinkling of a paper sack is my only reply.

CHAPTER 5

My dreams, or rather nightmares, are filled with various unnerving possibilities for Klang's death. In each scenario, Erick plays the bloodthirsty murderer and Klang the helpless victim. I finally tear myself from the grip of my horrible imaginings and snuggle against the warmth of Pyewacket, curled up beside me.

In the faint glimmer of dawn's first light, Pye studies me with a look that says he senses my agitation. He pushes his broad head against my hand and purrs softly.

"Don't take this the wrong way, Pye, but if this is what is meant by 'for better or worse,' I'm not sure I'm cut out for it."

"Nonsense, dear."

My heart seizes up in my chest, and the fears from dreamland are suddenly palpable. "Grams, again, I beg you to use the slow, sparkly reentry. I haven't slept at all. I'm a nervous wreck. Plus, I feel super guilty because a teeny-tiny part of me almost believes Erick is guilty."

"That's perfectly natural, Mitzy. Deep down, you know that Erick didn't do this, but you saw another side of him at the broomball arena. Accepting all of him is a process."

"What if I can't do it? What if I'm only attracted to gorgeous, kindhearted, generous Erick? What if I can't accept his shadow side?"

"I wish I had the answers, sweetie. But let's not forget, I had five husbands and more than a handful of special friends. I'm not sure I ever stuck around long enough to get to know anyone's shadow side. The closest I ever got was probably with your grandpa Cal, but even then I cut bait before anything was truly resolved."

"Great. My lone source of relationship advice is from a serial short-term monogamist."

She exhales sharply. "You don't have to say it like it's such a bad thing. I do have a lot of experience with getting relationships off on the right foot."

"Hooray." I raise my arms in a weak, halfhearted cheer. "I might as well get up and do some investigating before class. There's no point lying here and imagining the worst."

Grams pumps her translucent fist in the air. "That's the spirit. Get out there and prove Erick's innocent."

Hardly able to muster the enthusiasm to change

into my going out in public clothes, I can't begin to share Grams' excitement.

After bundling up against the freezing early morning temperatures, I pour my fur baby's breakfast and drive over to the arena.

There's already a truck in the parking lot, and when I try the back door, it's unlocked.

"Hello. Hello. Anyone here?"

The thrumming of an engine and an unpleasant scraping sound echo from the rink.

I thread my way through the back passageway and peer out of a doorway toward the ice. Not that I would know, but the enormous machine skimming across the ice like a polar lawnmower must be a Zamboni. The driver can't hear me, and I'm pleased to take the opportunity to snoop around unhindered.

There are two separate sets of locker rooms. One set appears to be public locker rooms for men and women, and the other is private locker rooms for the Abominables and the She-bominables. The guys' team got the better end of that naming scheme.

I try the door on the team's locker room and, since the handle turns, I take it as an invitation.

Inside the blue-and-gold shrine to the Abominables are the expected bank of lockers, each displaying a player's last name, but also a surprising number of amenities. A huge freezer filled with bagged blocks of ice and three stainless-steel whirlpools. Looks like they could be filled with either hot water or ice-bath therapies, based on the piping. I don't have a great deal of first-hand sporting experience, but I'm a walking Wikipedia of film and television. I've seen plenty of players forced to soak their aching joints in tubs filled with ice. I'm sure it helps, but it's definitely one more reason I have no interest in being a team player.

Each of the blue metal lockers is secured with a combination lock.

Except Harper's.

His lock is missing.

Noted.

A huge malodorous canvas cart with a metal frame and industrial-size wheels is solidly packed with used terrycloth towels and equally abused jerseys. I can't imagine the deputies took the time to stuff the dirty laundry down tight. That means that Erick's bloody jersey was right on top.

Also noted.

Moving on.

Other than the surprising cleanliness of the showers and the relatively mild stench in the rest of the locker room, there is nothing else to report.

As I step out of the changing room, the ominous silence is hard to miss.

Uh oh. Sounds like the Zamboni driver has finished, and without the guiding hum of the engine to pinpoint his location, my mind spins in search of a cover story as I return from whence I came.

One thing my vast media knowledge has taught

me is that looking guilty and running are two of the worst possible ideas.

My casual stroll toward the back door is expectedly interrupted.

"Hey, what are you doing in here? The rink doesn't open until six."

"Oh, there you are. I heard the machine, and then I got all turned around. My little Billy is crazy about ice-skating, and one of the other moms told me this is the place to get lessons. Is there a sign-up sheet or a list of available coaches?"

Luckily, my ditzy mom routine works like a charm.

"Look, lady, I'm sure your little Billy is going to be the next Michelle Kwan. The rink opens at six. Students and coaches will be here at *six*."

How convenient that this crabby old cuss is more concerned with making me feel stupid than determining my true purpose.

"Thank you so much! I will absolutely come back at six and see if I can get Billy signed up. Sure do appreciate the information. Have a wonderful day."

He grumbles under his breath as he turns toward the locker rooms.

Heading to the back door, I pause to inspect the lock.

One of my foster brothers taught me more than any girl should know about picking locks, and this one isn't particularly difficult. However, the person who forced their way into the arena didn't bother using a lock pick and tension wrench. The strike plate shows clear signs of forced entry. Seems like something even Paulson would've noticed.

I cannot wait to get my hands on those reports.

Back at amateur sleuth headquarters, Ghost-ma is swirling frantically around the apartment. She's pushed the rolling corkboard we affectionately call the murder wall into the middle of the room and she's had the audacity to make a card for Erick.

"Myrtle Isadora Johnson Linder Duncan Willamet Rogers! How dare you accuse my boyfriend of murder!"

"Listen, dear, you're the one who taught me how the murder wall works. For now, he's a suspect. He absolutely has a connection to the victim. It's your job to find the actual killer and clear Erick's name. My job is to put the cards on the board."

"Oh brother." I stomp into the closet, peel off my wonderful comfy clothes, and strap in to the wardrobe of ace archaeology student, Darcy Brown.

"You really are becoming an expert with wigs, Mitzy. You got that thing in place and securely fastened with bobby pins before I even had a chance to offer suggestions."

Her praise brings a smile to my face. "I had an excellent teacher."

She presses her hand to her bounteous bosom and a little tear sparkles in the corner of her eye.

"Don't you dare start crying, Grams. You and Pyewacket hold the fort while I go shake down some community college students." I give my wig a little tug and fluff the ends. "I promised to take Erick his dinner after school, but when I get back we'll recap my first day. Wish me luck!"

"You won't need it, dear. Everyone's going to love you."

I cross my fingers and hope that her statement results from an afterlife clairvoyant message, rather than the inclinations of a love-is-blind grandmother.

The Birch County Community College is not what I expected. The underwhelming architecture consists of rows of square buildings around a central greenbelt. However, the *quantity* of square buildings does not fail to impress.

Parking my Jeep in a visitor's space, I follow the signs to the registrar. The week before Thanksgiving has taken its toll on staffing, and many of the desks in the open-plan office area stand empty. I approach one of the service counters where a forlorn student worker scrolls through her phone in an effort to stave off boredom.

"Excuse me. Hi, I'm Darcy Brown. Today's my first day. Could you print out a schedule for me, or something? I'm an archeology student, but I think it's part of the Anthro Department here."

The girl's large brown eyes roll upward to meet my gaze. She swallows and stares. Her lack of a verbal response is perplexing.

I place a hand over my mouth, look around the space, and double-check my info. "Am I in the wrong department? Classic me. First day and I'm already making an idiot of myself. Please point me toward wherever I'm supposed to go, and I'll vanish."

She blinks twice. "You're starting today? Next week is Thanksgiving."

Yikes, I've captured a live one. "I know, right? Leave it to me to pull up roots and transfer at the weirdest possible time. It's totally the worst."

Something I said sparks her interest, and it appears I'll finally get the help I'm seeking. She leans toward me and lowers her voice. "I'm supposed to send people over to the kiosk, to print out their own schedules. But that stupid thing is always on the blink. I'll print one for you, real quick." Her fingers fly over the keyboard and, as the printer springs to life behind her, she finds even more words. "Oh, the anthropology department is in the science building, straight across the quad from us, and to your left two buildings. Do you want to buy your books before class? Some people like to buy them and try to impress the professors, and some people wait until after they get the syllabus. Do you know what you wanna do?"

"I have no idea. Like, I don't even know if I'll stay in this advanced class, or this town. I mean, my grades are good, but who's ever heard of Birch County?"

Her initial facial expression indicates I've offended her, but as her eyes take in my glorious hair and designer satchel, she changes her tact. "You don't have to tell me. This place has got to rank at the bottom of the list of best party schools, you know?"

I share one of my best fake giggles as she hands me my schedule.

She points to the class at the top of the list. "It looks like your lecture ends at 11:30. If you want to swing by, I can show you what to avoid at the cafeteria."

Taking the sheet of paper, I paste on a big smile. "Thanks. That's super nice. I have no idea how aggro my professors will be about me transferring so late. So, if I have, like, a mound of assignments, I may have to skip lunch. Thank you so much."

Slipping the useless schedule in my Marc Jacobs bag, my psychic senses confirm that the persona of Darcy Brown is working in my favor. Maybe Grams was right about the power of the bling!

After one wrong turn, I find the lecture hall where a "Mr. Willoughby" is taking roll.

He looks up as I enter and effortlessly masks any response.

While I attempt to descend the stairs as quietly as possible, in four-inch heels, the professor runs a finger down his roll sheet.

"Either you are Darcy Brown or Rebecca Jankowski."

Typical Silas. Even the simplest statement carries the threat of a trap.

I drop into the nearest empty seat and reply, "I'm Darcy Brown. I don't have my textbook yet, but if you have an extra syllabus, I'm sure I can pick it up this afternoon."

He harrumphs into his bushy grey mustache, and the fluorescent lighting bounces off his bald head as he peers up the stadium seating in my direction. "I think you'll find that in an advanced class, such as this, we will rely far more on field experience than texts." He selects a potsherd from a tray on the counter next to his podium and holds it up. "Who can tell me about this?"

An eager girl in the front row adjusts her messy updo and raises her hand.

Silas refers to something on his podium, most likely the roll sheet. "Yes, Miss Rey."

"That is a shard from an Anishinaabeg water vessel. Circa 1600s. The fragment displays the classic Anishinaabeg symbol for water." She leans back and smiles.

"Incorrect." He exhales and glances around the hall. "Miss Brown, please come down to the front."

Looks like I'm destined to be teacher's toy, rather than teacher's pet. My heels click down the steps, and three of the girls sitting in the front row, including Messy Bun, make no effort to hide their shoe envy.

"Hold out your hands, Miss Brown." The now familiar scents of pipe tobacco and denture cream accompany the command.

I do as I'm told, and Silas drops the broken bit of pottery into my palms. His milky eyes fix me with a meaningful stare. "What can *you* tell me, Miss Brown?"

Clearly, that simple phrase is code for, "Tap into your extrasensory perceptions, Mitzy." Time to impress the cool kids. I grip the shard in both hands, take a deep breath, and focus on the piece of history. "Yucatán Peninsula. 500 to 550 CE. Mayan. A ceremonial vessel used for blood offerings." The image that provided that last thread of information turns my stomach, and it's a genuine struggle to keep from dropping the sacred piece of history and running.

Professor Willoughby holds out his hand and I return the fragment.

Having had more than my share of experiences with Silas and his mysterious ways, I return to my seat without waiting for confirmation. This wreaks havoc on the calm disinterest of the front-row girls.

Messy Bun blurts, "Is that right? Is she right, Professor?"

Silas sets down the remnant and smooths his mustache with a thumb and forefinger. "Indeed. Algonquin pictographs tend to be syllabary, while Mayan glyphs are modular. Each hieroglyph contains several elements, as Miss Brown accurately deduced."

Messy Bun and her friends whisper and shoot me suspicious looks.

"She just got lucky. If I'd been able to hold it in my hands, I'm sure I would've been able to tell that the symbol wasn't Anishinaabeg. It really wasn't a fair test, Professor."

The subtle tilt of Mr. Willoughby's cranium tells me all I need to know. "Very well. Come forward."

Poor thing, she's in over her head.

Silas selects a piece with delicate carving, despite its heft, and a large green accent stone, and places it gently in her hands. "What can you tell me of this?"

She glances at her cohorts and gives a smug grin. "It's a Chinese carving. Liang Dynasty. 502 to 557 CE. Most likely a wedding gift. This elongated jade piece attached to the top is a fertility symbol." She hands the carving back to Silas.

"Incorrect. You may return to your seat."

Her eyelids twitch, and the rasp of her dry swallow reaches all the way up to the fifth row.

"Miss Brown, will you return?"

Once again I walk to the front of the room, and Silas places the carving in my hands.

An odd heat trickles up my arms and a series of ancient rites race through my head in a clairvoyant montage. "It is a form of jade, nephrite. However, it's known by the name greenstone, or pounamu in the Maori tongue. This item is a ceremonial adze. It's an item belonging to the chief, passed from father to son, marking rank and power in their society. This particular carving is from the time known as Classic Maori Material Culture, in New Zealand, 1400 to 1500 CE." The images of war and struggle tighten my throat and I'm unable to continue. I pass the powerful artifact back to its current caretaker.

The flood of information doesn't cease. Instead, as I grip the counter to steady myself, the words "deadly secret" throb in my skull. Unsure whether they're tied to the object I was reading for Silas or something else, I swallow uncomfortably and hurry back to my seat.

Messy Bun raises her hand.

Silas waves her hand away. "Miss Brown is correct on all counts. While the debate still rages over Polynesian versus Chinese influence on early Maori culture, this adze is a remarkable example of the carving style unique to the tribes of New Zealand."

He turns and writes three separate book titles on the whiteboard. "Take the last ten minutes of class to divide into three groups. Each group will present a critique on one of these volumes tomorrow."

Hands shoot up in the air, and whispers and grumbles spread across the lecture hall.

Silas picks up his tray of artifacts and exits through a back door.

The students, including me, are left staring at each other in speechless frustration.

Messy Bun and her two wing-women race up the steps toward my seat. "Darcy, do you want to be in our group?"

Back in the days of friendless foster care, my rules about protecting myself would've prevented accepting this offer. I would've tossed out a snarky response and marched out of the room, not much caring whether I had an assignment to turn in. But I'm here to prove my boyfriend's innocence, so I'll have to swallow my pride and pander to the lowest common denominator. Welcome to Mitzy 2.0!

I muster up some enthusiasm and reply, "Really? That's super sweet of you. Like, I don't know anyone, and I'm so worried about this project. I would totally love to be in your group. Thank you so much."

My two afternoon classes are entry-level science courses, and I don't bump into any of the students from the morning's advanced class.

No additional messages are delivered from the ether, and I make a firm decision to avoid these classes in the future. This way lies madness, and a dead end.

The road to information runs directly through Messy Bun and her cohorts. The best plan of attack is to lure them in with my fancy clothes, and then pump them for information while they're distracted by my accouterment. I have no idea if Klang's actual killer is associated with the college, but *this* archaeology student is definitely on a dig!

CHAPTER 6

BEFORE I MEET my super-awesome prehistory group at the dormitories, I barely have enough time to take Erick an early dinner.

There's no deputy at the desk when I enter the sheriff's station, and the overall feeling in the air is heavy and somber. So much so, that even someone without benefit of psychic perceptions could pick up on the negative energy. I head to the holding cells and am surprised to find Erick clean-shaven and in civilian clothes.

"What happened? Do I smell lavender? Was it prisoner makeover day?"

My tendency to use humor as a coping mechanism has the desired effect, and a weak smile flickers on his handsome face. "Not even Deputy Paulson can stop Gracie Harper."

"Are you saying that your mom was here? I thought she couldn't drive?"

"Oh, she can't. Her vision is atrocious." He shakes his head. "However, she went door-to-door in her neighborhood, make that *our* neighborhood, telling each and every one of the neighbors how I had been wrongly accused and was being held under horrible conditions, until one of them offered to drive her into town."

I hold up the paper sack containing a burger and fries and shrug. "Well, this makes my delivery seem pretty pathetic."

He strides across the cell and his hand lunges through the bars. "Is that a bacon cheeseburger? Please tell me that's a bacon cheeseburger."

"You know Odell would never disappoint you."

He eagerly takes the sack and mumbles several thank-yous under his breath as he returns to the metal bench seat to enjoy his meal.

"Silas left me a voicemail—"

Erick's assault on the french fries ceases. He looks at me and raises an eyebrow.

"Let me finish. He said the medical examiner had released her report but that I would probably want to talk to you about the findings."

He nods and picks up the pace of his chewing.

"Look, I'm not gonna spoil your dinner. Take your time. Enjoy your delicious burger and let me tell you about my day."

He swallows loudly. "Yeah. I definitely want to hear about college, and, if I didn't say so, that wig is amazing."

I primp the long, wavy ombré locks. "Why, thank you, Sheriff Harper."

He resumes the attack on his burger, and I bring him up to speed on my archaeology lecture, how Silas performed as a professor, and the cool kids clamoring to be in my group project. And, for once, our timing is perfect.

He wipes his mouth as I finish my tale. "So, this group project . . . You have to do that tonight?"

"Oh, yes. I have to head back over to the dormitories and hang out with Brooklyn, Hutton, Kaden, and at least three others, to put together a critique of the late professor Klang's fascinating book, *Norse Expansion in the New World*."

Erick chokes a little on his sip of soda pop. "Are those people's names or places?" He wipes his mouth and shakes his head. "Man, I do not miss college."

"They're names. I'm starting to feel like being named after a ball of Greek cheese is too basic."

He grins. "Never."

Brushing away his compliment, I ask, "Did you go to BCCC?"

"Nah, back in the day, my mom scrimped and saved and insisted that I go to a big state school down south. It was fine, but I honestly learned way more useful skills while I was managing personnel and battle strategies in the Army."

"Hey, what's this 'back in the day' nonsense? You're not that much older than me, but that sounds a lot like my experience. The fantasy of film school was a solid five stars, but the reality was barely a two-star experience."

His easy laughter warms my heart. "So, you could say it was a 'would not recommend'?"

"Can confirm."

The momentary levity fades, and Erick walks back toward the bars to hold my hand while he shares the rest of his news. His voice carries too much worry. "About the ME's report—"

I tilt my head. "The medical examiner's report will help us. Whatever she found gives me more to work with."

"Oh, you'll have plenty to work with. The report was basically inconclusive. Cause of death was most likely blunt-force trauma to the occipital, that's the back of the skull."

"Hey, I know where the occipital bone is. I'm a crime-TV junkie, remember?"

"Of course. Anyway, the rest of the injuries, superficial bruises and cuts, were deemed the result of the broomball fights. Technically, the blunt force trauma didn't appear to be fatal, but with his history of concussions, it could be the cause."

"Could be the cause? So they don't even have a confirmed cause of death and you're still sitting in this cell! Oh, Silas is going to hear about this. We're getting you out of here."

He shakes his head. "Don't bother. The last thing I need is to be sitting at home explaining to my mom why I can't be involved in the investigation." He exhales dejectedly. "Plus, the report hypothesizes that the blunt force trauma is a result of the victim's skull impacting the ice at the rink."

"Wait! So they're still trying to pin this on you?"

Erick nods and squeezes my hand. "If that punch is what killed him, then I have to be held accountable."

"But they're not even sure if the ice rink is the murder weapon."

He laughs bleakly. "An ice rink as a murder weapon. I never thought I'd live to hear that phrase."

I shrug. "You and me both. I think it's a bunch of baloney! It wouldn't be the first time that the medical examiner has made a mistake. In case you don't remember, she miscalculated the time of death during the investigation of my grandfather's murder. That little gem almost landed me in jail!" I throw my free hand in the air in frustration. "Silas is representing you, right?"

Erick knits his brow in concern, but nods.

"Perfect. The defense is going to demand a second autopsy. And the Duncan-Moon Philanthropic Foundation is going to make a hefty donation to Sheriff Erick Harper's defense fund. We're going to bring in the best forensic pathologist money can buy."

"That fancy foundation is just you, right?" Erick pulls me toward the bars and plants a soft kiss on my cheek. "Glad you're on my side, Moon."

I flip my luscious wig over my shoulder and kick

out a hip. "Yeah, you're real lucky. Don't you forget it, Sheriff."

His chuckle sounds hollow as it echoes off the cold brick, but I know an exit line when I hear one.

Next stop, the Piggly Wiggly to obtain proper snacks for an all-night study sesh.

The grocery store is relatively empty, and, since I'm in disguise, I get a full greeting from the checkout clerk rather than the locals-only head nod.

"Welcome to the Pin Cherry Piggly Wiggly. Can I help you find anything?"

"I'm good."

Grabbing a handbasket, I head to the snack aisle and load up with a variety of salty options. I finish off the basket with a couple bags of bite-size chocolate candies and grab a twelve-pack of caffeinated beverages as I walk toward the checkout.

When I arrive on campus, it takes a few passes around the quad to locate the signs for Manone Hall. Finding parking is an even bigger challenge.

The freezing temperatures mean that all spaces close to the dorms are taken.

I end up parking almost two blocks away. My "win" is that I don't have to lug my two bags of groceries through any snow. The big storm is coming—according to all the locals—but it's not here yet.

Of course, the front door of the hall is locked. Seems obvious now.

There's a nifty key card scanner to the left of the glass door, but I don't have a card.

Before I die of frostbite, a too-friendly jock returns from some sport or other and gallantly holds the door for me as I babble on about losing my stupid key.

"If you get lost again, I'm in room 239." He winks salaciously and jogs away.

I think we both know I'm too much woman for that little guy.

Fortunately, the elevator doesn't require a key card. Stepping out on the third floor, I search for room 333 and knock tentatively.

The door flies open, and laughter and loud music spill forth.

"OMG!" Brooklyn glances over her shoulder, tugs at her messy blonde bun, and announces, "Darcy's here, and she brought hella snacks, yo!" She turns back and grabs one of my bags. "Come on in. Grab a chair or a bunk."

I slip past her and flop onto an over-sized purple beanbag. This apparently qualifies as a chair. I have to remind myself that not everyone has a ridiculously wealthy Ghost-ma and a swanky apartment filled with fine furnishings.

"Darcy, your boots are like the best thing in life right now!" Hutton widens her kohl-rimmed eyes and drools over my footwear while Brooklyn tosses bags of snacks to eager hands.

Ainsley reaches down from the top bunk and her half purple/half mermaid-green textured bob temporarily covers her face. She catches a pack of cheese puffs, and sighs dramatically. "These are everything.

I'm doing a no-carb thing right now, so cheese is like my savior."

Far be it from me to point out that there is basically no cheese in a cheese puff. Let the skin-and-bones girl have a night off. Time to pour on the *Darcy*. "Stop. You guys are too much. These boots are totally over."

Brooklyn drops onto a zebra-print throw on the bottom bunk and rips into a bag of white cheddar popcorn. "I can't believe you brought so much grub. Do your parents give you a massive allowance or are you a Visa-card kid?"

Neither. I'm a rich heiress that can see ghosts and receive secret psychic messages in my magicked mood ring. Don't worry, I don't say that. Instead, I fan myself with one hand and say, "Massive allowance."

Ainsley and Hutton exchange a wicked grin. "Lush!"

The group is smaller than I expected. "I thought there were some dudes in our group. What gives?"

Brooklyn rolls her eyes, throws herself back on the lower bunk, and exhales sharply. "Ainsley is having a spasm about pretty-boy Kaden, so he's out. Tayton never misses hockey praccy, and he says we owe him one for some free tickets, or whatevs, and then there's Bodie . . ." She starts giggling.

The wonder twins join in, until the snickers reach a maniacal pitch.

I pop open a soda, take a slow sip, and wait for

the hilarity to die down. "What do I need to know about Bodie?"

Hutton is the first to catch her breath. She pushes her thick auburn curls back and winks. "He's got a med card, you know?"

First I'm hearing of this Birch County policy. "Like, for weed?"

Ainsley shoves another handful of puffs in her mouth and nods furiously. "Yeah, he's like totally useless."

The bad news: fewer suspects for me to question. The good news: these chicks can't keep their mouths shut.

It doesn't take a psychic to predict that these three will easily spend the rest of the evening gossiping, leaving me without a paper to turn in to Mr. Willoughby. Even though I'm only pretending to be a student, I find failure unacceptable. Time to push my agenda.

"So, like, what's the deal with Professor Klang? The reason I transferred to this school was because of him. Is this new guy any good?"

The trio exchanges a conspiratorial smirk, but the unofficial spokesperson, Brooklyn, takes the question.

"Um, Special-K, that's our secret name for him, was like the hottest professor ever. He came from an Ivy League school, or whatever. He was super smart and stuff, but mostly he was so plush."

They collectively swoon.

If you can't beat 'em, join 'em. "Right? That's my

whole deal. I was hoping to transfer in and get a TA position, or find some other reason to stay after class." I flash my eyebrows suggestively and struggle to ignore the nausea in my gut as I join in their lascivious chuckles.

"Yeah, even though Bodie is AFK like eighty percent of the time, the other half of the time he was always sucking up to Special-K." Hutton scrapes her wavy locks back into a casual ponytail and pulls a scrunchy off her wrist to hold the hairdo together.

For all you non-gamers out there, AFK stands for "Away From Keyboard." Sadly, there's no time to correct her 80/50 math. Out of nowhere, my *moody* ring envelops my left hand in an icy chill. I glance down and, as the wisps of black mist clear within the glass dome, the image of a cow crystallizes. The image alone doesn't mean a whole lot, but my clairaudience picks up on the word *Ainsley*. Now I need a clever segue.

"What about you, Ainsley? Were you hot for teacher?"

She blushes and shakes her head in an entirely non-committal maneuver, but she avoids any eye contact.

Brooklyn pipes up with the truth. "No. Little miss farm girl is fully hot for Kaden. The only reason she even changed her major to archaeology was to be in more classes with her all-American hero. Obvs." She nods knowingly and rolls her eyes.

Ainsley throws a stuffed Pachimari down on

Brooklyn and exclaims, "Shut up, B! It's not like that."

I hastily interject some reason. "Why does Brooklyn call you 'farm girl'?" Hopefully I'm on the right track.

Ainsley brushes the mermaid-green bangs out of her eyes. "My dad's like a big-deal dairy farmer. Brooklyn thinks it's hilarious to mention it at every possible opportunity. It's not like I live there now, you know? I live in the dorms like everyone else. I don't milk cows before I go to class anymore."

Brooklyn presses a fuzzy purple pillow to her abdomen and laughs uncontrollably. "Anymore!" She attempts to add to her clever quip, but her giggle fit prevents any further brilliance.

Yeesh! Can I get some useful information? "Were you guys close to Special-K?" Hopefully using their lingo will strengthen our budding bond.

Hutton's face grows somber, and she wipes an invisible tear from the corner of her heavily lined eye. "He was so gorgeous, you know? It's so cringe that he's, like, dead and stuff."

Oh brother! She and Grams would get along great. The horrible tragedy of handsome people dying! "What happens to his special projects? I was really hoping to get in on an active dig, you know?"

My extrasensory perception hums as Ainsley leans away from the group, and the sensation of her fear of discovery thickens the air.

"Ainsley, is everything all right?"

She peeks over the edge at Brooklyn for permission to speak and gets the nod. "The six of us were like his archaeology Defenders. He was going to take us all on—" She breaks into tears and can't finish.

"How did he end up in Birch County? I heard he was a professor at Princeton or something?"

Brooklyn squeezes the pillow snug against her midsection. "He was the youngest professor ever to be named department head at Durham. Then the whole Kensington Runestone thing completely crashed his rep. At least they, like, gave him the option to resign, but he couldn't get hired anywhere after that. I guess he knew someone up here, or whatevs. So he got hired at BCCC—but he was still salty about the conspiracy, you know? He was, like, badmouthing those British people and claiming that one day he would prove the runestone was on the right track, even if it was a hoax."

"On the right track? What does that mean?" I lean toward Brooklyn, perhaps too eagerly.

Ainsley's energy shifts deeper into the vibration of fear and panic.

Brooklyn moves to the chair at the study desk and gives her a nearly imperceptible headshake. And I say nearly imperceptible, because obviously I'm perceiving things on more levels than they can imagine. That was an unmistakable hush gesture from the Queen of the hive.

I push a little harder. "Seriously, what are you guys talking about?"

Hutton risks stepping into her own power. "He was, like, super obsessed with finding evidence of Vikings and stuff in North America."

I point to the book on the floor between us. "So this Norse expansion book . . . It's all theoretical?"

Ainsley whispers, "At the time."

Brooklyn snatches the book from the floor and grabs her laptop. "Look, it's late and we have to turn in this paper, like, tomorrow. The three of us already pretty much know this whole book by heart, so let's knock this thing out and crash. I need a solid six or I'll have wicked eye bags."

The sensation of finality floods through the room.

I'm definitely not going to get anything else tonight. I'm proud of myself, though. I made an impressive start and I have some juicy tidbits to work on.

To be fair, Erick is stronger than I give him credit for, and he'll figure out how to hang on while I find the truth. I'm desperately hoping that the truth points a nice clear finger at someone else. There's no place for blurred lines in this investigation.

CHAPTER 7

GHOST-MA HAS DONE a bang-up job of setting up the murder wall. As I lounge on the settee and write out cards for each of Special-K's ring of Defenders, I wonder if there are any additional broomball rivalries I should investigate. It seems unlikely that a bunch of kids killed a professor they worship. However, I'm not ready to write them off just yet. Any potential suspects, besides Erick Harper, are worth further scrutiny in my book.

I grab the tacks and put the six new names on the corkboard. Using the green yarn, I connect them all to Gerhardt Klang. A handsome man, by all accounts, in his early thirties with a towering form in peak physical condition. Not sure about the heavy beard, but maybe it was a nod to his Viking obsession.

As I conjure up a variety of scenarios hypothesizing the size and strength of his attacker, my fiendish feline leaps onto the coffee table and silently deposits a piece of plastic.

"It's a little late to be logging things into evidence, Pyewacket." I reach toward the stretched remnant from a clear plastic bag and attempt to decipher the logo, or what remains of it, between the puncture marks of my wildcat's teeth.

There's a distorted image of a grinning cartoon polar bear and the words, "HILLY BEAR?" I stare at Pyewacket and shrug. "Sorry, big boy, I got nothing. I'll keep it in mind though."

Morning comes far too soon, and the prospect of finding Darcy another knockout outfit does not entice.

"Don't worry, dear. I've got everything handled."

Sitting up, I rub the sleep from the corners of my eyes and scowl at Grams through half-raised lids. "Lips not moving. Ghost get out of head."

"Understood, sweetie. When you're ready, I have a lovely outfit laid out for you in the closet."

Oh brother! I can't believe the apparition-entitlement I have to endure. Not even a half-hearted apology?

She clears her ethereal throat, and I glare a warning.

After splashing some cold water on my face and throwing a thick robe over my pajamas, I'm greeted by my impatient caracal.

He drops into a casual seated pose and looks away, too above it all to beg for human assistance.

I receive his silent message loud and clear. "Yes, Master."

Stumbling down the spiral staircase, I feed the beast and brew a cup of coffee to tide me over. Silas agreed to meet me for breakfast at Myrtle's before we take our separate vehicles to the college.

Back upstairs in my "super closet," Grams has laid out a pretty bangin' outfit. The black skinny jeans slip nicely into a pair of riding boots, which will be far easier to walk in than yesterday's footwear selection, and the silk thermal shirt will keep me extra warm, while being carefully hidden under my cashmere boyfriend sweater.

The thought of "boyfriend," even in relation to a sweater, conjures images of Erick. Our private forensic pathologist should have the second-opinion report today, and I sincerely hope it clears Erick.

Time to get some yummy in my tummy.

Silas gives a brief nod as I enter the diner, and Odell offers his standard greeting through the orders-up window. My news about the special group of six students that served as some sort of secret archaeology club doesn't carry the shock I'd imagined.

Silas smooths his grey mustache and nods. "That fills the gap between what I know and what I assumed."

This guy is always talking in riddles. "Maybe I need another cup of coffee, but can you explain?"

Silas harrumphs. "After the lecture, I took the liberty of searching Professor Klang's office. He had an unusual number of locked cabinets for a community college employee. Several contained unremarkable items, such as manuscripts in progress, rare texts, and a journal. However, an entry in the journal led me to seek out a hidden compartment in his desk. That compartment contained an artifact of Norse origin."

"Well, he did literally write the book on Norse expansion. Is it so strange that he would have an artifact?"

"In this instance, yes. Unless I am severely mistaken, this particular unicorn-horn-and-meteorite chalice was part of a traveling exhibit that originated from a small dig on the eastern shores of Newfoundland."

"Unicorn horn? Is that a joke?"

Silas waves away my disbelief. "It has since been shown to originate from the tusk of a narwhal, but the 'unicorn horn' was thought to possess powerful magic."

"So you think this relic is stolen? Are you saying Klang was some kind of art thief?"

"I do not believe that is exactly the scenario. In fact, it is far more likely that he was either part of the team that uncovered the original site, or he may have purchased the item with some of the grant money he received before the Kensington Runestone disgrace. Additional research is required."

I take a long sip of my perfectly brewed wake-up juice and savor the warm liquid as it trickles down my throat. "So what gap did I fill with my information about the Defenders?"

"Ah, yes. The journal. He made a series of cryptic entries regarding a secret project and an angel investor. He never mentioned the other members of his team by name, simply referring to them as 'the defenders of historical truth.' I believe you stumbled upon those persons involved in his quest for vindication."

Finishing my golden-delicious home fries, I wipe my mouth and slide my cup to the end of the table for Tally's "nick of time" refill. "Thanks, Tally."

"Did you do something different with your hair, sweetie?" She doesn't wait for a reply, but bobs her flame-red bun and hurries to the table by the window to refill another local's mug.

I brush the wig back and chuckle to myself. "It's starting to sound like these students were more than hero-worshipers? Do you think they were actually involved in a working dig?"

Silas shakes his head and his jowls waggle back and forth. "I do not presume to know any concrete details of the group's activities. However, the entries in the journal indicate an elevation in Professor Klang's certainty, a much-needed infusion of cash that would help move things forward, but also the uprising of a seemingly immovable obstacle. It is precious little to go on, but if this immovable obstacle is in fact an individual, that individual may have had reason to halt the professor's inquest—permanently."

"Like, another suspect? Someone with an actual motive?"

Silas carefully wipes his mouth and mustache before answering. "Indeed. A suspect worthy of further scrutiny."

Glancing at my phone, I slide toward the end of the booth. "I better get going. What can I do to help us get to the truth faster?"

"I believe your current efforts to ingratiate yourself to the possible members of this secret club is our best option. In addition, our autopsy results will be available at the end of the day. Let us hope the new report provides another potential avenue."

"I do hope so. I'll meet you at the station after class. We can give the news to Erick together."

Silas nods, and I hurry off to school.

The lecture hall seems fuller today. Professor Willoughby is writing the presentation order on the whiteboard. As I make my way down the steps, Brooklyn turns and waves me to the front row.

Hutton, her auburn curls hanging loose, sits to her left and Ainsley is in the second row, snuggled onto the shoulder of the raven-haired man-boy who must be Kaden.

Asleep in the back row with his feet on the seat in front of him is surely the infamous stoner, Bodie.

Finally, I'll warrant a guess that the jock with the blond mullet on Kaden's right is Tayton. I pause for additional "extra" information to reveal itself, but nothing pops into my head.

Brooklyn removes her backpack from the seat next to her. "I added some stuff to our paper this morning. Needed a little kick, you know?"

As I drop into the available chair, I nod and smile. Like my mom always told me, if you don't have something nice to say . . .

"We will begin with the presentation on Professor Klang's book. I understand he was a renowned expert in Norse expansion." Remarkably, Silas sounds entirely sincere.

I stand, expecting the rest of the group to follow suit. Instead, a volley of whispers, giggles, and headshakes ensues.

In the end, Brooklyn and I are elected the de facto representatives of our ragtag band.

We step behind the podium, and Brooklyn lays the paper on the birch-wood surface. She begins to read the paper aloud—verbatim.

It's all coming back to me now. The memorization, the regurgitation, the lack of original thought. All the wonderful reasons why college was such a shattering revelation.

There has to be a way to unearth something useful in this sea of wannabe archaeologists.

I casually flip the paper over.

Brooklyn stutters to a halt. "What are you doing?" she hisses as she tucks a loose strand of blonde hair behind her ear.

Leaning toward her, I whisper, "Follow my lead."

A tentative smile curls the corners of her full lips.

"Actually, Kaden had some insight into what motivated Professor Klang to pursue his exploration of Norse expansion."

Ainsley's eyes are wide as saucers and she leans away from Kaden, while I gesture toward him. "Can you share your insights with the class?"

He crosses his arms over his chest and scowls. "Not cool, Brooklyn."

She shrugs her shoulders helplessly.

Beneath the tension, my extrasensory perceptions pick up a mishmash of emotions. The group holds a secret. It may be nothing more than what Silas has already uncovered in the journal, but, with a priceless artifact of questionable provenance in the mix, I intend to find out if anyone in this room knows about that possibly pilfered piece of history.

"My bad, Kaden. I thought you were, like, in the inner circle. I thought you knew about what he found."

Bodie wakes up in the back row. "Dude? Seriously? I thought I was your bro?"

Kaden shoves his way out of the row and marches up the stairs past Bodie's seat. "New girl doesn't know what she's talking about. We're out of here."

Tayton looks like a lost puppy. He definitely wants to follow his bros, but I'm assuming there are some academic requirements that hockey players must meet. A failing grade in this class would certainly impact his eligibility.

Turning toward Professor Willoughby, I attempt

a save. "Sorry, Prof. I'm still learning everyone's names and I clearly got mixed up. That's totally on me. The group wrote a super awesome paper. So you should definitely base their grade on that paper, and if anyone needs to take a hit for this hot mess of a presentation, I'll totally take one for the team."

Tayton nods, and, unsurprisingly, no one in the group argues with me.

"Very well, Miz— Miss Brown. You shall receive a zero for this assignment, and the other members of your group will receive a grade based on my review of their critique. Return to your seat."

Ouch-town. Population: me. I didn't expect Silas to be so brutal, but hopefully my self-sacrifice will gain me some much-needed "street cred" with the Defenders.

The other groups don't fare much better than the Defenders and me.

Everyone is eager to beat a hasty retreat at the end of class.

"Miss Brown, may I speak to you for a moment?"

Tayton stops on the stair above me and turns. "Thanks for grabbin' the slot in the sin-bin for that wack presentation. My GPA can't take another yard sale."

"No problem. Catch up with you guys later. I got this." I have no idea whether any of Tayton's hockey slang is good or bad, but he started with "thanks," so I think I did him a solid. Embracing my role as martyr, I let my shoulders slump and my steps slow as I return to the front of the room, casting worried glances over my shoulder.

Ainsley takes one last desperate look before ducking out with the rest of the group.

"What's up, Silas?"

He harrumphs, possibly for effect, but more likely as part of his consistent disappointment with my lax etiquette. "Follow me."

His tone is a tad serious for a ruse. I hope he's not planning on actually punishing me for failing to make a pretend presentation, under an assumed identity, in a cover class, at a college I don't even attend!

The thin, wood-grain plastic plate on the door says Gerhardt Klang, but, since Silas produces a set of keys, it doesn't take a psychic to predict that this is now his office.

"Is his stuff still in there? Doesn't he have any family or anyone?"

"The department secretary has put in a request for boxes. I generously offered to pack up Mr. Klang's belongings when those boxes arrive. There has been no official request from survivors, and the college must clear the space in preparation for a permanent, full-time archaeology professor." He pushes open the door and gestures for me to enter the immaculate room.

"Oh, right. You're doing such a bang-up job, I forgot it wasn't your real gig." My quip brings an actual chuckle to Professor Willoughby's face. "You are performing quite well yourself, Miss Brown."

I feign a curtsy. "I'm guessing you didn't bring me here to discuss packing. My experience consists of filling a black trash bag with a bunch of worn-out clothes, or, post foster care, throwing a few things in a backpack before running out on past due rent."

Silas shakes his head. "The Foundation has taken care of all your outstanding debts. It was your father's suggestion, and a wise one at that."

"No argument here. It's not that I didn't want to pay my bills, but barista money and crappy tips only stretch so far. I'm much better at managing my financial situation now."

Silas exhales. "Indeed, since it is in fact I who manage your financial situation."

"Rude." But I have to chuckle at his accurate summary.

"However, I did not bring you here to discuss packing or finances. I'd like you to use your gifts to examine the room and its contents before they are carted off to a storage facility to decompose in anonymity."

"À la *Raiders of the Lost Ark*," I offer.

The languor of Mr. Willoughby's thin eyelids is a clear indication that he does not get my reference.

"I'll see what I can do." Rubbing my magicked mood ring encouragingly, I take a few deep breaths to clear my head of distractions. Starting to the right of the doorway, I make my way around the room, pausing to examine photographs, artwork, certificates, and other items as I move in a counterclockwise pattern.

Silas sits patiently in a visitor's chair, with his fingers steepled and his jowly chin bouncing rhythmically on his pointer fingers.

Nothing of interest is coming to me until I draw near the desk. *Deadly secret.* There it is again. "Silas, it's the second time the words *deadly secret* have come to me in relation to Klang. Where's the artifact?"

He opens the top left-hand desk drawer to retrieve the item he'd previously pulled from a secret compartment.

He leans over and searches with increasing intensity. "Unfortunately, it is gone. I placed the item in this drawer before we spoke and now it is missing."

"Well, I guess we know why he kept it in a secret compartment."

Silas narrows his gaze, and a flicker of his alchemical power stirs his aura like heat rising off Arizona pavement in the summer.

I take a step back and swallow. "Sorry, I didn't mean that to come out as insultingly as it did. Where's the secret compartment?"

He removes the bottom drawer on the left-hand side and I kneel to examine the compartment behind that drawer. "That's clever. This drawer's a little bit shorter—"

"Incorrect. All the drawers are the same size. If one drawer were shorter than the others, it would be a clear indication of a secret compartment. However, with all drawers the same size, there would be no reason for the casual observer to suspect that anything is amiss."

"Copy that." I reach my hand in and let my psychic senses guide my feelers. They discover the concealed latch, and the compartment pops open. Again, I let my fingers do the walking. Along the top edge, I feel a strange shift in texture. As I slide my pointer back and forth over the spot, I recognize what I'm touching. Flopping down to my belly, I carefully use what little fingernail I have to grip the edge. Pulling out my find, I show it to Silas. "A negative."

Silas smiles like a proud parent.

Holding the single 35mm negative to the window, I examine the exposure. "It's a little girl—" As soon as I say "girl" a flood of images assault my senses. When the unbidden montage ends, I inhale sharply and lay the negative on the desk.

"What did you see?" He sits in absolute stillness.

I rub a hand across my forehead, and a shiver grips me before I reply. "The items are all Norse artifacts. The picture wasn't taken in a museum. The artifacts are piled on a coffee table. It's someone's . . . home!"

CHAPTER 8

In every movie I've ever seen, when two or more phones PING simultaneously, it is not good news.

Silas for the win. "Ah, it would appear our forensics report is ready. Shall I drive?"

"As much as I love you, *Professor*, there's no way I'm riding in a 1908 Model T in this weather. I'll drive."

The Pin Cherry Harbor morgue is not a place I've been before, nor is it a place I'd ever like to visit again. For a budding psychic, such as myself, the pervasive energy of death and the confusing cacophony of "last" messages are overwhelming.

The ever-vigilant Silas must sense my unease. "Would you prefer to wait in the car? I can retrieve the report and we will discuss the results en route to the sheriff's station."

"That sounds—" Without bothering to finish my

sentence, manners be dashed, I race back to the Jeep and get the heater running.

Silas returns in under five minutes.

I want to think positive, but the churning in my gut carries a visceral warning that's difficult to ignore.

Silas climbs into the vehicle with an upbeat smile lifting his round cheeks.

"It's good news? Your face makes it seem like it's good news."

"Whether the information is good or bad will be determined. However, it is complete."

This man and his hairsplitting! He could employ an entire race of follicle-based lumberjacks! "I accept your terms. What's the news?"

"The cause of death is no longer undetermined, nor is it in any way related to blunt-force trauma. In fact, the victim suffered two blunt-force trauma injuries in similar regions of the occipital on the same night. The examiner's best estimate is that the injuries were inflicted approximately two to three hours apart. The angle of impact varies, as does the velocity."

Faking a loud snore, I pretend to wake up. "Get to the good part. All of this nonsense about nonfatal blunt-force trauma is putting me into a trance."

"If Gerhardt Klang's death is what you refer to as 'the good part,' then here it is. He died of a fatal embolism."

My extensive television-based education merely

gave a cursory explanation of embolisms. "That's an air bubble, right?"

"It is. However, this particular air bubble was not a result of natural causes."

"What's that now?"

"Based on her expert analysis, the bubble of air that stopped Professor Klang's heart and starved his brain of oxygen was artificially induced."

And this is where Movie Medicine 101 fails me. "And by artificially induced, you mean . . .?"

"The local medical examiner did not see the need to perform certain tests. Our forensic pathologist performed a post-mortem CT scan, which revealed the air bubble, and, after removing the victim's thick beard, as part of a thorough search, she found an injection site into the external jugular, under the mandible."

"So, someone shoved a needle in his neck and pumped him full of air? And that killed him? Death by air?"

"I believe 'death by air' is the simplest explanation." Silas smooths his bushy mustache.

I'm smiling from ear to ear, but the sludgy feeling in my tummy refuses to vacate. No problem, I'm happy to continue to ignore it. "That obviously puts Erick in the clear. The death was clearly premeditated. Erick simply got in a fight with the guy after a broomball game. He didn't make an elaborate plan to devise a method of murder that would escape detection."

"Perhaps. Although, it did escape *initial* detection."

Nervous laughter battles with the doubts creeping along the edges of my mind as we drive to the station.

Silas and I nod politely to the deputy manning the front desk, and he stops at Erick's office to inform Deputy Paulsen we're visiting his client.

She nods. "Deputy Baird is processing the paperwork. Sheriff Harper is free to go." To be fair, her tone carries a note of relief. However, she can't leave well enough alone. "What's with the getup, Moon?"

Sucking in a quick breath, I open my mouth to sling a stinging retort her way, but Silas places a warning hand on my arm as he fields the question. "Miss Moon is undercover. We'll fill you in after we share the good news with my client."

I want to do a happy dance in the hallway and tell her to get her polyester-clad behind out of his office, but some of Silas's lessons have actually rubbed off. I withhold my celebration and, instead, imagine where I'll take Erick for dinner.

Silas regards my self-control with mild amusement.

Leading the way down the hall, I open the door into the holding cells.

"We have the new medical examiner's report! You're in the clear, and Paulsen is processing your release papers. Your self-inflicted quarantine is over.

Time for dinner at the restaurant of your choice, *Sheriff* Harper."

Erick gets to his feet and ambles toward the bars. "Before I get my hopes up, let me see the report."

Silas passes the recent information through the bars and Erick paces a tight circle as he reads. The shift in his energy extends through the bars like the tentacles of a deep-sea creature. Each circle he makes tightens the invisible constriction of my heart.

"What's wrong? It's good news. It was clearly premeditated murder. Nothing to do with the fight or the ice. You're—"

Erick collapses onto the metal bench and crumples the report into a ball.

"Mr. Harper, what troubles you?" Silas grips a cold metal bar.

"There's a gear bag in the trunk of my cruiser. The vehicle is county property. They don't need a warrant. Please tell Deputy Paulsen that she'll find a hand-pump with an air needle affixed to the nozzle." His head hangs. "Sometimes we have to pump up the balls at practice, and the compressor at the rink is always blowing a fuse." He tosses the crushed report to the floor, lies back on the metal bench, and laces his fingers together behind his head.

He doesn't look at us. He doesn't say goodbye. He stares at the cement ceiling and breathes in and out through clenched teeth.

Silas grips my arm and gently tugs me away.

And that's what I get for ignoring the horrible churning in my gut.

Outside the holding cells, I make my play. "Silas, I'm sure I can pop the trunk on Erick's vehicle. You head into Paulsen's office to distract her and I'll make that gear bag disappear."

Silas inhales slowly and his stooped shoulders square as he rises to his full, powerful height. "You will do no such thing, Mizithra Achelois Moon. Erick Harper is an honest man who has chosen to do the right thing. I will not stand by while you sully his good intentions with your misguided plots."

The words vibrate through my body, and the folly of my deception is revealed like a centipede under a lifted rock.

"Sorry. Honestly, I'm sorry. But I know Erick didn't do this, and it's killing me to see him suffer needlessly."

My mentor smiles warmly and places a comforting hand on my shoulder. "You and I will uncover the truth. In the meantime, we must settle matters with Deputy Paulsen. Perhaps you can see your way clear to include her in our solution. I believe that while her hands are bound by the law, her loyalty lies with the sheriff."

I roll my eyes. "As if."

Silas narrows his gaze and a wave of energy shimmers around him.

"All right! All right. I'll try."

He leads the way into the office that Paulsen occupies and places his weather-beaten briefcase on a chair. He rummages around inside and retrieves a second copy of the report, which he hands to Deputy Paulsen. "My client wishes to cooperate with the investigation and has informed me to instruct you to retrieve a gear bag from the trunk of his cruiser. He indicated the bag contains a hand-operated air pump, with a needle attached."

Paulson stares at Silas in confusion before running her pudgy finger down the pathology report in an attempt to decipher his message. "So he's confessing to the murder?"

That's it. End of rope reached. "No, he's not confessing to the murder, Paulsen. He's not guilty of the murder! You and I both know that. He's cooperating with the investigation. Clearly someone is setting him up!"

Paulsen drops the report on the desk that does not belong to her and crosses her arms stubbornly. "Look, Moon, I follow the evidence. If the evidence leads to Harper, I'll arrest him. I'm not saying that's where I want it to lead, I'm telling you how I run a legal investigation."

"What are you implying, Paulsen?"

She tilts her head with an irritatingly superior slant. "Another thing that you and I both know is the way you slip around the edges of the system." She gestures to my wig and scoffs. "You seem to think that the laws don't apply to you." She rises to her full five foot two inches. "Well, I'm here to tell you the law applies to everyone, even Sheriff Harper. If the murder weapon is in his gear bag, I will place him under arrest for suspicion of murder."

As I lunge forward, the unexpectedly strong arm of Silas Willoughby bars my path. "None of us will move any closer to discovering the true villain if we waste time squabbling amongst ourselves." He looks over his right shoulder at me, and his eyes spark with a fiery warning. Satisfied that his message is received, he returns his gaze to Paulsen. "If you will permit it, Deputy Paulsen, I would encourage you to allow Miss Moon to bring you up to speed on what she has uncovered at the community college."

I gasp and find myself at a loss for words. How can Silas throw me under the bus like this?

To my shock and awe, Deputy Paulsen's arms fall limp at her sides and she drops onto the chair with a sigh. "Something smelled rotten from the minute this got called in." She shakes her head. "According to dispatch, the call came from an untraceable number, despite the fact that the Zamboni driver claims he's the one who found the body."

Slipping past Silas, I slide onto the empty chair beside his briefcase. "Why wouldn't he have called from his own cell phone? Does he have his number blocked?"

Paulsen leans forward. "Absolutely not. I placed a test call to dispatch from his phone and the number showed up—no problem. There was also no previous call to dispatch in his call history."

"That's shady." I chew my bottom lip for a second. "So he placed a call from someone else's phone and has no memory of it?"

"He kept saying he found the body. He never actually answered me when I asked him if he placed the call."

"Weird."

Paulsen leans back in the chair and nods her head. "Definitely."

Land o' Goshen! I think Paulsen and I are working together. It's not terrible. I'm sure I could make a lot more progress if I had her cooperation than if I had to sneak around and obtain everything less than legally. "What do you say, Paulsen? Call a truce, just this once?"

She nods unconvincingly, but offers me her hand.

I grasp it, and seal the bargain with a handshake.

"I shall leave you two to discuss the potential suspects in the archaeology class. I must request some additional information from the pathologist. My findings will be shared the moment they become available."

A weak smile graces Paulsen's face. "Thanks, Willoughby. You always were a straight shooter."

Silas bows his head in gratitude, retrieves his beat-up valise, and exits the station.

After bringing Paulsen up to speed on my findings, we agree (I'm as shocked as you) that my continued presence at the community college could reveal additional leads.

In the interest of getting things off on the right foot, I chose to leave out a few details, like the secret compartment in Klang's desk and the missing unicorn-horn cup.

Once I get the negative of the little girl developed, I'll turn it over to Paulsen as an additional gesture of goodwill. I don't have to tell her exactly when I uncovered it. That's part of my mysterious charm.

Time to head over to the *Pin Cherry Harbor Post* and see if Quince Knudsen is home from college for Thanksgiving break.

Right after I take off this blasted wig and give my poor scalp a good scratching!

CHAPTER 9

THE LOCAL JOURNALISTIC house of integrity is showing its age. Winter-dormant vines steadily consume the brick corners, and the painted letters are fading from the plate-glass window. The logo appears to read: "Pin herry Harbo Pos ."

As I run across the street, an arctic wind whistles up from the great lake and bites my cheeks and nose. Luckily, I found a spare stocking hat in the car, to hide my disastrous post-wig hair and cover my tender ears. The metal handle on the glass door is so cold I can feel my bones icing through as I swing open the portal and rush indoors.

Previous visits to the newspaper have taught me not to expect a welcoming committee. I slide into the office behind the counter to see if Quince is in the adjoining darkroom, where the pungent odor of acids and ammonia lurks.

No such luck.

I'm forced to return to the lobby and ring the bell resting on the birch-clad counter. Much to my dismay, the elder Knudsen emerges from the depths.

Blink. Blink. Blink.

The juxtaposition of the diminutive man's height compared to the size of his eyewear never ceases to amaze. The massive lenses magnify his eyes to comical proportions.

"Good afternoon, Mr. Knudsen. I'm not sure if you remember me? Mitzy Moon."

His small mouth cracks into a grin beneath his enormous glasses. "I believe your philanthropic foundation was responsible for establishing a photo-journalism scholarship at the local high school. My son, Quincy Knudsen, was the fortunate inaugural recipient. I'm not sure if you're aware of Quincy's photographic accomplishments, but—"

"Quince and I are well acquainted. I'm so glad to hear he received the scholarship." I also happen to know that this man will literally never stop talking if left uninterrupted. "The reason I'm here today is because I need a negative printed. I was hoping to pay Quince for a quick turnaround. Do you happen to have someone helping you with photographs while he's away at school?"

Blink. Blink. Blink.

The issue with this man seems to be that he has trouble engaging his starter, but once the engine is running, he has that "1970s muscle car" tendency to run even after the ignition is in the off position.

"Negative you say? Are you referring to a 35mm negative or perhaps you have a vintage camera with a 110 cartridge—"

"It's a 35mm negative, Mr. Knudsen. Do you have someone?"

"There was a girl that was helping on Mondays and Wednesdays, but her younger sister's best friend had an incident at her after-school care provider—"

"Oh, how unfortunate. Is she here?" This man will be the death of me.

"The girl? Oh, no. It's Friday."

I nod and smile. "Do you know how to make a print and develop it?"

Blink.

"I'm sure someone must've taught Quince."

"Why, yes. When did you say you needed this print?"

"How about we get into the darkroom and develop it right now?"

"Well, I have to proof the stories for tomorrow's edition. And I still have to write the *Letter from the Editor*, so I am—"

"I tell you what, why don't you go and print this negative for me, and I'll draft up a letter from the editor for you. What were you planning on writing about this week?"

"Let's see . . . I believe folks should be prepared for the big storm. It's always good to stock up on canned goods, dry goods—"

"Agreed. I'll put together a wonderful storm-prep letter, and you can add your special touches. Deal?"

Blink. Blink. Blink.

I hand him the negative and smile as I gently steer him back toward the darkroom.

He shuffles and I follow. While he steps into the black cylinder that rotates and dumps out its occupant in the light-proof darkroom, I take a seat in the dilapidated office chair and open up a new document on the museum-piece computer.

He hums a jaunty tune as he works, and for some reason the sound of it seeping out of the photo lab infects me with a severe case of the giggles. The image of the tiny man in his large glasses, singing as he skips around the darkroom, reminds me of a children's story that should never be written.

Since I know next to nothing about prepping for a winter storm, I force my psychic senses to replay several enhanced memories from the diner. Regulars are always chatting about the weather, and no weather seems to get as much attention as storms. Once I've played enough clips to gather the required intel, I type up a rough draft and sign it "The Editor." I don't actually know Mr. Knudsen's first name, and that's not for lack of interest. It's straight-up, stone-cold fear. I'm afraid that if I ask his name, he would begin by saying, "In the beginning, Adam begat Cain and Abel, etc." I'm not sure I have time for that genealogy.

The cylinder scrapes around with a swoosh, and

Mr. Knudsen emerges, holding a black-and-white 8 x 10 print and my negative, now in a protective sleeve.

"Thank you, Mr. Knudsen. Your letter from the editor is on this computer. I wasn't sure if you wanted me to print it out."

"You're already done?"

"Well, it's a draft. I wasn't sure how long it needed to be, but I think it's a good start."

He shuffles over to the computer and pushes the chair to the side. At his height, five feet in boots, he doesn't need to sit down to get a good look at the screen.

"What do you think?"

He puts up a hand, indicating he's still reading.

As I wait for his feedback, my mood ring tingles on my left hand. I glance down at the photo and grin. It's unmistakably Ainsley, circa 2005 CE, sitting cross-legged on a coffee table next to a pile of what appears to be authentic Norse artifacts. "I better be going, Mr. Knudsen. Thanks again for this print, and please say 'hi' to Quince for me when he gets home next week."

He straightens up and turns. "You're very fast."

"Thanks, I think." I resist the urge to snicker or mumble, *That's what he said*. "Let me know if there's anything else I can do. I sure appreciate this photo. Bye now."

I can practically hear his eyelids blinking as I hurry out.

There are so few days left before everyone heads

home for the break, I better get back over to the dormitories and see if I can pry Ainsley away from the herd. Of course, that means I have to get back into the wig. Aargh!

Lady Luck smiles upon me when I arrive at the dormitories. A gaggle of giggling girls are clustered around the front door. One of them taps their key card against the scanner, and, when they all start filing in, I join the conga line.

They continue on toward the common area and I break left to the elevator. Up on the third floor, I meander down the hallway reading the various stickers, Post-its, and miniature whiteboards on the wooden doors. Eventually, I find one with the following message: "Ainsley. Had a late study sesh. Don't wait up. Hutton."

Knocking firmly on the door, I hope it sounds friendly and not like the resident assistant's knock.

"Hutton isn't here."

"Ainsley? It's— Um, it's Darcy. I was actually looking for you." Holy *Bourne Identity*! Forgot who I was for a minute there.

Ainsley opens the door, and her expression is one of confusion as she scoops her green bangs out of her eyes. "Me? Why would you be looking for me?"

"Can I come in?"

She steps back hesitantly. "My room's not as nice as Brooklyn's."

"No sweat. Brooklyn's room is a little over the top, if you ask me."

Ainsley instantly jumps onto this train. "Right? Like, that zebra comforter is cringe."

"Totally." I scan her room for anything I can possibly compliment. "You have a lot of books. I knew you were the smart one."

Her eyes sparkle and she blushes. "Thank you so much. I thought college would be me, living my best life. I didn't expect to spend every day in someone else's drama, you know?"

"Totally." Oh brother. I've got to come up with another response. "So, I'm pretty sure Professor Willoughby is going to throw down a pop quiz on Monday. He seems like the type, you know? Sounds like a lot of people are taking off this weekend and adding a few extra days to their break, and I think he wants to make sure they take a hit in their GPA."

"For reals? That would be bad. Like, super bad. You better go. I need to study."

Wow, she may not be as brilliant as I assumed. "Yeah, that's why I'm here. I thought we could study together. I mean, I'm so new and I've missed so much—"

"No way! You crushed that identification exercise. You are, like, pro-level. But, yeah, let's study."

Smile and nod, Mitzy. "I saw the note on the door. Does Hutton stay out late studying very often?"

Ainsley turns and rolls her eyes dramatically. "Hutton? Studying on a Friday night? That's such a load of cow manure. And, trust me, I know cow manure." She chuckles at the self-deprecating reference to her farm upbringing.

After a forced courtesy laugh, I ask, "Oh. Where is she?"

"Her and Brooklyn are— They don't think I know. I mean, it's not a big deal."

My psychic senses finally kick in. "You don't think they're with Kaden, do you?"

"Yeah. Kaden is totally stepping out on me. But the joke's on him, or at least it was."

Right as I'm about to snatch a juicy extrasensory tidbit about her slimy boyfriend from her subconscious, her walls go up. "What do you mean 'was'?"

"Skip it. Stale doughnuts. Let's just study, okay?"

Foiled again. Time is running out and I can't afford to be patient. Time to push the boundaries. "Do you have any soda? I mean, pop? Or water?"

"OMG! I'm so sorry. You brought all those super lush snacks the other night and I'm, like, not giving you anything. I'm such a potted plant."

"Don't worry about it. I wasn't trying to be all that, but I'm kinda thirsty."

She grabs two glasses, which may or may not be clean, from the counter above the mini-fridge, and pulls a two-liter bottle of root beer from the middle shelf. "Is root beer okay?"

"Totally." That word is like sour milk in my mouth. I hate the sound of my own voice.

She fills the two cups and passes one to me. I take my glass and follow her toward a low table between the two bunk beds, where all of her books are haphazardly stacked.

As I walk behind her, I sink my finger into my root beer and carefully trace the truth symbols that Silas so painstakingly taught me. As I focus on drawing the symbols accurately and in the correct order, I can hear his voice echo in the back of my mind.

"This is no parlor trick. This is a powerful transmutation, and you should know better than most how truth can be a double-edged sword. It is not a skill to be abused. It is a potent tool, to be wielded with the precision of a scalpel."

She sets down her glass and turns to organize the books and make room for me.

I place the alchemically transmuted cup of root beer next to hers and swap their positions like a sleight-of-hand magician. Part of me feels a flash of guilt, but the rest of me is absolutely all right with doing whatever is necessary to get to the truth. I keep the untainted glass in hand and take several big sips, hoping that my thirst-quenching act will encourage her to take a drink.

Finally!

She downs half the glass in one go.

That's my girl. "So what do you think Hutton and Brooklyn are really doing tonight?"

Her eyes widen, and her mouth seems to move despite her efforts to prevent it. "Brooklyn's secretly dating Kaden. She thinks I'm too stupid to notice."

"That's rude. Why did you say it doesn't matter?"

She blinks and a brief flash of fear darts through her eyes. "Everyone thinks I transferred to archaeology because of Kaden, but it was really because of Special-K. Kaden is—was—just his errand boy, or whatever."

I'm starting to regret my decision to use any means to get at the truth. "What do you mean?"

"Like, I was kind of— It all started online. I kind of had a thing with the professor."

She may be eighteen and everything, but I definitely have to hide my shock and focus on keeping her talking. "I get it. He was super yummy. How did you meet a professor online?"

"No, I met Kaden in this online dinosaur game. He invited me to his Jangle server for a private chat and said he was into archeology for real."

"That's cool."

"I guess. Whatevs. I tried to impress him by saying that I had authentic Viking stuff and then he wanted to MIRL."

"Merle? Who's that?"

"OMG, Darcy. Isn't it obvs? Meet In Real Life. Kaden wanted me to bring one of the artifacts and meet him on campus."

Her energy is struggling against the truth symbols and time is running out. "Did you meet him?"

"When I got there, Special-K was there. I was kinda swoony. I showed him this ultra-fancy cup. He said it was the goddess Freya, carved into a unicorn-horn chalice, and he touched my hand and— He was super smart, and he was totally gonna prove his theory about Norse expansion. I was helping him on a secret project. He had this investor that was going to fund our dig, and the cup was gonna be, like, collateral. He said the two of us were going to *remake* history."

"I thought all the Defenders were helping him?"

Her eyelids slide open so far I fear her eyeballs may pop out of her head. "You know about the Defenders' secret project?"

"That's why I came here. Professor Klang invited me to be part of the group." I sincerely hope she doesn't ask me too many questions, since I have zero information about the inner workings of the Defenders.

She narrows her gaze and a thick wave of suspicion rolls toward me. "Show me."

"I'm afraid I can't do that. You'll have to show me yours first." Again, totally spitballing here.

She reaches into the pocket of her skinny jeans and produces a runestone that looks like it's carved from a piece of antler. The symbol is a "Y" with an extra line in the middle. I recognize it from one of Silas's books, but I don't remember its meaning. "Now you," she says.

Great. The stress is shutting down my psychic talents, and I clearly have no runestone to show her. Time for some B-list acting.

I *accidentally* spill my soda on her textbooks.

She panics and drops the stone as she struggles to rescue her books.

"I'll grab some paper towels. I'm so sorry. I'm such a stupid klutz." I scoop up the stone with my left hand as I run toward the kitchen.

She's desperately clearing away her papers and flicking sugary liquid from the textbook covers, but calls after me, "Don't even. It's my fault. I usually don't bring soda in here."

Shoving the runestone in my pocket, I grab a wad of paper towels from the roll. But, as I walk back, a strange whispering swirls up my spine toward the nape of my neck.

Trust only me. Trust only me.

I toss the wad of paper towels at Ainsley as the overwhelming need to climb out of my own skin consumes me. "I'm super sorry. I'll buy you new textbooks or whatever. I've gotta go! I forgot I have to pick up my cat from the vet before they close."

Racing down the hall toward the elevator, I claw the runestone from my jeans and drop it in the pocket of my puffy jacket. The whispering doesn't cease entirely, but it's quieter. I can resist it.

I scramble into my Jeep, fishtail out of the parking lot, and gun it back to the bookstore.

CHAPTER 10

My heart is pounding in my chest like a war drum, and I can't seem to catch my breath as I pull the heavy metal door closed behind me and lock my-self into the bookstore. Now that I'm safely home, I grab my phone and shout for Grams while I dial Silas.

She pops into existence right in front of me as Silas answers the call.

"It's a bit late to be calling your professor for extra credit." He chuckles over the speaker and Grams smiles along with him.

Unfortunately the next two words out of my mouth will seriously murder their mood. "Rory Bombay."

Silas grumbles. "On my way." The line goes dead.

Grams swirls around me protectively. "What do

you mean, Rory Bombay? Is he here? In this bookshop? He's dangerous, Mitzy. We're not prepared. I'm not sure if the protections Silas put in place all those months ago will still hold up. What should we do?"

"I'd say we should take a deep breath, but only one of us needs oxygen. Take it down a couple notches on the paranormal panic dial."

Ghost-ma crosses her bejeweled limbs over her designer gown and tilts her proud head. "You don't get to march into my bookshop, drop that man's name like a used handkerchief, and then tell me to calm down."

I raise my finger in protest. "Correction, *my* bookshop. I appreciate everything you left me in the will. However, by definition a 'last will and testament' means the end of one thing and the beginning of the next thing. I'm the *next* thing."

"Oh my, I would've expected a little more gratitude, especially this time of year."

I wag my head back and forth. "Fair point. And since we'll be waiting until Silas gets here to dive into this Rory Bombay mess, maybe this is a good time to talk about Thanksgiving?"

"What do you mean by that?"

"Well, Dad asked me if I had any plans. Which, of course, I don't. I haven't had holiday plans since my mother was killed. I'd love to spend Thanksgiving with Dad and Amaryllis, but I'd like Erick to be there. If he's out of jail by then."

"He better be! I'll haunt the hind end off that Deputy Paulsen—"

"Easy, *Atomic Blonde*. I think we were talking about Thanksgiving."

"Oh, well in that case, Twiggy always does Thanksgiving."

"Always? I don't remember anything about it last year."

"You were new in town. I think she took the dogs and went to visit her sister. It was an odd year for everyone. Kind of a reset year, if you will. But now you're here to stay and a tradition is a tradition. You better check with Twiggy before you make any plans. Also, ask her if she can host the meal here. I don't think it's fair to leave me out."

"All right." I bow with a flourish. "The last thing I want to do is put a burr under Twiggy's saddle or exclude a ghost that can't eat!"

Grams giggles and her shimmering hand pushes playfully at my shoulder.

It's an odd sensation to be touched by a ghost, but there's so much love in her energy field that it almost always brings a smile to my face.

"Mitzy, we may have been gifted with too much junk in the trunk and a random assortment of psychic gifts, but neither of us got any patience. Tell me what happened! You can give Silas the shorthand when he gets here."

"Copy that." I slip out of the puffy jacket, hold it

away from myself as though it's a poisonous snake, and carry it upstairs to the apartment.

By the time Silas arrives, I've filled Ghost-ma in on all the interpersonal relationships between Professor Klang's inner circle of acolytes, plus the added bonus of a possible teacher-student affair, and we've placed a 3 x 5 card bearing Rory's name on the murder wall. To be clear, it's not his first appearance on my infamous corkboard of suspects.

"Good evening, Mizithra. I do appreciate the key. Thank you for seeing to that."

Grams zooms down to our level and Silas shivers with a quick flash of ghost-chills.

He reaches into one of the many pockets inside his tattered tweed jacket and slips out his special spectacles. Carefully unfolding the wire arms he hooks the brass curves behind his preternaturally large ears and scans the room for the phantom. "You are looking well, Isadora."

She smiles and gestures for me to bring him up to speed.

"So the connection between Ainsley and Professor Klang definitely deserves further investigation, but the *pièce de résistance* is this." I reach for the puffy coat, tip it sideways, and shake until the runestone clatters onto the coffee table.

Silas reaches toward it.

"Don't touch it. You taught me well, Mr. Willoughby. That little beauty is as cursed as cursed can be, and the mantra that it chants is very reminiscent of a charm previously used by the devious Mr. Bombay."

Silas withdraws his hand and nods at me approvingly. "It gives me great pleasure to note that my lessons are not in vain."

I brush away his compliment with a flick of my wrist. "There will be time for praise later. What I need to know is can you break this curse or uncurse this stone?"

Silas smooths his mustache with a thumb and forefinger. "To what end?"

"Oh!" I slap the heel of my left hand on my forehead. "Did I not mention that every one of the Defenders has one of these cursed runestones? Or at least that's what I assume. Possibly only Ainsley's stone is cursed, but with all the weird stuff going on, it makes more sense that if this token is a symbol of membership to the inner circle, all the tokens are cursed."

Silas points to the mark etched on the surface of the cursed stone. "The rune of defense. Used as a tool to control. A clever and deadly ploy. Certainly of the type we've come to expect from Mr. Bombay."

"This is what I'm saying. I'm ninety-nine point nine percent sure he's the mysterious 'angel investor' you found mentioned in the journal. But I need you to uncurse this one so I can use it as my buy-in to the inner circle and find out for certain. Can you do it?"

He lowers himself onto the scalloped-back chair,

steeples his fingers and bounces his chin on his pointers.

I exhale and pace around the murder wall/corkboard.

While each of us is engaged in our own mental gymnastics, neither of us notices the furry fiend slinking along the perimeter.

Out of nowhere, Pyewacket leaps onto the coffee table, drops something from his mouth, and hisses vehemently at the cursed runestone. He leaps off the table and runs to hide underneath the four-poster bed.

"What did you bring us, Mr. Cuddlekins?"

Grams swirls closer. "That's my smart boy." She floats off to congratulate him, while I take a seat opposite Silas and wait for his input.

The chin bouncing stops, and a brief smile flickers beneath his bushy mustache. "Ah ha! A solution comes from a most unlikely source."

Looking back and forth between the two runestones, the cursed one, and the one delivered by Pyewacket, doesn't bring a matching smile to my face. "I get that they have the same symbol, but they look nothing alike. That smooth, wooden one isn't going to fool the Defenders. Can you fill me in on the good news, Silas?"

He pats his round belly and leans back with a satisfied sigh. "The obliteration of a curse is a next to impossible task. The energy used to create a hex cannot be destroyed. It can be transmuted, but some portion of the curse's original stain may always linger. A much simpler and efficient method, as Robin Pyewacket Goodfellow has shown us, is transference."

"Sounds great." I smile halfheartedly. "What's transference?"

"It is the process of moving energy from one place to another. If I can move the curse from this runestone to the one Pyewacket provided, I have a means to keep the curse intact, while freeing the original item from any negative influence. The more similar the two items are in size, shape, and intent, the easier and more permanent the transference."

"You done good, son," I call to the whiskered face peeking out from under the dust ruffle. "He's not gonna pull that cursed-item malarkey on us."

"Re-ooow." Not in my house!

Turning to my mentor, I offer my assistance. "What do you need from me?"

Silas gets to his feet and shuffles toward the Rare Books Loft. "I must consult a text or two, but I believe I possess all the ingredients required."

I bet he does! What I wouldn't give to get a peek at all the secret pockets in that man's jacket. "Will it throw off your mojo if I make some microwave popcorn?"

My use of the term mojo produces a hearty laugh from my mentor. "That should be fine. And if it's not too much trouble, I would love a cup of that hot chocolate that you brew."

"No problem." I'm sure he knows it's a packet mix, but I'm glad he likes it. I'm feeling very positive about our chances, and I skip down the treads of the wrought-iron staircase two at a time. In fact, my bravery extends to hopping over the chain at the bottom.

And, as the saying goes, "Oh Icarus, you flew too high." I manage to tuck and roll, and avoid any serious injury, other than my pride.

"Everything okay down there, Mizithra?"

"Yes. Please pretend you didn't hear that."

A ghostly snicker drifts through the ether.

"I'm warning you, Isadora. I can wear your vintage Chanel and forget to dry clean it at a moment's notice. Don't push me, woman."

She laughs outright, and my heart swells with love. It feels good to belong somewhere. To have people who answer my call for help and genuinely have my best interests at heart. I won't say it was all worth it to get to this point, but I will say the painful memories get a little dimmer each day.

The delicious smell of popped-buttery goodness fills the bookshop. Once upon a time, there was a terrible instance of burnt microwave popcorn, which triggered a silent alarm to the fire department and something called a halon fire-suppression system.

Thanks to my ghostly resident's hasty instructions, I was able to shut down the halon, but I was not spared an embarrassing visit from the, less than pleased, Fire Chief. So, I pop my popcorn for two minutes and twenty seconds—and not a second more.

I can handle a couple of old maids at the bottom of my bowl. Way easier than a ladder-truck full of apparently disappointed firefighters.

Getting comfortable on the settee, I toss a popped kernel in Pyewacket's direction.

He leaps at least eight feet in the air and snatches the popcorn with the deadly precision of a laser targeting system.

Grams claps her hands, but adds, "I would hate to be a bird in that beast's line of sight."

Since my mouth is stuffed full, I simply widen my eyes and nod.

Silas clears everything from the coffee table except the two runestones. "I will require silence and concentration during this transmutation. No more feline aerobatics, and no otherworldly horseplay between you and your interfering grandmother."

I swallow my popcorn and make a face at Grams.

She giggles insufferably. "I best go work on my memoirs. I never behave more poorly than when someone tells me to behave well."

Chuckling, I share her admission with Silas, and he nods furiously. "Exactly my point. Good day, Isadora. All my best on finding a publisher for your life's story."

She vanishes through the wall and her disembodied voice calls out, "Tell him thank you for me."

"She says, thanks."

He harrumphs. "As with any alchemical procedure, it behooves you to pay careful attention. You may not be prepared or trained to perform such complex transmutations, but exposure to the processes will open new pathways in your psychic array."

Inexplicably, that speech makes me think of the Star Trek Enterprise. At least I possess enough awareness to realize this is not the time to share that tidbit with my mentor. "Copy that." I cross my legs, pull a cozy throw over my shoulders, and diligently munch my popcorn.

Silas produces three glass vials and a small metal tin from inside his coat. The two amber vials he sets to the left of the cursed runestone. The metal tin he sets to the right of the un-cursed runestone.

He lifts the clear-glass vial and removes the stopper. He pours three drops of clear liquid on the uncursed stone. He replaces the stopper and slips the bottle inside his coat.

Next he opens the small metal tin. That type of container reminds me of the salve my mother used to rub on my arm when I would get too close to the jumping cholla cactus. Somehow the goo pulled the needles from the flesh and helped the wounds heal. Tangent! I lean forward to get a closer look at the contents. Fine jet-black powder. Yet, as I stare into the tin, the flecks seem to shimmer with a metallic nature.

He opens one of the amber vials and pours white

crystals in a circle around the two stones and the open tin.

My clairaudience hears *salt*. My eyes agree.

Silas places his hand over the cursed runestone and utters a rhythmic series of three Latin-sounding words. His hand pulses above the stone with each repetition of the chant. He pulls the stone's energy upward—forming an invisible ball.

All at once the invisible becomes visible, and it looks as though he holds a plasma globe beneath his right hand. Forks of purple, blue, and silver lightning spark within the clawed grip of his fingers. He then moves that sphere of energy over the un-cursed stone and chants a new Latin phrase. This one he repeats twice and forces his hand down firmly.

The sphere of lightning detaches from him and spins around the stone like a spider encasing its prey in the threads of its silk. The energy tightly envelops the stone, and before my very eyes the two become one.

Silas draws a shaky breath, and for the first time I glance up at the man performing this ritual before me. The color has drained from his face and his stooped shoulders seem to bear a great weight.

I want to ask him if he's all right, but he gave me strict instructions not to speak.

He retrieves the final amber vial, pulls the stopper, and gently pours one glistening black drop onto the formerly cursed rune. The liquid falls in slow motion, and when it touches the Defense rune it seems to be absorbed into the original etching, and travels down each ligature at equal speed. When it has completely filled the symbol, an audible pop emanates from the small disc.

A moment after the sound, Silas picks up the newly cursed runestone and drops it in the black powder. The fine ebony grains swirl in a counterclockwise tornado around the runestone.

I can't help but hold my breath, and I'm certainly not able to eat any more popcorn.

The tiny cyclone swirls on and the silver flecks bounce in the light.

Silas picks up the lid, and floats it above this miniature storm. I watch in awe as the storm sucks the lid down with ear-popping pressure. He breathes a sigh of relief and drops, exhausted, into the scalloped-back chair.

"So, that was amazing, but you look spent. What do you need?"

"I'll take that hot chocolate now."

"Oh, right." I jump up and race out of the apartment, down the stairs, and zap the cup in the microwave for a thirty-second hotter upper.

My distraction with hot-buttered goodness got the best of me earlier, and I left the cocoa on the table in the back room.

When I return, some of the color is coming back into his cheeks. I hand him the mug, handle first, because I still got mad tolerance for hot mugs. Barista skills, you never really lose them. I toss a few more kernels toward Pyewacket, but he's lost the thrill of the hunt and waits until they hit the carpet to casually retrieve them.

"Can you explain what happened? And what everything is?"

He takes a long sip of the hot chocolate, wipes his mustache, and exhales. "Certainly. The clear vial is holy water. To remove any residual energies from the target object. We don't want the curse to be altered in any way."

"Got it." Not gonna ask him where he sources his holy water. He'll tell me if I need to know.

"The second vial is salt. This particular formula is specially created to set a firm boundary which the energies cannot cross."

I nod, pretending I understand that there are different kinds of salt.

"The third contains alchemically altered squid ink, which protects the cleansed runestone against re-contamination."

Despite my best efforts, I can't help but murmur, "Squid ink. Cool."

"The canister contains a finely crushed dust comprised of activated carbon and ferric oxide. It anchors the cursed object and allows the energies to be contained within the metal clamshell."

"And the swirling cyclone?"

He smiles and his eyes twinkle. "A bit of showmanship."

My eyelids pop up like a breakfast pastry out of a toaster. "Silas Willoughby, you showboater."

He bows his head. "Perhaps you should check on your grandmother. I do need a moment to rest."

When I reach the third floor of the printing museum, Grams is hunched over her writing desk and utterly oblivious to my presence.

I'm certain she's using that fancy quill pen to forge my signature on another batch of query letters, but I'll let it slide. I hope she finds a publisher for her precious memoirs. She'll be the first ghost to top the New York Times bestseller list—or will she?

What an odd thought. I can't possibly be the only person in the world who can communicate with ghosts, which means she can't possibly be the solitary ghost. Is that comforting or creepy? Is there a club? A secret society? Oh, the possibilities are making my head spin.

It's best if I leave her to her craft and return to Silas.

Blowing her a silent kiss and wishing her luck, I thread my way through the large printing presses on the first floor and return to the apartment.

"Ah, Mizithra, would you escort me to my vehicle?"

"Sure. Everything all right?"

"Indeed. I wish to return home and partake of my restorative tinctures. You will keep me posted on any news of our foul friend?"

"Count on it."

CHAPTER 11

The bookshop is closed for the weekend, and possibly even on Monday. Twiggy headed south to scoop up a treasure trove of rare books at an estate sale that she's had her eye on for some time. When I pointed out that it's morbid to circle like a vulture above a dying animal, waiting for a well-known book collector to pass through the veil, she assured me it was a common practice in our line of work.

Since I have zero knowledge about collecting rare books, and it's more her line of work than mine, I'm in the unenviable position of needing her more than she needs me. So I nodded my agreement and offered to pay for her trip.

She scoffed away my generosity and hung a "Closed for Collection Trip" sign on the front door.

Generally, the empty bookshop feels safe and adventurous. The scent of possibility fills the air, and shelves and shelves of books speak of other worlds and other lives. However, amazing escapes at my fingertips don't have the same frivolous intrigue with the possibility of Rory Bombay slithering around in the shadows—nothing is truly safe. I have to keep busy to prevent my mind from spinning out of control.

Today, I'll head down to Grand Falls to see if Bombay Antiquities and Artifacts has had any recent visits from its absentee proprietor.

A scratch at the alleyway door flicks all of my senses into high alert. I tiptoe toward the door and press a hand to the cold metal. "Pyewacket, is that you?"

"Reow." Can confirm.

I unlock the heavy deadbolt and push the door open a crack. "What are you doing outside? It's freezing. Actually, let me rephrase that question. How did you get outside?"

Pyewacket struts past me and straight into the back room. He rests on his haunches, looks up at me, and tilts his head with an air of superior tolerance.

"Never mind. You go out when you want to go out. Who am I to question the activities of my feline overlord? Let me get you some Fruity Puffs."

He waits patiently while I grab a bowl and dispense a portion of his guilty pleasure.

I have no idea what he does or eats when he's outdoors, and I am perfectly fine keeping it that way.

Opening the cardboard flaps of a leftover container, I inspect the sweet-and-sour chicken. "Smells okay to me." I pop the container in the microwave and brew some coffee while my breakfast reheats.

Ghost-ma drifts in, looking especially vaporous.

"Everything all right, Grams?"

"I had a breakthrough."

This may be my first spectral existential crisis. "Care to share?"

"I was making some edits on my memoirs. As I read through several chapters, covering three different relationships, I was struck by the idea I may have been a tad self-involved."

Thank heavens I don't have a slug of coffee in my maw, because there would be a very large spray of java covering the back room on that spit take. "This is a revelation?"

Her apparition shimmers. "I was a busy woman, Mitzy. I was on the boards of several charitable organizations, and I traveled extensively collecting arcane texts for this bookshop. I didn't have a great deal of time for self-reflection."

"And now?"

"Well, I have all the time in the world now, don't I?"

The idea generates a slow ache in my heart. "But I don't."

"What do you mean? Did someone threaten you?"

Shrugging, I reach for my cup of coffee and retrieve my breakfast from the microwave. "It's nothing. I need to eat."

Grams peers into the partially open container. "I must say, I don't miss eating as much as I thought I would."

I pull out a chair and pick at the best pieces of chicken from my day-old Asian experiment.

Grams chuckles. "Day-old? Whatever you need to tell yourself, dear."

"I believe we were talking about you, Isadora."

"Oh, yes. You enjoy your coffee while I— We can discuss my spiritual growth later. I'm concerned about your doom-and-gloom outlook. We'll always be together, sweetie."

"I don't think so. When I die, I'll cross over like most people. If you're tethered to this bookshop, I'll never see you again."

Grams flickers in and out of focus. "When the time comes, I'm sure Silas can reverse my situation."

"Silas? You think Silas will still be alive when I die? Do you know something I don't about his longevity, or are you expecting my demise a lot sooner than I am?"

Grams taps a perfectly manicured finger on her coral lip. "I hadn't— I assumed— I need to make some notes." And without so much as a "good luck hunting for bad guys," she pops out of sight and I'm left with my subpar breakfast, my lukewarm coffee, and some afterlife anxiety.

"What about you, Pye? Do you think I'll have any luck tracking down Rory Bombay?"

He pauses in his ablutions, with one large tan

paw in mid-whisker swipe. He looks like a tiny feline villain in an old silent movie.

"No comment?"

As an afterthought, his golden eyes fix me with a warning, and he gives a halfhearted hiss.

"Copy that."

Upstairs, I layer up for the day's adventures and pull my pilfered handgun from the back of the scarf drawer.

I'm not sure whether I hope to find Rory or hope not to find him, but either way I want to be prepared.

With sweaters and a thick winter coat padding my person, shoving the gun in the back of my waistband doesn't seem like a plan for easy access.

The large pockets of my puffy jacket will have to do. Checking to make sure the safety is on, I slip the Springfield EMP in my coat.

Phone, keys, and I'm out the door.

Heading south, toward Grand Falls, the dark clouds thin by the time I reach the antiquities shop, and a pale blue sky shines with the light of a crisp winter sun.

As I case Bombay Antiquities, I'm surprised to see that it's open.

It never occurred to me that the estate sales and antique collecting would continue in Rory's absence. I park a block and a half away and cautiously approach the shop.

Before going in, I scroll through the contacts on my phone and select the direct number to the sheriff's station, slipping the cell into my pocket—at the ready. If he's here, I'm not going to try to be a hero. I'm calling for backup on the spot.

I push open the door, take a sudden interest in vases, and struggle to ignore the smell of mothballs.

"Welcome to Bombay Antiquities. Is there anything in particular that I can help you find?"

That hint of a Southern drawl sounds vaguely familiar. Seems like Rory kept more than Gershon's inventory of antiquities when he scooped up the business after the previous owner's sudden death. "Oh, I need to browse a little."

The petite redhead steps from behind her immaculate Louis XVI desk and daintily crosses the room as quickly as her snug, narrow pencil skirt will allow. "Don't I know you? Seems like you've been here before." She puts a hand to her forehead. "Ah, yes. You purchased a collection of armed services medals, if I'm not mistaken."

Wow. This chick is no slouch. Although, to be fair, there aren't a lot of twenty-two-year-olds, with pure white hair, frequenting antique shops. Time to see if she's as innocent as she sounds, or if she's Rory's accomplice. "Oh, yes. That was a while ago. How's business been?"

No change in her energy.

"It's a little slow this time of year, but there have been some lovely estate sales. We're fortunate to have several new items." Her voice is almost as soothing as a kitten's purr.

Maybe a more specific query will trigger her defenses. "Does the owner collect items from out of state or are all of these antiques local?"

Still no shift in her general vibe.

"We bring in objects from all over the world." Her gentle smile widens. "I rarely see the new owner. He travels extensively. I handle the local business and he ships items from abroad whenever he finds something he thinks will suit his clientele."

"How nice. He really trusts you to keep an eye on things here."

A whisper of defense floats upward. "I do my best."

"Have you received any shipments recently?"

The invisible defense thickens, and she shifts her stance. "Let me see." Her smile remains sweet and her eyes bright, but she chews her bottom lip thoughtfully.

I sense that she's stalling. "Nothing new?"

"Let me check." She steps behind her desk, and one hand shuffles a stack of papers from the left to the right.

"You take your time and think about it." Maybe she's pressing a button that sounds a silent alarm. Better make good use of my remaining time. "I hate to ask, but is there a restroom I could use?"

She's definitely uncomfortable now. "Well, it's technically not for customers." Her soft Dixieland charm is wavering.

"Gosh, I'm in need of several things for my new

apartment. I'm sure it would be worth your while if I could stay and shop without being so distracted." Dangle the ol' money carrot. That should work.

"It's through that door there. Mind your step. I'm unpacking some things in the back."

"Thank you so much." The singsong emphasis on "so" is a little snark I learned at college. I step through the door and reach out with all of my senses. Is he here? Did she send him some kind of message?

A quick scan confirms she has definitely been unpacking a new shipment. I snoop through the items, but there's nothing of interest and nothing cursed.

Much of the storeroom is carefully organized, and several of the items are shelved with certificates of authenticity or carefully notated provenance tags.

Circling around the second set of shelves, I walk back toward the restroom. There's a lamp on at the work desk in the corner.

Pulling out my gun, I click the safety off and approach slowly. So much for my promise to "not be a hero."

The lamp is very hot; the bulb has been on for some time. I slip around the desk where a copy of *Norse Expansion in the New World* is open to the chapter on Newfoundland.

The top left-hand drawer is ajar. My claircognizance fills me with a strong sense of knowing that something of importance lies within that drawer. I slide it open carefully, and in an instant the message is confirmed.

The chalice of narwhal tusk, etched with an image of the goddess Freya.

How did it get here?

A light scraping comes from somewhere beyond the shelves, and my skin crawls with fright. If I take the item, he'll know I was here. But if I leave it . . . It might be a critical component to some scheme he's building.

What would Silas do?

Take it.

The phrase resounds inside my head, and I shove the object inside my puffy jacket without a moment's hesitation.

The door from the retail space opens. "You all right, Miss?"

I carefully push the drawer closed, flick the safety on my gun, and shove it in my pocket.

Tiptoeing away from the desk, I make my way down the aisle before I reply. "I think I got turned around. I don't see a bathroom over here."

Her heels click rapidly on the cement floor and her eyes are bright with concern when she rounds the corner. "You shouldn't be back here." Her gaze flicks nervously toward the desk, and her sweet down-home Southern accent has vanished. She's angry, and a little afraid.

"I'm so sorry. I'm terrible with directions. I have ambulatory dyslexia. If I'm moving at all, I don't seem to know my left from my right. Could you point me in the right direction?"

She squeezes her eyes closed for a moment as she struggles with my wearisome presence, and recovers her charm. "It's right over there, sweetie."

"Thank you." I hurry into the bathroom, close the door, and lean against it as I catch my breath. She's been in contact with Rory. There's no mistaking that flicker of fear. Whether she stole the artifact from Klang's office or he did, someone has been doing some research.

I flush the toilet and turn on the taps to complete the ruse.

When I open the door, she's waiting with her arms crossed. "I didn't want you to get lost again. Let me show you the way back to the store."

Rude. "Thank you. I'm wondering if you have any Art Deco pieces?"

One grossly over-priced lamp and a hideous white panther bookend later, I've paid penance for my guilt. With no intention of further tempting fate, I hustle back to my Jeep with the packages—and my prize.

CHAPTER 12

Since Grams and I don't know a great deal about narwhal tusks, or their potential use in magic and alchemy, I opt to call in the big guns. Unfortunately, Silas is otherwise engaged. He promises to pick up doughnuts and coffee from Bless Choux in the morning and delve into a deeper Rory Bombay discussion at that time.

Pyewacket is deeply disturbed by the recovered relic, and circles warily around the coffee table. In the end, he takes up a position atop the wardrobe and sleeps with one eye open.

I've had all the excitement I can stand for one day, and a long hot bath with one of my new rainbow bath bombs is just what the doctor ordered. Or would be, if doctors gave orders for spectacular soaks.

"I'll search for that book while you're luxuriating in the tub, dear. The unicorn horn reference has a real ring of familiarity. One of the secretive arms of the Rare Books mezzanine must contain what I'm looking for. If I can't find it tonight, you can text Twiggy in the morning."

"Copy that, Grams. And to make sure we're all on the same page, there's no popping in the bathroom while I'm luxuriating in the tub. Capisce?"

Grams throws a sparkling hand to her forehead and pops a salute. "Aye, aye, Captain."

Oh brother. I grab my warmest pajamas, thickest socks, and my robe.

Pyewacket continues to feign sleep from his perch, high atop the antique furniture.

Splendid steam fills the bathroom and the wall heater hums to life. This has to be the coziest space in all of Pin Cherry Harbor.

The bath bomb emits a warm spiced-apple fragrance as it circles around the bathtub sputtering its rainbow trail. Eventually we get to the end of the rainbow, and I slip into the delicious liquid.

Resting my head against the soft, air-filled pillow suctioned to the back edge, I replay the incidents at the antiquities shop to see if I can collect any extrasensory information about the suspicious events in the back room.

Starting the memory-clip with my hand on the front door, there's a strange flash of familiarity. I can't discern whether it's the place or a person, but it's worth noting. There are two or three items on the carefully lit shelves that draw my attention as I walk through the psychic recall—they scream *stolen.*

No surprise there.

I fast-forward to the moment when the pretty Southern belle steps behind her desk to check her inventory. The left hand shuffles papers, while the right hand slips out of sight.

The extrasensory replay allows me to zoom in and confirm that she indeed presses a button.

The light blinks on and off in the back room. I hadn't noticed that in the shop, but this tidbit supports my suspicion that she was alerting someone to my presence.

Fast forward to me searching the shelves and desk in the storage area. There's that sound.

I rewind the scene. With all of my inexplicable perceptions engaged, the replay reveals that the sound is definitely the shuffling slide of a foot. The energy is twisted in some way—almost as if it's masked. For me, that's authentication enough. Who else would be hiding in the back room of Bombay Antiquities and cowering behind a magical shield?

Allowing myself to slip under the water, I release the replay as the heat and fragrance envelop me.

Silas will know what to do.

Tomorrow.

Tonight's program includes: relaxation, recharging, and reheating—

"If you say reheating sweet-and-sour chicken, I'll find a way to ghost vomit!"

I shoot out of the water like a surfacing submarine. "Grams!"

The ghostly form has its back turned, for what that's worth. "I'm sorry, dear. I know I broke the rules, but I found the book, and I can't manage enough physical substance to pull it from the shelf. So when you're done in here—"

"Oh, I'm done. Trust me, relaxation obliterated." I lift the drain plug and scowl. "Skedaddle, so I can at least get dressed in peace."

"Thank you, dear. You are a treasure."

"Flattery will get you nowhere, you peeping ghost!"

She snorts as she vanishes through the wall.

Out on the elegantly curved left arm of the mezzanine, that long ago surrounded the huge brewing vats that were part of this historical distillery, I slide the ladder across the shelving to the point where Grams is bouncing up and down like a toddler who has OD'd on birthday cake.

"It's here. It's right here. See, *Unicorn Magic of the Norse.*"

I climb carefully up the ladder, not wanting a repeat of the fall that could've killed me several months ago . . . but that's another story. Reaching the shelf where Grams is anxiously pointing, I toy with her for a minute. "Is it this book? This one right here?"

Her pointing finger becomes a fist and lands on her curvy hip. "Don't you get smart with me, young lady."

Laughing at my own joke, I retrieve the book and slowly back down the ladder.

The tales prove less enthralling than the title led me to believe, and I'm shocked awake when the voice of Silas Willoughby crackles over the apartment's intercom. I drifted off so quickly last night that the reality of daylight leaves me confused and disoriented. Surprisingly, I'm still holding the book of "unicorn" lore—or, rather, bore.

"Coming!"

"He can't hear you until you push the button, dear." Grams gestures toward the wall.

Not being a morning person, I glower and snap. "Thanks, Vasco da Gama. I've had the intercom orientation." I put on a false voice and recite the lesson. "The mother-of-pearl-inlaid buttons are the way to respond. The one on the left lets you talk and the one on the right is the 'call' button to ring the back room. The middle rings the museum."

Grams crosses her arms and tsks. "You had better adjust your attitude before Silas gets up here. He won't tolerate sass."

I push the button on the left and attempt some congeniality. "Come on up, Silas. I'm desperate for doughnuts."

Ghost-ma snickers behind me. "You should put *that* on a T-shirt."

Pushing the plaster medallion above the intercom, I turn as the bookcase door slides open for Silas. "I deserved that. Sorry for snapping at you. You know me— and *early*."

Grams crosses her bejeweled limbs and lifts her chin. Vindicated at last.

Silas enters with a large box of pastries and two steaming cups of java. He places everything on the coffee table and takes his favorite chair, as I lunge for a cup of black gold as though it's the antidote to a poison.

He speaks while I glug. "I uncovered a plethora of alarming facts. How did your research progress?"

Grams laughs openly at his query, and both of us glance toward the open book peeking out from under the folds of the down comforter.

"Not that great." I take another glorious sip of coffee before I continue. "I kind of nodded off. But, in my defense, it was the most boring book in the history of ever."

He carefully chews his pastry and politely wipes Bavarian cream from the corner of his mouth. "Which text put you to sleep?"

"Something about Norse unicorn horns . . ."

Silas nods. "Ah, yes. A fanciful attempt to disguise the truth. Once the myth of the unicorn horn had been put into play, narwhal tusks escalated rapidly in value. There would've been little benefit to hunters to correct the inaccuracy."

My bottom lip juts out in a mock pout. "So you're not about to tell me that unicorns are real? Because with all the ghosts and stuff, I was really hoping for unicorns."

Silas chuckles and reaches for a second pastry. "I

wish for it as well. However, in the long years of my life, I have never had the pleasure to prove or disprove that myth. There are yet places in the world I have not visited. Perhaps, one day . . ." His musings are terminated by a mouthful of éclair.

Grams rockets down from the ceiling in frustration. "I think the two of you have had enough to eat. Let's get down to business. Why is Rory Bombay after that unicorn horn chalice?" She gestures violently toward the relic next to the doughnuts.

"Yikes. For your information, Grams is getting a little pushy. I think we better wrap up breakfast and get down to the deets."

Silas smooths his mustache. "I'm not familiar with Dietz. Is this a relatively new author?"

The burst of laughter that erupts from my mouth carries a small puff of powdered sugar along for the ride. "Um, no. It's short for details. All this time at college has affected my vocabulary."

Silas harrumphs. "Not for the better, I see."

"You're not wrong."

"My time with arcane texts proved quite valuable. The chalice was carved from a narwhal tusk, the stem and ornate base were crafted from iron ore extracted from a meteor. The symbol on the cup is indeed the mark of the goddess Freya."

"So why does Rory want it?"

"Certainly not to transmute poison. It was proven in the 1600s that narwhal tusk, then known as unicorn horn, did not possess any properties of merit in that arena."

"So what's he after?"

"It is far more likely the power of this cup is linked to the seiðr magic instilled by the high priestess of Freya. According to my research, it is believed that this vessel once held the power of illusion. Perhaps it plays into a scheme of Mr. Bombay's to conceal himself from authorities."

I reach for a third doughnut, but Ghost-ma's gasp forces my hand back to my lap. "So he drinks something from this cup and becomes invisible?"

Silas tilts his head back and forth slowly. "In a manner of speaking. It would be a complicated transmutation, resulting in an intricate delusion. I do not believe Mr. Bombay possesses the skill. However, he is delving deeper into these murky secrets than I would deem safe."

"Do you mean he could get sick, like what happened to Grams?"

She sputters with offense. "Look here, young lady, I wasn't devouring mystical texts in search of supreme power."

I arch an eyebrow and translate for Silas.

He leans back and chuckles. "I had no intention of impugning your reputation, Isadora. There was no malice in your search for knowledge. Perhaps you were a bit greedy and depleted your body faster than it could replenish. It's not a judgment. It is simply the truth."

Sadness and regret vibrate my grandmother's apparition. She floats through the wall without a word.

"She didn't argue, but she did leave."

"Understandable."

Picking up the chalice, I turn it in my hand and trace the gentle swirl of the unicorn horn. "Do these whales still exist?"

"Narwhals are severely endangered. Apart from the Inuit peoples, no one is permitted to hunt them in this day and age. This cup may, in fact, have powerful magical properties, but it is also worth a veritable fortune."

"Wow." I gingerly set the chalice on the coffee table.

"We must protect it and see that it is gifted to a museum for proper display."

"Sure. Whatever you recommend. I'm not really comfortable owning something made from an endangered species."

"Indeed."

"Should I go back to the antiquities shop and confront Rory?"

Silas leans into the over-stuffed chair and laces his fingers over his paunch. "That would be ill advised. One man is already dead. I believe we've uncovered a probable motive. I will continue my research here, in the loft. Tomorrow we shall see what we can pry from the lips of the Defenders. Perhaps today you can visit Mr. Harper and update him as you see fit."

"Am I giving any of this information to Paulsen?"

"Perhaps it is time to hand off the negative. A gesture of goodwill should keep her on our side."

"Copy that."

Silas retires to the loft to page through history, while I shove a judgment-free third doughnut in my mouth and finish my coffee.

Down at the station Paulsen is in an uncharacteristically foul mood, even for her.

"Hey, Deputy. I found something that may or may not help the case."

She scowls up from the mountain of paperwork on Erick's desk. "Look, Moon, I don't have time for hunches. The evidence against Harper is stacking up." She leans back and sighs heavily. "And despite what you think, I don't like that."

I nod and pull a small envelope from my coat pocket. "This negative was recovered from Professor Klang's office. I'm not sure if it will help, but it appears to depict some Norse artifacts. Maybe he was engaged in some black-market trading? It's a potential lead."

Paulsen takes the negative. "Okay. I'll get this over to the lab and get a print made." She puts one of her pudgy hands on the telephone and pauses. "Thanks."

"No problem. We both want the same thing, right?"

She nods and picks up the receiver.

That's my cue. I exit the office and walk toward the holding cells. The heaviness in my heart is sure to affect the expression on my face. As my hand rests on the door handle, I attempt to access some positive energy reserves and paste a smile on my frustrated face.

"Harper? You awake? I brought doughnuts."

His sexy fingers reach through the bars and grip the cold grey metal. "This promises to be the highlight of my day, Moon."

I smile and pass the doughnuts through the bars. My eyes widen as I take in the redecorated cell. "First it's prisoner makeover day, and now it looks like an episode of *While You Were Out*. What's going on in here, Harper?"

His cheeks redden, and he rolls his eyes. "You would be looking at the efforts of holding cell interior designer, Gracie Harper." He sits on the metal bench, now covered by a small mattress and a handmade quilt.

"Your mom is a pistol. If you're in here much longer, she's liable to paint a mural on that back wall."

The smile on his face is everything. "You have no idea."

Given Erick's history with Rory Bombay, I keep the update to the 35mm negative and a possible connection to black-market artifacts.

He nods, but I can feel his desire to jump into this investigation.

"I'll stop by after school tomorrow and let you know if Silas and I get any more info from the students."

He sets down his pastry and walks to the bars. His hand reaches through and brushes the snowy hair from my face. "It's nice to see the real Mitzy, too."

His kind words stir my heart, and my cheeks flush a self-conscious shade of pink. "Thanks, Sheriff."

He presses against the barrier and pecks my cheek. "Keep sayin' that. It gives me hope."

That one little phrase keeps me toasty warm all the way back to the Bell, Book & Candle, despite the howling winds and threatening clouds.

The remainder of my Sunday fun-day is frittered away listening to Silas drone on about narwhals and unicorn horns.

No smoking gun is revealed and we opt for calling it a day and hoping for a breakthrough tomorrow.

CHAPTER 13

THE COMFORTING WEIGHT of Pyewacket sprawled across my chest wakes me. As I scratch between his black-tufted ears, I offer my thanks. "I appreciate your protection, Pye. I'm sure you heard us talking about Rory—"

HISS.

"I couldn't agree more, but I'm a little scared, you know? He's already so many steps ahead of us. I don't think I can handle it if he gets away with murder—again. If there's anything you know that could help me, I'm open to all suggestions. Don't hold back, boy. I need all the players on my team to give me a hundred and ten percent."

A sparkling ball of energy slowly drifts toward the bed.

"Thanks, Grams. After the fright of discovering Rory's back in town, I definitely can't take any of your apparition hijinks."

Ghost-ma twinkles into the visible realm and smiles warmly. "Pyewacket was on alert all night. He never left your side."

For some reason, this news chokes me up more than I would've thought. "Of course, that means you also never left my side."

She shrugs her designer-gown-clad shoulders and looks away.

"We're gonna get him this time. I don't care what inter-dimensional laws I have to break, Rory Bombay is gonna wish he never met me."

Grams floats up to the ceiling and her essence flickers pensively.

"What is it? I can tell something is troubling you."

She hovers near the tin-plated ceiling and gazes down at me. "Well, who's thought-dropping now?"

"Touché. But seriously, do you have any ideas?"

"Not yet. Give me some time and I'll definitely come up with something. For now, you should get to school and ask Ainsley about that photograph."

"The photograph! I completely forgot. When I felt the curse emanating from that runestone, I lost my mind and ran. She probably thinks I'm completely insane." I gently push Pyewacket to the side and throw back my thick down comforter. "You better have an extra special outfit for today. I'm gonna need to win friends and influence people faster than Carnegie ever imagined."

"I'm on it!" The ghost of grandmothers past

blasts through the closet wall with the conviction only a fashion diva can hold.

"Come on, Mr. Cuddlekins. Let's go scrounge up some grub before I have to face the potentially cursed Defenders."

I slip into my fuzzy dragon-claw slippers and the two of us shuffle down to the back room. As I approach, I smell coffee brewing. "Twiggy?"

My heart shouldn't be looking for a place to hide inside my rib cage, but knowing that Rory Bombay is loose in Pin Cherry makes even the most mundane things seem suspicious.

"Yeah. What's up, doll?"

Whew. "Welcome back. Did everything go all right at the estate sale?"

Twiggy chuckles. "Well, look who's all interested in the business. Yep. I was the first collector on site and I had the good stuff locked up before JB's plane even landed."

"JB is another collector?"

She pretends to spit on the floor. "He's a washed up bookmobile chaser."

I don't think I want the backstory on JB. Time for a change up. "Grams said I should ask you about Thanksgiving. I don't want to put any pressure on anyone, but my dad and Amaryllis brought it up, so . . . I don't have any plans."

She pours some questionably dated half-and-half into a cup of java and hands it to me.

Now I'm doubly suspicious. "Are you all right? You don't seem like yourself."

"Trust me, kid, I was already pouring the coffee. Don't go thinking you're special."

Now, that's the Twiggy I know.

"I always have a big potluck out at my place. Your dad and Amaryllis are more than welcome. Tell them to bring the pumpkin pie and you can bring rolls." She tilts her head. "And please, buy a bag from Piggly Wiggly. I don't want anyone breakin' a tooth."

"Gee, thanks. What about Erick and his mom? I mean, I'm sure I'll get him out of jail by then. There's no way he murdered anyone, and now that Rory Bombay—"

"Whoa! That good-for-nothing, green-eyed serpent is back in town?"

Swallowing, I nod slowly. "I'm ninety-eight percent sure. I found a cursed runestone in the dorms Friday night, and it's exactly his kind of tactic."

"You let me know if there's anything I can do. These biker boots are happy to stomp on anything that gets out of line."

We share a chuckle, and I nod. "Thanks. I'm kind of hoping Silas has a trick or two up his sleeve."

She laughs out loud. "That man has more tricks than either of us could count."

"Copy that."

"I'll feed the beast. You get changed for school, kid."

I shake my head and exit without reply.

The echo of her cackle follows me as I retreat to the safety of my apartment.

"All right, Grams, I had a few sips of coffee and I'm ready for whatever six-inch-heel-based outfit you've got planned. I'm at your mercy."

Her shimmering image appears at the closet doorway, complete with a smirk. "Perfect. Then I can't wait to show you what I've chosen."

Stepping through her, I glance at the pieces carefully placed on the padded mahogany bench.

"What do you think, dear?"

Tears spill from my eyes. "Every time I think I've got you figured out, you pull another supernatural trick out of your invisible back pocket. Thanks for believing in me."

"I'll never stop. I love you."

"I love you too, Grams."

She rushes off, and I run my fingers over the items she's lovingly chosen. My favorite pair of skinny jeans. My comfortable, well-worn high-tops, and a long-sleeved T-shirt with a picture of a cat filing one of its claws. Beneath the brazen feline it says, "Sure, underestimate me. That'll be fun."

I'm not ready to go full Mitzy Moon, so I bobby pin the wig into place. I feel practically invincible as I slip into today's wardrobe.

Silas is taking roll when I walk in. "Thank you for joining us, Miss Brown."

Five heads spin toward the door at the back of the room. The painfully obvious absence of Ainsley's face among the crew pricks a warning hum in my psychic senses.

Brooklyn's messy bun tips to the side as she gazes disapprovingly at my attire. "Those shoes are so cringe, Darcy. Did you oversleep?"

I don't have time for this girl's multitude of hang-ups. "Where's Ainsley?"

"Ouch. Down, girl." She glances at Hutton and smirks.

I look past her and address Hutton directly. "Where's Ainsley?"

Hutton twirls an auburn ringlet around her finger. "She was AFK when I got home last night. I think she bugged out early to add some vacay days to her break, you know?"

"No doubt," chimes Bodie.

I stride up to the lectern and whisper to Professor Willoughby. "Ainsley is missing and I'm sure it's no coincidence. Can you get the rest of the crew into your office and give me an opportunity to brandish my club membership?"

"Certainly, Miss Brown."

Returning to the seat next to Brooklyn, I plunk down and cross my arms.

Silas clears his throat. "Today is the perfect opportunity for field research. Return to your critique groups and visit one of Pin Cherry's historical sites. If you are unfamiliar with the area, the Pin Cherry

Harbor Historical Society provides maps, free of charge. You will present these field reports on Wednesday, for half of your total semester grade."

Gasps of shock ripple through the student body.

Silas collects his things and walks toward the exit next to the whiteboard. "Oh, and Miss Brown, bring your group to my office at once."

Brooklyn rolls her eyes and adjusts her hair. "Great job. Now we're, like, totally going to get slammed with extra work."

She links her arm through Hutton's elbow and drags her out the door after Professor Willoughby.

The three male members of the group eye me suspiciously and follow Brooklyn as though it was their idea.

Once we're all crowded into the late Professor Klang's office, I pull out the now un-cursed runestone I swiped from Ainsley and show it to the group. "I thought this was supposed to mean something. When Professor Klang invited me into this program, he assured me that the Defenders looked out for one another. I can't believe that Ainsley has been missing for almost twelve hours and none of you bothered to report it."

Shocked expressions adorn every face in the lineup, but no one else produces their stone.

"Maybe you guys aren't in the club? I assumed that since Ainsley was in the club, and she hung around with you . . ." I let my voice trail off and wait, hoping they take the bait.

Brooklyn produces her stone. "As if. Ainsley was, like, the last one to get a stone. And I'm not even gonna tell you what she had to do to get it."

Silas sends me a very clear, but invisible, message. My clairaudience hears the phrase *all the stones*.

Kaden fishes around in his front pocket and thrusts his runestone in my face. "See? BTW, you don't know what you're talking about, New Girl. Klang didn't give us these stones. The angel investor passed them out at a special after-hours meeting. He said that only members who had these stones would share in the profits from the dig's treasures. If we lost 'em, or whatevs, we got nothing."

"Well, let's see everyone else's. What I'm about to say is exclusively for the inner circle."

Hutton digs in her backpack, while the two remaining boys reach into their various pockets. Within seconds, five hands are extended forward to display five cursed runestones.

Silas mumbles something in a strange tongue, which I've never heard before.

The five Defenders go glassy-eyed.

"What did you do? Did you stop time?" I stare open-mouthed at the frozen coeds.

"It is a weak counter-measure that locks them in a temporary loop. Use these tongs to collect all the stones and place them in this pouch. Then you must quickly trace the reversal runes on each of their hands and erase their memory of this meeting."

"Seriously? You told me those symbols are incredibly dangerous and shouldn't be used willy-nilly, or whatever."

"Indeed. Time is running out to find Ainsley and catch Rory Bombay. In this instance, my powers must remain as secret as yours. You have little time. Start with the blond boy on the left and work quickly, but with deepest focus."

A chill creeps across my shoulders and the hairs on the back of my neck stand on end. Since solving my mom's murder, I understand that sensation means she's watching over me, and it bolsters my courage. I grab Tayton's hand, take a deep breath, and visualize the words and actions that took place in this room as I carefully trace the four symbols, in the exact order taught to me by Silas.

As soon as I finish, I move to the next. That's Bodie, done. Kaden, done. Brooklyn, done.

"Make haste, Mitzy."

Easy for him to say. I grasp Hutton's hand, and as I'm tracing the third symbol, she blinks her black-lined eyes. My heart skips a beat and I have to hold my breath to maintain focus. My finger is drawing down the last ligature of the final symbol when she fully awakens.

"What is your issue? What are you doing to my hand?"

"Nothing. Cool ring." I step back and try to act casual. "You guys better get over to the historical society and get those maps. I'll catch up with you in the dorms later."

Silas opens the door, and the five vaguely confused, slightly foggy Defenders of nothing shuffle out in single file. He closes the door and breathes a sigh of relief. "Impressive. Your focus is expanding daily. And your ability to receive messages is also vastly improved."

I collapse onto one of the visitor chairs and pant, as apprehension drains from my body. "I was so worried. I lost my focus a little at the end. I drew the right symbol, but Hutton was coming around."

Silas places a calming hand on my shoulder and I sense nourishing energy soaking into my being. "You performed the runes exactly as you were taught. There was no mistake, no damage. You removed their memory of this meeting and only this meeting. Now you should rest."

"Yeah, I feel kind of empty."

"I would never ask you to do more than you are capable of, Mizithra."

I stumble across the wind-swept quad toward my Jeep, and the image of curling up under my down comforter with Pyewacket at my side warms me from the inside out.

Unfortunately, once I start the engine, my hands seem to have plans of their own.

For some reason, I'm not afraid, but I'm hoping this isn't Rory's doing.

The next thing I know, I'm turning down a dirt

road next to an enormous sign for McClintock's Divine Dairy.

Is this the farm owned by Ainsley's father? Did I know where this was? If I didn't know where it was, how did I get here? Either way, I trust he knows where his daughter is, because I'd hate to be the one to tell him she might've been kidnapped by a deranged practitioner of the dark arts.

The two-story farmhouse bears the typical coat of white paint and has a large screened porch enclosing the entrance. Three huge red barns stand like sentries to the right of the house, and farm implements, too numerous to mention, are strewn about the property.

I approach the front entrance hesitantly and ease the screen door closed behind. Sure, I could let it slam like every screen door in every country song you've ever heard, but I'm not entirely sure why I'm here and I prefer to take a more subtle approach.

There's no doorbell.

However, there is a large metal triangle hanging from a sturdy steel arm. Since I'm not here to call the hired hands to dinner, I'll go with a more traditional option.

Knocking softly at first, and then with increased volume, I wait.

A large man with rough red cheeks and a redder neck answers the door. He smells of earth and hard work, and an unfriendly expression weighs down his features. "We don't support no charities except our own, and I ain't had time to read a magazine since 1975." He begins to push the door closed.

"Mr. McClintock?" It's as good a guess as any. "I'm actually a friend of Ainsley's. We're in the archaeology program together at the community college."

The gap widens an inch or two. "She ain't takin' no visitors, ya know."

A sigh of relief escapes my lips. "She's here? She's all right?"

The door opens a bit farther. "What do you know about it?"

"I know she was working on a special project with Professor Klang before he was killed . . ." I reach into my jacket and slip out the photograph of Ainsley next to the pile of artifacts. "And I think it might've had something to do with this."

The door flies open wide, and he reaches to his right.

Before I can say "got milk," I'm staring down the double-barrel of a shotgun.

"Get off my land. Get back in whatever devil wagon brought you here and don't come back." His finger rests solidly inside the trigger guard. "No one is gonna dig up my farm, and that's final. Now, get!"

Slowly backing toward the screen door, I worry what this man might do to someone who doesn't take no for an answer. I'm not sure what to say to him, but this is my one chance to get a little piece of information. "Mr. McClintock, I don't want to cause any trouble. I'm trying to find out who killed the professor. I'm worried that Ainsley might be in danger, especially if those artifacts are the real deal."

He fires a warning shot past my head, and buckshot rips through the rusty screen.

I shove the screen door open, let it bang shut for all to hear, and run to my Jeep. The frigid air stings my cheeks and burns my throat, but it's nothing compared to the pain of being shot if I stop running. At some point I drop the photograph, but with the negative safe at the sheriff's station, there's no point risking buckshot in the behind to pick it up.

Diving into my vehicle, I kick up a rooster tail of dust and gravel as I tear out of the Divine Dairy.

And no, the nomenclature-based irony is not lost on me.

CHAPTER 14

It's never a good day when someone shoots at you, but, on the upside, Ainsley is safe at home and not being held against her will by Rory Bombay.

I need a decent cup of hot chocolate and an extravagant pastry to help me process all of this information.

Next stop, Bless Choux patisserie on Third Avenue.

The crowd is thinner than expected for the afternoon rush, but the proprietor, Anne, is bustling around as though the line stretches around the corner. When I get my turn at the counter, I order an extra-large Mexican hot chocolate and a chocolate croissant. "You seem awfully busy. You wouldn't happen to have time to teach a girl how to make a pie, would you?"

She chuckles, and her eternal smile shines on me. "I'd be happy to teach you how to make pie eleven months out of the year, Mitzy, but November isn't one of those months. I have orders for pumpkin, pecan, apple, and strawberry rhubarb pies longer than both my arms and legs. And every single one of them has to be baked and boxed by this Wednesday. But I tell you what, if you'd like to place an order, I'm happy to tell everyone you baked it yourself."

Her kind accommodation always surprises me. "I'd like to order a pumpkin. I'm not sure how many people will be there. Is one pie enough?"

She sets my chocolate croissant on a plate and shakes her head playfully. "One pie is never enough. If you're headed out to Twiggy's shindig, you better take a pumpkin and an apple. I happen to know that's her favorite."

My mouth waters at the sight of the croissant. "You know everything that happens in this town, don't you?"

We share a chuckle and I confirm my order for the two pies. "Hey, on the topic of knowing everything, what do you know about the McClintock's and their dairy farm?"

For the first time since I stumbled into her patisserie, the smile on her face fades. "That was some bad business."

My extrasensory antennae tingle with anticipation. "Something bad happened out at the farm?"

She glances at the short line behind me and leans across the counter. "Give me a minute to take care of these folks, and I'll stop by your table."

"No problem." I pay for my snack and my pie order, and take the croissant to a corner table.

A few minutes later, Anne appears with a beautiful mug of Mexican hot chocolate, topped with a healthy portion of whipped cream and a gentle sprinkling of cinnamon.

She sets the mug on the table without spilling a drop and takes the seat opposite. "Mrs. McClintock was attacked when Ainsley was a little more than a year old. They never caught the man responsible. Rumor has it, he was one of the hired hands, and he moved on, as the seasonal workers always do. Poor Clyde found his daughter wandering down the dirt road and came home to find . . . Well, best not talk about it. Mrs. McClintock was in the hospital for almost two weeks. Clyde was never the same. He got real, you know, protective."

"So he shoots at everyone that shows up unannounced?"

Anne claps her hand on the table and leans back, wide-eyed. "You went out to the farm?"

"Ainsley didn't show up at class today, and I wanted to make sure she was all right."

Her broad smile returns and she chuckles as she points to my wig. "Oh, that explains the getup."

"What do you mean?"

"You know how folks talk in a small town. I've heard a story or two about you wearing disguises and going undercover to solve crimes. When you do good, word gets out."

"I'm trying my best to do good, but I'm not having any luck proving Erick's innocence."

Anne reaches across the table and squeezes my hand. "We all know he's innocent, sweetie. You'll figure it out. I have as much faith in you as I do in my great-grandma's *pâte à choux* recipe." She pats my hand and returns to her kitchen.

It's time to bring Erick up to speed. He'll be angry, but it doesn't feel right to keep him in the dark about Rory. I'll grab a dozen doughnuts to soften the blow.

Furious Monkeys is busy tapping and swiping on her phone when I arrive at the sheriff's station.

"Care for a doughnut?"

Shockingly my offer receives real live eye contact. "Set a jelly-filled next to me. I'm only two coconuts from leveling up and can't stop now."

I place a jelly doughnut on top of the stack of reports next to her and make my way to Erick's office. I am not looking forward to running into Paulsen, but she doesn't seem the type to say no to a doughnut.

"Can I interest you in a doughnut, Deputy?"

"It's Acting Sheriff, and yes." She reaches into the box and grabs a large bear claw.

Now to test the waters with my news. "Hate to be the one to tell you, but I'm pretty sure Rory Bombay is behind Gerhardt Klang's murder. I think he purposely set up Erick to take the fall."

Her mouth is already full, and she chews slowly as my words sink in. She swallows and wipes the crumbs from the corner of her mouth with the back of her hand. "You got any evidence?"

Since I can't really tell her about cursed runestones or psychic messages I'm left with a gigantic pile of nothing. "Not yet."

"Well, if it's a setup, it's a good one. The trace came back on that needle today—victim's blood inside. The outside had been wiped clean. I'm afraid we'll have to charge Harper, but I'm gonna keep him in our holding cell as long as I can. County jail is no place for a sheriff. If we don't find something to clear his name before the holidays, my hands will be tied. He'll have to transfer to County and await his trial."

If ever there was a gloomier sentence, I haven't heard it. "I'll find something. I'm sure I'll find something." As I turn to leave the office, she calls out.

"Moon, you shouldn't tell him about Bombay. He's like a powder keg back there, and I'm afraid that name will light the match."

"All right. For now. But if I get you some evidence, you'll— I mean, you know he's innocent, right?"

"My opinion isn't the law. Like I told you before, I have to follow the evidence, just like the sheriff would if he was in my position."

"Copy that." At least there's a hint of apology in her tone. That's something.

The hallway outside the holding cells seems narrower, the paint more disheartening, and the air colder than I remember. Erick gazes toward me as I walk in front of the bars, but his eyes don't light up.

"I brought you doughnuts."

He laughs once. The sound is sharp and hollow. "My last meal, eh?"

Tilting the box, I pass it through the bars and set it softly on the cement floor. "Absolutely not. In fact, it's a celebration."

His eyes dart up, and the weight of his hope threatens to break my heart. "You found something?"

"Yes, but I can only tell you if you promise to remain calm."

He stands and stalks to the bars. "I don't know if I can make that kind of promise, Moon."

"You have to. *Acting Sheriff* Paulsen made me promise not to tell you, but I can't stand seeing you like this."

"Look, they've got my jersey with the vic's blood, the murder weapon from my gear bag, and I've got no alibi. Even if it's more bad news, it's better than nothing, I guess."

"I hope you still feel that way thirty seconds from now." I take a deep breath and ignore the burning ring of fire on my left hand. I'm sure the universe at large is screaming at me to keep my secrets, but when I look into those helpless blue eyes, I'd do anything to change his fate. "It's Rory Bombay."

My extra senses pick up on the building rage, and I step away from the bars. Erick kicks the box of doughnuts, grabs the quilt his mother brought him off the bench, and throws it across the tiny cell. "What has that guy got against me?"

I swallow and whisper, "Me."

His wild, fierce anger vanishes faster than a Sedona sunset. "You? Don't you dare try to take responsibility for that madman."

I step toward the cell and place my hands on the bars. "It's true. If I'd just given him what he wanted." I choke back the tears and try to continue. "He would've never come after you. He would've taken what he wanted from me, picked up his stupid relics from McClintock's farm, and you'd still be sheriff."

Erick exhales loudly and he places his hands lovingly over each of mine. "I still am sheriff. You and I are the best crime-solving team north of the Gulf of Mexico. Let's stop feeling sorry for ourselves and put our giant brains to use."

I lean against the bars and our lips meet in a passionate kiss, as a tear trickles down my cheek.

My mood ring has no time for lovey-dovey nonsense. The heat is so intense it feels as though my ring finger is on fire. I pull my hands away and look down. Ainsley has a gag in her mouth and she's weeping. I don't need to see any more of the image to know that Rory has taken her. My new commitment to honesty is going to have to be shelved.

Erick leans against the bars with concern. "What's wrong? Not to toot my own horn, but usually you don't pull away from a kiss like that."

When in doubt, lie it out. "Yeah, sorry. The kiss

was amazing. Something popped into my head . . . I need to talk to Silas." I hold a hand to my head as though the pressure can force a solution to the surface. "Should I send someone in to clean up the doughnuts?"

Erick blushes shamefacedly. "Nah, I'm gonna eat 'em off the floor as penance. That's where I'm at now, Moon. Will you be back today?"

"Let's say by morning. It's a bit of a drive out to Silas's place, and I'm not sure how long it'll take to get the information I need. Do you want breakfast from the diner or the patisserie?"

"How about you surprise me?" A weak smile touches his lips.

I turn and march toward the door, and hear him call after me. "Don't do anything stupid."

The man knows me too well.

There's no time to actually drive out to see Silas. A call will have to do. I put the phone on speaker and drive, hoping for psychic guidance.

"Good afternoon, Miss Moon. How may I be of assistance?"

"Silas, Rory has taken one of the girls as bait. I know he won't hurt her—yet. There's something to those artifacts in that picture of Ainsley. I need your expertise. We have to figure out what he wants and give it to him. I hate to let him get away again, but I don't want anyone's blood on my hands."

"I shall meet you at the bookshop. Bring the photograph."

"Yeah, about that . . ." As I drive back to the Bell, Book & Candle, I bring Silas up to speed on the unholy events at McClintock's Divine Dairy. He assures me that with minor coaching, I should be able to recall every detail of the photograph.

Since there's no time to get Mr. Knudsen to develop another print, my psychically enhanced recall is our best bet.

Twiggy has already left for the day, so I don't have to update her on the Thanksgiving menu change-up. My dad and Amaryllis can bring dinner rolls. I can't believe Twiggy thought I couldn't make a pie. I mean, technically I'm not the one making a pie, but po-tay-to, po-tah-to.

CHAPTER 15

Grams bursts through the wall separating the bookshop from the printing museum. "Oh, thank goodness. I was worried sick."

"Why? What happened here?"

"He was here! That snake, Rory Bombay! He couldn't use any of his wily tricks. At least the protections Silas put in place did that much. He tried to steal a book, and Twiggy had to pepper-spray him!"

I shake my head in disbelief. "Good for her. Did he get the book?"

Grams places a ring-ensconced fist on each hip. "You've met Twiggy, right, dear?"

Despite the tension, we both chuckle.

"Silas is on his way over. He'll definitely want to know which book Rory was after. Do you remember?"

"Of course! I went and made a card and tacked it

on the murder wall as soon as Twiggy got rid of that viper."

"Wow! You might need to open your own afterlife detective agency."

"Oh Mitzy! You're such a hoot."

A key slips in the lock, and the thick metal door from the alley swings open. I'm not sure I've ever been happier to see Silas.

"Rory was here. He tried to steal a book, and Twiggy gassed him."

Silas calmly slips his key into his jacket pocket, dons his bespelled spectacles, and smooths his mustache with a thumb and forefinger. "Is he dead?"

"I should've been more specific. She pepper-sprayed him. He didn't get the book, but he got away, and now he's got Ainsley."

Taking off my thick winter coat, I toss it on a chair in the back room. "We need to figure out what he wants, get our hands on it, and then set a trap. And this time it needs to be a trap that won't fail."

Silas harrumphs. "Easier spoken than executed. He is a cunning man of many deadly talents, and dark powers. Each time we meet, I fear he grows more powerful. Would you not agree, Isadora?"

Grams nods her translucent head.

I cross my arms over my chest and scoff. "Well, I'm not above killing him." I do my best impression of the classic Robert De Niro nod, in every movie he's ever made. "I have a gun."

"Mizithra!" Silas and Grams remarkably admonish me in unison, even though he can't hear her.

The tears that I carefully kept at bay at the sheriff's station come tumbling out. "They found Klang's blood in the needle on that hand pump thingy. They're charging Erick with murder, today! It's not all right, and I can't handle it. I let myself care for someone and the same thing that always happens, happened again. He's going away. He's going away and he's breaking my heart."

Grams is the first to rush to my side. She slips an ethereal arm around my shoulders and coos softly into my ear. "There, there, dear. Erick isn't abandoning you. A nasty, horrible rat of a man has set up the good sheriff. It's our responsibility to turn the tables."

I translate for Silas.

"Without impugning any additional parties," he adds.

"All right, but I'm just saying." I swipe at my cheeks and pantomime cocking my finger-gun.

"There will be no need for firearms, Mitzy. Let's proceed upstairs and review the evidence. We know far more about this case and the true culprit than Deputy Paulsen."

I snuffle loudly and wipe my nose with the back of my hand. "Yeah. We're the Scooby Gang, and he's the crooked real estate developer."

As I walk toward the spiral staircase, Grams and Silas share a confused shrug.

Not bothering to explain my TV reference, I unhook the "No Admittance" chain and defiantly leave it hanging.

Silas takes his usual place in the scalloped-back chair and I arrange myself comfortably on the settee.

Pyewacket issues a low growl from his perch atop the antique armoire, next to the secret door.

"I hear your complaints, Pye. We're definitely going to get him this time. So if you have any other clues you were saving for a rainy day, today's the day."

"RE-OW!" Game on!

"I couldn't have said it better myself, son." I fold an arm under my head and take a deep breath. "What must I do, all-knowing mentor?"

Silas refuses to take the bait. "The process of psychic recall is delicate. Your opinions can alter the accuracy of your perceptions. You must release all of your preconceived notions and endeavor to describe the items in the photograph exactly as they appear."

"Copy that. No creative license."

Silas steeples his fingers, and as he leans back and slowly bounces his chin, he delivers the instructions. "Close your eyes and clear your mind of distractions. Count down from ten and, after each number, exhale any unwanted thoughts that appear."

I close my eyes and begin the count. "Ten, nine—"

"You may recite the count silently. Picture yourself descending a staircase, and each number represents a step farther down. When you reach the bottom, you'll see a beautiful door. Open it."

The door is magnificent. In fact, it looks very similar to the wooden door at the front of my bookshop. A thick timber slab intricately carved with whimsical vignettes. A centaur chasing a maiden through delicate woodland. A faun playing a flute for a family of rabbits dancing around his cloven feet. The shadow of a winged horse passing in front of the moon. A wildcat stalking a small boy—and the cat bears a striking resemblance to Pyewacket. I reach for the handle and it turns easily.

"Step into the room. In front of you, there is a lavender-colored screen. On this screen you may call up the memory of your choosing."

Staring at the projection screen, I wonder how I've not come to this room before. There are so many things I want to see. Maybe I could call up a memory of my mom.

"Your breathing indicates distraction. Push the other thoughts away. You may return to this room any time you choose. It is your inner world. For today, right here, right now, you must call up the image of the photograph."

It takes a moment to steady my breathing and let go of selfish desires. As soon as I turn my attention to the crisp black-and-white photograph printed for me by Mr. Knudsen, it blooms to life on the screen in front of me, like an inkblot spreading across paper.

"Good. Now, take your time as you examine the

image. Start on the left and let your eyes drift over the picture. Each time you see something of interest, describe it to me."

There's little Ainsley, probably about two years old, wearing an adorable floral sundress. "The photo was taken in the summer."

"Excellent. What else do you see?"

I shift my gaze to the pile of artifacts. "There are nails. They look handmade, probably iron. There are some small metal discs; they could be rivets. There's a piece of stone, kind of cone-shaped, but smooshed. It has a wide rounded base and the top is flat, with a hole all the way through. I don't know what that is."

"It's not important for you to know; simply describe things to me. What you're seeing is likely a spindle whorl, most assuredly carved from soapstone. Is there anything else?"

I never realized how soothing Silas's voice could be. My focus drifts and I have to pull it back to the photograph. "Yes, there's a bronze pin. I think it's a cloak pin."

"Very good. Anything else?"

"Yes, a piece of jewelry."

"Excellent. Can you describe it?"

A strange feeling of *otherness* comes over me, and words I've never heard come out of my mouth. "It is the golden torc Brísingamen. Made for the goddess Freya by the dwarven tribes. It holds the power of the sorceress of seiðr. It carries the power to make the wearer irresistible."

Gasping, I'm ripped from the mystical room. I fall back into my body with a frightful thud.

Silas stands and places a hand on my forehead. He mumbles, "Requietio," and I fall asleep.

When I open my eyes, Pyewacket is curled up in the curve of my body and Silas is sipping a cup of tea while an arcane tome lies open in his lap.

"You did wonderfully, Mitzy. Your description of the torc was spot on. Isadora showed me the book Rory was attempting to steal. It is a hand-written compilation of the rituals of Freya. The power of her gold torc is not to be underestimated. I believe we have stumbled upon the exact thing our nemesis seeks. The question is, where is it now? And how can we see that no harm comes to this Ainsley, and yet preserve the priceless artifact?"

I sit up and rub my eyes. My entire body aches with a grogginess I've never before experienced. "Isn't Freya a mythological figure? I mean, a Norse goddess isn't an actual person, right?"

"Whether the goddess chose to take human form is not our debate. We seek the torc as a means to rescue the girl."

The details of my vision are seeping back in like smoke under a door. "Did I say it makes the wearer irresistible?"

Silas nods affirmatively.

"That sounds about right. I guess Rory figured if he couldn't woo me the old-fashioned way with gifts of cursed jewelry, he'd mesmerize me by wearing a necklace that would make him irresistible. *Dirty Rotten Scoundrels,* part two!"

Pyewacket snarls and Grams nods furiously. "That man has been up to no good for far too many decades. I'm reconsidering your suggestion on guns."

Grams' brazen flip-flopping makes me chuckle, and Silas tilts his head questioningly.

I quickly interpret. "Oh, it's Grams getting on board with my gun idea."

"That will not be necessary. We know he doesn't possess the torc. If he did, he would have no reason to kidnap the girl."

"But how did he get her? Her dad pulled a gun on me ten seconds after I got there, and I wasn't even acting threateningly. Plus, how do we know where this picture of her was even taken? Maybe they were at a friend's house or something."

Silas fixes me with his uber-mentor stare. "How indeed?"

"Oh, right." I close my eyes, take a deep breath and seek the answer. "They definitely took the photograph at the Divine Dairy. We have to get in there and somehow get these artifacts. I mean, technically Clyde shouldn't have them, right? Why do you think he didn't report his findings to someone? This seems like a very important archaeological discovery."

Silas harrumphs. "There is more to Mr. McClintock than meets the eye. We may need to take the necklace by force."

"Should I get my gun?"

"Settle down, Annie Oakley. We have far more subtle tools at our disposal." Silas pats his coat of many pockets.

"Should I tell Paulsen about the kidnapping?"

"What evidence do you have to offer other than your vision?"

"Yeah, I see what you did there."

He smiles encouragingly. "Let me finish this passage and transcribe the remainder of my reference notes, and then I believe we shall take a drive out to the heavenly milk house."

"It's Divine Dairy, Silas."

"To be sure."

Grams flits around in a panic, and in her agitated state can't manifest enough corporeal form to open the secret panel underneath one of the built-in bookcases in the apartment.

"Let me get that for you, Grams." I press the panel, and the long wide drawer eases open.

She attempts to dig through the contents, but again her phantom fingers let her down.

"What are you looking for? Tell me. I can find it."

"It's a bracelet. It will protect you from Rory, I think."

"You think a bracelet will protect me? It would be great if you could be more certain."

Silas clears his throat as he approaches the open drawer. "Alchemy is a blend of science and the supernatural. Science maintains a degree of predictability, while the supernatural is slightly less compliant." He reaches into the drawer, slides over a smudge bundle of sage, and retrieves the copper bracelet. He slips the cuff over my right wrist. "If you feel Mr. Bombay's subtle manipulations swirling toward you, hold the bracelet in front of you and say, 'Ektrépo'."

I press a hand to my chest and stifle a giggle. "Like Wonder Woman? You seriously just gave me a Wonder Woman bracelet?" Hugging the bracelet to my heart, I gaze at the copper cuff and smile. "I love my life!"

Grams swirls through Silas and he steps back with a shiver. "Listen, young lady, this is no joke. That bracelet saved my life, once or twice. Not the last time, but I was sick. That's different. You wear it, and don't get smart."

I stand in the position of attention, with my fists at my sides. "Yes, sir, Major Ghost-ma, sir. Private Moon acknowledges."

My silliness softens her concern, and she chuckles as she drifts toward the ceiling.

"You know your way to this dairy, Mitzy?"

"I do. Let's rock . . . and ride!"

Silas scrunches up his face in confusion, but as I walk toward the Rare Books Loft, he follows without comment. It's the battle cry from *Biker Mice from Mars*, if you were wondering.

Time to save the girl, rescue a priceless mythological artifact, and crush an obsessed sorcerer.

You call it a blockbuster movie; I call it Monday night.

CHAPTER 16

As WE BUMP along the gravel road to McClintock's Divine Dairy, my misgivings about the plan, and concern over potentially getting shot, consume me. "Clyde wasn't in a very generous mood earlier. I'm betting that hasn't improved."

Silas nods and his jowls brush the collar of his shirt. "I would tend to be in agreement, if it weren't for one variable."

"Which is?"

"The disappearance of his daughter. We know that Mr. Bombay shies away from getting any dirt directly on his hands. However, his scheme to force Gerhardt's students to do his bidding with the cursed runestones collapsed in a dead end. Perhaps he attempted to pressure Professor Klang into stealing the remainder of the relics and Klang refused."

"Or Klang planned to double-cross him, and Rory chose to eliminate a traitor."

"A fair point." He nods as he ponders. "A father's love for his daughter is a powerful thing. For some reason, which I cannot grasp, Mr. McClintock watched his daughter be carted away rather than turn over the relics." Silas smooths his mustache and grumbles under his breath.

"You're assuming he had a choice. What if Rory secretly took Ainsley, or took her by magical force, and intends to use her as ransom?"

A heavy dread settles over the car as we make our final approach to the dairy.

In the gloaming, the white farmhouse looms with a sinister vibe.

"What's our next move?"

Silas exhales and cracks his knuckles. "I shall attempt a civil request for entry. If civility is denied, I shall be forced to immobilize Mr. McClintock while we search the property."

"Copy that. Am I waiting in the car for a sign, or do I follow you in now?"

"A valuable query. Since your earlier interaction with the farmer was less than positive, perhaps it would be best if you delay, and await the sign." Silas exits the vehicle and closes the door without indicating what sign I'm waiting for, but hopefully it's a clear one.

A soft yellow glow spills from the two windows to the right of the front door. When Silas knocks, the harsh white porch light flicks on, casting a sharp shadow against the screen.

Mr. McClintock answers the door, gun in hand, and an angry voice cuts through the frosty stillness. "No cops!"

He seems momentarily confused to see a doddering old man on his stoop, but after a brief exchange he aims the gun threateningly.

Silas appears to grow several inches in height, and I can feel the vibration of his deep voice in the soles of my feet.

Mr. McClintock lays down his weapon and steps back.

Silas turns toward the vehicle, snaps his fingers, and a flash of blue light pops in the twilight.

There's no mistaking it. That's the sign. I hop out and hurry to his side.

Mr. McClintock walks like a zombie into the living room.

"Be seated, Mr. McClintock."

The farmer drops into his well-worn recliner and folds his hands in his lap.

Silas turns to me. "It is up to you to find the items we seek. Focus. Breathe. Locate."

"Understood." I take a deep breath, and, I must admit, the multiple dishes of potpourri do little to disguise the underlying bouquet of manure.

Having learned a thing or two about the architecture of homes in almost-Canada, I head straight to the basement. You don't get a lot of basements in Arizona, and the creepiness factor still has a palpable effect.

I pull the string hanging from the single bulb and, as the light creates a circle around me, I clear my mind and reach for the torc.

Nothing.

Moving around the damp, musty cement space, I extend my hands as though I'm playing a game of blind man's bluff.

No messages. No feelings. No pretty pictures in my moody ring.

Clearly, I overestimated the importance of basements. Back on the main floor, I continue my extrasensory search. As I enter the bedroom at the end of the hallway, I'm startled to discover a woman asleep in the bed. I gasp and step back. The snafu blows my focus, and it's all I can do to close the door quietly.

Slipping into the living room, I share my news. "There's someone asleep in the bedroom."

"Perhaps it is Mrs. McClintock. Have you met her?"

"No. I heard a story about her from Anne at the patisserie, but for some reason I thought the woman was no longer with us."

Silas flourishes his hand. "She will continue to sleep. Finish the search. I fear time is running out for Ainsley."

At the sound of his daughter's name, Clyde flinches in his chair. Silas turns and tends to the man. "Remain calm. We are friends. We intend to save your daughter."

Clyde blinks once and slips back into the stupor.

I march up the stairs and search the bedrooms on the upper floor.

Nothing, aside from more cloying potpourri.

As I return to the top of the staircase, a pinching pull touches my chest. I turn and glance up and down the hallway. Finally, the psychic in me connects and my head whips back to see an access panel in the ceiling.

"The attic! Of course."

I have to locate a chair or stool. I find what I'm looking for in what must be Ainsley's room, based on the decor. Lots of pop-star posters, a laptop, and a massive collection of Funko Pop! figurines.

I slide the chair under the opening and pull the handle. As it lowers, an attached ladder is revealed. Folding it out, I climb up and use the light on my phone to search the space.

It's chokingly dusty. There are creepy-crawlies lurking, and I don't wish to disturb any of them. A hanging spider web catches in my hair and I freak out as I try to get the sticky strands off of me.

In the confusion, I drop my phone. As soon as it hits the floor, it's as though a barrier has been lifted. An invisible rope circles around my heart and pulls me forward.

There's an old metal chest, with wooden bands encompassing it. I kneel and open the chest. Without the aid of a light, I reach in and retrieve a heavy stone box.

There are runes carved in the lid.

I scrape the lid to the side and lean it against the trunk. Grabbing my phone, I illuminate the contents. Inside are all the items from the photograph, plus two smaller pieces that must've been absent from the picture, as was the chalice. There's a woven bag on the left-hand side. I pull it open and the golden gleam of the torc shocks me. I expected an item of such age to be tarnished. The goddess Freya has been watching over her jewelry.

Slipping the phone into my pocket, I reach for the stone lid.

The torc *calls* to me, and part of me yearns, in the worst way, to place it around my neck. As I move the lid closer to the box, a push like opposing magnets shoves the top away from the bottom.

"No. You are not for me." Saying it out loud breaks the trance and the lid drops into place with a stony thud.

I exhale with relief, take a deep breath, and choke on attic dust.

Time to grab this box and get the heck out of Creepytown.

When I return to the main floor, Silas's pinched expression evaporates the moment he sees the box. "You found it?"

"I did. It kind of tried to possess me or something."

"Yes, an item of such power would be eager to be wielded. We must depart with haste. The McClintock's will be unharmed. The immobilization will wear off in a few minutes."

When we reach the paved road, I hesitate and turn to Silas. "Where am I going?"

He calmly replies, "Where is Ainsley being held?"

"I don't know. The image showed her face and the gag in her mouth. That was it." I shrug and rub the steering wheel.

Silas harrumphs and exhales patiently. "Close your eyes and recall the image."

When he answers a question with a question, it always means a lesson is right around the corner. I should've seen this coming. That's on me.

Taking a deep breath, I do as I'm told. The visual of the fear in Ainsley's eyes is hard to ignore, but I have to look past it. I have to search the edges of the image and find something that— "Pipes! Freezers!"

Silas nods. "And what does this tell you?"

"Rory has her at the ice rink. I saw the pipes from the hydrotherapy whirlpools and the coolers with all the blocks of ice. She's in the locker room. The Abominables' locker room."

"Very well. Drive on."

I wouldn't have said no to a little fanfare, perhaps some overzealous praise, but that's not my mentor's way. I turn onto the paved road and proceed to the fieldhouse. As we approach, I turn off my headlights and pull to the side of the road. "I'm going in alone."

Silas inhales sharply.

"Don't argue with me. I've got this bracelet, and I've dealt with Rory before. You keep the torc and go for backup. I don't care what you have to tell *Acting Sheriff* Paulsen or what spells, I mean, transmutations, you have to perform. You get her and some deputies over here as fast as you can. I can keep Rory talking, but don't leave me tap dancing too long."

Silas grumbles indiscernibly. "I do not care for this plan, Mitzy."

"Neither do I, but it's all we've got. I'm going in, and I'm counting on you to make sure I come back out."

I exit the Jeep and leave the door open.

Silas comes around to the driver's side and places a comforting hand on my shoulder. "Do not let him in. Do not entertain any of his fanciful attempts to control you. Use your gifts, use the bracelet, and remember *everything* I've taught you."

There's a strange hum to the word everything and my skin buzzes with a knowing I can't ignore.

"Copy that. See you on the other side, Willoughby."

He shakes his head, and his jowls waggle as he climbs into the driver's seat. The door slams, and I stoop as I slink into the darkness encompassing the venue.

I've seen enough action films to know that it's important to stay low and move in the shadows. As I inch my way toward the rear entrance of the ice rink, the taillights of the Jeep disappear into the night.

My courage wavers as I face the truth: I truly am alone.

Hopefully, Silas can work his alchemical wizardry on Paulsen and get back here with a posse before Rory gets the best of me.

With my hand resting on the door handle, I run through a few scenarios and whisper softly to the blackness, "No matter what, Ainsley makes it out alive."

Whatever forces linger beyond the veil, I hope they've heard my plea and take it seriously.

CHAPTER 17

The door is unlocked, as I'd hoped. More than likely Rory is expecting Clyde McClintock to show up with the torc, in exchange for his daughter. He's probably got the back door under surveillance, so it's best to proceed as though he's watching me right now.

Regardless, I continue to move as stealthily as my natural clumsiness will allow. Rather than draw unnecessary attention with the light from my phone, I move cautiously in the dim red glow of the "EXIT" signs.

As I approach the Abominables' locker room, an eerie chuckle reverberates through the arena.

"How perfect. I should've known you would come to that Boy Scout's defense."

The best defense is a good offense. I'm sure I heard that somewhere. No point letting Rory know that I have any doubts about my ability to succeed this evening. "First of all, Erick isn't a Boy Scout. And I'm not here to defend him. I'm here to take Ainsley home to her family, and you better not get in my way."

He laughs out loud and steps from the shadows. "Your concern for others will be your downfall, Mitzy."

I twist the handle of the locker room door. Pulling it open, I dash inside. He'll surely follow, but if I can get to Ainsley, maybe I can offer her a moment of reassurance.

As I round the corner her terrified eyes meet mine and shift from surprise to confusion. I rip the gag out of her mouth and, shockingly, the first thing she says is, "Darcy, what did you do to your hair?"

Oops. I kind of forgot that I wasn't wearing the wig on this mission. "It's a long story, Ainsley. I'm going to get you out of here, all right? I need you to do exactly what I say. No questions asked. Got it?" The smell of fear hangs in the air.

The thud of Rory's boots on the cement floor echoes in the empty locker room. "She loves to be in control, Ainsley. She's very much about people doing exactly what she says." He snarls under his breath. "I hate to be the one to burst your bubble, Mitzy, but if you didn't bring me the torc, neither of you are leaving this locker room alive."

The panic rushes back into Ainsley's eyes and her mermaid-green bangs fall across her face as she cowers against the metal therapy tub.

I turn to face him, and even in the dim lighting, his green eyes sparkle with malice. "That's not how this is going to end, Frank. You're not getting the torc. Mr. McClintock isn't coming. In fact, he no longer has the item you seek." I choose to use his childhood name in a feeble hope that stabbing beneath his "Rory Bombay" façade, to the real Frank Freeman, might throw him off.

My extra senses pick up on a flash of surprise and a soupçon of fear, but Rory quickly adjusts his attack.

I feel the tingle in the air that I've come to recognize as his singular brand of manipulative magic. I raise the copper bracelet over my chest and hold the word "Ektrépo" firmly in my mind.

The venom in his eyes shifts to shock, followed by desire, as he stares at the bracelet and lusts to possess it.

I lift my chin and press on. "Toss me the key to her handcuffs. If you cooperate, I'll let you walk out of here."

He scoffs and squares his shoulders. "Your natural talents are still amateurish, and no match for my skills. I have studied texts that you and your bookshop merely dream of owning. If that wannabe druid Silas Willoughby has the torc, he will deliver it, or he will lose his last apprentice." The edge of hatred in Rory's voice cuts through the air like a knife.

I'm not sure what I expected, but I had no idea he would be willing to kill me to get what he wanted. So much for thinking I was the prize. Clearly, I'm simply another meaningless pawn in his great game. New plan. "You know Silas better than I do. He won't negotiate with you. I'm sure he'd rather not have me killed for no reason, but he certainly won't hand you a powerful relic in exchange for my life. He may care for me, but he'll weigh one life against the greater good. You know he can't be manipulated."

"We shall soon find out." And like a cobra striking, he lunges for me. Ripping the bracelet from my wrist, in its place he loudly clicks a handcuff. Rory yanks me toward the pipe and claps the other end around it.

I twist my wrist in the cuff and glare at him. At least I still have my mobile.

"Before you get any bright ideas, I'll be taking this." He pulls my phone from my back pocket and smirks as I sink to the floor next to Ainsley.

"This isn't over."

He sneers and turns his back to me. "Let me place a quick call and put your theories about Silas Willoughby to the test." He dials and utters a single phrase. "Bring me the torc or they both die."

Ainsley begins to cry.

Ignoring the young girl's whimpering, I slide my handcuff up the pipe and get to my feet. "Why Klang? Was it random, or did you have a score to settle with him?"

Rory smashes my phone against the cement floor, cracks his knuckles, and grins. "It is dangerous to disappoint me. As you well know."

I roll my eyes.

"Gerhardt Klang was one of the most promising archaeologists to enter the scene in decades. I was certain I could manipulate his passion for history into a lucrative stream of artifacts for my network of collectors. If he happened to uncover anything of magical significance, all the better for me." He bows as though accepting a standing ovation.

"Was this partnership voluntary, or did you control him with a cursed object as well?"

Rory's throaty, devilish chuckle makes the hair on my arms stand on end.

"In the beginning it was voluntary. He was desperate for funding for his research, and I was happy to accommodate him. However, when he got mixed up in the Kensington Runestone debacle, he lost his prestigious appointment at Durham, and I lost a powerful rook in my game."

"So why not find another desperate nerd to control?"

"Tsk tsk. You reveal so much of your naïveté with these questions, Miss Moon. The subtle magicks that bend others to your will are difficult to maintain. A willing participant is far more valuable than one such as yourself."

The harsh tone in his voice forces me to swallow uncomfortably, but I have to keep him talking. "So you followed him back to Birch County and renewed your partnership?"

He shrugs. "In a manner of speaking. Our falling

out was financially disruptive to my business, and he suspected my hand in the blacklisting that followed his disgrace. He was none too eager to do me any favors." Rory runs a hand through his jet-black hair and sighs. "Then I discovered his little group of fawning minions. What better way to influence the puppet master than to possess his puppets? I insisted Gerhardt call a meeting of his so-called Defenders to announce my financial backing of their yet-to-be-approved dig, and I passed out the runestones as valuable tokens, binding them to glory and riches when the treasures were uncovered."

Ainsley's sobbing subsides, and she leans toward her captor. "Special-K didn't want to sell the artifacts. He wanted us to publish a scholarly paper and have an exhibit." She chokes and sniffles. "He didn't want the money. He wanted vindication."

Rory crouches beside her. "You are as foolish as you are trusting. Gerhardt Klang was no more in love with you than I. His manipulations may have led to a different reward than mine, but both of us wanted the artifacts—and nothing more."

Ainsley's weeping resumes.

My psychic senses feel an added layer of broken heartedness in this new wave of sorrow. "Why kill him? If you both had the same goals . . . Why the murder?"

He steps a hand's breadth from me and stares down into my eyes. "He wanted to change the rules. No one changes the rules but me."

I shudder and step away. "And Erick? Did you frame him just to hurt me?"

Rory strides away, laughing uproariously. The fact that his humorous outburst is mostly a performance does not escape me.

"Serendipity, my dear. I attended that broomball game with the sole purpose of putting an end to Gerhardt's life. When I observed the brutality on the ice, the plan simply unfolded before me."

"But the air pump? Erick drove his cruiser to the lake. How did you plant that evidence?"

"Ah, yes. That twist was not predicted. I assumed he would drive you home and celebrate his win like a real man. I had no idea he'd sink into introspection and wander off to sulk in solitude. In fact, I was late to my meeting at the fieldhouse with Klang because of the added delay of driving out to the lake. Luckily, your precious sheriff had passed out in a drunken stupor. I had more than enough time to finish off Klang and replace the hand pump."

"You'll never get away with—"

"I already have."

I wish I could slap that smug grin right off his face.

"Enough banter. I need to place some *sentries* around the perimeter." He winks at me and continues, "You two girls get acquainted. I'll be back before you know it. Try not to miss me too desperately, Mizithra."

Oh, it's on. He knows I prefer Mitzy. Well, two

can play that game. "No problem, *Frank*. Take your time."

He leaves to set what I'm sure are a series of magical traps, which will alert him to the arrival of any intruders, and his throaty chuckle lingers behind him, making my skin crawl and my stomach churn.

When the locker room door clicks shut, I breathe a sigh of relief.

"Ainsley, we have to hurry. Listen to me carefully and don't ask any questions. There's no time. I'll explain everything later, once I'm sure you're safe."

She whimpers. "Who are you? Why does he keep calling you Mitzy?"

"No questions, remember?"

She sobs and gasps for breath. "Okay. Okay. Please don't let that creepy guy kill me."

"Copy that."

If I have any chance of keeping my promise to Ainsley, I need to work fast. I close my eyes and place my free hand over the lock securing the cuff around my wrist. Using the transmutation that Silas taught me the first time we were in a holding cell together, I picture ice changing state from solid to liquid. I can feel the mechanism release inside the lock.

Pulling my hand free, I grip the lock on Ainsley's cuff next.

"What are you doing? You know how to pick locks?"

It's pointless to keep reminding her not to ask

questions. The best approach seems to be to simply ignore her.

The lock releases and she rubs her red wrist as she clutches it to her chest. “What if he comes back?”

“I’m counting on that.” I place a hand on either side of her face. “Ainsley, look at me.”

Her big brown eyes stare up at me, and her bottom lip quivers.

“I want you to go sit on that bench and cry. When he comes through the door, you tell him I broke free and left you behind. You cry, you scream, whatever you have to do. Make sure he doesn’t take his eyes off you.”

She shakes her head. “I can’t do it. What if—What about you? Where will you be?”

“Look, kid, the less you know the better. If you want to get out of here alive, you do what I say. Now get on that bench and cry your eyes out—like your life depends on it.”

She hugs her arms around herself, sits on the bench and rocks back and forth as she sobs.

It’s definitely not an act. I reach out with all of my senses, searching for anything that I can use as a weapon.

The equipment is locked up. There’s no time to . . . and then—

The smiling cartoon polar bear.

“The ‘C’ was missing! CHILLY BEAR. Pyewacket, I love you.” I open the door of the freezer and grab a ten-pound block of solid ice by its plastic-bag handle.

Pressing myself against the wall next to the door, I ready my arm, like a catapult, and wait for Frank Freeman, a.k.a. Rory Bombay, to return.

He chuckles wickedly as he pushes open the door. "Help has not arrived, gir—" He stops with one hand still on the doorknob.

One thin metal door separates us. I hold my breath.

"How did you get out of your handcuffs? Where's Mitzy?"

Ainsley screams, and when he steps forward, I swing the block of ice with all my might.

It connects solidly with the side of his skull. He teeters and falls like a tree in the forest.

I've never been able to grasp the purpose of the random philosophical thought experiment, "If a tree falls in a forest and no one is around to hear it, does it make a sound?"

But today it all makes sense, and someone is here, and someone hears it. And I couldn't be more pleased.

"Ainsley, run."

For once, she doesn't ask any questions. She races out of the locker room like a jackrabbit with a coyote on its tail, and the door slams behind her with the ominous clang of a portcullis.

I am alone. No help has arrived.

All at once the word *everything* rings in my head, and my entire body buzzes with a purpose.

The reversal runes.

I have to use them.

I have to make him forget he ever knew me.

It's the only way to protect the people I love.

Crouching with one knee squarely in the center of his back, I place my finger on his cheek.

My heart is beating so fast. I'm worried I'll never find the focus I need.

The thing that pops into my head is Pyewacket. *Mr. Cuddlekins, you gave me the weapon, now help me get the win. I need to focus. I need to calm down.*

And for a moment I can feel the coarse fur of his back under my hand. The vibration of his purring soothes my chest.

I close my eyes and trace the first symbol on Rory's cheek as I hold the image of our initial meeting at Myrtle's Diner. Simple, casual, no sign of the havoc it would unleash. As I draw the next symbol, I pull up additional memories, and with the third symbol I witness a montage of images displaying his vendetta against Erick.

A deep calm settles over me when I lift my finger to begin the fourth and final symbol.

The locker room door bursts open and Deputy Paulsen, gun drawn, shouts at the top of her lungs, "Hands in the air. Nobody move."

CHAPTER 18

My hands instinctually fly up, and the final symbol is left undone.

Rory groans beneath my weight, and strong arms pull me to my feet.

"Erick?" I stare in disbelief. "What are you doing out of jail?"

He hugs me protectively, while Paulsen slaps the cuffs on Rory.

Silas observes from the hallway, a somber expression pulling his hangdog jowls lower than usual. He must see the fear in my eyes. He steps forward as Paulsen pulls Rory to his feet. "Mizithra, you are quite pale. Is everything all right?"

I shake my head.

Rory regains consciousness and scans the faces in the room. "What's going on? Where am I?"

Silas tilts his head ever so slightly, and every fiber of my being knows the question in his eyes.

I shake my head again and struggle to swallow.

Paulsen jerks him roughly toward the door. “Rory Bombay, I’m placing you under arrest on suspicion of murder—”

“Who’s Rory Bombay? I’m Frank Freeman.” He tugs against the cuffs. “Frank Freeman. I live at 718 Thornwood Ave. I grew up around here. I went to Pin Cherry Harbor High School. Don’t you recognize me?”

Paulsen pushes him toward two waiting deputies. “Take him down to the station and process him. Rory Bombay, Frank Freeman, whatever he wants to be called today. Put him under arrest and list all the names.” She turns to me and rests her right hand on the handle of her holstered gun. “You’ll need to come in and make a statement.” Her eyes dart from Erick to me and back. “Sooner, rather than later.”

Sheriff Harper tightens his arm around my shoulders. “10-4, Deputy.”

Paulsen licks her lips and shakes her head, but she waddles off without another word.

I shrug and turn toward my mentor.

Silas nods silently, and I feel his acceptance. It may not have been exactly what he intended when he told me to use everything he taught me, but I sense no remorse on his part.

Erick hugs me close and kisses the top of my head.

I inhale his woodsy-citrus scent and lean into his chest. “Thanks for coming to my rescue.”

He laughs dryly. “If you say so. How exactly did you knock him out?”

I point to the block of ice melting on the cement floor to our left. “Same way he knocked out Gerhardt Klang. A nice flat block of ice that would perfectly mimic Klang’s earlier injury on the ice rink.”

Erick leans back and looks down at me with admiration. “One of your hunches?”

Shaking my head, I give credit where credit is due. “Actually, you can thank Pyewacket for that tip.”

“You and that cat. Someday, you’re going to tell me what the two of you are really up to, right?”

I shrug and paint my features as the portrait of innocence.

His well-educated gaze scans the room. “Two pairs of handcuffs. Are you planning on telling me how you got out of those?”

“I pick locks. You know that.”

“Mmhmm. And what were you doing kneeling on Frank Freeman? You told me you had a thing for bad boys, but I thought you’d gotten over him. It looked like you were touching his face when we came in. Do I get to hear that explanation?”

Uh oh. Think. Think. “I was checking for a pulse. I hit him pretty hard. I was worried that I might’ve actually killed him, you know?”

Erick loosens his hold and lets his hands slide down to my waist. “You remember when I mentioned you had a *tell*?”

I nod slowly, attempting to ignore the knot tightening in my stomach.

"Yeah, you've still got it. I think we're getting to the point in our relationship where we don't have so many secrets, Moon. Being honest with each other is an important part of moving forward, don't you think?"

"You're not wrong."

"And you're dodging." He pulls me closer. "It's been a long day. You look exhausted. Please, don't take that the wrong way." He grins apologetically. "Let me take you home. Paulsen can clean up this mess."

I swallow my secrets as surreptitiously as possible, and smile and nod. "I can drive. Give me a chance to freshen up, and then you can check in on me."

Erick gives me a squeeze. "If you insist."

As we pass by Silas in the hall, his hand brushes my shoulder. A wave of something very close to approval passes between us. I hope he's telling me he understands that I didn't do what I did on purpose. I mean, I fully intended to complete the series of runes properly and only remove the memories pertaining to Erick and me. But the interruption resulted in a wipe of a much larger swath of memory than I ever meant to erase.

If Frank Freeman was being honest, it seems that I erased everything that occurred from the moment he changed his name and assumed the identity of Rory Bombay.

Perhaps it's for the best. If Rory's obsession with arcane knowledge and dark magic is what drove him to murder, and manipulate others to murder, maybe we're all better off with a "Rory-free" Frank Freeman.

I hope the nauseous feeling in my stomach indicates my conscience is intact. I have no intention of using my powers for anything but good.

As we meander back to the bookshop, the burden of what might've been, what is, and what could come to pass rests heavily on my young shoulders.

In response to the unspoken weight of my world, Silas harrumphs. "You did what had to be done. The right path is not always the simple path. You saved a life and potentially prevented the suffering of many more."

My grip tightens on the steering wheel. "I guess. It's that *potentially* part that's tripping me up." I draw a shaky breath and continue. "I intended to trace all the runes properly. I held my focus on the reversal of his memories of me, and his negative feelings toward Erick. But Paulsen barged in—"

"You owe me no explanation, Mizithra. And, furthermore, let your conscience be clean. Your intentions were pure, and the universe intervened. The growing darkness within Rory Bombay was far too dangerous to be left to its own devices. This Frank Freeman may be the solution that our little corner of the world needs right now."

Silence settles over us again and my mind spins off to the possibilities Frank Freeman might bring to bear. "He'll still be charged with Klang's murder, right? I mean, regardless of what name he was using at the time, he is the one who killed the professor."

"I fear there is good news and bad news on that front. Deputy Paulsen pulled a partial print from the trunk of Erick's cruiser, which matched the prints they had on file from Rory's previous arrest."

"I'll go out on a limb and say that's the good news."

He nods. "On the matter of standing trial, this rift in Frank's psyche may push his defense toward an insanity plea."

"So you don't think he'll go to jail? He'll get to sit in a nut house somewhere eating tapioca pudding and playing checkers?"

Silas rests his hands in his lap and takes a deep breath. "You say that as though it is a reward."

"Good point." I turn down the alley, pull into the garage, and Silas and I exit the Jeep in silence.

He stops beside the alley door and places a fatherly hand on my shoulder. "Your powers are indeed growing. I am most pleased to see that your concern for others and your capacity for love is expanding at an equal rate."

Despite his high standards of etiquette, I throw my arms around his neck and cry a few tears into his fusty coat. "Thank you for being my moral compass. I couldn't have asked for a better guide." I wipe a finger under each eye. "Now, I need to scrub all this drama off, change into some clean clothes, and get ready to entertain a gentleman caller."

Silas laughs until his cheeks turn cherry red in the glow of the streetlights. "I look forward to spending Thanksgiving with you and the rest of Twiggy's band of misfits."

I pause with the key in the lock. "Wait. Band? Who else is invited?"

"Oh, Twiggy's been quite busy. From what I was able to gather, in addition to the two of us, she's invited her on-again/off-again special friend, Wayne, and invitations were also extended to your father, Amaryllis, Erick, his mother, and Odell. I believe that is the entire roster."

"Wow! I'm glad I ordered two pies. I mean, I'm glad I'm going to make two pies." I wink at Silas and he chuckles. "What about you know who?" I point to the ghost lurking inside.

"I must bid you adieu, but I wish you the best of luck with that endeavor." He nods politely as he strolls toward his Model T parked on First Avenue.

CHAPTER 19

THE FIRST ENTITY TO greet me when I open the door is Robin Pyewacket Goodfellow.

"Greetings, wise and furry one. Once again, I will have to award you the title of 'Most Valuable Player' on the investigative team. You were one hundred percent right about the devious Rory Bombay pulling the strings of this entire scheme, and you correctly identified the use of CHILLY BEAR ice in the murder plot. Rory used the ice to knock out Klang and then loaded him into the laundry cart, on top of all the towels and jerseys, where he injected the bubble of air, and finally, dumped the professor at the service entrance. Klang was a big boy, and, while Rory is crafty, he's not strong enough to carry a man that size all the way from the locker room."

"Ree-ow." Soft but condescending.

"Yes, I've already acknowledged your massive intelligence. Now, where's our ghost?"

Before Pye has a chance to share his intel, Ghost-ma blinks into being.

Her shimmering arms encircle me. "You're alive! I knew you could get the best of that serpent."

I return the hug and play the pity card. "I'm sorry I caused you any worry, Grams. Can we postpone the debrief? I could use a hot shower."

She pulls away and looks me up and down. "Go ahead, try *not* to think it."

And like a hypnotist's suggestion, my reunion plans with Erick flood into my mind.

Grams giggles. "Oh my! Let's keep it PG, Mizithra."

A frustrated huff escapes as I stomp up the circular stairs. "I'm taking a shower. Then I'm hanging out with a friend in my apartment. I forbid all ghostly intrusions until noon tomorrow." It's none of her business, but I'm not *planning* on having Erick spend the night. I simply want to leave the window open to possibilities.

She swirls around me grinning ghoulishly. "Noon tomorrow? My, my. Don't count your chickens before they hatch, dear." She continues to snicker.

Without acknowledging her taunt, I walk into the sacred closet and grab her vintage Oscar de la Renta silver-sequin halter gown.

"Mitzy, what are you doing?" She flickers with panic.

I lay the treasure on the floor and raise my foot above its glimmering folds.

"Don't you— You wouldn't!"

"Noon. Tomorrow." I flick one finger toward the exit.

She whooshes out of the apartment grumbling something about an unnecessary tantrum.

Even a ghost has its vulnerabilities. I carefully pick up the gown and return it to the closet. There's no need for her to know that I would never follow through on my fashion threats.

By the time the telltale "BING BONG BING" of the alleyway bell sounds, I'm fresh as a daisy and fully dressed. In jeans and stuff, nothing daring, in case you were wondering.

As I approach the side door, I trip on absolutely nothing and all my cool vibes vanish in an instant. I take a moment and try to recover some semblance of allure as I push open the door. "Good evening, Sheriff."

He takes my hand, bows deeply, and kisses the curve of my fingers. "I come bearing tidings of gratitude for the Dame Mitzy Moon."

Pulling my hand back as though a bee has stung it, I giggle and blush. "Who? What are you talking about?"

He stands and avoids my gaze. "It's freezing out here. How about you let me come in, and I'll explain?"

I step back and wave him through. "All right, fess up."

His eyes sparkle with mischief, and his gentle

chuckle warms my heart. "I had to look it up on the internet. Since you were my knight in shining armor this time, I wanted to present an appropriate speech, but I wasn't sure what they called 'lady knights.' Apparently, they're called 'dames.' Go figure."

"Thanks, but you were never a damsel in distress."

He exhales and runs his fingers through his long loose bangs. They fall enticingly over his eye, and I'm happy to see he's operating pomade-free this evening. "If you say so."

"Come on up. I have snacks."

He gestures chivalrously. "After you."

When we enter the apartment, I catch sight of the murder wall and hurry to roll it away.

He catches my elbow. "No, no. Leave it. I really want to see how the mind of Mitzy Moon works."

I have no intention of telling him how little of my mind is on that board. I'll let him draw his own conclusions.

He paces in front of the board and runs his finger along the green yarn connections. "I'm a little surprised to see my name up here. I thought you were trying to prove my innocence?"

"You were connected to the victim. You know that no one can be ruled out—until they are."

He turns and strides toward me.

My tummy flip-flops when I catch sight of the look in his eye.

"You really did save my bacon. If you hadn't

brought in that second pathologist and discovered the true cause of death, the investigation would've stalled out."

"But the cause of death made you look even more guilty!"

"I don't disagree." He turns and glances at the board. "But somehow, you followed that trail of twists and lies to Rory Bombay." He pulls me close and leans down to whisper in my ear. "What do I have to do to make you reveal your methods?"

And . . . I'm dead. My heart has stopped beating, I can't breathe, and my knees are jelly. What does he have to do? It's done. His interrogation techniques are irresistible.

His strong arms embrace me and keep me from collapsing into a puddle on the floor. "You okay, Moon?"

After pulling some air into my lungs, I recover my defensive wit. "You're not gonna break this witness, Harper." I disengage myself and head for the sofa. "Can I interest you in a sweet or savory nibble?"

A heart-melting grin spreads across his face and he joins me on the couch. "I got an unexpected invitation while I was in the slammer." He holds up a finger to put my snarky comment on hold. "Somehow, me and my mom got invited to Twiggy's Thanksgiving potluck. Was that you're doing?"

I shrug. "Maybe. Indirectly. My dad asked me about my plans, and I haven't had any plans since my mom—you know."

He squeezes my hand and nods. "I know."

"I ran the question past Twiggy, and the next thing you know she's invited everyone to her place. Which is great. It's not like I have a kitchen." Nervous laughter tightens my throat, and he smiles wickedly.

"I was wondering about that. Can you cook?"

I pull my hand away and cross my arms. "Depends what you mean by cook. Can I boil water? Yes. Can I heat absolutely anything in my microwave without alerting the fire department? Pretty much. Can I make duck à l'orange served on a pillow of nutmeg air? Not on your life."

He chuckles and grabs a handful of pretzels.

Pyewacket saunters in and circles the settee expectantly.

"Hey, I understand I owe you a big thanks for the tip about the Chilly Bear ice, big guy." Erick grins and tips his head toward Pye in that way that insinuates he's doffing a cap.

Pye stops, flops onto the Persian rug, and cleans his left paw.

"Would a box of Fruity Puffs be an acceptable tribute?"

The caracal's tail flicks once, and he squeezes his eyes as he gazes at Erick. "Reow." Can confirm.

I open my mouth to translate, but Erick beats me to the punch. "Understood, buddy. I got your back."

Mr. Cuddlekins turns his narrow gaze on me and tilts his head.

I toss him a cheesy puff, and he catches it with one agile paw, clamps it in his fangs, and stalks off to the closet.

The night slips away like sand through an hourglass as we discuss Thanksgiving memories, the importance of family, and canoodle on the couch.

It's nearly 3:00 in the morning when the conversation vanishes and the canoodling takes center stage.

My extra senses flash a warning light and we're clearly approaching the tipping point. I gently disengage. "I'm gonna grab a drink of water. You need anything?"

The heat in his eyes is more answer than I can handle.

As I rush into the powder room to splash some cold water on my face, Erick checks the time on his phone. "Wow, I didn't realize it was so late. I should probably go."

My heart is screaming, *No, don't go. You can stay.* But my new, levelheaded brain is saying, *Take it slow. You're worth the wait.* I return and smile. "Yeah, time got away from us. Breakfast at the diner?"

He shakes his head with regret. "I wish. I'll be eating stale doughnuts at my desk. Paulsen is a great deputy, but she really sucks at administration. I have a mountain of paperwork to catch up on before the holiday, plus I have to prep for the interrogations." He flashes me a half grin. "Mom and I will definitely see you at Twiggy's, though. Sound good?"

Sounds terrible. Sounds like the abrupt ending to

a perfect evening, and an entire day moping around on my own. Boo. Hiss. Of course, I don't say any of that to him. "Sounds good. I totally understand. I'll walk you out."

When the bookcase door slides open, Pyewacket emerges from the closet and meows in a tone I don't recognize. It's almost like he's asking me what went wrong. Silly cat, don't judge me. I'll deal with you later.

As we're circling down toward the stacks, a happy distraction pops into my head. "By the way, I can't wait to observe the Frank Freeman interrogation tomorrow."

He shakes his head in defeat. "I'm not going to waste my breath. That's not an official invite. Not that you've ever needed one."

Before Erick braves the frosty air outside, he pulls me close and kisses me too well and for too long. These trembly legs are never going to make it back up the stairs.

"I'll text you tomorrow, with the interrogation info. Sleep tight, Moon." He glides his hand along the side of my cheek as he exits.

My skin is on fire. My heart is thumping like it ran a marathon. That man will be the death of me, but oh, what a way to go!

I lock the deadbolt and set the alarm.

Maybe if I'm especially good, and the universe is feeling generous, I'll see Sheriff Too-Hot-To-Handle in dreamland.

CHAPTER 20

Luckily, I closed the blackout shades earlier this morning before I collapsed into bed, and Grams keeps her word and steers clear of the apartment. So, it is my distinct pleasure to wake up to a late-morning text from Erick.

"Freeman interview in 20."

Yeesh! Time to get crackin'. I hit the button and the shades roll up to reveal a thick layer of swollen grey clouds.

Maybe I should take this whole storm thing more seriously?

I give Pye a good scratch between the ears and roll out of the rack.

Splashes of cold water, a quick pass with a hair-brush, and a last minute swipe of lip tint.

The reflection in the mirror shrugs. "Good enough."

"You're much better than good enough, dear." Grams gestures to the large four-poster bed. "I see you're alone. Did things not go as you planned?" Her perfectly drawn brow arches.

"Erick left around 3:00, which is fine. Things are moving at the exact right pace."

She clutches her pearls and swoons comically. "You're a stronger woman than me!"

"Grams!" I shake my head and march into the closet. "I could use a little moral support."

"You've come to the wrong ghost if you're looking for morals."

We share an eye-watering laugh as I scamper into my clothes.

"I'm off to the station to make sure Rory Bombay is truly 'no more.'"

"Good riddance!" Her eyes widen. "To him, not you, sweetie."

"Copy that."

Since the partial print that Deputy Paulsen recovered from the trunk lid of Erick's cruiser is a match for Frank Freeman's middle finger on his left hand, and the guy kidnapped a couple of people and threatened to kill them, all charges against Erick have been dropped and he's back on the case.

As I sit quietly in the observation room, sandwiched between Interrogation Rooms One and Two at the sheriff station, I stare through the one-way glass at Frank Freeman.

I've tried every trick in the book. I've reached out with my array of psychic senses, searching high and low for any sign of Rory Bombay. I've held back and quietly waited for extrasensory messages to be delivered as Erick pursues various lines of questioning with Mr. Freeman.

Absolutely no trace of the person calling himself Rory Bombay remains. Every memory that Frank Freeman possesses, of persons or events, are all things that occurred prior to the date he changed his name, over thirty years ago. He has no memory of purchasing Gershon Antiquities (now Bombay Antiquities and Artifacts) in Grand Falls, and he does not understand why he's being questioned in connection to the murder of Gerhardt Klang.

A consummate actor like Rory Bombay could likely fool even a seasoned interrogator like Erick. But under no circumstances would he have the skill to avoid all of my psychic powers. Whatever happened in that moment when Deputy Paulsen interrupted the reversal runes has permanently deleted Rory Bombay.

I wish I could say I feel regret, but I don't. Rory Bombay was a selfish, manipulative, dangerous man. The residents of Pin Cherry Harbor are better off without him. Not to mention, my life and my future look a lot brighter without the specter of Mr. Bombay looming over my shoulder.

Erick completes his questioning and asks Deputy Johnson to prepare the lineup and bring in the witness.

Witness? He didn't mention anyone to me. Does he mean Ainsley? I thought she was still in the hospital for observation.

With my curiosity piqued, I lean forward and await the arrival of the mystery witness.

A few minutes later, Deputy Johnson escorts Kaden Soder into Interrogation Room One.

I crack my knuckles and grin. The speaker is still on from the previous questioning, but I pull my chair closer to the glass. This oughta be rich.

Deputy Johnson leads the sullen sophomore to the chair opposite Erick. The wiry, dark-haired boy drops and arranges his body in a carefully constructed pose intended to send the message that he doesn't care. However, my extra senses can confirm otherwise.

Erick rolls through the basics and Kaden Soder mumbles his replies.

"Look, son, we got an online chat history between you and Ainsley McClintock that puts you in line for an accessory to murder charge and possibly even conspiracy to kidnap. You better sit up and answer my questions like your freedom depends on it." Erick crosses his arms and lifts his chin.

I'm running through the list of charges in my mind and things don't add up. There's absolutely no way Kaden had anything to do with the murder, and

I don't think conspiracy to kidnap is even a real charge. Kudos to Erick, for picking up on some of my techniques.

Shockingly, Kaden complies.

"What was your relationship with Ainsley McClintock?"

He scoffs. "She was like a total online stalker. We played this dinosaur game on the same server, you know? A lotta people play. It's not like she was special."

"Seems like she was special enough for you to invite her to join your private Jangle server, and continue the chat outside the game world. What was the purpose behind that?"

Massive eye roll. "She was bragging about some artifacts. I told my professor—"

"This would be Professor Gerhardt Klang?"

"Yeah, Klang. So, I told him some stuff she said, and he was super into it."

Erick nods. "And then?"

"He wanted me to get her to MIRL and bring me the whale horn thing she had."

Erick exhales and uncrosses his arms. "By 'whale horn' you are referring to the narwhal tusk chalice?"

Kaden offers a minuscule head nod.

"And did you set up the real-life meeting?"

"Yeah, sure." Kaden leans forward and taps his finger on the table for emphasis. "Like, I didn't even go to that meeting, okay? I set it up, whatever. But

Klang is the one who met with her. She gave him the horn thing."

"The evidence we have supports that claim. However, I'm far more interested to know how the cup came into the possession of the man you knew as Rory Bombay."

Kaden swallows and leans back. "You mean the guy in the lineup?"

Sheriff Harper nods once.

Kaden crosses his arms tightly and curls his shoulders forward. "Yeah, that guy was weird, man. He offered me a lot of money, and, you know, Klang was already dead. It's not like he needed the cup, right?"

So, that was definitely Rory's partially masked energy I felt in the back room at the antiquities shop. He was holed up there doing research, and I almost caught him.

Erick summarizes the witness's statement, and Kaden confirms that he took the chalice from the top left-hand drawer of Professor Klang's desk—right where Silas left it. Kaden insists he dropped it at the store in Grand Falls and some woman gave him cash. He claims "lineup guy," as he calls him, wasn't at the drop.

Sheriff Harper stands and opens the door. "You're free to go, Mr. Soder. We'll be in touch if we need anything further. Leave your home address with the deputy at the front desk in case we need to contact you over Thanksgiving break."

Kaden unfolds himself from the chair and skulks out without another word.

Standing in the hallway between the observation room and Erick's office, I overhear the sheriff instructing Johnson to prep Frank Freeman for transport to the county jail, where he will undergo a complete battery of medical tests and a psychological evaluation. Sounds like the cursory examination he received from the paramedics last night indicated a type of amnesia, resulting from a severe blow to the head.

Guilty as charged. I whacked him senseless with a ten-pound block of ice, and I'd do it again in a similar situation. He threatened to take two lives; I handled the situation, without taking any.

I step back into the observation room and wait for Erick. I don't want to get caught eavesdropping.

The amnesia diagnosis should assuage the fears of all the laypeople involved in the investigation. Silas Willoughby and I are the only ones who know the truth. Well, and Grams and Pyewacket, of course.

Erick opens the door and steps into the observation room. "I asked Frank every question I could think of and I'd have to say the amnesia is real. There's no trace of Rory Bombay."

Nodding my head, I breathe a sigh of relief. "There's no permanent brain damage, right?"

"Whatever you did was in self-defense. There's been absolutely no mention of any charges. He hasn't even asked for a lawyer."

"Will you be able to get some additional trace evidence from the laundry cart or the freezer doors?"

"We have a team over there checking everything, including the dumpsters. Johnson found the combination lock from my locker in the trunk of Bombay's, or, rather, Freeman's car. That places him in the locker room and explains how he got my jersey."

"You didn't throw a bloody jersey in the cart to get washed?" I raise an eyebrow and scrunch up my face in concern.

He looks at the floor and bites his lip. "It's a weird superstition. As long as we keep winning, I don't wash the jersey."

"Disgusting, but all right." I shiver as I imagine the stench wafting off that thing. "That's further proof that your jersey would never have been conveniently lying on top of the pile of laundry, where Paulsen found it."

He nods. "We're dusting the freezers for prints and we've got Clyde McClintock coming in to see if he can pick Freeman out of a lineup. According to his statement, two different men visited the farm and asked about the artifacts. Professor Klang wanted permission to launch a full-scale archaeological dig, but the other man didn't give a name and was solely interested in the torc."

"That's the one thing I don't understand."

Erick leans against the one-way glass and crosses his arms over his chest in that yummy way that makes his biceps bulge. "There's just *one* thing you don't understand?"

"For now. Why didn't McClintock authorize the dig?"

He nods as though he had been thinking the same thing. "I think Ainsley may have accidentally shed some light on that. She claims that the man who attacked her mother didn't simply move on with the rest of the seasonal workers. Of course, she was a toddler at the time of the actual attack, but it was the arguments she overheard as a young girl that caused her to doubt her parents' story."

"Are you saying there's more than artifacts buried at the Divine Dairy?" I chuckle.

Erick nods and tilts his head. "We'll have to piece together a few more things before we can get a warrant, but I'm certain we'll find that a body was buried somewhere on that property within the last seventeen years."

"Now, that makes sense. Clyde wouldn't want a team of archaeologists scouring the property for artifacts or evidence of a Norse settlement, when he had evidence of something far more incriminating tucked away." I tap my finger to my temple and he grins.

Erick uncrosses his arms and offers me his hand.

I accept, and he pulls me close. "Thanks for never giving up on me, Moon."

Leaning in, I tilt my head up toward his full lips. "I keep my word, Sheriff. When Mitzy Moon takes a case, she doesn't quit until it's solved."

He leans down, brushes the tip of his nose to mine. "You seriously didn't suspect me for one second?"

"Are we being totally honest?"

His breath is warm on my lips. "I think I've mentioned that we're moving into that phase of our relationship."

I struggle to ignore the weakening in my knees. "There was a part of me that wondered, but only for a second, and it was a teensy tine-ty part. Hardly worth mentioning."

His kiss is warm and inviting.

My heart flutters and my tummy flip-flops.

The door blasts open and Deputy Johnson stammers hopelessly.

Erick blushes like a radish and I look everywhere except at people.

I'm the first to recover vocal abilities. "Well, I gotta get busy with storm prep and whatnot." I didn't say it was an amazing segue.

Sheriff Harper nods officially and Johnson steps out of my way.

I pause in the hallway and catch a tidbit about Clyde positively identifying Frank. My work here is done.

Time for me to head over to the Piggly Wiggly and stock up on canned goods, dry goods, toilet paper, bottled water, and, most of all, coffee—exactly like I wrote in that Letter from the Editor.

The storm is scheduled to obliterate the entire

Great Lakes area on Thanksgiving day. Weather advisories are encouraging folks to leave a day early, if possible, or cancel their plans entirely. No one should be traveling on Thanksgiving.

I'll believe it when I see it.

CHAPTER 21

As I WATCH Erick carefully guiding his mother over the uneven cobblestone pathway leading to Twiggy's front door, my heart swells with pride and love. How anyone in their right mind could have thought for one second that this man was responsible for murder is beyond even my vast imagination.

The door of the two-story Arts and Crafts, prairie-style home opens and two dogs burst forth.

I tighten my grip on the precious apple and pumpkin pies.

One pup is tan and compact. He sports a holiday sweater, festooned with fall leaves and pumpkins. The other is a massive Husky with piercing blue eyes, thick blue-black fur, and a white belly.

"Bartles and Jaymes, sit." Twiggy's stern command receives an instant response.

Two puppers plant their bottoms on either side of the walkway. The smaller one whimpers and fights the urge to assault the guests with tail wags and tongue licks.

Erick waves. "Twiggy, you know my mom, Gracie, right?"

"Sure do. I hate to admit it, Gracie, but I wasn't sorry when you quit playing bingo. You had an unnatural lucky streak that severely interfered with my winnings."

Gracie laughs warmly and clutches Erick's arm. "Well, you know how Ricky worries about me when I'm out after dark."

Chuckling at my favorite nickname for Sheriff Harper, I stop between the two obedient dogs. "Am I allowed to pet them?"

Twiggy descends the short run of steps from her porch and skirts around the Harpers. She steps up beside the smaller dog and makes an "okay" symbol with her left hand. "Say hello, Jaymes." She swings the symbol toward me. Jaymes instantly rises on his back legs and waves his right paw manically.

"You better take the pies. You know how uncoordinated I can be."

She rescues the pastry perfection, and I immediately reach down and shake his adorable brown paw. "Pleased to meet you, Jaymes."

By this time Bartles is whining, and his little rear end is twitching with anticipation.

Jaymes drops onto all fours and Twiggy gives Bartles the signal. "Say hello to Mitzy."

The black Husky rises on his hind legs, and when

he wiggles his right paw, it nearly reaches my shoulder. I shake it hastily. "Pleased to meet you, Bartles."

He drops and the two dogs chase each other around the yard as Twiggy and I head indoors.

"They are really well behaved."

Twiggy tilts her head. "What did you expect, doll?"

"Touché."

The multiple banks of narrow, vertical windows flood the neutral décor with northern light, and the open-plan kitchen/dining area is a bustle of activity. Odell has taken over the cooking, and the much-recovered Amaryllis is pouring wine for everyone. A luscious mélange of roasting turkey and bubbling gravy fills the space, making my mouth water.

Silas appears next to me and whispers, "How is Isadora?"

"Furious. She gave a lengthy speech about never imagining she'd be treated more unfairly in death than in life."

He snickers. "Good thing she can't leave that bookshop, eh?"

My fervent nod agrees. "This sweater is punishment enough."

He inspects my colorful autumnal fashion and struggles to hide his grin. "Very festive."

Rolling my eyes, I reply, "That's one word for it." I grasp his arm as he moves away. "Did you find a proper home for the torc?"

"The artifacts were purchased by an anonymous

collector, on behalf of the *Norwegian government*, I believe." He places one hand on his rounded belly and chuckles.

My eyes spark with worry. "Did Frank get his 'Rory' memory back? Is Rory the anonymous collector? That doesn't seem like something to joke about."

Silas smooths his mustache with a thumb and forefinger and his eyes twinkle with the immense power lurking beneath his unassuming exterior. "The torc will remain safe in my vault. Now that we know its true power, we must protect it from those who would twist it toward darkness. The chalice, along with the balance of the items, will form the core of a Norse Expansion in North America exhibit, which will be augmented as additional artifacts are unearthed." He nods toward Erick. "The sheriff has agreed to cooperate with a team of archeologists to conduct a search of the Divine Dairy's acreage for the alleged modern-day corpse."

Gracie Harper releases her hold on her son's arm and accepts a glass of wine.

"Just one, Mom. You know you're not supposed to mix alcohol with your medication." Erick shakes his head.

She shrugs innocently and introduces herself to my father as he nods politely and slips by to greet me.

"This was a great idea, Mitzy. It's nice to spend this holiday of gratitude with all the people we care about." His eyes dart lovingly toward Amaryllis before he pulls me into a warm hug.

"It is, Dad. Glad we found a way to make things work, even if Grams will hold it against us for all eternity!"

Erick pats Jacob on the back, and they exchange a handshake. "Is it just me, Jacob, or does she spend an awful lot of time talking about a woman she supposedly never met?" His blue eyes sparkle with mischief.

My father expertly avoids the loaded question and instead offers his own teasing banter. "Welcome to the Frequent Felons Club, Harper. My daughter and I are founding members."

Erick blushes, shakes his head, and looks down at his own feet. "I had that coming. After spending a little time on the other side of the bars, I have a new appreciation for my freedom and a new understanding for people who are in the wrong place at the wrong time."

My father claps a hand onto Erick's shoulder and looks him in the eye. "Hey, I deserved what I got—mostly. I made some bad choices and some even worse friends, but you're a decent guy, through and through. Paulsen should've known better."

Erick shrugs. "She was doing her job. I would've made the same choice if our roles had been reversed."

And as though the mere speaking of her name summons her, the front door opens and in waddles Paulsen and—

Leaning toward Erick, I rise onto my tiptoes and whisper, "Who is that with Paulsen?"

He looks down at me as though I've gone insane. "Her husband. Greg Finley."

You could've used a forklift to pick my chin up off the floor. "She has a husband?"

Erick elbows me. "Behave."

Paulsen approaches me with slightly less than her usual disdain. "Greg, this is Mitzy Moon."

Greg sizes me up, looks at Erick, and looks back at me, before extending a hand. "Pauly's told me lots about you."

Oh, the things I wish I could say. Instead, I give his hand a friendly shake. "Nice to meet you, Greg." The conversation opener falls flat, since out of the corner of my eye, my attention is pulled toward a surprising spectacle.

Twiggy steps up onto the piano bench. Yes, she has a piano! She clinks her wineglass with a fork.

Once the room settles down, she proceeds. "Now that everyone's here, I'd like to make a toast. To the friends we make and the family we choose. May we meet for half an hour in heaven before the devil knows we're dead!"

"Hear! Hear!" Odell raises his glass.

Obligatory clinking of glasses passes through the gathering of friends, and Wayne reaches up to support Twiggy as she jumps down from her perch. Jacob smoothly moves in next to her and attempts to whisper, but even I can hear him as he asks, "Can we turn on the game?"

Twiggy throws back the rest of her wine and

replies to all. "The game is on in the rec room. And Wayne here will make drinks for anyone needin' somethin' stronger than grape juice. What time are we eatin', Odell?"

He opens the oven, lifts a few lids from the pots on the stove, and glances at the clock. "Dinner in two hours. Don't be late, or Mitzy will eat all the mashed potatoes."

The room erupts in far more laughter than I feel is necessary.

Amaryllis and I help set the table and arrange the trivets on the sideboard, while the rest of the attendees practically sprint to the rec room.

Shouts of "There's beer!" "Look at all these snacks!" and my personal favorite: "A pool table!" can be heard from the dining area.

Amaryllis places the pumpkin pie on a literal pedestal and turns to give me a wink. "That decorative oak leaf and acorn accent in the center reminds me of something." She taps a finger on her lips. "I can't quite—"

I sidle up next to her and hiss, "All right! You found me out. I went to Bless Choux to see if Anne had time to teach me how to make pumpkin pie, but, of course, she's too busy making pumpkin pies for the rest of Pin Cherry to have time to give baking lessons. I thought it would be in everyone's best interest if I simply bought a couple of her delicious pies, rather than potentially expose the group to some type of food poisoning."

Slipping an arm around my shoulders, Amaryllis gives me a squeeze. "Your secret's safe with me. If my options were bake a pie or face the noose, you could say goodbye to this elegant neck." She gestures to her lovely ballerina neck.

We share a laugh, and a little flame flickers in my heart. I may not be able to spend Thanksgiving with my mother, but I'm definitely warming up to the idea of spending many more with my soon to be step-mom.

Emotions are bubbling, and I need some air. "Can you handle things in here? I'm gonna step out on the porch for a minute."

She smiles and kindly ignores the tears threatening at the corners of my eyes. "Take your time. I've got the trivet situation handled."

The crisp air clears my head, as a deer disappears into the birch and pine forest surrounding Twiggy's property.

Leaning against the porch post, I take a sip of wine and smile. The family of my choosing. That sounds like exactly the kind of family I want. These people, this town, these memories—it's all part of a beautiful new life I'm building.

Touching the dream catcher necklace resting on my lurid Thanksgiving sweater, I whisper a message of gratitude to my dear, departed mother. "Happy Thanksgiving, Cora."

And, as if by magic, the first snowflakes fall.

Stretching out my hand, I catch one in my palm

and smile as the one-of-a-kind crystal warms to a drop of liquid.

Erick's arms circle around me from behind and I lean back against his chest. "I'm sorry Coraline isn't here to see what a wonderful human being she made. But I'd like to think she's looking down on you from heaven, and she's even prouder than me."

I set my wineglass on the railing and swirl into Erick's embrace. Happy tears trickle down my cheek and, for the first time in more than a decade, I truly am grateful. "I have a lot to be thankful for this year, Sheriff."

"Me too." He kisses me sweetly and gives me a crooked grin. "If this storm lives up to the hype, we might be at Twiggy's for more than a meal."

"You mean we could be snowed in? Overnight? All of us?"

He nuzzles into my neck. "Mmhmm. It's a house full. We'll have to double up, you know. Do you wanna be my bunkmate?"

Gulp.

This promises to be one heck of a Thanksgiving . . .

Come on, winter, hit me with your best shot!

End of Book 10

A NOTE FROM TRIXIE

Thank you to each and every one of you! Another case solved! I'll keep writing them if you keep reading . . .

The best part of "living" in Pin Cherry Harbor continues to be feedback from my early readers. Thank you to my alpha readers/cheerleaders, Angel and Michael. HUGE thanks to my fantastic beta readers who continue to give me extremely useful and honest feedback: Veronica McIntyre and Nadine Peterse-Vrijhof. And big "small town" hugs to the world's best ARC Team – Trixie's Mystery ARC Detectives!

Another thing I'm truly grateful for is my editor, Philip Newey. I always look forward to Philip's direct, actionable feedback. I'd also like to give some heartfelt thanks to Brooke for her tireless proofreading! Any errors are my own, as my outdated version of Word insists on showing me only what it likes and when it feels so moved.

FUN FACT: One of the two concussions I received in my lifetime was during a broomball game!

My favorite quote from this case: "I never behave more poorly than when someone tells me to behave well." ~ Grams

I'm currently writing book twelve in the Mitzy Moon Mysteries series, and I think I may just live in Pin Cherry Harbor forever. Mitzy, Grams, and Pyewacket got into plenty of trouble in book one, *Fries and Alibis*. But I'd have to say that book three, *Wings and Broken Things*, is when most readers say the series becomes unputdownable.

I hope you'll continue to hang out with us.

Trixie Silvertale (November 2020)

PARANORMAL COZY MYSTERY

Hopes & Slippery Slopes

TRIXIE SILVERTALE

Sittin' On A Goldmine Productions L.L.C.

CHAPTER 1

THE DARK TENDRILS of dreamland refuse to loosen their hold. I can't shake the weight of dread following me back to consciousness. What I need is some of that fresh air everyone raves about and massive quantities of java. Time to get this rig rolling.

Outside the Bell, Book & Candle, I squint my eyes against the bright sun and walk through little clouds of my own breath as I meander down Main Street toward Myrtle's Diner. Behind my shop, the great lake resting in the harbor of the town that tech forgot is, at long last, cloaked in white.

Born and raised in Arizona, I never imagined living in a place like Pin Cherry Harbor. Of course, the old me was too consumed with trying to make ends meet on a broke barista's salary to have dreams. I ran with a gaggle of fake friends and bounced down a list of insincere, unworthy boyfriends.

Today, the new me gets to enjoy my favorite

breakfast, with a good-hearted, gorgeous man, at an amazing diner named after my dearly departed grandmother and operated by my surrogate grandpa.

An entire string of words that little orphan Mitzy never imagined uttering. Tragically losing my mother at eleven and churning my way through a series of mostly unsavory foster homes left me underwhelmed and expecting little from life.

But when a mysterious old man with a marvelous mustache knocked on the door of my should-be-condemned apartment and handed me a manila envelope holding an unbelievable new future, my world literally flipped upside down and inside out.

The malodorous bus that ferried me across the country to almost-Canada certainly disguised the hidden potential in my sudden relocation.

Now I have a philanthropic foundation, a fascinating three-story bookshop and printing museum, a surprise father, an annoyingly endearing feline, a wonderful but interfering Ghost-ma—and did I mention the kind and handsome boyfriend?

The warm welcome of Myrtle's Diner envelops me, and I wave to Odell as he gives me the standard spatula salute through the red-Formica-trimmed orders-up window.

Sheriff Erick Harper occupies the booth in the corner, and his inviting smile melts my heart.

I slide onto the bench seat opposite him, and the flame-red bun of the best waitress in town appears beside me.

"Morning, Mitzy." She slides a mug of coffee onto the table and checks to make sure I have enough individual creamers in the pale-green melamine bowl.

"Good morning, Tally. How is your brother doing?"

She smiles proudly. "He's got the whole veterinary clinic retrofitted now. He can conduct examinations, surgeries, and even run the front desk from his wheelchair."

"That's wonderful. He's hands-down the best vet in Birch County. I'm glad he was able to work things out." We exchange a knowing look, and neither of us wants to mention the horrible hit-and-run accident that left her brother paralyzed. That's another story.

Erick reaches across the table and grabs my hand, sending tingles up my arm. "We sure were lucky to have Mitzy Moon on that case, wouldn't you say, Tally?"

She nods fervently. "From your mouth to God's ears, Sheriff."

I shake my head and flush with embarrassment.

Tally whisks away to see to the handful of other customers, and Odell approaches with our breakfasts.

I kind of love coming to a place like this. No need to order. Just sit back and wait to have exactly what you didn't know you wanted, but absolutely needed, delivered.

Odell slides a stack of pancakes in front of Erick

and I get a plate of scrambled eggs with chorizo, golden home fries, and a bottle of Tabasco. He slips a small side-plate bearing an English muffin on the table and I look up in confusion.

The lines in his weathered face deepen and his eyes twinkle as he grins. “Figured you’d better carbo-load. It’s gonna be a mighty long, chilly day at the races.” He raps his knuckles twice on the table and returns to the kitchen.

“If you say so. Smells delicious,” I call after him.

Erick nods. “That’s right. You and your dad are headed out to the snocross today.”

Having already shoved an enormous forkful of home fries into my mouth, I return the nod, and grin.

He chuckles. “Don’t let me interrupt your breakfast, Moon.”

I wash it all down with a swig of black gold. “Oh, don’t worry, I never would.”

His blue eyes dance with delight, and a satisfied silence settles over the table while we tuck into our meals.

I’m not ashamed to say, I finish first. “Let me regale you with the latest gossip while you finish your breakfast, slowpoke.”

His head shakes with laughter and a little swath of his beautiful blond hair swings loose from his pomade.

And I thought my *breakfast* was yummy! Fortunately, I’ve learned to keep thoughts like that safely locked in my head—most of the time. Instead, I turn to the event on everyone's mind. "Did you receive your invitation to my dad's wedding?"

He nods and politely swallows his food before answering. "Yes. An outdoor wedding on New Year's Eve! I'm looking into parkas and sled dogs as we speak."

We share a snicker. "You're not allowed to raise a single complaint. This is Amaryllis's wedding, and she's allowed to take off her corporate lawyer hat for a minute and indulge in a winter fantasy. Her day, her way. Plus, it's just the reception that's outdoors. According to my dad, the ceremony is going to be inside my bookshop."

Erick shrugs. "If you say so. The town's not that big. I'm sure everyone will end up at the right place."

"So you're not going to the races?"

He pushes his bottom lip up and shakes his head. "Not unless there's a riot. I have a mountain of paperwork and a whole county to monitor. The drag races may be noisy, but they're generally quite civilized. Good group of guys that just enjoy going fast."

"I can respect that." I reach for my cup of wake-up juice, but stop mid-motion.

Erick leans across the table and lowers his voice. "Really? Because if memory serves, you're the girl who wanted to take it *slow*. But if you're ready to speed things up . . . I'm your guy."

Tingly shivers run up and down my spine and my belly flip-flops. I definitely have to remember never to play poker with this man. He's far too ready to call my bluff.

A boisterous group of eight to ten men burst into the café and stomp the slush off their boots. They fill two booths and one of the four-tops by the front window.

Tally swoops in with menus and mugs, and makes small talk.

"You folks here for the snocross?"

"Oh yeah, you betcha. I got two boys runnin' in the junior and junior novice divisions."

Tally nods, and another red-cheeked patron pipes up. "My daughter's running in the junior novice division, and she's gonna take that title with one hand tied behind her back."

A heated but friendly debate ensues.

Erick walks his fingers across the table and turns his palm upward.

I slip my hand into his and he gives it a little squeeze. "See, they're passionate but respectful. I'm sure you and your father will have a great day. Dress warm and be sure to take earmuffs."

"Earmuffs? I have a stocking cap. Isn't that enough?"

He shakes his head and furrows his brow. "Trust me, you're gonna want the earmuffs."

Rolling my eyes, I slide out of the booth. "Thanks for breakfast, Sheriff. I better get back and see what Gra— great ol' Twiggy needs before I head out." My eyes are saucers, and I hope he didn't notice my almost slip.

"One day, you're going to finish that sentence, Moon. I promise you." He polishes his badge with his knuckles and narrows his gaze teasingly.

I choke on a nervous giggle, bus my dishes, and wave to Odell as I leave.

Tramping back down Main Street toward my bookstore, I smack a mittened hand on my own forehead. I really need to stop almost talking about my supposedly dead grandmother in front of my highly observant boyfriend.

Gripping the handle on the intricately carved wooden door, I smirk at the figure that so closely resembles my present day wildcat. I'm not the only one with secrets, am I, Pyewacket?

Pulling open the door, I brush through the quiet stacks and run my fingers along a row of novels. Some days it's hard to believe that this whole book-filled place, from thick carpets to tin-plated ceiling, is mine. I step over the "No Admittance" chain at the bottom of the wrought-iron spiral staircase and head up to the second-floor mezzanine.

The Rare Books Loft is strictly off-limits to patrons, except for one day a month, when scholarly research is allowed by appointment only. I still don't understand the full value of what I possess, but as I tread across the loft between the neat rows of oak tables, each with their brass reading lamps and delicate green-glass shades, a warm feeling of home wells up inside.

I turn and stretch my arms out, mimicking the curve of the balconies extending on either side of the mezzanine. There used to be huge fermentation tanks on the first floor of this famous brewery. My grandpa Cal bought the historic landmark for my grandmother, and she spent her entire life converting it into this magnificent bookstore and printing museum.

Inhaling the scent of age-old mysteries, I abandon the view and approach the secret door to my apartment. Reaching up to the candle sconce, next to my special copy of *Saducismus Triumphatus*, I tilt it down and the bookcase door slides open.

The ghost of Myrtle Isadora swooshes out of the closet with glee. "Good, you're back. I've got the perfect thing laid out for you to wear. Plenty of layers, and those special boots I was telling you about."

"Good morning to you too, Grams."

Her apparition shimmers, and she places a bejeweled fist on one hip as she smooths the folds of her burgundy silk-and-tulle Marchesa burial gown. "Don't take that tone with me, young lady. You'll be thanking me when you're out there freezing your ample behind off on the mountain."

"Far be it from me to argue with a fashion expert such as yourself."

She flutters her translucent eyelashes and giggles. "Sass all you want. You know I'm right."

Heading into the closet I've nicknamed *Sex and the City* meets *Confessions of a Shopaholic,* I'm pleased to see that today's outfit does not include high heels. There's at least one big check mark in the "pros" column for snocross.

"Don't you worry, dear, I'll be sure to pick out a nice pair of Christian Louboutin's for your wedding attire."

I point a sharp finger toward my lips. "Grams! You know the rules about thought-dropping! If these lips aren't moving, you don't get to comment."

She throws her ethereal limbs into the air. "Not even in defense of fashion?"

"Especially not for that." I begin the arduous process of layering my silk long underwear and wool socks underneath the rest of the garb Ghost-ma has selected. "Where's Pyewacket?"

"I haven't seen him this morning. He may be patrolling in the museum. The mice tend to be rather active indoors this time of year."

"Ew."

"Mr. Cuddlekins always earns his keep."

I chuckle at her fierce defense of the furry fiend and finish my transformation into a polar explorer. "Well, it looks like I'm ready to conquer Antarctica!"

"Mitzy. You're such a hoot! You have fun with your dad today and be sure to thank him for agreeing to get married in the bookshop. You know how much it means to me."

"I will, Grams." As I circle down the treads to the

first floor it occurs to me that Isadora always got her way in life, and not a whole lot has changed in death.

A voice from the ether whispers, "I heard that."

"Get out of my head, woman!"

A patron in the historical mysteries section looks up in confusion.

My expression mirrors her shock. Despite owning a bookshop, customers here are an especially rare sight. I smile self-consciously and rush toward the glowing red EXIT sign above the door leading into the alleyway between my building and my father's.

CHAPTER 2

Having my own key to my father's place across the alley is convenient, but it's still a little unsettling to be creeping around the big empty building on the weekend. We exchanged keys for convenience and safety, and also because I'm not quite ready to connect our two buildings with the Frida Kahlo/Diego Rivera style walkway that my father keeps proposing.

The impressive Duncan Restorative Justice Foundation is a miniature replica of the most famous building in all of Birch County: City Hall. A picture-perfect structure that always reminds me of a scene from *To Kill a Mockingbird*. The original, in the town square, stands about fifty feet tall. Three stories of solid granite with copper parapet walls, featuring original terrazzo floors, ornamental plaster cornices, and marble walls at the elevator lobby. It's truly the height of architectural design in Pin Cherry. My dad didn't miss a detail when he recreated the lavish, yet slightly miniaturized, version of the architecture for his headquarters.

He may have spent fifteen regrettable years in Clearwater State Pen for a crime he mostly didn't commit, but he definitely used the experience to turn his life around. His foundation provides a legal defense fund for wrongly convicted prisoners and a job placement resource for ex-cons.

Walking toward the life-size statue of the grandfather I never had the opportunity to meet, I stop and read the dedication plaque for the first time.

In memory of Calvin Jacob Duncan

Father, husband, and grandfather

May his efforts to protect the town he built, with jobs and commerce, via the Midwest Union Railway, and his love for his family, remain his undying legacy. It's never too late to choose love.

I dab at the tears under my eyes with my woolen mittens, before removing them and shoving them in the pocket of my puffy coat. I wish my dad could've had a chance to hear about grandpa Cal's change of heart before his untimely death, but, like so many of the relationships in the Duncan family tree, the truths revealed after the fact seem to build bonds that last beyond the veil. They may have had a terrible falling out in life, but Grandpa Cal uncovered the truth and changed his will. That act cost him his life, but it went a long way to healing the rift with his son, and laying the groundwork for my chance at a better relationship with my dad.

Continuing into the marble enclosed elevator lobby, I drop my defenses a fraction of an inch and let myself bask in the warmth of family as I ascend.

PING. The elevator doors slide open and I find myself right in the middle of an argument.

So much for the family-love vibe. "Um, should I come back later, Dad?"

Two guilty faces spin toward me, and my father runs a nervous hand through his ice-blond hair, but it's his fiancée who comes to our rescue.

Amaryllis smiles and shrugs her petite shoulders. "Don't worry, Mitzy, it's not a real argument. Your father is trying to convince me to go to the snowmobile drag races today. However, while I'm extremely proud of my soon-to-be husband and his record number of Junior Snocross Champion titles, my schedule is overflowing with wedding-planning duties."

She arches an eyebrow, and the golden flecks in her brown eyes sparkle as she gives me a conspiratorial wink.

I tug my stocking cap off, shake out the bone-white hair I inherited from my father, and breathe a sigh of relief. "Look, Dad, she's right. You and I can manage the races. You can present the trophies, or whatever, and Amaryllis can take care of the wedding stuff. New Year's Eve is coming up fast, and I don't know very much about weddings and even less about winter, but it seems to me that it will take quite a bit of preparation to keep your guests from straight up freezing to death at an outdoor reception!"

Amaryllis chuckles as she refills her coffee cup. "I keep telling Jacob that it's more complicated to plan a wedding than he thinks. But you know men!" She imitates my father's voice and jokes, "Just tell me what to wear and when to be there." She laughs and rolls her eyes. "That's his mantra."

My dad covers his face with one large, strong hand and offers no defense.

She pours another cup of coffee, adds a splash of Irish cream, and flashes her eyebrows as she hands it to me. "You'll need that extra kick to keep you warm. You're going to be surprised by what it feels like to be outdoors in the heart of winter at near-zero temps for an entire day."

I grasp the mug of liquid alert and inhale the comforting aroma. "At least you don't have to pay for a wedding venue. I mean, I wasn't planning on charging you for the bookshop." My hilarious comment meets with crickets.

My father shakes his head, and his eyes widen in fear as an uncomfortable silence grows.

Amaryllis sets her mug on the black granite countertop and transfers a hand to her hip. "Jacob Duncan, is there something you're not telling me?"

My dad and I exchange a worried glance.

He takes the lead. "My mom was hoping—always hoped—that I'd be married in the bookshop."

She narrows her gaze and scans the unspoken exchange between my father and me. "I may not be litigating cases in a courtroom, now that I'm official counsel for the Duncan Restorative Justice Foundation, but I haven't lost my ability to read people. You two are hiding something, and you're not leaving this penthouse until I find out what it is. Why you would wait until the last minute to drop this in my lap, Jacob, is beyond me."

My dad's moose-sized shoulders sag appreciably. "It's not important."

The hairs on the back of my neck tingle and the magicked mood ring on my left hand delivers an icy chill which creeps up my arm at a deliberate pace.

Her eyes widen with concern, and she walks around the counter to slip an arm around my father's waist. "Jacob, something really is wrong, isn't it? I thought we agreed to have no secrets. A lawyer marrying an ex-con is scandalous enough, but I understand what led you to commit the robbery—and they framed you for the murder. You served your time—and then some—and paid your debt to society. What else is there? I can't imagine there's anything worse?" Her voice shakes, but her eyes are full of compassion.

Little beads of sweat pop out along my father's brow.

My psychic senses deliver a volley of highly charged messages. Doing my best to ignore all supernatural information, I shift my weight from one foot to the other, cross my arms, and pretend to admire the artwork on the wall.

Amaryllis pulls away from my dad, and her expression grows cold. "Listen, you two, no secrets means no secrets. I've dreamt of getting married on New Year's Eve since I was a little girl, but I will cancel the Veuve Clicquot order and put this entire thing on hold until I get to the truth. Reality is far more important to me than a childhood fantasy."

Jacob looks at me, and his eyes beg for forgiveness.

My entire body vibrates with fear as I shake my head in warning.

He takes a deep breath and launches into his explanation. "Amaryllis, honey, my mother's ghost lives in the bookshop. Mitzy can see ghosts. And talk to them. And my mom wants us to get married there. I know it sounds crazy, but you have to believe me."

The stern look on her face vanishes, and a slow smile lifts her heart-shaped mouth as a single tear trickles down her cheek. She closes the distance between us and hugs me tightly. "I knew it! I knew you had the gift, Mitzy. You remember that time— Never mind." Turning to my father, she offers him absolution. "Of course we'll get married in the bookshop, Jacob. You'll be astonished at what I can accomplish in a week! I can redirect the vendors and put a notice in the paper to alert the guests to the change. Easy peasy." She squeezes me one more time and the love in her eyes nearly breaks my heart. "Mizithra, I know

I can never replace your mother, but I hope you'll let me try."

Now I'm crying. "You don't think I'm a freak? I mean, it's not every day you meet someone who talks to ghosts."

"I always knew you were special. How can any child of Jacob Duncan's be anything less than extraordinary? Do you think Twiggy will assist me in getting things sorted for the ceremony?"

The belly laugh that grips me comes out of nowhere. "I think you mean, can *you* assist Twiggy?"

We all share a hearty chuckle at the thought of anyone telling Twiggy what to do.

My volunteer employee, Twiggy, was my grandmother's best friend in life and currently runs the bookshop for me, while refusing any form of payment other than my, generally public, embarrassments. Part of me is sure she would take a bullet for me, but until that moment comes, she'd much prefer to laugh at my natural clumsiness and relationship foibles.

My father wipes his forehead and exhales loudly. "Whew! That's a load off. Trust me, Snugglebear, I didn't enjoy keeping that secret." Jacob breathes deeply and squares his relieved shoulders. "Even though it wasn't really mine to tell, hopefully my amazing and brilliant daughter will forgive me."

His big grey eyes stare pleadingly into mine and I shrug. "Flattery will get you everywhere, Dad. I may not be strong enough to tell Erick about it yet, but now that Amaryllis is part of the family, I think she deserves to know the truth."

She places a hand on my arm. "You haven't told Erick? I thought you two were getting rather serious?"

Fidgeting and staring at the floor, I avoid a direct response. "Things are fine. I'm taking it slow. I made a lot of bad choices in my past, and I kinda hope things work out with him—long-term. You know?"

Her gaze immediately drifts to my father and they exchange a heart-melting eye-hug. "I know exactly what you mean."

Oh brother. Snugglebears and eye-hugs! This is way too much mushy stuff this early in the morning. I'm not entirely comfortable baring all my emotions for anyone, and I certainly don't need to watch someone else do it. Time to get this train out of the station. "We better get going. I don't want Dad to be late for his runway walk!"

Amaryllis laughs so hard she snorts. "All hail the King of Snocross."

My dad shakes his head in mock frustration, but he takes the hint.

As the elevator descends, he slips an arm around my shoulders, leans down, and kisses the top of my head. "Thanks for letting me bring her into the inner circle, sweetie. I know we can trust her."

"Yeah, I feel that way too." In the alleyway between my father's foundation/penthouse and my bookshop, a thick layer of snow blankets the ground, nearly hiding my earlier boot prints, and the gently falling flakes create a fairytale wrapped in a hushed mystery.

I insist on taking my Jeep, because it has better heating than my dad's 1950s pickup, but he insists on driving, since I'm a bit of an amateur in the snow.

"Far be it from me to argue with the eight-time Junior Snocross and Drag Race Champion!"

He scoffs and shakes his head in embarrassment.

CHAPTER 3

The early morning drive out to the old Fox Mountain Ski Resort is as beautiful as a Hallmark movie's midwinter sleigh ride. The thick flakes are falling in earnest, and the windshield wipers swipe them away with a rhythm all their own. Luckily, the deer moving toward shelter in the deep pine and birch forest stand out starkly against the folds of white.

"Nice driving, Duncan."

My father replies with a sing-songy lilt. "Thank you kindly." He takes the last sloping turn on the winding road and pulls into one of the few available spots.

The parking lot is packed with vehicles, trailers, and pop-up tents. "Holy *Snow Day*! I think you undersold this, Dad."

"Well, the winter is long and the residents of Pin Cherry Harbor are mighty creative."

I tug my hat down over my ears, and make sure my scarf is tucked inside my jacket, before slipping my wool mittens inside bigger leather mittens called choppers, if I'm remembering that correctly, and bravely step out of the Jeep. I barely make it four steps when I skid on a patch of ice, hidden beneath the fresh snowfall, and land on my well-padded backside.

My father comes to my rescue in a flash and helps me to my feet. "How about you hang on to me until we get you to the grandstand?"

"Grandstand? Like actual stacked seating where more than five or ten people will be watching?" I grip his arm and shake my head in awe.

"The ski resort is closed for renovations, Mitzy. What did you think all these cars were here for?"

"Copy that." As a film-school dropout, new experiences always tend to fall into one of three categories: blockbuster, box office flop, or cult classic. The jury's still out on this event, but one thing it does not lack is volume.

The engines are whining in well over fifty sleds. That's the cool insider name for snowmobiles, in case you live south of the Mason-Dixon line. At least a hundred sleds are being removed from trailers, revving up for no reason, or whipping around the brightly lit track, on what I can only assume are test laps.

According to my father's brief lesson during our car ride to the competition, there are two categories, with divisions for several age groups. There's snocross, which is a lot like motocross, but with snowmobiles on a hilly snow-packed oval track. There are also a day's worth of snowmobile drag races, which sounds similar to quarter-mile time trials, but once again, in the snow and going uphill. Snowmobiles can reach speeds of one hundred and fifty miles per hour in the drag races, so the uphill configuration allows for a safe cool down path. All I can think of is how much I wish I'd listened to Erick and added a pair of earmuffs to my outfit, to dampen the whine of the two-stroke engines.

"Duncan! Jacob Duncan!" A small man in a bright-orange parka and a fluorescent-green neck gaiter waves both of his arms wildly.

I elbow my dad and nod toward the shenanigans.

He leans down and whispers, "That will be the mayor. Looks like my official duties are about to begin. You get yourself some hot chocolate and a spot in the grandstand. Try to find a seat on the first row or two. The view is better from the top, but so is the windchill."

"Copy that, Champ."

His shoulders shake with laughter as he walks toward the mayor.

Hopping into the hot chocolate queue, I wonder if they sell it in pints? Maybe if I sip on a steady stream of warm chocolate goodness, I can survive the frigid festivities.

Although, as I take in the rows of porta-potties

along the outskirts of the temporary race venue, I come to terms with the realities of weighing my warmth against my eventual need to relieve myself in the certain-to-be frosty facilities. Maybe a small cup of hot chocolate is the better plan, and I'll keep moving to stay alive.

The guy behind me in line offers a friendly smile and starts a conversation I didn't know I'd be having. "Spectator or racer?"

While I'm flattered that he thinks I might be able to handle a snowmobile, I don't know nearly enough about the sport to make any false claims. "Absolutely a spectator. I'm just here to support my dad."

"Nice. Your dad runnin' in the snocross or the drags?"

"Oh, he's not racing today. He's presenting some awards and probably other stuff."

"Wow. I didn't know I was in the presence of snocross royalty." He bows and lifts one eyebrow. "You're Jacob Duncan's kid?"

I'm not sure how I feel about being referred to as a "kid," but I'm not here to make a scene. "Yep. Eight-time Junior Snocross Champion."

The guy whoops and nods in admiration. "Actually, he was three-time Junior Snocross Champ, two-time Junior Stock Drags Champ, two-time Junior Modified Drags Champ, and one-time overall King of the Winter Circuit."

My eyes widen and I bite hard into my tongue to

keep from cracking up. "Wow. He really was the king, huh?"

Ignoring my comment, the guy shouts to his friends, "Bristol, AJ, Eli, this here's Duncan's kid." He gestures frantically with his high-tech articulated leather gloves.

What is happening? My throat tightens and I instinctively step back.

Three fresh faces join the crowd and a mother in line behind us, with two young children, mutters something about manners and cutting in line.

"Excuse me, miss, why don't you and your kids go ahead of us?"

Her face flushes with guilt. Clearly she thought her comment was subsonic. I can't honestly be sure whether I heard it with my five regular senses or if my clairaudience delivered the message. Either way, she herds her pack ahead of us while my new friend brings the group up to speed with exaggerated tales of the amazing Jacob Duncan.

One of the newcomers nods his ski-mask-covered face in my direction and rolls up the part covering his face. "So, you here for the whole day?"

I shrug. "I'm here as long as my dad's here. I suppose the trophies don't get handed out until the end of the day, so probably, yes?"

The additional trio calls out in rapid succession.

"Cool."

"Sweet."

"Noice."

The group's original spokesperson thrusts out a mittened hand. "I'm Crank. This beast is AJ, the little guy Eli won junior drags last year and he's already the number three seed in the pro-stock drags this season, and Bristol's fourth in the women's snocross circuit. Points-wise, I mean."

Good thing he clarified. Because? I take a moment to remind myself that the universe brought me here for my pops, and not to *snark*, before I reply. "Nice to meet all of you. I'm Mitzy Moon. My—"

Bristol steps forward, pulls off her jester-style beanie, and takes a knee. "Dude, I'm your humble servant. I read a bunch of stories about you online and all the, like, mysteries you solved and stuff. You're my hero. For reals."

The others nod in agreement, and it would appear my sleuthing has eclipsed my father's championship status. Even though this strange meet up is turning out better than I anticipated, I'm eager to duck out of the spotlight and melt into the crowd. "Hey, forget about it. I just do what I can to help out, you know? Today is all about snowmobiles and my dad, all right?"

Bristol jumps to her feet. "No doubt. No doubt. If I win, though, I'm gonna full on dedicate my trophy to you."

"Thanks." It comes out as more of a question than I intended, but this tough snocross fangirl is throwing me off my game.

AJ and Eli snicker and jab elbows back and forth,

and the super-sized AJ nearly knocks Eli off his feet. The small racer drops his decal-covered helmet and immediately retrieves it. He busies himself wiping off the snow covering his sponsors' logos.

Crank is not a guy to take a hint. "Where you sittin'? You can totally hang with us. I'm here as support crew, but it's truly cool if you want to hang out in the pits, you know, learn all the behind-the-scenes stuff from a top mechanic."

And he's humble, too. "Thanks, that's a super sweet offer, but I kinda promised my dad I'd be there for him, in case he needed anything. So, you guys go tune-up your sleds, and good luck. I'll be rooting for you, for sure."

This time the whole quartet sounds off.

"Cool."

"Sweet."

"Noice."

"Awesome, man." Crank gives me a "guy nod" before slugging AJ playfully.

The foursome tramp off toward the din of revving snowmobiles, and I breathe a sigh of relief.

Time to get back in that hot cocoa line and see if I can come up a winner.

"Mitzy. Mitzy, come on over here. I want you to meet someone." My father beckons me toward a running snowmobile, saddled with a rider in a full-face helmet with the visor pushed up.

Looks like it's going to be a "no joy" on the hot

chocolate. I hustle to my dad's side and he wraps a friendly arm around my shoulder.

"Mitzy, this is Trey Lee. He's top seed in the current points standing in the pro-stock division and Mr. Jablonski coaches him."

I reach out and give the young rider a fist bump. "Jablonski? The taxidermist?"

The kid nods his helmet up and down. "Yeah, Coach Jawbone is the best. I'd never be top seed without him, you know?"

I have no intention of telling him that I do not know. My only interaction with the creepy taxidermist left my skin crawling and my feet racing to put distance between us. "Oh, sure. That's great that he's coaching you. Does his son ride? Does he coach anyone else?"

Both my father and Trey scoff openly.

My dad pats Trey on the back and nods toward the pits. "You better get your sled checked out. I'm sure Coach will be here any minute."

Trey flicks his visor down, revs the snowmobile so hard it wheelies, and heads into the pits.

"The taxidermist is a snowmobile coach?"

My father's eyes drift to a faraway place in his memory. "Yeah, he was a champion on the circuit, and the second he retired, your grandpa Cal paid him a fortune to coach me."

My eyebrows arch under my stocking cap. "He was your coach? He coached the king of the slopes?"

I can no longer contain my laughter, and my father's cheeks redden with more than the bite of winter.

"I deserved that. I was pretty full of myself back then. Jablonski was pushing me to move out of the junior division and go for the bigger prize money on the pro circuit. That was about the time my rebellious streak kicked in."

A knowing sensation of dread floods over me. "You and Cal didn't get along."

He leans away, and for a moment Jacob looks a little surprised. "Oh, right. Your psychic messages."

"As Pyewacket would say, 'can confirm'."

He walks toward the grandstand, and as I follow he compresses the catalyst of his fall from grace into a few brief sentences.

"Cal never came to any of the races. He wanted to brag about me in boardrooms and country clubs, but he never spent any time with me. He put all my prize money in a trust and wouldn't let me touch it. So, once I was king of the circuit, I quit. Jablonski was furious and didn't coach anyone else for almost five years. I started spending most of my spare time with less desirables—"

"Like Darrin?"

"Like Darrin." Jacob shakes his head and stares at the ground. "After his dishonorable discharge from the Navy and my dropping out of college, we started to plan the robbery."

We stop next to the grandstand and he hugs me tight.

The emotions are bubbling close to the surface, and I need to stuff them back down. "Cut to—amazing father and daughter reunion, and the king of the circuit is back to hand out trophies!"

Jacob chuckles and pats me on the back. "Grab those open seats on the second bench. I gotta check in with the mayor, but I should be able to join you for the first few drag races. The snocross doesn't start until later this afternoon."

"Here's to the races, Duncan."

My father wanders off, and I thread through the blankets, coolers, and children's games of chase, to take a seat in the second row.

The junior novice drag race is up first, and the small snowmobiles and young riders force me to wonder what kind of a dumpster fire I'm about to witness. Despite their stature, these eleven- to thirteen-year-old guys and gals know how to get it done. I'm surprised by the control they have over their sleds. One little guy even pops a wheelie like the big boys.

Asking the parka-encased human next to me to save my seat, I wander off to get some hot chocolate. Finally successful, I return to my seat in time for the pro-stock drags.

Each sled and rider is accompanied to the starting line by one support crewmember. I recognize Crank behind the sled on the far right and assume that Eli is at the helm of that snowmachine. The rider closest to the grandstands is the favorite, Trey, but he doesn't have a crewmember at his side. Maybe it's one of Coach Jawbone's rules.

The announcer's voice crackles to life. "Hang on to your seat cushions! This is the most talked about race of the day! Number one seed Trey Lee is here to protect his pro-stock title, and Eli McGrail is here to take it away!"

The riders rev their engines and plant their feet firmly on the running boards. Support crews take their cue to step behind the protective wall and the light tree blinks down.

Yellow. Yellow. Yellow. GREEN!

The roar is deafening!

"And they're off and running!"

All six sleds rear back into powerful wheelies and rocket down the track.

"Lee fights for the lead. McGrail is only a ski behind," the announcer shouts.

The crowd cheers and stomps their boots.

The entire grandstand shakes.

"Looks like Wiggins is fighting for control of—" The announcer stops in mid call.

The rider in lane two loses control of his sled and crashes into Trey.

"Wiggins flips his sled! Lee is forced off the track!"

Trey's sled skids off the groomed track and careens into the tree line.

I search the starting line for his coach, but I'm not

sure I could identify Jablonski covered in layers of winter gear.

However, I do recognize my dad running up the slope.

I hop over the railing, into the snow, and follow. "Dad! Is he okay? Is he moving?"

My father moves like a charging bear. He leaps off the groomed track and pushes through the waist-deep snow amongst the trees.

Medics and a couple of mechanics from other crews are finally catching on. My father shouts instructions down the hill. "Get a stretcher. Trey's not moving! And somebody get a winch up here for this sled."

I stop at the edge of the groomed track, not confident enough to follow my father into the sinkhole of snow. "Dad, what can I do?"

He looks up from his perch next to the crumpled body of the young boy and whispers, "Is he alive? Are you getting any messages?"

I reach out with my psychic senses, and a sickening knot tightens in my stomach. Before I can share my message, other people arrive on scene and push past me to attach the winch's hook to the back of the sled.

The announcer is droning on in the background, but my ears feel clogged and I'm wrapped in a sound-deadening bubble.

The paramedics carefully make their way to the

boy, as crewmembers from other teams slowly winch the sled back toward the track.

As the skis slide out of the deep powder, a single red streak drags across the white.

"Stop!" I wave my hands wildly and grip the arm of one of the mechanics. "Stop the winch. There's blood!" And that's when the knot in my stomach unfurls.

Someone *is* dead . . . but it isn't Trey.

CHAPTER 4

This morning's fog of inexplicable dread now makes perfect sense. You know that scene in the movie when time seems to slow down and the edges of the main character's vision get fuzzy as he or she laser focuses on one pivotal thing? That's exactly what's happening to me right now, and that one pivotal thing is a crimson slash in the otherwise pristine snow.

My stomach swirls, and the burning message from my mood ring must be ignored, as I hoof it up the slope and deposit this morning's breakfast behind a birch tree.

Despite my father's preoccupation with getting Trey safely strapped onto a backboard, he calls out to me. "Mitzy, you okay?"

Picking up a handful of icy flakes, I clean my mouth before replying. "I'll live." Oh brother! What a poor choice of words.

"Hey, can you push back the crowds? I'm gonna find Trey's parents and his coach."

The word "coach" seems to freeze in the air like a group of floating icicles, and the burning message in my mood ring's black cabochon can no longer be avoided. I yank off my layers of mittens and gaze into the glass dome. The unmistakable face staring back at me nearly brings up another batch of home fries.

Shoving my hand back into the mittens, I jog down the hill and call out to my father. "Dad, I need to talk to you."

He sees the panicked look on my face and pats the paramedic on the back as he struggles back onto the stability of the hard-packed drag track. "What is it?"

I gesture hesitantly toward the site of the accident, but refuse to turn my head. "Under there, the body . . . It's Mr. Jablonski."

The color drains from Jacob's face. "Are you sure? You're positive it's Jawbone?"

Nodding my head slowly, I grip my dad's arm as icy tears form in the corners of my eyes. "You know what that means, right? Stellen's an . . . He's . . . an orphan."

Jacob holds me tight, and for a moment his love keeps the horrible montage, pressing at the edges of my consciousness, at bay. Stellen may not be eleven, but even at the sort-of-grown-up age of sixteen, losing both your parents in the space of five years is going to leave scars. "I need to get out to his place. I don't want him to hear about this when some deputy shows up on his doorstep."

Jacob nods solemnly. "Somebody needs to clear this area, though."

"Yeah, it's definitely a crime scene. I'll call Erick. You go find Trey's folks. I've got a fan club that will handle crowd control, and then I'm heading out to find Stellen."

"Fan club?" He lifts an eyebrow and shrugs. "I'll be over to check on you tonight."

Drawing a ragged breath, I struggle to hold it together. "Thanks, Dad." I slip my phone out and risk baring a hand to call the sheriff. Erick's friendly voice nearly cracks my fragile exterior. "Hey, it's a long story, and I promise to explain tonight— What? Yes, it's a corpse, but— You can tease me about it later. The victim is Mr. Jablonski, the taxidermist."

"Hey! Hey, no civilians on the drag track. If you're not wearing official race-staff safety gear, you better get off my track. I'll have you arrested—or worse."

An official-looking man in a bright-orange safety vest with a clipboard in his left hand is running up the hill toward my father and me.

My dad calls out. "Look, pal, I know you think you're in charge, but we have an emergency situation. You're going to have to cancel the races."

The man plants his feet on the track and shakes

his head firmly. "I *am* in charge. And you and this girl better get off my track or heads are going to roll. I don't make empty threats."

My father points to the carmine stain in the powder and shakes his head.

I give Erick the two-second update and place him on speakerphone as I aim the device at Mr. Hothead.

A calm, official voice takes control of the situation. "Mr. Bennett, this is Sheriff Harper. You need to shut down the drags and the snocross immediately. No one is to leave the grounds. No additional races are to take place. I have deputies en route to secure the scene and take statements from the eyewitnesses. Do you understand?"

The all-bark-and-no-bite official nods.

I kick out one hip and tilt my head. "You'll have to give a verbal answer for the record, Mr. Bennett."

"Yes, Sheriff. Yes, I understand. I'll take care of it right away." His suddenly cooperative head continues to nod.

"Thank you, Mr. Bennett." Erick swallows and exhales audibly.

I tap the speaker off and press the phone against my beanie. "Don't worry, I'm headed out to break the news to Stellen. I feel so awful for him."

My wonderful boyfriend attempts to console me, but I can't risk it. The tears are too close to the surface. "I gotta go. Dinner at the bookshop? Yeah, I will. Bye."

As I slide the phone into my pocket, a movement

on the hill catches my eye. A jester hat bobs up the slopes. "Bristol!"

She sees me and lopes forward with the determination of a hungry lone wolf.

"Bristol, get AJ up here and clear these people out. Find some rope or something and set up a perimeter. This is a crime scene."

She bows clumsily, turns, and shouts down the mountain with shocking volume. "Mitzy Moon is on the case."

I hang back until I see her and AJ headed up the slope, dragging long strands of plastic pennant-flag garland in their wake. All right, they've got this. Now it's time to deliver the worst news any kid could ever receive.

The Jeep seems to drive itself out to the old Jablonski farm. I certainly can't see the road. Tears blur my vision and I allow it to happen now, so I can be strong for Stellen.

Making the final turn by the crumbling silo—excellent landmark—I frown at the bare-limbed trees arching over the road. The grey skies hang heavier, as the road narrows to a single track through the deep snow. This drive has all the makings of a scary movie intro.

The old taxidermy shed looms into view and my skin crawls with the unwelcome thought of what it houses. I park in front of the dark and dreary main cabin, mount the steps and knock on the door.

No reply.

There's no bell, so I try the handle.

The door opens and I push my way inside. "Stellen? Stellen, it's Mitzy Moon. Are you in here?"

No reply.

He could be out visiting his memory meadow, the place where we cemented our friendship over the loss of loving mothers. However, my psychic senses tell me he's in the taxidermy shed. The absolute last place I want to go.

Time to put on my big-girl pants and woman up.

I trudge across the driveway and brush the falling snow from my face. Hopefully, the cold temperatures will shrink the puffiness under my eyes and it won't look like I've been crying for twenty minutes.

The handle turns easily, and I step inside. Before I can call out, my gaze locks onto a pair of black-tufted ears—frozen in time. The horrible sight of a stuffed caracal, eternally leaping in the air to grab a bird, sucker punches me right in the gut. "Pyewacket!" I lunge forward, grab the statue and force myself to look at its face. Is this why he was missing?

Stellen appears between a mound of prepared hides and the naked armature of a mountain lion. "Mitzy? What are you doing here?" He takes in my terrified expression as I clutch the mounted caracal, and he thinks he's solved the mystery. "Oh, that's not . . . It's a really long story. Don't worry, I would never let my wacko dad stuff your cat." He shakes his head and laughs a little.

The mounted cat has no scars over its left eye,

and my panic evaporates. But, before I deliver my heartbreaking news, I'll let the kid have this moment. I'll let him have the last laugh he'll have for—possibly years.

He steps forward and helps me right the stuffed wildcat. "My dad's not here. Big snowmobile race at the mountain, you know?"

Taking a deep breath, I struggle to find an ounce of courage. "That's why I'm here, Stellen. Maybe you should sit down?" In the movies, they always tell people to sit down before bad news. I suppose it's to keep them from injuring themselves when they faint, but nowadays fainting doesn't seem to be nearly as common as it was in the Victorian era.

He shrugs. "I'm fine. What's going on?"

"There was an accident during the drag races, and—"

"Oh no. Did Trey get hurt? If Trey got hurt my dad's gonna be furious. He was counting on his take of the winnings to pay his entry fees into the Taxidermy World Championships."

Despite the horrible news I'm trying to share, the thought of the Taxidermy World Championship momentarily pulls my focus. "There's a world championship?"

Stellen rolls his eyes dramatically. "You don't wanna know. Anyway, is Trey gonna be all right?"

"I don't know for sure. I had to leave. There's more. It's your dad."

The young boy's eyes widen, and his uncanny

intuition jumps ahead. He stammers, "My . . . my dad was injured? In the accident?"

This is uncharted territory for me. I can't very well tell the kid that a snowmobile skewered his father's buried body! There's gotta be some of that decorum Silas is always talking about hidden inside me somewhere. I search my brain for the right words.

Stellen lowers himself onto the pile of hides. "It's bad, isn't it?"

"I didn't want you to have to hear it from the sheriff, you know?"

He nods and blinks his watery eyes. "How bad is it?"

"Stellen, I'm afraid your father is dead." I could've used some cheesy euphemism, but it's better to give it to him straight. It's not going to make it hurt any less if I confuse the kid with a "no longer with us" or a "slipped away." At the end of the day, his dad is dead. Nice words won't change that.

His gaze slowly scans from one side of the shop to the other, taking in all the treasures and trophies his father held in such high regard. "What am I gonna do with all of this?"

"You don't need to worry about that. There will be an investigation. I'm sure the sheriff will send a team out to look for evidence—"

The young man jumps to his feet and steps toward me. "Wait, it wasn't an accident? He wasn't killed in the race? You think he was murdered?" His breathing is rapid and shallow.

Placing a hand on his shoulder, I offer the only comfort I can. "I think he was murdered, and I'm going to find out who did it."

Stellen paces a tight circle and taps his forehead with two fingers on his right hand. "What am I gonna do? Where am I gonna live? Maybe I can petition the court to become an emancipated minor. I don't have any—" He stops and his right hand slowly falls to his side like the lazy flakes outside the window. His eyes glaze over and his jaw hangs slack.

The crippling overwhelm. I know it too well. "I tell you what, let's go inside and pack up a bag or two. I'm sure you have schoolbooks, projects, favorite clothes . . . You can come and stay with me until everything is settled. All right?"

The boy's intelligent green eyes narrow and he tilts his head of dark-brown curls with concern. "I'm not sure Child Protective Services will allow me to stay with someone who's not a relative."

"I hold quite a bit of sway over the sheriff. You let me and him worry about CPS." I slide a friendly arm around his shoulder and intend to guide him into the house.

Instead, he turns into me and weeps. It's all I can do to hold it together and be a rock.

A few moments pass and Stellen turns away to wipe his eyes, too embarrassed to look at me.

"Hey, I was only eleven when I lost my mom. I cried for a solid week. You never have to feel self-conscious around me. All right? Let's go get your stuff, and you can help me find the real Pyewacket when we get back to the bookshop."

He swipes at his tears and silently leads the way into his empty house.

Stellen pulls a carry-on-sized suitcase from under his bed, unzips it, and places the open clamshell on his bed. As he collects random items from around his room, his inner world pours out of his mouth.

"My dad always wanted me to ride, you know? It's not my thing. I can't play sports, I wasn't into taxidermy, and I don't like snowmobiles."

He places a stack of books next to the stack of cards, still tucked in envelopes, he'd pulled out of his bedside table. "I guess I was a disappointment to him. He wanted some kind of super manly jock for a son, and I was a nerdy bookworm."

He picks up a picture of his mother from a small desk, shoved into a poorly illuminated corner, and holds the frame as though it could disintegrate in his hands at any moment. "Will I ever be back? Should I take the photo albums from the living room?"

"I'm not going to let anything happen to this place, Stellen. It'll be here as long as you need it to be here. You don't have to worry about making any major decisions today, all right?"

He nods and places the photo of his mom in the suitcase.

I hate to interrupt his process, but the bag is half full, and it doesn't contain any clothing. "You should grab some clothes. Stuff for school, and something nice for the—funeral."

"I have a suit, but I haven't worn it since her— It probably doesn't fit."

"No sweat. We'll take care of that later. Just grab some school clothes, pajamas, and you can bring your pillow if you want."

He sits down on his bed and stares at me with sadness and a hint of apprehension. "I don't have pajamas. I usually sleep in my clothes. My dad never checks on me."

This kid is crushing my heart, piece by piece. "That's all right. Do you have some sweatpants, or something comfortable? I don't mean to freak you out, but there's only one enormous studio apartment at my place. I'll set you up on the sofa, but I'd hate for you to have to sleep in jeans."

For the first time since I offered him a place to stay, Stellen seems to be processing the reality of moving in with me. My regular and psychic senses pick up on an increase in his discomfort.

"Don't worry. You'll have some privacy. We'll set up a bathroom schedule, and— We'll make it work. You'll get settled in no time. I promise."

He nods and retrieves some items of clothing from the floor of his closet.

Never let it be said that teenage boys are neat freaks. Despite his above-average intelligence and bookworm tendencies, he's still a dyed-in-the-wool slob.

He zips the suitcase and grabs his pillow. "I'll get my winter gear downstairs, and I have to set the alarm on the shop before I leave."

"What about the house?"

"There's nothing in here anyone would want. All the valuable stuff is in the taxi shop."

Turning the lights off in his room as we leave, I follow Stellen down the narrow staircase and try to ignore the hollow emptiness that threatens to swallow us. There's nothing left in this building. Once upon a time, long, long ago, it may have been a home, but I think it's barely been a dwelling since his mother passed.

True to his word, Stellen does not bother to lock the house. He slides his suitcase into the back of my Jeep and jogs over to secure the taxidermy shed.

I jump in the vehicle and get the heater running.

He climbs onto the passenger seat and sits quietly as I maneuver around in a seven-point turn to exit the property without hitting any trees. "I need to make a quick call, is that all right?"

He nods and stares out the window mournfully.

No need to explain to Stellen the reasons why I need to call my attorney and secret alchemical mentor. I'm hoping that my wise teacher will read between the lines and help me navigate this strange situation.

"Hey, Silas, I have a project for you and I need a bit of legal advice."

He harrumphs at my lack of proper etiquette, but makes no objections to my request.

"Unfortunately, Mr. Jablonski was found dead this morning at the snocross event on Fox Mountain. I picked up Stellen Jablonski—you met him once at the bookshop—and I offered him a place to stay until we get things sorted out."

Silas jumps in to warn me of the possible legal ramifications of taking in an under-aged child without proper paperwork.

"I know you can sort out the legal side of it for me, and I'm sure even call in a favor from Erick. But the real reason I called is that I'd like you to protect the property from any potential transfer of ownership. Can you find out if Mr. Jablonski had a will? And, also, file whatever injunctions you need to make sure the property can't be sold until Stellen decides what he'd like to do?"

Silas mumbles something about meddling, but I cut him off. "I know it's a lot, but I'm sure you can handle it. Thanks. I look forward to your update tomorrow." I end the call before he can protest.

Stellen presses his cheek against the cold glass, and I know exactly the swirl of emotions and fears coursing through his body.

There's no need to push him to discuss things he's not ready to explore.

Silence can be healing.

It's enough for him to know that I'm here—for as long as it takes.

My eyes scan the road as my mind drifts off to memories of the days following my mother's death. I can't change the past, but at least I can pay it forward.

CHAPTER 5

As though I've slipped into a scene from *Dune*, I seem to fold space and arrive at the bookshop in the blink of an eye. Stopping the vehicle next to the alleyway door, I gesture to the back of the Jeep. "Why don't you grab your bag and wait here while I park this thing?"

"Okay," he mumbles.

Once he's retrieved his suitcase and safely closed the hatch, I pull the Jeep into the garage and take a deep breath.

Unlocking the side door, we step inside and immediately catch Twiggy's attention.

"Who's the tagalong?" She tilts her head and scrutinizes my sidekick.

"Hey, Stellen, how about you head up that circular staircase over there, and I'll join you after I fill Twiggy in? All right?"

He nods and rolls his bag toward the stairs.

Stepping into the back room, I bring Twiggy up to speed on the horrifying events of the morning.

"You're one heckuva corpse magnet, kid. It was good of you to take in the boy, though. I'll call over to the Elks Lodge and see if I can pick up a cot. He can't sleep on that settee for more than a night or two."

I'd like to explain to her how teenage boys can sleep absolutely anywhere, but I know she's trying to help in the only way she can. "Thanks. That would be great."

Out of nowhere she calls out, "You better hook that up behind you, kid."

Wow! I didn't even hear him unhook the "No Admittance" chain. Maybe I'm not the only one with psychic senses. "Go easy on him, Twiggy."

She runs a hand through her short grey pixie cut and shifts her weight from one biker boot to the other. "He ain't made out of glass, Mitzy. The sooner things return to normal, the better off he'll be."

There may be some truth in what she's saying, but I know from experience that nothing in his life will ever return to normal. My best bet is to change the subject. "Did you hear from Amaryllis? About the wedding?"

Twiggy shoves a hand in the pocket of her dungarees and nods. "Yep. I gave her a list of rules for the venue and vendors approved to work on the premises. We should have everything sorted out in a couple of days." She leans in and whispers conspiratorially, "It sure will make your Grams happy to have the wedding here."

I snicker. "Don't I know it? I better go get Stellen settled. Thanks for everything."

"All in a day's work." She returns to her rolly office chair and I tempt fate by stepping over the chain at the bottom of the stairs. The universe smiles down and allows me to pass without a trace—or a tumble.

Upstairs, in the Rare Books Loft, Stellen stands next to one of the oak tables and waits patiently.

"So, now that you're gonna be staying here, you need to learn a few of the secrets. Why don't you do the honors?" I gesture to the candle sconce on the wall and force a smile. "You just tilt it down."

He wheels his suitcase over, reaches up with his left hand, and pulls.

The bookcase door slides open with a satisfying whoosh. Despite Stellen's horrible morning, he manages to mumble, "Sweet."

Chuckling, I invite him into the apartment and gesture toward the settee. "I'll get some blankets for you. You can sleep here for now, and Twiggy said she'll get you a cot. Which may or may not be more comfortable."

Grams blasts through the wall from the loft into the apartment and it takes all of my self-control not to shout at her.

"Mitzy? Who's the boy?" She gestures at Stellen, who thankfully has his back turned.

I pinch my lips tightly together and take advantage of her ability to read my thoughts. *This is Stellen Jablonski. His father was murdered, and we found his body at the snowmobile drag races this morning. He's staying here indefinitely, and the last thing he needs right now is to be frightened to death by a ghost. So vanish!*

She crosses her arms over her ample bosom and kicks out her hip. "I was here first. He can't see me or hear me, so it doesn't matter if I'm in here. Besides, I came to let you know that I found Pyewacket in the printing museum."

That's great. We'll debate ghost versus guest rules later. For now, make yourself scarce.

She shakes her translucent head and mumbles loudly. "Well, I never."

I shoot one last thought in her direction as she disapparates. *We both know that's not true!*

Her giggle echoes through the ether.

"Mitzy? Sorry. I don't mean to interrupt your thoughts or whatever you—"

Oops. Looks like Stellen may have been talking to me while I was thought-scolding Grams. "Oh, you're fine. I was running through a mental checklist, you know?"

He nods. "Would it be okay if I walk down to the Piggly Wiggly to grab a few things?"

"Of course. Do you need any money?"

He shoves a hand in the pocket of his jeans and pulls out a few crumpled bills. "No. I think I have enough for bread and peanut butter."

How can I be such a dork! The kid probably hasn't eaten all day. "Hey, why don't I take you to lunch at the diner. I'm actually kinda famished." I'll spare him the explanation involving most of my breakfast being left on the mountain.

A hint of color returns to his face and he almost smiles. "I can pay."

"Look, I don't mean to sound like a snobby rich chick, but as long as you're my ward, let's agree that I can definitely afford to feed you. Got it?"

He nods. "Thanks. I don't know why you're being so nice to me. But it means a lot right now."

"I've been where you are. I'm just doing what I wish someone would've done for me. Now, let's go grab some grub. We can't very well hunt wild bookstore caracal on empty stomachs."

And for a split second, the corners of his mouth turn up.

I did that. And that's everything.

Despite his traumatic morning, Stellen has a gargantuan appetite.

Two perfectly cooked cheeseburgers, surrounded by matching mountains of french fries, and a pair of chocolate malts grace the table before us.

Tally refills our waters and tilts her head in that "poor little lamb" way—I remember it all too clearly from my childhood.

The scrape of the spatula against the grill in the kitchen stops, and I look up as Odell approaches.

"You Stan Jablonski's kid?"

Stellen's mouth is far too full to facilitate a verbal answer, so he nods slowly and wipes his mouth with a thin paper napkin.

The lines around Odell's eyes crinkle as he forces a smile. "Sorry about your dad. He was a good guy, and a great taxidermist."

The rate at which news travels in this quaint town never ceases to amaze.

My new roommate swallows roughly and takes a quick sip of his water. "Thanks. You know— knew my dad?"

"Indirectly. My brother Walt, God rest him, used to run the Walleye Lodge out on Fish Hawk Island."

Stellen nods knowingly. "Oh, yeah. My dad did a lot of quick turnaround fish mounting for that guy. He ran charter boats, too, right?"

Odell nods appreciatively. "Smart kid. You two oughta get along great."

I blush a little at the compliment, but smile with gratitude.

My surrogate grandfather puts one hand on our table and leans down as he gestures toward me with his thumb. "I got this one on the free burgers and fries for life plan. I'm happy to offer you the same deal whenever you're in town."

Stellen's face kind of freezes, and my psychic

senses feel his emotions swirling too close to the surface.

Time for me to jump in and create a distraction. "You might regret that, Odell. Stellen is bunking with me until Silas gets everything sorted out with Mr. Jablonski's will."

Odell stands up and chuckles. "Well, it's too late now. A deal's a deal." He raps his knuckles twice on the silver-flecked white Formica table and returns to the kitchen.

Stellen blinks rapidly and avoids my gaze.

"You ready to head back to the store and look for that wildcat?"

He grabs his napkin, and, as he pretends to wipe his mouth, swipes at each of his eyes. "Yeah. Sounds good."

I stack our plates, and, before I can say a word, he picks up both of our empty malt cups and follows me to the dish bin behind the counter. He definitely has more than the average teenager's intuition, and manners to boot. I might enjoy having a roomie.

We make slow progress down Main Street, and Stellen clears his throat two or three times. Even someone without the benefit of psychic senses could tell he needs to say something.

"Just a reminder, you can tell me anything you want any time. No judgment. I promise."

He exhales, and I can sense his relief. "I really appreciate everything you're doing for me, and I don't want to sound ungrateful, or whatever."

"You won't. What do you need?"

"I don't know the bus schedules around here. So, I'm not sure how I'm gonna get to school on Monday."

Wow! I can't believe he's thinking about school. That would've been the last thing on my mind at his age. In fact, at his age, I was deep into the undesirable crowd, skipping school, shoplifting, and practicing my lock-picking skills whenever I could. Maybe I should be *his* ward. "Are you sure you're ready to go to school on Monday?"

"No. But I'm sure I don't wanna sit around all day and think about what might've happened to my dad."

"All right. You let me know how you're feeling Monday morning. If you want to go to school, I'll drive you to school. If you want to stay home, I'll have Silas take care of everything."

We take a few more steps before Stellen asks another question. "So, um, Silas Willoughby is your attorney, right? He does a lot of stuff for you. It almost seems like he's family."

Now it's my turn to uncomfortably blink back tears. "I guess he's a little bit of both. He started out as my attorney, but over the last year or so he's definitely taken a more important role in my life." There, that's truthful and yet vague enough to keep all our collective secrets.

We cross First Avenue and I retrieve the hefty,

one-of-a-kind brass key that opens my special front door.

Stellen runs his fingers over the carvings and mumbles little phrases out loud as he traces the characters. "Chiron and Hippodamia. Pan and the gift of Aphrodite." When his hand reaches the carving of the wildcat, he crouches and leans his face close to the timber. "This looks like a caracal."

I have to chuckle. "It definitely does."

His touch moves over the cat's face. "Looks like he was injured."

"Again, I'd have to agree."

A frosty gust of wind curls around the corner of the building from the harbor, and my teeth chatter. "Not to rush you, but do you mind if we continue this discussion inside?"

His eyes snap up, as though he's only just realized he wasn't alone. "Yeah. Sure. Sorry."

We walk into the bookstore, throw our heavy coats over the "No Admittance" chain, and I lead the way into the printing museum.

"Is that a real Gutenberg press?"

I give a low whistle and nod. "Impressive guess. What do you think you know about ancient printing technology?"

He proceeds to download more information than I ever wanted to hear on the topic.

My eyes widen with each additional fact. "That'll do, *Wikipedia.*"

His cheeks flush self-consciously and he kicks the

toe of his shoe at an invisible rock. "I read a lot of books and watch way too many YouTube videos."

"I didn't have a lot of friends growing up either." Giving his back a friendly pat, I continue toward the stairs. "Now let's find that cat."

As we approach the landing, I call out. "Pye? Pyewacket, I have someone to introduce to you."

We complete our search of the second floor and come up empty-pawed. When we're about to walk into the third-floor exhibits, I send a quick mental message to Grams. *Please don't scare the boy. We're just trying to find Pyewacket.*

As we turn the corner, I see the drawers open on the antique writing desk, and the stack of papers representing Ghost-ma's memoirs has nearly doubled since my last visit to her writing alcove.

Next to the stack of papers, Pyewacket is stretched lazily over the top of the desk, feigning a deep sleep. Unfortunately, the ghost of Myrtle Isadora is seated at her writing desk, with one shimmering limb scratching between Pyewacket's tufted ears and the other busily writing with a quill pen.

The next irreversible sequence of events occurs almost simultaneously.

Pyewacket growls.

Grams drops her quill pen and flickers out of sight.

Stellen gasps and stops moving, but instead of screaming with fright, his eyes sparkle with hope.

I hustle in to erase the obvious. "Well, there's

Pyewacket. Let's head back to the apartment and make some microwave popcorn." And the award for lamest distractionary technique goes to . . .

"Was that a ghost? Is this museum haunted? That's so lit!"

Forcing a dismissive chuckle, I stride toward Pyewacket and make up a story as I go. "Oh, I think Pyewacket was just playing with some of the props. You know how cats are with feathers." I whisper to Pye, "Help me out, buddy. We gotta get the kid back to the apartment."

Pyewacket stretches his glorious tan form, leaps off the desk, and races down the stairs.

"Let's head out." I gesture like a children's television host trying to make room cleanup sound fun.

Stellen's momentary spark of life drifts away and his eyes glaze over. "I guess you don't believe in ghosts, huh?"

When in doubt, lie it out. "I don't know. I never really thought about it. Why?"

"Never mind. It's stupid." He shuffles down the stairs.

"It's not stupid." I toss some encouragement over my shoulder as we cross the main floor. "Say whatever you want."

He follows me silently into the apartment and I motion for him to sit on the sofa.

He chews on a fingernail and casually wipes a little tear from the corner of his eye. "My mom's ghost used to visit me sometimes. Like when I was sick, or after my dad would yell at me. I'd go up to my room and just sit in the dark and wish that she was still alive, you know?"

"Yeah. I know exactly what you mean." Raw emotions scratch at my heart. "Did you actually see her?"

"I don't know, maybe. Never mind, it makes me sound crazy." He looks away.

"It doesn't make you sound crazy. What I meant was, was it a feeling? Like, did you feel her spirit in the room, or did you actually see her ghost?"

Stellen crosses his arms over his chest and curves forward. "Promise not to laugh?"

"Absolutely. It helps to talk about it. Honestly." As I sit in the scalloped-back chair, normally reserved for my mentor Silas, it feels strange to be the one asking the difficult questions, rather than struggling to answer them.

Stellen rocks almost imperceptibly, and his voice is faint and uncertain. "She looked like before—before she was sick. She was wearing that dumb dress that my dad gave to the funeral home. She wanted to be buried in her favorite jeans and a sweatshirt I gave her for her last Mother's Day." He sniffles. "My dad said it was undignified."

"What did the sweatshirt say?"

A wry grin tugs at the corners of his mouth. "Secretly hoping CHEMO will give me SUPERPOWERS."

My heart aches for this grieving boy, but the shirt

is mad snarky. “Sounds like your mom had a great sense of humor.”

“She really did. Right up until the end, you know?”

“I wish I could’ve met her.”

He nods and swallows loudly.

“How many times did you see her ghost?”

“Quite a few. I kind of lost track. I started to take it for granted.” He looks at me and bites hard on his fingernail. “What if she can’t find me here?”

I have no idea how to answer that, but his story sounds too believable and my concern for the area of impact widens. “Have you seen other ghosts? I mean, besides your mom?”

Stellen’s crossed arms remain tight against his body, but his spine straightens. “Mostly animals. That’s why I hated my dad’s shop.”

Leaning against the chair, I exhale and let my head fall back. Staring at the ceiling, I’m at a complete loss for words.

“Do you believe me?” His tone borders on desperation.

I bend forward and place an elbow on each of my knees as I gaze directly into his worried green eyes. “I do. I do believe you.”

He sighs, gulps in air, and leans back.

My psychic senses uncover a flood of relief rushing through him.

Before I have a chance to recap or throw him one of my amazing conversation starters, Twiggy’s voice blares over the intercom. "Sheriff Harper's here. Want me to send him up?"

Stellen jumps and a measure of his earlier unease returns. "Do you want me to leave? Or wait outside?"

"What? Why would I want you to leave?"

"Well, I thought you guys were, like, hooking up."

An unexpected surge of laughter grips me, and I cover my mouth with one hand as I nod. "Um, we are *dating*. But I'm pretty sure he's here on business."

Stellen's face falls. "Oh, about my dad?"

His half question, half statement hangs in the air as I walk to the intercom and reach for the button. "Yeah, send him up." Turning to Stellen, I offer the only reassurance I have. "I'll handle this, all right? Let me do the talking."

He nods, but his energy is giving off a decidedly "freaked" vibe.

CHAPTER 6

Pressing the twisting ivy ridges on the plaster medallion, I paste on a smile as the bookcase slides open.

Erick walks across the mezzanine in his perfectly pressed tan uniform with his dark-brown winter jacket draped over his left arm, and my heart speeds up a few beats per minute. His eyes catch the light and he flashes a crooked grin.

My brain is telling me he's here on business and it's a standard-issue uniform, but that man could make a burlap sack look sexy!

"Hey, Moon. We need to talk about your kidnapping."

My eyes widen. "I wasn't kidnapped. Obviously, I'm standing right here. Clearly not abducted." I gesture magnanimously toward my person.

He walks into my apartment, tilts his head toward the minor posted up on my settee, and scrunches up his face.

"Oh, that kidnapping." My confident gaze falters. "He wasn't coerced. He needed a place to stay." A sudden angle pops into my head and bolsters my courage. "He's my ward."

"Look, Moon, you're not Bruce Wayne. There are rules for a reason. Minors can't give consent."

My clairsentience picks up on an instant heightening of fear, and Stellen jumps to my rescue.

"Mitzy is just letting me stay here until everything gets sorted out with my dad. She fed me lunch and she's gonna take me to school on Monday, and everything."

Erick's features soften and he smiles wistfully. "I wish it was that easy, Stellen. But—" His cell phone interrupts the lecture. "It's the station. I gotta take this." Erick steps back into the Rare Books Loft and Stellen fidgets nervously.

Gesturing toward the boy, I wave my hand in a "simmer down" motion. "Don't worry. You're not leaving this apartment. I still have a few tricks up my sleeve."

Stellen gnaws on another fingernail.

Erick slips his phone into his pocket. A frustrated, but unsurprised, grin spreads across his face as he returns. "You really are something else."

"Thank you for noticing." I take a bow. "Can you be more specific?"

"That was Silas Willoughby on the phone. They

patched him through from the station. Apparently he's representing the minor Jablonski and has arranged for Mizithra Moon to take temporary custody."

I look over my shoulder at Stellen and wink. "See, all legal and above board, Sheriff."

Erick offers me a tantalizing smile and my tummy flip-flops as I forge ahead. "So, did you just come to arrest me for kidnapping, or is there more to this house call?"

"I need to ask him some questions. Stellen, do you want your attorney present?"

Stepping forward, I place a firm hand on Erick's arm. "You don't think for one minute that—"

"Easy, Batgirl. I need to get some background information, and anything suspicious he may have noticed in the last week or so. He's not a suspect."

Stellen nods nervously. "It's okay. You can ask me whatever you want."

"Thanks." Erick turns to me and hits me with his irresistible puppy-dog eyes. "Can I trouble you for a cup of coffee, Miss Moon?"

"No trouble at all. It'll only take a sec." I hurry to the back room and bump into Pyewacket on the circular stairs.

Crouching down, I whisper a quiet warning to the fiendish feline. "I know you don't like guests, but Stellen lost his dad, and he's all alone in the world. We're gonna take care of him until Silas works things out. All right?"

"Reow." Can confirm.

"Oh, and I'm fairly certain he can see ghosts. So play it cool, and help me keep Grams out of the apartment."

Pyewacket tilts his head, narrows his eyes, and replies, "Ree-oow." Conspiratorial agreement.

By the time I return with two mugs of coffee and a can of pop, Erick is seated across from Stellen and has his notepad and pen in hand. I set a mug on the coffee table in front of Erick, pass the soda to Stellen, and take a seat next to him on the settee.

Sheriff Harper hits him with the standard barrage of questions about rival coaches, unhappy snowmobile students, and wonders if Stellen ever overheard his dad arguing with Trey Lee or his parents.

"I'm really sorry I can't be more help, Sheriff. I'm not into snowmobiles, you know? That part of my dad's life was totally separate. He hated that I didn't ride. It was one of the things him and my mom argued about the most."

Erick puts away his pad and pen, picks up his coffee, and leans back in the chair. "Thanks for your help. I know it's hard to talk about. We should have the medical examiner's report in a day or two, and once we establish time of death I might have a few more questions for you. I hope that's okay?"

"Yeah. It's fine."

An awkward silence falls between us.

Sheriff Harper manages a bumpy topic shift.

"Hey, you guys mind if I order some pizzas? The investigation ran through lunch and I'm so hungry I could eat my own boot."

Stellen gives me a sideways glance, and I easily interpret his response.

"I think that sounds great. What's your favorite topping, buddy?"

The boy shrugs. "Whatever you guys like. I'll pretty much eat anything."

Erick leans forward. "Let's say it's your birthday, and money is no object. What kind of pizza would you order?"

Stellen chews his bottom lip and stammers. "Is it — Do I have to— Can it be more than one thing?"

The sheriff gives a friendly laugh and nods. "There's no limit. You want all the toppings on one pizza? You got it. You want just pineapple and nothing else? You got it. Come on, what's your dream pizza?"

For the first time since I picked Stellen up from his house, I sense a shift in his energy. For a moment, he's actually forgotten he's an orphan. Bless Sheriff Harper's little heart.

"Okay, this is going to sound weird, but I would get pepperoni, bacon, jalapeños, onions, and pineapple."

Erick slaps his hand on his thigh. "Now that's what I'm talking about. That's a pizza. What about you, Moon? You got a favorite?"

"I'm feeling like barbecued chicken with green onions and extra cheese? Can you guys handle that?"

My amazing boyfriend pulls out his phone and apparently has a pizza place on speed dial. He tips the phone away from his lips and whispers, "Do you have more soda, or should I order some?"

"I've got plenty of pop." It still gives me a little giggle to use the local colloquialism for soft drinks.

He nods, and his voice is all business as he places the order for our two outrageous pizzas, plus a large Italian sausage.

Rubbing my hands together to create the appearance of anticipation, I attempt to lighten the mood. "You guys wanna play a board game or something while we wait for the 'Za'?"

Stellen smiles, an actual almost-cheerful smile. "Is it lame if I say Scrabble?"

As if on cue, Pyewacket struts into the room, plops down at the end of the coffee table and fixes our new guest with a golden-eyed stare.

"Funny you should mention Scrabble. My grandmother literally won ol' Pyewacket here while betting in an off-the-books Scrabble game. But you didn't hear that from me, Sheriff."

Erick unbuttons his collar and comically places a hand over his badge. "Let's drop the formalities. We're just hanging out, getting to know each other. Keeping it casual. No titles. Sound good?"

Stellen nods. "Sure. Sweet."

I wink. "Whatever you say, *Ricky*."

Sheriff Too-Hot-To-Handle blushes a delightful shade of crimson when I use his mother's nickname for him.

I fetch the Scrabble game and the play quickly shifts from friendly to intense. I always knew Erick was above average, but his skill with the tiles is impressive. Oh, and let's not forget little Stellen! The kid has a shockingly advanced vocabulary. Some of the medical terms and names of bones he's throwing onto the board would be awe-inspiring coming from a neurosurgeon.

BING. BONG. BING.

Erick jumps up. "I'll get the door. Don't look at my tiles while I'm gone."

I giggle and cover my mouth with one hand.

As he walks out of the apartment he says, "Yeah, I was talking to you, Moon."

"Where did you learn all of this medical terminology?"

Stellen takes a deep breath and rubs both palms on his jeans. "I have to help my dad. I hate it in the taxi shed, but he gets really busy, and it's—it was—our only income, besides coaching."

"So what does helping your dad stuff animals for hunters have to do with your vocabulary?"

I can almost see the light bulb flick on in his head. "Oh that. The basis of any good taxidermy is anatomy. I didn't like mounting the pieces, but I used all the knowledge of anatomy and stuff to help prepare me for college, you know?"

"What do you want to study?"

"I want to be a veterinarian. Maybe I can make up for all the money my dad made dealing in death by saving a few animals' lives."

"That's an awesome idea." And suddenly a light bulb clicks on in my own head. "Hey, could you handle a *new* after-school job?"

"Do you think I should finish the orders that my dad was working on?"

Rubbing my chin for a moment, I struggle with the question. In the end, I offer Stellen the permission he needs to quit the family business. "Anyone who had an order in with your dad will understand that it's not going to get completed. Maybe you can help Silas sort through all the pending ones and he can contact people to pick up their projects—as is. I don't want you to have to stuff another dead thing as long as you live."

He breathes an enormous sigh of relief. "Thanks. So, what kind of after-school job? Like bagging groceries at the Piggly Wiggly?"

"Nope. What would you say to being an apprentice to Doc Ledo at the Pin Cherry Animal Hospital?"

Stellen's eyes widen with disbelief. "Are you messing with me?"

Erick returns with the pizzas, just in time to jump on the bandwagon. "If she said something that's too good to be true, let me be the first to break it to you, it's true. She's got an uncanny thing with hunches." He places one pizza on the coffee table and two on the floor. "I hope you guys don't mind this buffet arrangement?"

Stellen leans forward and exhales with force. "Are you serious? You could actually get me a job with Doc Ledo?"

"Of course. But, if you want to get into veterinary medicine, your grades are going to have to be way above average. How many hours a week can you work and still keep your academic record in tiptop shape?"

Stellen smiles and there's a positive tone in his voice that surprises me. "As many hours as he wants. I'm so far ahead, at school. I've been doing extra projects, and even some independent study. I can totally work every day. Even weekends. Whatever he needs."

Erick chuckles and wipes some tomato sauce from the corner of his mouth. "I wish I had a couple deputies with that much energy."

"I'll call the doc tomorrow and set everything up. For now, let's dig into our amazing creations."

Stellen nods eagerly. "Yeah, I'm starved." He grabs a paper plate and loads it up with half a pizza.

Everything is going swimmingly and the guys are taking turns throwing meat projectiles in the air for Pyewacket to retrieve.

My fur baby does not disappoint. He leaps with deadly grace and never misses his target.

One more Scrabble game turns into three and the pizza eventually disappears. At the end of the evening, Stellen is the big winner, but refuses to take any credit. "I just got good tiles, you know? Luck of the draw."

Erick chuckles. "Come on, man. Take the win. You definitely earned it."

Nodding, I wipe a streak of pizza sauce from my chin. "Yeah, clearing your board not once, but twice, and hitting three triple word scores is a little bit more than the luck of the draw."

He shrugs. "Okay. I guess I played pretty good."

Sheriff Harper stands and retrieves his jacket. "There's no 'pretty good' about it. You crushed us."

The young man allows himself a smile, but continues to stare at the floor.

"Moon, I'll let you know if the ME's report comes in tomorrow." Erick heads for the door, and I jump up to follow.

"I'll be back in a minute, Stellen. I need to set the alarm after Erick leaves."

Stellen looks up at me and smirks. "Sure. Whatever you say."

"Mind your own business, kid." I toss him a playful glare. It's none of his business if I plan to sneak in a goodbye kiss before I set the aforementioned alarm.

He turns, folds the board, and dumps the tiles into the bag.

At least we gave him a few hours' reprieve from the day's tragedy.

"Wait up, Sheriff. I'll walk you out."

Erick pauses at the top of the spiral staircase and glances over his shoulder. “For a minute there, I thought I might have to beg.”

Shoving him gently, I snicker and hurry downstairs.

Under the crimson glow of the EXIT sign, he slips his arms around my waist and pulls me close. “You’re lucky that you have Silas to cover your tracks. Next time, try filling me in on your harebrained schemes. I know people at CPS too. I could’ve gotten the temporary custody order for you. Remember, I’m on your side—most of the time.”

Before he can offer any additional lectures, warnings, or admonitions, I push up on my tiptoes and plant a kiss on his full lips. “Copy that.”

He tips his head and departs out the side door. “See ya tomorrow, Moon.”

“You absolutely will.”

CHAPTER 7

Morning dawns without ceremony and I take the first bathroom time slot. I gesture silently to Stellen when I exit the facilities, and he takes his turn. We bundle in our winter gear and trudge down the street to the diner. Neither of us has the energy to navigate the checkerboard of shoveled and un-shoveled sections of the sidewalk. Instead, we keep our boots low and kick a path straight to breakfast.

Odell gives us a greeting, and as we slide into a booth Tally sets down a steaming cup of coffee and a luscious mug of hot chocolate with whipped cream.

"Morning, Mitzy, and guest."

"Good morning, Tally. Looks like you're playing favorites already." I gesture to the cocoa.

"You know me, I've got a soft spot for kids."

She turns to leave, and I suddenly remember one of my promises. "Oh, Tally, do you have a minute?"

"For you? Always."

"Stellen here is a whiz with anatomy, and he's planning to go to veterinary school after graduation. Do you think—?"

"Glory be! You must be psychic or something, sweetie. Ledo called me just last night to say that one of his vet techs had to go out on maternity leave. He sure could use an extra set of hands—as soon as possible."

Stellen looks at me and shakes his head in disbelief. "There's something about you . . . How can I ever make it up to you?"

Tally answers for me. "Pshaw! You don't owe anybody anything. Mitzy only wants what's best for you, and you'll be helping out my brother, not the other way around. Can I tell him you'll start tomorrow?"

I raise my hand and attempt to buy Stellen some time. "Tomorrow is a little soon. Let's say he'll start Wednesday. We have a few things to work out. I'm sure you understand."

"You betcha. I'll let Ledo know he can expect a new apprentice on Wednesday." She smiles at Stellen. "You know, if you take the bus that runs through The Pines, you can jump off on Gunnison before it makes that last turn and it'll take you right to the clinic."

I see a cloud pass over Stellen's eyes, and I jump to his rescue. "I'll take him over and make the introductions. I'd love to see the doc and check out the modifications he's made at the clinic."

Tally nods, and her scarlet-red bun bobs up and down. "Sounds good."

As she ducks behind the counter to grab the coffeepot, Odell approaches with our breakfasts.

I know I'll be getting what I want, but I can't wait to see what he thinks Stellen might have wanted.

He pushes a plate in front of me, and I smile with satisfaction. As he sets the second plate down in front of Stellen, I watch the boy's eyes widen with surprise and a hint of trepidation. "How did you—?"

Odell fixes the boy with a kind gaze. "I usually have a pretty good idea what folks need. Enjoy." He raps the table twice and disappears into the kitchen.

Stellen picks up a fork and pauses as he admires his breakfast. "I haven't had french toast since my mom died. It's my absolute favorite."

My mouth is already stuffed full of delicious home fries, so I nod and smile. Once we finish our breakfasts, which doesn't take long, we walk back to the bookstore where Twiggy is unboxing a recent shipment of rare books from Eastern Europe.

"Hey, kid."

Both Stellen and I answer the call.

Twiggy cackles mercilessly and gestures to Stellen. "I was talking to the new recruit. Can you spare him for an hour or so? I could use some help cataloging this shipment."

"I don't really have anything else planned for us. I need to head over to the station later and check on the reports. Until then, you're free to do as you please."

He nods. "I'm happy to help. They look like rad books."

Twiggy chuckles. "Yeah, they're super rad, kid."

"I'll leave you two to handle this, and I'll—"

"I told you she'd be here, man."

"Yeah, not a big stretch, Bristol. She, like, owns the place." Crank shakes his head.

Blerg. Looks like my fan club found my lair. "I'll handle this, Twiggy."

She crosses her arms and a sly grin spreads across her face as though she's swallowed the Cheshire cat. "I'm definitely not gonna miss this."

With a heavy sigh, I step toward the advancing trio. "How can I help you?"

Bristol removes her jester-style stocking cap. "We heard some stuff on the mountain. We thought you should know. You know, for your investigation."

Twiggy lets out a low whistle behind me. "I didn't realize you were starting a club, doll." She cackles and elbows Stellen playfully.

Stifling my snark, I herd the gang into the children's section under the mezzanine, hopefully out of earshot of my volunteer employee. "Sure, what did you guys hear?"

AJ is the first to share his intel. "So, that organizer guy, Mr. Bennett, that went all aggro on you and your dad, some redhead said she overheard him arguing with Jawbone Friday during the qualifiers."

"Did she say what they were arguing about?"

"Um, no. Like, she couldn't hear what they were saying, just that they both looked angry and the organizer guy shoved Jawbone."

"That could come in handy. Was there anything else?"

Crank takes the next at-bat. "There was some scuttlebutt in the pits. Sounds like Jawbone was gonna take on another student. Priest. His mechanic said Jawbone was inspecting their sled on Friday."

"I thought Mr. Jablonski only coached one student at a time. What changed? And is 'priest' a name or a profession?"

Crank nods furiously. "Totally. You're totally right. But he was gonna cut Trey loose and coach Freddy Priest, the number four seed. Trey's dad was *not* happy. He thought maybe Jawbone was, like, squeezing them for more money, you know?"

"That definitely sounds like motive." I rub my chin and wait for a psychic hit.

Bristol smacks Crank firmly on the back. "See, dude, I told you that was major. Follow the money, right?" Her big brown eyes hold far too much adoration.

"Absolutely. This is great stuff, guys. Thanks for taking the time to come and see me."

No one moves.

"Was there something else?"

Bristol swallows and shifts her weight.

"What is it? Even the smallest details can help, Bristol. Did you hear another argument?"

"No. I just thought it was weird that Jawbone was wearing a helmet—when they pulled the body out, I mean. What would he be doin' out on the mountain with a helmet and no sled?"

"Excellent observation. Seriously, this has been a huge help. I've got to get back to—"

"You gotta set up the murder wall, right?" Bristol nods and grins with anticipation.

If she were a puppy, her tail would be wagging hard enough to clear a coffee table. "I do. I'll put all this information on there. Again, thanks."

"Cool."

"Sweet."

"Awesome, man."

I show the acolytes to the door and thank them one more time for the information. Attempting to sneak upstairs before Twiggy can take another crack at me meets with epic failure.

"Looks like you got yourself a fan club. How does it feel, doll?"

"It's nice to be appreciated." I step over the chain and march up the stairs in a huff.

Once I'm safely inside the apartment, and the bookcase has whooshed closed behind me, I have to laugh. I never would've imagined a fan club, but I'm not going to look a gift horse in the mouth. They brought me some good leads. "Time to set up the murder wall."

I pause for the interruption that doesn't appear.

Grams must be working on her memoirs. It's not like her to miss interfering with the murder board set up. In her absence, I carefully write out all the cards myself. The rivalries within the snowmobile world sound awfully intense. I wonder how much of this information Erick's deputies gleaned yesterday? Maybe I'll walk down to the station. I need to check on the medical examiner's report, anyway.

The crisp blue sky hugging the harbor belies the sub-zero temps. I turn up my collar against the icy winds, and hustle down the block.

Deputy Baird, or, as I like to call her, Furious Monkeys, after her favorite phone app, gives me a head nod, and I push through the crooked wooden gate into the bullpen. The normally empty desks are crowded with deputies, and typewriter keys are clacking madly. Slipping through the chaos, I peek into Erick's office. "What's going on out there?"

He looks up from a large stack of files on his desk.

"We've gotten over one hundred and fifty tips since yesterday. These guys are working overtime, trying to separate actual leads from dead ends. Not to mention, we've received about thirty calls from the race organizer, demanding to know when he'll be allowed back onto the mountain. Apparently there's another race in the series in two weeks and they need to gather their equipment. So, I brought in some extra guys, and even pulled a few deputies from Broken Rock to help move things along.

"Anything I can do?"

"Sure. You can keep your nose out of this and leave the investigation to the professionals. But saying that out loud feels like throwing an extra gallon of water over Niagara Falls."

An easy laugh escapes. "You're not wrong. I have some information to share. It could be helpful."

"And what do you want in exchange?"

"Just a teensy weensy peek at the medical examiner's report."

He flashes a devious smile. "Let's see how generous you're feeling, Moon. I don't have the report yet, but if you pay it forward, I'll let you sneak that peek tomorrow."

"Deal."

I take a seat on one of the scarred wooden chairs, specifically designed to keep visitors from getting too comfortable, and spill the intel I received from the *Scooby Gang*.

Erick taps his pen on the desk. "I definitely have my opinions about that Bennett character. He's a genuine piece of work. I'll bring him in, but I have a feeling he's more of a typical blowhard than a murderer. However, I'm not ruling anything out."

"What about Trey Lee's dad?"

"That is news. Who did you say your source was?"

"I didn't."

He leans back and crosses his arms behind his head.

Unable to resist, my eyes dart downward, on the off chance that his shirt comes untucked and I get a sneak peek at something better than a medical examiner's report. Although the memory of his abs is never far from my mind, an occasional first-hand account doesn't hurt either.

"Moon? Did I lose you?" His smirk is far too tantalizing.

"I don't know what you mean." The pinkish hue on my traitorous cheeks is all he needs to see.

"Hey, how about I bring some Chinese food over for you and Stellen tonight?"

"Tonight?"

"Yeah. We can watch a couple movies, eat some popcorn, you know . . ."

"I don't think there's going to be any, *you know*, while I have a houseguest, Sheriff."

And now he gets to blush. "Hey, you know what I meant."

"Do I?"

He refuses to take the bait. "Am I bringing the Chinese food or not?"

"Sure. I think Stellen really enjoys hanging out with you. If you bring any movies, though, they have to be VHS tapes."

Erick gasps and leans forward. "Did you say V-H-S?"

"Yep. Grams likes to— liked to keep it old-school."

His gaze narrows. "There's something going on, isn't there, Moon?"

"See you tonight. I've got plenty of microwave popcorn." As I beat a hasty retreat, I hear Erick shout a thank you from his office.

Upon my return to the bookshop, I'm shocked to see the progress Twiggy and Stellen have made on the shipment.

"I'm going to be sorry to see you head off to work for Doc Ledo. You're handy to have around."

Stellen smiles wistfully. "It helps to keep busy."

"It absolutely does. Also, Erick plans to stop over tonight with Chinese food and movies. Sound good?"

He pauses with a large leather tome in hand. "Does he need to ask me more questions?"

"Nope. Nothing official, just to hang out."

"Sweet."

The mood ring on my left hand burns with a message, and when I glance down, I'm surprised to see the face of Silas Willoughby staring back at me. This can't be a coincidence. "What's that book you're holding?"

Stellen glances at the ancient manuscript and shrugs. "My Latin is mostly genus species stuff. Otherwise it's not that good."

A scoff and a chuckle escape before I quip, "It's gotta be better than mine, which is nonexistent." As I walk toward the book, the hairs on the back of my neck tingle. "Hey, Twiggy, we need your help out here."

She stomps out of the back room and fixes me with an impatient stare. "Open the box. Take the book out of the box. Check off the title on the packing list. Seems simple enough to me."

"What's the story behind this one?" I point to the book in Stellen's gloved hands.

Stepping forward to get a better look, she emits a tiny squeak. Twiggy grabs a pair of gloves, slips them on, and snatches the book from his hands. "This is for Willoughby. I'll take care of it."

Stellen looks at me and shrugs.

"Don't worry, you didn't do anything wrong. You keep unpacking boxes, and I'll check back with you later."

Traipsing into the back room, I plunk myself onto a chair. "What's the story with the book?"

Twiggy places the tome into a protective bag, seals it, and slowly turns toward me. "As far as I know, there's only one copy of that thing in the entire world. Willoughby asked me to track it down. He gets first crack at it, and then it's added to the inventory in the loft. Research purposes only. By appointment only."

"Sounds expensive? How much did we pay for it?"

She tilts her head and grins. "Don't worry, Princess, I didn't empty the coffers. Willoughby has this place on a tight budget. He went fifty-fifty on this one."

"Can you read Latin?"

She shrugs. "I've picked up a few things over the years."

"What's it say on the cover?"

Turning toward the book, she gazes through the protective archival sheath and reads aloud. "*Loca Sine Lumine, Loca Sine Lege.*" She chews the inside of her cheek and hums. "It's something about places without light or laws. You'll have to check with Willoughby."

"That sounds sketchy. What's Silas up to?"

She chuckles and shakes her head. "I learned a long time ago not to ask that question, doll."

The burning message from my ring and the tingling in my spine push me to delve deeper into *el misterio del libro*. Yeah, not big on Latin, but I know a little *Español*.

BING. BONG. BING.

"Are you expecting anyone?"

Twiggy shakes her head and spins back to the computer.

It's too early for Erick, so I inch open the side door. "Can I help you?"

The sweet face of Amaryllis peeks through the crack. "I don't have an appointment, but I was hoping you'd have time to go over some wedding stuff. Any chance?"

Pushing the door open wider, I welcome her inside. "Of course. This is the perfect time. Did you want to go to the apartment?"

She rolls her head from side to side. "Well, I

wanted to walk around and get a feel for the place. I need to decide where to put guests, where to have the ceremony . . . You know, all the mundane stuff. Maybe you can help?"

"I'd love to. Let's go up to the mezzanine. I think it's the best view, and will give you a better idea what we have to work with. I'm sure we can move—"

"Nope. Nothing gets moved. Check the rules." Twiggy's disembodied voice echoes from the back room as she references the non-negotiable instructions.

Amaryllis and I exchange a silent giggle and hurry up the circular staircase.

"About how many people have you invited?"

She taps her pearlescent fingernail on her lip and hems and haws. "Your dad wanted to keep it extremely small, but it's my first wedding, so I leaned toward more of a spectacle."

"You never married?"

She rolls her eyes. "I know. I know. The truth is, law school consumed me and I started working for Cal Duncan right after graduation. He opened so many doors for me—it was astounding. He had a team of lawyers, and I learned more in those first few years as a junior attorney than in all my time at law school. I sort of lost myself in the work, and barely even dated."

"Well, I want you to have everything exactly as you imagine it. So if—" I lower my voice, lean toward her, and whisper "—we need to move things, I'll make it happen."

She smiles and puts her hand on my shoulder. "Thank you. And thank you for welcoming me into your family. I know you only met your dad last year, and it must be difficult to think about sharing him so soon, but I promise there will always be more than enough room in our lives for you. Any time. I swear."

The urge to hug her overrides my natural tendency to stuff my emotions. "Thank you. I'm looking forward to all of it. The wedding, the extended family, everything."

She chuckles and shakes her head. "You might want to hold off on saying that until *after* you've met my parents."

My eyes widen. "Anything I should know?"

She leans toward me and whispers, "They definitely don't need to know about my otherworldly mother-in-law."

I clap a hand over my mouth and nod. "Good to know."

We while away the rest of the afternoon planning where guests will sit, who will monitor the guest book, and how we can transform my dusty old bookstore into a sparkling fairytale wedding. When we finish making our lists and sketches, we head back downstairs, just as Stellen is coming up.

"Oh, Amaryllis, this is my houseguest, Stellen Jablonski."

The name sends a flash of recognition across her

face. "I'm so sorry for your loss, Stellen. It's nice to meet you, and let us know if there's anything we can do. Jacob and I are just across the alley."

He nods self-consciously and looks down at his feet. "Thanks. Mitzy's helped a lot."

Amaryllis smiles and pats me on the back. "She's rather amazing. I'm sure she'll see that you're well taken care of. Do you have relatives coming to pick you up?"

He shakes his head. "My dad was an only child, and my mom—" His voice catches in his throat and I jump in.

"I'm going to walk Amaryllis home. The apartment is all yours. If you need anything, let me know." I grip my almost-stepmom by the elbow and tug her down the stairs. As we say our goodbyes, she lowers her voice. "He really doesn't have anyone?"

"I don't know the total story, but Silas told me the family angle was not a viable option. So there's no one. Well, on one side of the family there's no one, and on the other side of the family there's no one who cares. A Catch-22 that I'm all too familiar with. I'm hoping Silas can help me find a suitable foster family for him, so he can finish out the school year without too much upset. Once he turns eighteen, he can take possession of the property and we'll make sure there's a caretaker to look after things while he's at college."

She smiles tenderly and nods.

"He's going to veterinary school, and he starts an

apprenticeship with Doc Ledo this Wednesday," I quickly add.

Amaryllis exhales and rubs my arm. "What a bright young man. So lucky to have you watching out for him, Mitzy. Now, I better get home and figure out what to make for dinner. Thanks for all the great wedding ideas. I'll be in touch."

As the alleyway door creaks closed, I rub my mood ring absently. Maybe you could send me a nice little psychic message about the perfect foster family for Stellen? He can't live on my couch until graduation.

Cold black mists swirl within the glass dome of my antique mood ring.

No messages.

Not a single hint of help.

CHAPTER 8

WHEN SHERIFF HARPER shows up with our takeout feast, I'm busy working my way through a bag of chocolate-chip cookies and Stellen is parked in the Rare Books Loft poring over some anatomy reference books.

As I open the door, I give a little bow. "Good evening, Sheriff."

He glances at the nearly empty bag in my hands. "I hope you didn't ruin your appetite."

"You've met me, right?"

He chuckles and nods his agreement. "You want to grab some plates and forks? Are we eating up in the apartment?"

"We are. And, if you behave yourself, I'll even bring napkins."

His shoulders shake as he walks toward the wrought-iron spiral staircase.

Bringing up the rear, and having more than a

passing obsession with film, I must get more information about this evening's entertainment. "So what epic big-screen sagas have you brought for us?"

Stellen looks up from his pile of reference material. "What time is it? Is it suppertime already?"

"You really are a bookworm. Don't tell Twiggy, but I'm giving you permission to leave all of your books on the reading table so you can continue your research tomorrow."

"Tomorrow I have to head back to school."

Erick shakes his head. "We all lost track of time, with the upsetting events of the weekend. It's winter break. There is no school."

"Right. I totally knew that. I've been— Everything's so— No school. Got it." Stellen leans back in the chair and runs one hand lovingly over the large volume open in front of him. "Perfect. I'll head straight over to the veterinary clinic in the morning, and I can keep reading when I get home."

Harper and I exchange a look of wonderment.

"Are you for real?" I shake my head in disbelief. "You've got to be the most studious teenager I've ever met."

Stellen shrugs and looks down.

Erick jostles the bags he's carrying. "Enough studying. Let's dig into this food and let the James Bond marathon begin."

I choke on my words and pat my chest to regain control. "James Bond? Seriously?"

Stellen pulls the candle handle and leads the way

to the apartment. He grins as the bookcase door slides open. "I've seen all the Bond movies. Even though I was only three when *Casino Royale* came out, I streamed it and the other two before I saw *Spectre*, so I'd have the back story."

Placing a hand over my mouth, I shake my head in disbelief, but it's Erick who responds to the innocent oversight.

"I hate to be the one to break it to you, Stellen, but Daniel Craig is about the sixth actor to play James Bond. We're gonna kick it old-school tonight, and you're going to learn about the genealogy of Bond, while you're entertained."

Stellen flops onto the settee and looks at Erick as though he's crazy. "For real? There's other James Bonds?"

Erick inhales sharply and sets the food on the coffee table. He walks toward the VCR with his sack of tapes, pulls one out and holds it up for both of us to see. "Behold, Sean Connery, the original James Bond. Prepare for *Goldfinger*."

Passing out the plates and opening the takeout containers, I'm pleased to see my favorite sweet-and-sour chicken among the main-course options, along with potstickers, egg rolls, and wontons. The man definitely knows a thing or two about my appetites.

Stellen picks up a plate, bites his lower lip, and whispers to me, "Which one do you want? I'll just have whichever one is left."

"You can have some of everything. That's the

whole deal with Chinese food. Everything is up for grabs."

He stares at the variety of entrées, appetizers, and rice options and shakes his head. "You guys blow my mind on the daily." A half smile brightens his face as he glances toward Erick. "Thanks for all the food, Sheriff Harper. If you need me to do anything at the station, or wash your squad car, just let me know."

Erick pushes play, walks toward Stellen, and places a friendly hand on his shoulder. "You don't owe me anything. Any friend of Mitzy's is a friend of mine. You've got your hands full. Let us worry about your care and feeding for a while, okay?"

Stellen nods and loads a plate with our myriad options.

The piracy warning and the previews slide past, and I can't help but snicker as the familiar tune of the *Goldfinger* theme song fills the apartment.

Stellen is shocked and excited to learn the vast history behind the James Bond he grew up believing was the one and only.

The spy movies do their job and transport the young boy out of his world of misery and into the wonderful distraction of villains and gadgets.

I snuggle closer to Erick on the settee and he whispers softly in my ear, "What's that note on your corkboard about a helmet?"

And the dream of secret snuggles vanishes like a cartoon balloon that meets with an oversized straight pin. However, I don't miss the opportunity to lean closer and turn my lips toward his stubbled chin. "That was the one thing I forgot to tell you before. The racers who stopped by today mentioned that Jawbone was wearing a helmet, but there was no sled abandoned on the track."

Erick nods and turns toward me. "I'll look into it. Unfortunately, all the previous night's tracks were scraped away by the groomer, and no one runs a sled without gloves. I doubt we'll get any evidence, even if we figure out which snowmobile he might've used."

I nod and pull his arm tighter around my shoulders.

"Although, that does beg the question: How did you know the identity of the victim if he was wearing a helmet?"

My throat tightens and I search for a way to climb out of the corner I've painted myself into. "I don't remember. Someone must've recognized Jawbone's helmet or something."

A soft chuckle escapes from my boyfriend and he leans over and kisses my cheek. "Sure. That sounds very plausible, Moon."

Ignoring the implication, I point to the credits rolling up the television screen. "Time to put in the next one, Harper. We don't want the James Bond train to stop now!"

He teasingly tosses the blanket up over my head as he slides off the sofa to swap out the VHS tape.

By the time we get to Pierce Brosnan's Bond interpretation in *GoldenEye*, everyone is full, comfortable, and a little punchy. We crank the volume and our three voices badly belt out the theme song. Some of us know more of the words than others!

Right about the time we're going to hit the chorus for a second time, Grams rockets through the wall ready to launch a noise complaint, when—

Stellen's finger shoots in the air, and he points at the apparition and shouts, "Right there! Do you see it?"

I desperately try not to look at Grams, but the shock on her face is hard to ignore.

"He can see me? Mitzy, why didn't you tell me he could see ghosts?"

I fire off a quick thought message. *When was I going to tell you? I've been kinda busy with wedding planning, and it was only a suspicion that surfaced when we were searching for Pyewacket. He might've seen you at your writing desk in the printing museum. I couldn't exactly have a conversation with you then. What am I gonna do now?*

She crosses her bejeweled limbs and shakes her head. "I'd go with plausible deniability, dear."

Stellen sets his plate on the coffee table, chugs some soda to rinse down his broccoli beef, and gets to his feet. "She's right there. It looks like she's talking to you. Can't you see her?"

Erick shifts in the settee and fixes his eyes on me with anticipation.

"Her who? What do you think you see, Stellen?"

Grams nods. "Good. Good. Keep him on the ropes."

My ward looks from me to Ghost-ma and back again. "Seriously, she's talking to you right now. You can't hear it?"

The only thing that pleases me about this current disaster is that *he* can't hear it. "I'm not sure what you think you see, but shouldn't we get back to the movie?"

Erick leans forward as though he's got a suspect cornered. "I think the flick can wait. I'm pretty interested to hear more about what the kid thinks he sees."

I clench my jaw and fire off a warning to Grams. *Get out of here! If Stellen starts describing you—*

And my worst nightmare comes true.

"She's older."

Grams scoffs. "Older? The nerve of that kid."

Stellen continues. "She's got a real fancy dress on and lots of pearls, and some diamond rings."

Erick leans forward. "Sounds kind of familiar. Is the dress sort of a dark reddish-purple? Very expensive looking?"

Stellen nods. "Yeah, totally."

Ghost-ma fixes Stellen with an ethereal glare. "Can you believe this boy? He doesn't know a Marchesa when he sees one!"

I roll my eyes and force myself to look at anything except my grandmother's ghost.

Sheriff Harper narrows his gaze. "You said older, right?"

Stellen nods.

"Would you say she's in her sixties?"

The kid shrugs. "I'm not that good with age, or whatever. But I think ghosts can look different after they die. Maybe she was older and now her ghost is changing its appearance."

Grams arches a perfectly drawn brow. "This kid seems to know more about my realm than I do. Let's get him on the payroll, Mitzy."

"Give it a rest, Grams."

Erick drops his plate in his lap. "I knew it."

I clap my hand over my mouth, but it's too late. Every human— and ghost—in the room heard me. I lost my focus, and I said it out loud.

Stellen smiles brightly and puts a hand on my shoulder. "Did you hear? Because it looked like she was talking to you. Could you actually hear what she said?"

Isadora sighs dramatically. "You can't put this genie back in the bottle, sweetie."

The only thing that matters to me right now is the next words out of Erick's mouth. Is he going to think I'm a freak and walk out on me? Or will he be able to accept the part of me that's secretly been talking to my dead grandmother for more than a year?

Our eyes meet over the *moo goo gai pan*, and he shakes his head. "You could've told me, Moon. You could've trusted me." He sets his plate on the table, collects his coat, and strides out of the apartment.

Now I'm crying and Stellen is patting my back. "It's okay, Mitzy. I think there are more of us out there than you realize. Or maybe not. But I can see her, so you're not alone, you know?"

"Thanks, but I think I just blew up the only genuine relationship I've ever had."

"I've never been in a . . . or had a . . . I'm no relationship expert."

He pats my back again, and I wipe the stupid tears from my face.

Stellen looks over his shoulder. "Should I go talk to him or something?"

"Nah. He needs some time. He's right. I should've told him." A frustrated moan escapes me. The best thing I can do is keep busy. I'll distract myself with some otherworldly introductions. "Myrtle Isadora, this is Stellen Jablonski."

Grams gives the boy a friendly wave.

His eyes light up. "She waved to me."

She zooms through him, and I watch the goosebumps rise on his flesh.

"Whoa!" Stellen laughs out loud. "Yeah! She flew straight through me."

"Grams, he's not a toy. He's our guest. Give him privacy when he needs it and no thought-dropping."

She makes an "X" across her chest. "Cross my heart and hope to . . . Well, you get the idea."

I roll my eyes.

"I saw you moving that quill, up in the museum. Can you do other stuff?" Stellen shoves another potsticker in his mouth while he awaits her demonstration.

She claps her ethereal hands with glee.

"I'll leave you two to get acquainted. I need to call Silas."

CHAPTER 9

Despite the complete lack of blips on my psychic radar, I search the entire first floor of the bookshop for Erick before I call my mentor. Sure, it's a long shot, but I thought maybe he would be somewhere down here waiting for me to chase after him. Clearly, that's not his style.

Slouched on the rolly office chair in the back room, with my feet kicked up on the built-in desk, I call Silas and flick on the speaker.

"Good evening, Miss Moon. How may I assist?"

"I'd appreciate it if at no point during this conversation you say the words 'I told you so'."

"Understood. Proceed."

"Erick came by with dinner and movies. He was being really awesome to Stellen."

"I am pleased to hear that news. However, your tone indicates there is more to this story."

"How about I drop this tidbit, 'Stellen Jablonski can see ghosts,' and let you fill in the blanks."

Silas harrumphs, and in my mind's eye, I know he's carefully smoothing his bushy grey mustache.

"Did you hear what I said? Stellen can see Grams. He totally called me out in front of Erick."

"And what is the rest of the story, Mizithra?"

"Erick was kinda mad, and he stormed out." Slight exaggeration, but I'm looking for sympathy anywhere I can find it.

"Hmmm, for a psychic, with a fair degree more perceptive ability than the average human, your emotional vocabulary is stunted. Did Mr. Harper say anything before he left?"

"Yeah."

"Would you care to enlighten me?"

"Fine. He said I could've told him, that I could have trusted him."

"Ah, and there it is."

"Don't say it. Don't even think it."

"I have always counseled you to rely on truth as your best ally. I understand your misgivings, and your hesitancy to reveal your deepest secrets with abandon. However, I believe that what you are now experiencing is something we call the consequences of actions."

"Touché. Leave it to you to find the most elegant way possible to say I told you so. Yes, your alchemical wizardry reigns supreme. I should've been honest. I should've told Erick about the ghost thing. But I didn't. What am I supposed to do now?"

"A useful exercise, that I often employ, is to imagine one's self in the other party's circumstances."

"So I need to be an adult? You want me to imagine what it would be like if our situation was reversed?"

"Indeed. If Erick had been the one to keep such a vital secret at this stage of your relationship, how do you imagine that would affect your opinion of him?"

Silence hangs in the air between us as I struggle with *adulting*. Silas is right. He's always right. This is no exception. "I get it. I should've been honest with Erick when things started to get more serious. He suspected something was up, and I kept dodging. But it's too late now. The cat's out of the bag, and—"

"Ree-ow." Soft but condescending.

"Perhaps Robin Pyewacket Goodfellow is correct. You must bear this result until the tide shifts. Give Mr. Harper time and space. He's proven himself a good man, Mitzy. He will let you know when he's ready to discuss things."

"That's just it. I can't give him space. I promised Stellen I'd figure out who killed his dad. I'm bound to run into Erick on this case. What am I supposed to do then?"

"Maintain professional decorum. And let me know if there's anything I can do to assist."

Exhaling loudly, I almost end the call. "Oh, there is one thing. Stellen said that his father had several orders in process. Can you help him go through the receipts, or records, and contact the clients to have them pick up their carcasses, or whatever you call half-stuffed stuff?"

"I knew Mr. Jablonski to be quite meticulous in his record keeping. I shouldn't need the boy's help to fulfill this request."

"Well, there's a whole alarm system . . ." I laugh dryly. "Never mind. Alchemical transmutations should see you through. I'm sure an alarm system is nothing you can't handle. Thank you. I appreciate the advice, and Stellen will be relieved to hear that he doesn't have to go back to the taxidermy shop."

"Any time. Be sure to tell Isadora that I wish her well with her new friend."

Silas ends the call, and I lean back in the chair to think about his last words. She does have a new friend. I'm not the only person in the world who can see her now. I wonder if that means she'll love me less?

"Not on your life, young lady!"

The shock of her sudden appearance throws me off balance, and I flip over backward in the office chair.

She chuckles mercilessly, and two seconds later Stellen rounds the corner and his laughter joins hers.

"Great, now I have two humans and a ghost to laugh at my mishaps. Twiggy will be over the moon."

Grams ghost snorts, "No pun intended, I'm sure!"

Oh brother. I push myself to a seated position and rub my bruised elbow.

Stellen steps into the back room and clears his throat.

"Out with it, Jablonski."

He smiles and looks down at his feet. "I'm sorry I outed you in front of Erick. Isadora wrote it all down, and I guess you were trying to keep it secret. I can go down to the station and try to fix it for you."

"Hey, it's not your fault. You've been through enough. I'm a big girl. I can take care of myself. Let's enjoy the rest of our takeout and finish the movie marathon. You let me worry about Erick. Got it?"

He nods and points to the chair. "So, stuff like that happens to you all the time?"

"Yeah, I'm a klutz and a ghost hunter. It's a two-for-one deal."

He grins. "Sweet."

The soft buzzing of my cell phone on the bedside table wakes me. With one hand I reach for the phone and with the other for Pyewacket. One hand comes up empty.

The incoming call is from Silas, so I'll have to answer it. And I use the dim blue glow from the mobile to quickly search the room as I tiptoe to the bathroom.

Pyewacket is curled up on top of the soundly sleeping Stellen.

"Traitor," I whisper before closing the bathroom door.

"It's too early for etiquette, Silas. This better be important."

He harrumphs and draws a long breath. "What was the state of Mr. Jablonski's taxidermy building when you and the young boy departed?"

"The state of the building? What do you mean? It's a taxidermy shed. It was full of mounts, hides, some metal frames, tools . . . I don't know."

"And you're sure the boy secured the door and set an alarm?"

My extrasensory perception finally decides to join the party, and a single word echoes in my mind. "Was there a break-in?"

"Ah, there is my ever-brilliant student. Indeed, there was. I had hoped to spare the boy another trip to this unsettling place, but in light of recent events, I will need his input. We must ascertain what was taken, and perhaps get the authorities involved."

The idea of facing Erick, especially on an empty stomach, doesn't sit well with me. "We'll grab a walking breakfast at the patisserie and join you in about thirty minutes. Is that all right?"

"It will have to be."

Setting down the phone, I splash warm water on my face and run my fingers through the haystack of hair looking back at me from the mirror.

As I approach the settee, Pye stares up at me with defiance.

"Look, Mr. Cuddlekins, I'm the one who knows where your favorite breakfast cereal is kept, so you best remember that when you're playing favorites."

I gently shake Stellen's shoulder. "Hey, buddy, we gotta get up."

He groans and rolls over.

Pyewacket leaps to safety and avoids getting pinned between the flip-flopping boy and the sofa cushions.

"See! I would never do that to you, ya Benedict Furball."

Looks like I'll have to take extreme measures. Returning to my bedside, I hit the button that rolls up the automatic blackout shades. The apartment is flooded with the bleak grey light of winter's morning.

Stellen yawns, stretches, and calls out without opening his eyes. "What time is it?"

"Time to go get some breakfast. There was a break-in at the taxidermy shed and Silas needs you to tell him if anything was stolen."

He sits up abruptly. "A break-in? Seriously? Is the cash missing?"

I shrug and roll my eyes. "How would I know that?"

He rubs his face and groans. "Right. Sorry. Mornings are tough."

"We've got that in common. Do you drink coffee?"

He chuckles. "No, but I might start today."

Inside Bless Choux, the line of patrons is astonishingly long considering the early hour. When Stellen and I finally reach the counter, the effervescent face of the patisserie's owner, Anne, falls on the boy.

She pinches her lips together and tilts her head downward. "How are you doing?"

Stellen shrugs, looks at the floor, and imperceptibly slides behind me.

Anne looks up at me. "I'm so sorry to hear about the tragedy, but it certainly is wonderful that you've taken him in."

Yeesh! There is no confidential living in this town. And now that Erick knows my secret, my life could get a whole lot more front-page.

"Mitzy? You drifted off, sweetie. What can I get you two?"

"I'll take a ginormous coffee and a slice of quiche." I tip my head over my shoulder. "What do you want?"

He mumbles something about whatever I'm having, so I place an amended order.

"And he'll have a half hot chocolate, half coffee and another slice of quiche." I pull a wad of cash out of my pocket, but Anne waves it away, almost angrily.

"Your money's no good here. You did a nice thing, and I'm returning the favor. Is this for here or to go, sweetie?"

"Unfortunately, it's to go today. Thanks."

Stellen and I step over to the display case containing travel mugs, holiday ornaments, and Bless Choux T-shirts.

He seems to be trying to shrink inside himself, and I recognize the fresh surge of pain that being out in public has caused.

"Don't worry. We'll be out of here in a second, and I promise no more shopping trips."

He leans toward me and stammers softly. "But I need . . . for the, you know."

"Right, a suit. After we take care of things with Silas, I can take you to Broken Rock for—"

He grips my arm urgently. "Can you just take me to the vet clinic? I don't care if the suit fits that good. Just guess my size. I'd really rather work with Doc Ledo today."

"No problem. I'll handle the shopping trip, and you can enjoy your first day of apprenticeship. Deal?"

He nods, and a flood of relief races across his face.

"To-go order for Mitzy Moon." The boisterous announcement bounces off the low ceiling.

Ignoring the tennis match-esque whipping of heads, I hand the bag containing our quiches to Stellen and grab our hot beverages. "Thanks, Anne."

The welcome blast of cold air on Third Avenue does wonders to relieve my embarrassment.

We load into the Jeep with our slices and wake-up juice and head out to the Jablonski's desolate place.

Silas was not idle while he waited for us to join him. He's plowed through the order book and made half a page of notes.

"Thank you for agreeing to assist, young man. Is there anything missing?"

Before Stellen can answer, I blurt out my own observation. "The cat! That caracal that scared me half to death on Saturday . . . It's gone."

Stellen's well-trained eyes scour the contents of the shed. He nods in agreement. "You're right. There are also some expensive hides missing." He walks along the tool bench and I can almost feel him ticking off boxes on his mental inventory. "There are some tools missing. Nothing super valuable, but I thought I should mention it."

Silas nods. "Mention it all. You'd be surprised how the most insignificant things come to have great import."

He scans the space more slowly, shakes his head, and walks back toward Silas. "Three of the most valuable mounts are missing. *Eretmochelys imbricata, Panthera pardus orientalis,* and *Gymnogyps californianus.*"

My alchemical mentor nods as though speaking Latin is perfectly normal. He leans toward the ledger and runs his finger down the list. "I see no mention of a hawksbill turtle, an Amur leopard, or a California condor. Was your father working illegally? Those species are on the critically endangered list."

"No. No way. My dad always insisted on permits

and letters from the U.S. Fish and Wildlife Service before he produced educational mounts."

Silas smooths his bushy grey mustache. "Why would they be missing?"

"Wait!" I step forward as the word "missing" rattles around inside my head. "Look. A page has been torn out of the ledger."

Stellen hurries to the desk and flips the pages back and forth. "Yep. There were at least six other orders on that missing page, including the caracal." He glances around a third time. "I don't think they took anything else, though."

"What about the money?" I ask.

Silas tilts his head and the furrows in his brow deepen.

"Stellen mentioned that his dad kept a lot of cash in the shed."

Stellen slides a stuffed mountain lion away from the back wall, kneels, and spins the combination on the safe back and forth. The door swings open and he breathes a sigh of relief. "Looks like it's all here. My dad and I were the only ones who knew where he kept the cash."

"Perhaps we should move the currency into a holding account while we settle the estate. The cash may not have been taken for a number of reasons. Not the least of which would be the difficulty in cracking that particular model of safe. However, if the intruder is determined, they may return."

Stellen nods and retrieves a small leather bag

from beneath the workbench. He transfers the money into the bag and hands it to Silas.

I peer into the satchel and whistle. "Why did your father keep so much cash in here?"

He leans against the counter and sighs. "I told him it was dangerous. I told him we needed to get some kind of electronic payment system, but the wi-fi is super sketchy this far out of town, and he didn't want his clients to get mad. All of his transactions were in cash, or sometimes checks."

"I believe we must involve the authorities." Silas lifts his milky-blue eyes and raises one bushy eyebrow. "Shall I call the sheriff or will you, Mizithra?"

Crossing my arms over my chest, I shake my head and sigh. "You call him. I'll stay here and search for clues, while you take Stellen to the animal hospital." I turn to the boy. "Are you all right with Silas making the introductions?"

"Sure."

Silas gathers up the ledger and several other papers, shoves the lot into his dilapidated briefcase, and shuffles toward the door.

In his wake, I turn to Stellen and whisper, "Oh, I should mention you'll have to ride in his 1908 Model T. You might want to grab a blanket or one of these pelts to keep warm." I chuckle at my joke, but the kid has a completely different reaction.

"Awesome. Can I crank it?"

"Follow me, young man. I'm pleased to see that someone from your generation appreciates history."

CHAPTER 10

As THE GUYS sputter away from the Jablonski property in a slice of automotive history, the weight of my waiting settles over me like a dark cloud. This will be my first time seeing Erick since the *incident,* and it fills the pit of my stomach with dread.

Wandering back inside, I attempt to distract myself with some good old-fashioned investigative work. Since stress and worry are blocking my psychic abilities, and my cantankerous ring refuses to offer any assistance, I'm going to rely on my five regular senses.

Let's start with a visual inspection of the door.

Obvious signs of forced entry. Some type of crowbar or prybar was employed to wrench the door open, and a breaker was tampered with to disable the alarm. It stands to reason they could've picked the lock. It's a standard single-cylinder deadbolt. The thief chose the obvious break-in for one of two reasons: they were in a hurry; or they were attempting to disguise their true abilities.

Walking between the rows of creepy critters, I explore my theory further.

If their reasoning was distraction, maybe they took the additional items to hide the true target. Then, removing the page from the ledger, they assumed no one would be able to figure out which specific trophies went missing.

I run my hand along the workbench and pause. Why tools? Did they need the tools or was that another part of their plan to muddy the waters?

I'll check with Stellen and see if he knows exactly which tools were taken.

Also, if the stolen mounts were endangered animals, they would be worth a fortune on the black market. That points to financial motivation.

Tires crunching down the snowy drive break my concentration and send a fresh wave of nausea through my gut.

Should I wait here? Should I greet them out front? I'd prefer to disappear, but I don't currently possess enough calm or focus to do anything but mildly hyperventilate.

Hurrying to the front of the shop, I have the displeasure of being greeted by none other than the trigger-happy Deputy Paulsen.

"Birch County Sheriffs, we're coming in. Hands where I can see them."

"Paulsen, it's me. I'm the one who called this in."

"False. Silas Willoughby called in the break-in."

"Well, I was here when he called it in." I scoff and roll my eyes. "Don't shoot, I'm leaving." In my haste to slip past her short, squat frame, I nearly crash into Erick. I school my features into a calm I don't possess and keep my tone professional. "Sheriff Harper."

His response is equally cloaked in disinterest. "Miss Moon. We'll take it from here."

I open my mouth to protest, but I have no bargaining power.

Erick gestures toward my vehicle. "You're free to go. Please let Mr. Willoughby know that there is a copy of the ME's report waiting for him at the station."

"Don't you need a statement from me?"

"Not at this time. Once we conduct our investigation and ascertain the scope of the burglary, we may follow up. Until then, you're free to go."

"Copy that." Trudging through the snow toward my vehicle, I feel like Atlas, and the weight of the world is crushing me. The hurt in Erick's eyes will haunt me all day.

I'm fresh out of ideas on how to fix my messed up relationship, so I'll head back to the bookshop and see if Silas can get his hands on that report. Maybe the additional information about time of death and cause of death will unblock my extrasensory perceptions.

Slipping my cell phone in the bracket clipped to

the heater vent, I call Silas and place it on speakerphone.

"Good morning, Mitzy. Did the sheriff arrive at the Jablonski's?"

"Yeah."

"It would appear the encounter was less than satisfactory."

"Understatement of the century."

"Were you able to uncover any useful information before the deputies arrived?"

"Hardly. The stress and worry sent my psychic senses packing. Forced entry, and some theories about the motivation, but nothing else."

Silas pauses to contemplate my meager offering. "Never underestimate the fragments that you gather. The devil is in the details."

Yawning with boredom, I struggle to move the focus away from the detritus that is my personal life. "There's a copy of the medical examiner's report waiting for you at the station. Do you want me to meet you there?"

"I'm currently conducting research at your bookshop. I shall retrieve the report during my luncheon interval."

"Copy that. See you in ten."

As I cross the Rare Books Loft, Silas looks up from his stacks of papers. "Ah, at last. May I use your apartment for a brief experiment?"

"Why not?" Opening the door, I step out of the way as Silas transfers the Jablonski ledger from an oak reading table to my coffee table.

He plants himself in the scalloped-back chair and nods for me to close the bookcase.

Taking my standard position on the settee, I lean forward, ready for the action. "Whatcha doin'?"

Silas ignores my playful query and pulls items from the secret pockets within his tattered tweed jacket.

Rubbing my hands together, I grin eagerly. "Oooh, is someone doin' some alchemy?"

"I'll thank you to take this seriously, Mizithra Achelois Moon."

Oops. Formal name territory. I crossed the line. "Understood. May I observe?"

"Certainly."

He opens the ledger and runs his finger along the torn edge of the missing page.

I gasp. "Are you going to summon the page from the ether?"

"Must I continually remind you of the differences between magic and alchemy?"

Sitting back, I cross my arms. "No. Carry on."

He selects a stem of dried herb and shows it to me. "Mugwort."

I nod.

Silas lights the dried twig of mugwort with the snap of his fingers, and I have to throw a hand over my mouth to keep from exclaiming my admiration.

Luckily, my psychic senses detect his secret satisfaction. I'm starting to understand his subdued, showboating nature.

He lets the ash fall into a small silver bowl and picks up a second vial filled with a crimson powder.

"Crushed dragon's blood."

I open my mouth, but a single commanding finger stops me from speaking. "It is a root, not a mythical animal's dried blood."

Closing my maw, I swallow awkwardly. It's almost as though he can read my mind.

He circles the first two fingers of his left hand above the bowl and the dark ashes and red powder swirl together. Carefully lifting the bowl with his right hand, he sprinkles it lightly over the right-hand page of the ledger.

My eyes widen in anticipation.

Once the powder is distributed, he waves his right hand over the book. The fine grains align like a formation of micro-soldiers marching over the page. He then lifts the book to his eye-level and gently exhales across the paper. The dust quivers and quakes over the page.

My jaw drops open as I watch the granules fall into the crevasses that appear on the sheet's surface.

When the motion ceases, he lowers the book to the table. "I fear success is not in our pantheon on this day."

Circling around to his side of the table, I kneel in front of the book. I can see where the substance has fallen into the marks caused by the pen pressing through the missing page and into this sheet that was left behind. However, whoever wrote those entries had a gentle hand. The marks are shallow and few.

I flop onto the floor, cross my legs, and gaze up at the alchemist. "Is that your best trick?"

He harrumphs and glares at me.

"I mean, do you have another idea? I know I said the wrong thing. Don't look at me like that."

His fiery gaze continues to bore a hole through my snark. "That was indeed my best trick, as you so eloquently put it."

Shrugging, I offer some encouragement. "We pretty much know what was taken. Maybe Stellen will remember the other two entries from that page, but for now the theme is clearly valuable endangered species. Let's just run with that."

He leans against the chair and laces his fingers over his round belly. "Indeed. At least we have that fragment."

"Oh shoot! I forgot. I have to get a suit for Stellen. He needs something to wear to the funeral."

Without missing a beat, my mentor has the answer. "You'll be wanting to see Rivail Gustafson in Broken Rock. He is the proprietor of A Stitch in Time."

"Of course you know a tailor. However, I don't care how many stitches he can make in time, he can't make a suit in time for this funeral."

"While he specializes in bespoke menswear, he

will also have a selection of off-the-rack vestments for your perusal."

"Yeesh." While the word bespoke always makes me cringe internally, I don't share this with Silas. Instead, I take his recommendation without retort. "I'm on it. By the way, how'd it go at the clinic?"

He makes a sound that could be construed as pleasant. "Quite well. Doctor Ledo is thrilled to have help, and Stellen's passion for the profession would be obvious to even a casual observer. You've done a good thing, Mitzy."

"Well, that still leaves me in the losing column, but it's something to build on."

"Once you allow yourself to trust in the sheriff's true nature, a solution will present itself."

I can barely prevent my eyes from rolling dramatically. "Thanks for the info about the tailor. Will you still be here when I get back?"

"Indeed. We shall discuss the report and perhaps your gifts will grace us with some guidance."

"Sounds good. See you later."

Once inside the Jeep, I type in the name of the tailor's shop and let my GPS take over. The drive along the Black Cap Trail, past Pancake Bay, provides a magnificent distraction. The intricate ice floes and the beautiful snow-dusted scenery succeed in taking my mind off my problems for a short while.

A Stitch in Time is an inviting slice of history. A

cleverly painted exterior and the faux-thatched roof harken back to images of an old European village. The wares displayed in the window show careful craftsmanship and pride in product.

As I open the door, a lovely bell tinkles. Nothing brash, nothing off-putting—a light, welcoming sound that makes me feel cared for.

A willowy wisp of a man strides from the back room. His wild mop of white hair rivals my own, and his astonishing mustache must hold several world records.

"Good afternoon. Welcome to A Stitch in Time. What may I create for you today?"

This definitely seems like the type of establishment where name-dropping is essential. "Good afternoon. Silas Willoughby referred me."

"Ah, yes. That sly old fox. He's due for a new suit, most assuredly."

All I can think is that Silas was due for a new suit about twenty years ago, but Grams has taught me that "more flies with honey" is the best approach. "I'll definitely remind him. However, today I am here to buy something off the rack."

His shoulders and mustache sag simultaneously.

It's all I can do not to laugh out loud. "I'm caring for a young man who lost his father this past weekend, and he needs a suit for the funeral."

No sooner are the words out of my mouth than the man's entire aura shifts. His eyes sharpen, his mustache perks up, and he adjusts the cloth tape measure draped around his shoulders as though it were an ermine stole.

"My condolences to your young friend. Right this way, Miss—"

"Moon. Mitzy Moon." My recent Bond marathon has had an unfortunate side effect.

"Ah, your reputation precedes you, Miss Moon. You are the granddaughter of the illustrious Isadora Duncan, are you not?"

"If you're referring to Myrtle Isadora Johnson Linder Duncan Willamet Rogers, then yes, I am she."

His knowing smile marks him as one of my grandmother's many "special friends." "A lifetime ago . . ." He smiles wistfully and sighs. "Shall we focus on the task at hand? What is the boy's size?"

I chew my bottom lip. "I'm not great with sizes. He's a junior in high school, if that helps?"

Mr. Gustafson chuckles and fluffs one end of his luxurious mustache. "Why don't you describe him to me, and I shall do my best. Let's start with height."

A series of images flash through my mind. "He's about here, just below my nose."

Mr. Gustafson whips the tape measure from his shoulders and flourishes it in front of me. "Five feet and six inches. And about how wide are the boy's shoulders?"

The focus on the task at hand allows a flicker of a psychic replay to pass through, and I can see Stellen standing in front of me in my mind's eye. "About the same as mine."

Another flourish of the tape measure. "And is he a thick boy or more of a waif?"

"He's quite thin. He eats like a horse, but he's skinny as a rail."

"I imagine he's not done growing. I should think he'll have quite a growth spurt in the next year or two." Gustafson struts over to the rack with the confidence and grace of a runway model and selects three items. "Do you prefer a traditional black, a charcoal, or a midnight blue?"

"I suppose we should stick with tradition."

"And the boy's coloring? Perhaps we can pull a bit of color into the shirt or tie, to offset the harsh effects of such a deep color."

"His hair is dark brown, curly, and his eyes are green with little flecks of gold."

Mr. Gustafson's mustache wiggles as he smiles broadly. "You are exceptionally observant. An excellent trait."

He runs his finger over the rows of neckties and selects a deep green, with tiny black and gold fleur-de-lis. "Now, to pair this with the proper shirt." A moment later, he has selected three options and shuffles through them. He tests the tie and the coat with each combination. "I believe the dark green gives us the most bang for our buck, while remaining subtle and respectful. Would you not agree?"

Don't get me started. "I think that's fantastic. I'll take all of it." As I walk toward the counter, a surge of generosity washes over me. "If I wanted to get a gift for Silas, what would you recommend?"

Mr. Gustafson winks at me and takes a little bow. "What a lovely thought. I would highly recommend a silk pocket square. Mr. Willoughby is a huge fan of the perfectly folded pocket square."

This news hardly surprises me, but I'm happy to have the opportunity to repay a portion of my mentor's kindness. "Would you select one for me and add it to the order?"

"Of course."

He carefully packages the items with tissue and gold seals, and fits the suit into a garment bag.

That's when it dawns on me that I definitely don't have enough cash for this transaction. I pull out the plastic and offer it hesitantly. "Do you accept this form of payment?"

He waves it away. "Isadora has an account with me. She's no longer with us, God rest her magnificent soul, but I'm sure none of the particulars have changed."

"Well, I'm sure you're correct." Having visited the bank in Pin Cherry Harbor back when I first arrived, I was shocked to learn about passbooks and NCR paper in the town that tech forgot. It makes perfect sense that none of the account numbers would've changed. "I hope I have another reason to visit you, Mr. Gustafson. You've been more than helpful."

"I wish the same, my dear." He hands me the garment bag, and another carefully wrapped parcel. "Again, my condolences."

"Thank you."

Silas is returning from his "luncheon interval" by the time I get back to the Bell, Book & Candle.

"What does the report say?"

"We shall examine it together." Silas takes a seat at one of the reading tables in the Rare Books Loft and lays the report on the polished oak surface.

"Time of death?"

"Estimated time of death is between 8:00 and 10:00 p.m. on Friday evening."

"And they're taking into account the weather, the body being buried in snow, all that stuff, right?"

"Indeed. They list the details of the factors used in the calculation in a footnote."

"And what about cause of death?"

Silas moves his gnarled finger down the page and shakes his head with displeasure. "Gruesome. Perhaps it is best if we simply refer to it as a stabbing and gloss over the details."

He turns the paper toward me and taps a finger on the description.

My expression grows more horrified with each sentence. "Ew. That's so . . . violent. Also, it was either a super lucky strike, or the attacker knew exactly where to stab someone for the quickest result."

Silas nods. "While the unfortunate snowmobile

collision with the corpse has obscured some evidence, at this juncture I believe we must entertain both scenarios."

"Does the other report mention if they found a murder weapon on scene?"

He peruses the attached crime-scene report and shakes his head. "No murder weapon has been located, and they refer to the place where the body was discovered as a possible dump site. The suspicion seems to lean toward a working theory that the murder took place elsewhere, and Mr. Jablonski was placed in the deep snow beside the track, likely in the hopes that the body wouldn't be uncovered until spring. Possibly the assailant assumed decomposition and predation would prevent discovery altogether."

"What are the specs on the alleged murder weapon?"

"They're hypothesizing a screwdriver, with at least a nine-inch shank." Silas holds his hands apart to show me a visual estimation of the length.

"That definitely points to someone involved in the snowmobile racing world, wouldn't you say?"

"A likely assumption. However, without an actual murder weapon, it would be difficult for the authorities to make an arrest. Perhaps you can inspect the report and see if you receive any additional messages."

I scan through the medical examiner's report and the crime-scene report, but my psychic senses continue their vacation. "Nothing. Nada. Bupkus." If I have any intention of receiving extrasensory help on this investigation, it seems like I'm going to have to patch things up with Erick. The stress and the constant roiling in my gut are blocking any and all access to any of the four "clairs."

"When Stellen returns from the animal hospital, perhaps he can recall some additional details about his father's coaching. I would be interested to know if Trey Lee's father made any visits to the Jablonski property."

"Right? It sure seems like he would've been upset about losing such an excellent coach, when his son was poised to take the title and collect all that prize money."

Silas smooths his mustache with a thumb and forefinger. "You are correct." He hums for a moment before leaning forward in anticipation. "Were you successful in your visit to A Stitch in Time?"

"Geez! I left everything in the car! I'll be right back."

Thundering down the wrought-iron staircase, I'm met by the scowling face of Twiggy at the bottom of the stairs.

"Look, doll, you're disturbing the customers. Maybe you can stop running around like a herd of elephants and let people shop in peace."

I glance around the deserted first floor and stifle a chuckle. "I'll do my best." Before we get into an argument about disturbing invisible customers, I hurry out the side door and retrieve the packages from the Jeep.

"Mr. Gustafson is so skilled with his tape measure. I hope the suit fits Stellen."

Silas nods. "I'm certain you meant to say that you hope it *still* fits him in the spring?"

"What do you mean *still*?"

"Ah yes. I continue to underestimate your lack of experience in the customs of the far north. In a land where permafrost often reaches four feet deep and grave markers are obscured by layers of snow, the burials for deaths occurring in January, February, and March are almost always postponed until late April or early May. Memorial services and cremations are conducted during the winter, but we postpone interments. I will review Mr. Jablonski's last wishes, but I believe he was slated for burial, which will take place in the spring."

My jaw hangs open like that of a broken ventriloquist dummy. "What do you mean postponed? Like, there's just a room full of bodies somewhere, waiting for spring? You can't be serious?"

Silas tilts his head and fixes me with an iron gaze. "Mizithra, when have you known me to jest? The realities of our brutal winters cannot be ignored. Mortuaries have storage vaults, and storing the deceased during the harshest months of winter is a common practice. Do not fret. I'm sure Mr. Gustafson can adjust the hem on the trousers if young Stellen happens to hit a growth spurt before the service."

My gums flap a bit, like those of a fish out of water, and I almost forget the gift. Almost. Reaching into the bag, I retrieve a small tissue-wrapped parcel held together by a lovely golden seal. "Here. I got you this."

Silas straightens his spine and a look of surprise grips him. "What is this? A gift? The Yuletide has passed. Why would you present me with this token?"

A self-satisfied smile finally overrides my flapping jaw, and I nod happily. "Don't act so surprised. Do I need a reason to get you a present?"

"Perhaps not. I'm not one to make a fuss."

"Well, I'm making a fuss. Thank you for all your excellent mentoring!"

Silas harrumphs into his mustache, suppresses his emotions, and continues to unwrap his present. "What a lovely pocket square. Exactly what I needed to perk up this old coat."

He removes a tattered grey pocket square from his ancient tweed jacket and replaces it with the lovely navy-blue silk square that Mr. Gustafson carefully folded for me.

"That looks great, Silas. Do you like it?"

He fumbles unnecessarily with the item and clears his throat twice. "It is a thoughtful and welcome gift. Thank you, Mizithra."

"You're welcome. I'll spare you the embarrassment of a big hug, but you should know that I think you deserve one."

He tugs at his jacket, smooths his mustache, and shuffles the papers on the table.

Poor little guy. I've embarrassed him with my sappy comments. I'm all too familiar with the discomfort of raw emotion. I'll spare him any further agitation. "I guess I'll head over to the station and see if they're bringing Mr. Lee in for questioning."

"A wonderful idea. I shall continue my efforts with the Jablonski estate paperwork." He pats the stack of legal documents and leans forward studiously.

CHAPTER 11

Bundling up for the short trek, I play through various movie scenarios inside my head. When I open the door of the station, will Erick sense my arrival and step out of his office? Will he be happy to see me, or will he banish me from the premises?

Maybe I should've taken the time to put on a sexy outfit or a seductive shade of lipstick?

All the handy little gimmicks that work so well on the silver screen seem like empty, hollow gestures. The truth is, my heart is broken and I owe Sheriff Harper a massive apology. No plunging neckline or luscious berry lip tint is going to solve this problem.

Inside the bustling station, two deputies are fielding calls and making notes in the bullpen, while Furious Monkeys has had to put her phone down to handle the growing line of real, live humans queuing up in front of her desk, to file complaints about the canceled snocross or offering useless tips in an attempt to score a juicy tidbit to share with their coffee klatch. She fires me a put-upon side eye and nods her head sharply. Clearly, she hasn't heard that Erick and I are on a break.

Taking any opportunity given, I push through the crooked swinging gate and enter the bullpen.

Just when I think I'll make it safely across the room, Deputy Paulsen launches out of Erick's office with a red face and veritable steam coming out of her ears. "What are you doing here, Moon?"

When in doubt, lie it out. "I had some information for Deputy Johnson." Deputy Johnson and I are loosely acquainted, and he mostly knows me as the sheriff's girlfriend, so he fidgets nervously behind his desk as his eyes dart back and forth between Deputy Paulsen and myself. A tentative smile finally breaks his stern expression. "Give me one second to finish this gentleman's statement, Miss Moon."

Nodding pleasantly, I flash a grin and offer a triumphant head nod in Paulsen's direction. "Looks like everything will be handled in a moment. Don't let me keep you from your investigation."

She growls openly and storms through the front of the station.

Johnson pulls the report out of his typewriter, grabs a pen, and hands it to the concerned citizen. "Just sign your name at the bottom, and you're free to go. Thank you for coming in today." He looks up and gestures his thumb toward the interrogation rooms.

"Sheriff Harper is questioning a suspect right now. Did you want to wait in his office?"

Not bad for a newbie. For a minute there, I thought Johnson actually believed my story. But clearly he saw through my ruse and kindly chose to support my alibi. "Actually, that sounds great. Thanks for covering for me."

He rolls his eyes ever so slightly and winks.

Walking toward Erick's office, I'm overcome with curiosity about whom he's questioning. A quick glance over my shoulder reveals Deputy Johnson deep in conversation with the concerned citizen. Before he can look up, I slip into the observation room between Interrogation Rooms One and Two. Activating extreme stealth mode, I flip the silver switch above the speaker and hold my breath . . .

"Look, Mr. Lee. We know that Coach Jablonski was leaving your team to coach Priest. With your son poised to win $75,000 on the circuit, I don't think you could afford to lose a coach, and you certainly couldn't afford a coach as good as Jablonski to defect to a competitor's team."

Mr. Lee rubs his hands together and leans forward, his face a mask of worry. "Sheriff, please, you have to believe me. I went to the track Friday night on good terms with Jablonski. Jawbone had given Trey every advantage, but Trey had outgrown him. The fact that he was moving on to coach Priest was a mutual decision. We had a conversation, I told him I understood, and he offered us a refund."

"And now that he's dead, my deputy noted that you've hired an attorney to recover those coaching fees."

Mr. Lee exhales in frustration and leans back. "Sure. But only after I found out about his death. We had a gentlemen's agreement. There was no reason for me to kill him."

"The evidence points to the attacker having more than a cursory knowledge of anatomy. The blow that killed Mr. Jablonski was expertly placed at the base of the skull. Death would've been nearly instantaneous, with very little blood loss. I'm sure you can understand how incriminating that is, Mr. Lee. You're a doctor. A surgeon, if I'm not mistaken. Precisely placing that incision would've been second nature for you. I have deputies up on the mountain searching for the murder weapon. I'm afraid if we find your prints on it, we will make an arrest."

Mr. Lee bends forward, places his elbows on the metal table, and hangs his head in his hands.

I lean toward the glass in an attempt to hear his soft whisper.

"Sheriff, my boy is in the hospital with severe injuries. He could be paralyzed. He could have suffered brain damage." The man lifts his head and gazes directly at the sheriff. "I have a temper, I'll admit to that. Maybe I wasn't happy when Jablonski told me he was going to quit coaching Trey. But I promise you, we parted on good terms Friday night. He was alive and well when I left him on that mountain. Now please, can I go back to the hospital and sit with my son?"

My forehead bumps the glass, and I jump back and inhale sharply. The intense emotion of Mr. Lee's last statement caused me to lose my spatial awareness.

Erick's shoulders tense and it doesn't take a psychic to guess that he suspects *someone* of eavesdropping. He hastily gets to his feet. "You're free to go, Mr. Lee. We'll be in touch as the investigation develops."

Mr. Lee slowly stands. His shoulders are slumped and his spirit is broken. "I understand, Sheriff." He walks out of the interrogation room and Erick spins towards the one-way glass.

Busted.

There's no point in running, he'll step out of that door and intercept me before I make it two steps down the hallway. Better to sit tight and take my lumps like a big girl.

He strides out of the interrogation room and my stomach swirls uncomfortably.

I fix my eyes on the door handle of the observation room, but it doesn't twist. I lean toward the one-way glass and try to see around corners, but there's no sign of Sheriff Harper.

Well, I'm not going to sit in here like a child in timeout.

Taking a deep breath, I square my shoulders and open the door. The short hallway outside the interrogation rooms is empty, and the door to Sheriff Harper's office is tightly closed.

Message received.

I stalk out of the station and stomp down Main Street toward my bookshop.

The nerve of that guy! It's not like I cheated on him or lied about being married before! I kept a little secret about a ghost living in my bookstore. Is it really that bad?

The cell phone in the pocket of my puffy coat rings and the shock wave sends a flash of guilt across my face.

"Stellen? Is everything all right?"

"Everything was amazing. Doc Ledo is the best. Should I walk back to your apartment, or is someone picking me up?"

I thunk my head with the heel of my mitten. "I'll be there in five minutes." Stuffing the phone back in my pocket, I pick up the pace and hop into the Jeep. Having a kid is more work than I imagined. I completely forgot that Stellen was at his apprenticeship. What if he was only two or three years old? He wouldn't know what to do. He wouldn't know whom to call. It's official, I'd be a terrible mother. Maybe I'm just one of those people who's not cut out for long-term relationships or procreation. Maybe I'm destined to be a lonely, selfish, secret-keeping spinster.

Taking the final turn at an unsafe speed, the Jeep fishtails as I round the corner onto Gunnison Avenue. Shockingly, my instinct to counter steer is the correct one, and I get the vehicle under control.

When I turn into the parking lot of the Animal Hospital, Stellen is waiting outside.

"Thanks for coming to get me, Mitzy, but I can totally walk next time. You don't have to change your plans for me."

"Nonsense! And next time, wait inside. It's freezing out here."

"Inside? My dad always liked me to wait outside, so I wouldn't waste his time when he picked me up from stuff. With the coaching and the taxidermy gigs, he really didn't like making trips into town for no reason."

To hear the young boy refer to himself as "no reason" breaks my heart. I have no right to judge Mr. Jablonski, but I'm going to. This sweet, sensitive kid lost his mother to a horrible disease, and his father offered him nothing in the way of comfort. A roof over his head is not what this little soul needed. "I don't mean this to sound harsh, Stellen. I'm sure your father was dealing with his own pain surrounding your mother's illness. But you're important, and you deserve a good life. Don't ever think of yourself as an inconvenience. All right?"

He gazes out the passenger-side window and nods his head.

"I'll see how long this temporary custody thing will last, but no matter what type of foster home you have to go to, never give up on yourself. You're gonna graduate, and you're absolutely going to veterinary school. Promise me you won't let the system break you."

Stellen's small Adam's apple struggles to swallow the emotion welling up inside him. "I don't think my dad was upset when my mom died."

The words slice into my heart like a hot knife through butter. "Why would you say that? I'm sure he loved your mom."

Stellen sniffles and continues, "Maybe. After she passed away, all he ever talked about was the mountain of medical bills. The reason he had to work so hard, and take on so many taxidermy projects, was because of her. He always used to say that the cancer was the worst thing that ever happened to him."

My hand smacks against the steering wheel, and I exhale. "Well, he was wrong. What your mother went through was terrible. She fought it as long as she could so that she could be there for you. Every treatment she endured was to buy a few more days with you. And if your father didn't appreciate that, and he thinks it was money wasted, then maybe he got what was coming to him."

Stellen's eyes widen in shock and he hugs his arms around his torso.

Pulling into the garage, I turn the engine off and wipe the stream of tears from my cheeks. "I'm sorry. I don't know where that came from. It's none of my business, and I'm sure your dad did the best he could."

Stellen tentatively reaches out a hand and places it on my arm. "I think you're right. I know you're not supposed to speak ill of the dead, or whatever, but—"

Our tear-filled eyes meet, and I finish his sentence. "You'd pay any amount of money to have just one more day with her."

Stellen nods, and I offer him a hug.

After drying our eyes, we head into the bookshop to discover Amaryllis and Twiggy deep in an argument, and the volume is growing.

"Like I told you before, we ain't moving nothin'."

"Don't be ridiculous, Twiggy. How are we going to fit guests in here with all of these bookshelves in the way?"

"Run the chairs between the aisles." Twiggy places a defiant fist on her hip.

Amaryllis gestures wildly. "And how will they see?"

I lean toward Stellen and whisper, "You see what you can find to eat in the back room, and I'll throw some water on this fire."

He smirks and nods.

"Ladies, may I offer my assistance?"

Twiggy turns on me. "Look, kid, I told you I'd handle this. We have a creative difference. I'll take care of it."

Amaryllis shoots me a pleading stare, and right as I'm about to put my foot down with Twiggy, an enraged ghost rockets down from the mezzanine.

Grams heads straight for Twiggy, and instead of

passing through her, she freeze-frames. The prolonged ghost chills send Twiggy into a violent shiver. "Is it Isadora? Tell her to get off me!"

I wait a beat, like any good movie villain. "Isadora? Don't force me to deface one of your designer gowns."

Grams finally finishes passing through Twiggy and floats behind her. The shimmering features hold an expression full of menace, and Ghost-ma is ready to dish out additional retribution at a moment's notice.

"Twiggy, I don't know how to tell you this, but I get the distinct feeling that if you don't do exactly what Amaryllis says, Grams is seriously planning on possessing you."

Twiggy makes the sign of the cross with her fingers and backs away from me. "You tell that ungrateful Myrtle Isadora that she'll lose her last friend if she doesn't keep her creepy ghost fingers off me."

Grams crosses her arms over her ample bosom and winks.

"You're really not in any position to bargain. Why don't you hire a company that you trust to box up the books, and we'll store them in a weatherproof, safe location, and then we'll let Amaryllis make all the decisions about decorating the main floor for her wedding? Do we have a deal, Twiggy?"

Twiggy frantically searches the air around her and rubs the gooseflesh on her arms. "Nothin' gets packed up without my supervision."

"Absolutely. I wouldn't have it any other way. Hire whoever you want and send me the bill."

Twiggy makes no further argument. She shakes her head and stomps her biker boots with unnecessary force as she heads into the back room to make the arrangements.

Amaryllis sighs with relief and offers me a namaste-style bow of gratitude. "You got here just in time. That woman was driving me crazy. Can you imagine? Guests sitting in little rows as though they were riding a train, not able to see anything? It's enough to drive a woman to drink."

"I hear ya. However, Grams deserves all the thanks. I wouldn't know the first thing about running this bookstore without Twiggy, so I have to tread lightly, but I think Isadora's little stunt gave us the bargaining power we needed. If there are any other issues that come up, just let me know. Twiggy's a good person, she's just kinda set in her ways, you know?"

Amaryllis nods too easily. "Speaking of people who are set in their ways, Jacob is still living under the misguided impression that I kept the guest list small. Do you think I can wedge a hundred chairs in here?"

I chuckle and shake my head. "I guess you'll find out. I need to call Silas. Is there anything else I can help you with?"

She hooks her arm through my elbow and smiles from ear to ear. "Just one thing."

"Name it."

"Will you be my maid of honor?"

An entire movie montage of horrible bridesmaid's dresses flashes before my eyes. "Sure. Of course."

She breathes a sigh of relief and squeezes my arm. "I'm so glad you said that, because I already bought your dress. I hope it fits!"

Dear Lord baby Jesus. "I'm sure it will."

"Perfect, I'll bring it by, and you can try it on and we'll talk about what we're going to do with your hair."

"Sounds great." I clumsily disengage my arm and head upstairs before I say something I'll regret. Bridesmaid's dresses? Hairdos? Heaven help me! How do I get myself into these things?

CHAPTER 12

THE SECRET BOOKCASE SLIDES OPEN, and, as I walk into the apartment, I experience the distinct feeling of being watched. Spinning around, I find Pyewacket perched atop the antique armoire with one eye open. His golden orb is fixed on me with a mixture of impatience and doubt.

"Sorry to keep you waiting, Mr. Cuddlekins. I had to pick up our houseguest and prevent an attack of Bridezilla. But I'm here now. How can I be of service?"

The large tan ball of muscle leaps from the wardrobe and lands with the grace of a prima ballerina. He drops onto his haunches, stares intently, but makes no vocalization.

Walking toward the fiendish feline, I crouch and await further instruction. "I'm here. I'm listening, but you're not telling me anything."

His black-tufted ears twitch, and he leans forward.

I instinctively offer my palm as he drops a small item from his mouth. "I'm going to go out on a limb and assume this has something to do with my case?"

"Reow." Can confirm.

I roll the red shard back and forth in my hand and shrug. "I've got nothing, Pyewacket. I mean, it looks plastic, but other than that—"

"How's the investigation going?"

I can't believe I didn't hear the door slide open. I must've been focusing harder than I thought. However, despite my best efforts, my psychic senses are still on the fritz. "Hey, Stellen, we got the reports from the sheriff's station." I place the chunk of red debris on the coffee table, stand, and brush some cat hair from my knee.

The boy flops onto the settee with a bowl of Fruity Puffs.

Shockingly, Pyewacket neither comments nor attacks.

Stellen swallows his mouthful of sugary cereal. "What'd the medical examiner say?"

"Are you sure you're okay to talk about this?"

He shrugs and sets his snack bowl on the table. "I don't know. Not talking about it isn't going to change anything. Maybe knowing the truth will help me deal, you know?"

"Yeah, I understand. If you change your mind, though, it's okay to tell me to stop talking."

Grams bursts through the wall, already chuckling. "Well, good luck with that task. Tell him what I said, Mitzy."

Rolling my eyes, I pick up my duties as an afterlife interpreter. "Grams thinks that it's too great a task to get me to stop talking."

Stellen gazes at the elegant ghost hovering above us and grins. "It's so cool that she's here all the time."

Sighing, I know he's thinking about his mother, and the only way I can change the topic is to talk about his dead dad. Wow, what a great option. "The medical examiner places time of death Friday night between 8:00 and 10:00 p.m."

Stellen laces his fingers behind his head and stretches out on the sofa. "Makes sense. That was part of my dad's ritual. Every night before a big race, he'd wait until the venue had cleared out and then he would ride the track, as well as walk the track. Both the drag track and the snocross track. He said it was to check for imperfections, but I think he was superstitious. One time when I was sick and my mom was in the hospital, he had to stay home with me and didn't get to perform the ritual inspection. Trey had his only loss of the season the next day."

"So you didn't think anything about him being out late?"

"Nope."

"What about in the morning? Didn't you wonder where he was at breakfast?" I tilt my head.

Stellen shakes his head sadly. "We didn't really eat together, you know?"

My heart squeezes with pain and I'm at a loss for words.

Pyewacket casually climbs onto the coffee table and brazenly plunges his face into the unprotected bowl of Fruity Puffs.

Stellen smiles. "They're all yours, boy. Sorry I didn't ask."

Pye lifts his head and squeezes his eyes closed as he stares at the usurper.

"Well, he didn't yell at you, and he didn't thwack you with his razor-sharp claws. I think he actually likes you."

Stellen reaches a hand toward the caracal's arched back.

"Wait! Do not touch him when he is eating. I mean, not to be that person, but—"

Stellen chuckles. "Thanks. I owe you one. The last thing I need is an injured hand when Doc Ledo is giving me so much responsibility at the clinic." He chews the edge of his fingernail and stares at the tin-plated ceiling. "Did they have a cause of death?"

"Yeah, we're calling it a stabbing."

He nods. "Okay." Sitting up, he rubs his hands on his knees. I get the feeling he wants to say something, but neither my useless mood ring nor my semi-retired psychic senses offer any assistance.

He reaches out and picks up the red shard from

the coffee table. "Where'd this piece of taillight come from?"

I lean forward eagerly. "You know what that is?"

"Yeah. Oh, for sure. It's a broken piece of taillight from—" he holds it up and runs his thumb along the edge as he inspects it more closely "—the right taillight. Seems like it might be an older vehicle, just based on the opacity and the diffusion texture."

I let out a low whistle. "Turns out you're pretty handy to have around. How do you know so much about cars?"

He turns the debris over in his hand as he answers. "I like patterns. I like the way cars have consistencies and the way they evolve over time. When I was real little, I thought maybe it would be something that I'd have in common with my dad. Turns out he's not really into cars. But once I started studying the patterns, I just couldn't let it go. The things that change, the style, materials, I just sort of absorbed it. You know?"

Nodding, I chew my bottom lip and reply, "I do. I think that's how it is with me and movies. There are so many tropes that repeat over and over again, but there are also subtle differences, unique interpretations. It's all swirling around in here somewhere." I tap my finger on my temple.

Reaching across the table, I open my hand and he drops the bit of crimson plastic into my outstretched palm. As soon as the plastic touches my skin, the word "tracks" hits me like a brick wall. I see an image of a tire track in the snow. "I have to go back to your house. I think whoever took the endangered species from the taxidermy shed left some kind of tire track."

Stellen sits up and shakes his head. "We drove in and out of there a few times, and didn't you say the sheriff and the deputy drove both their cruisers down the road?"

I nod.

"Doesn't seem like you'll be able to find anything, plus it's snowed a little off and on. I bet any tracks that were left would be covered."

I jump up from the couch and grab my coat. "One thing you gotta learn, kid. When I get a hunch, it's always worth following."

"RE-OW!" Game on!

Stellen stands and scratches between Pyewacket's ears. "I better come with you. You don't know anything about tires."

"Rude. But you're not wrong."

The sun sparkles off the fresh layer of white powder blanketing almost-Canada. The bright, upbeat scenery lies in stark contrast to our mission. However, the ominous Jablonski estate does not disappoint. The weather-beaten cabin still holds every ounce of its inherent dreariness.

Rather than drive through and potentially further obscure the tracks we seek, I park in the driveway and Stellen and I hop out.

"Where did the chunk of taillight come from?" He stops at the front of the Jeep and waits for me.

"My co-investigator, Pyewacket, delivered that tidbit."

Stellen raises his eyebrows and his mouth makes a little surprised oh-shape. "Does he always help you?"

As I stop to ponder the question, it surprises me to take stock of the number of times that wildcat has saved my skin or provided key information. "Now that I think about it, yeah. He seems to be in tune with information that's somehow beyond my human perception."

Stellen nods in agreement, as though my statement is as commonplace as adding cream to coffee. "So you don't actually know where the taillight was broken, right?"

Taking a page from Pyewacket's book, I reply, "Can confirm."

He pauses in the curve of the driveway and scans the surroundings. "If it happened here . . . What would he, or she, have hit?"

As soon as my sidekick mentions a collision, my clairvoyance delivers a flash of a taillight impacting a tree. Sadly, there is no extended visual on the vehicle or the driver, just pitch blackness surrounding— "Look! Is there bark scraped off that tree?"

Stellen shifts his gaze toward a huge old pine tree whose branches are weighed down with the burden of fresh snow.

I make a beeline toward the tree, but my cohort grabs my arm. "Wait. There could be part of a track still visible under those huge branches. They would've blocked the snow from covering it. We need to take pictures, or measurements of the track, right?"

"Hey, you're a natural. We absolutely need to do all of those things. Does your dad have a measuring tape in the shed?"

The kid whips out his phone. "I've got an app for that."

We share a giggle and inch toward the scarred pine tree.

Stellen squeezes my arm in excitement. "Right there. That's a track from a BF Goodrich All-terrain T/A KO."

"I'm not even going to ask how you know that."

He shrugs. "Tread patterns. It's one of those things. But that's an older tire. It's been discontinued. Maybe that'll help the sheriff narrow down his search for the vehicle?"

He snaps a few pics and uses the app to measure width and depth of the track.

I pat him on the back. "And it will have a busted right tail light, too."

He nods. "Yeah, that scrape wasn't there before the—you know—the accident."

"It stands to reason that whoever stole the leopard, sea turtle, condor, and the tools, is the same person who hit this tree."

"Yeah, but I still don't get why they stole them. I

would've handed them over, or I could've finished them if they really needed me to."

"So you're pretty good at taxidermy?"

"Not to brag, but they have the world championships every two years, and my dad's placed in the top three for the last five competitions. Three of those mounts were more than half my handiwork. But he puts on the finishing touches, so who knows."

"I'm sure your work made a difference." An awkward silence threatens, but my spinning brain offers a different distraction. "Hey, what about the tools? When we were here the other day with Silas, you mentioned they stole some tools. Do you know which ones?"

"I can totally tell what's missing. I organized that whole tool bench for my dad. Let's go back inside and make a list."

He scans the wall behind the bench and calls out the names of the MIA tools. "Let's see, they took the shaving knife, the hone, the eye scoop, the curved spring forceps, and the broad sculpting spatula."

"Those tools all sound really specialized. Can you show me what they look like?" Taking a deep breath, I steel myself, and promise not to think about what the tools are used for.

He quickly calls up some pictures on his phone, but as he mentioned on our last visit, the internet lags and it takes some time for the pictures to load.

As he scrolls through the shots and points to the types of tools that were taken from his dad's workbench, my breath catches in my throat. "What's that one? The super long piece?"

"Oh, it's called a hone. We use it to restore the edge on other tools."

"And that was one of the things that was taken?"

"I'm pretty sure."

"Is this long part kind of strong? It's made out of metal, right?"

"It's steel. The one we had was about nine-inches long. It's important to keep after the curl on the edge of skinning tools and stuff. If the blade wilts, it affects the precision."

There's only one part of his mini-lesson that interests me. "Nine inches? You're sure?"

"Yeah, why?"

"The description of the murder weapon mentioned something with a nine-inch shank. The medical examiner hypothesized a screwdriver."

The color drains from Stellen's face. "If it was the hone . . . My dad might've been killed here, in the shop."

I scan the porous wooden floor. "I don't think so. We would've seen bloodstains on a floor like this."

The young boy steadies himself on the bench. "Not if it happened in the back." He gulps down some air and whispers, "I call it the grim reaper room."

Now it's my turn to feel queasy. "Do I even want to know what that is?"

He shakes his head. "You better call Erick, I mean Sheriff Harper."

Great. Another opportunity for me to disappoint my possibly *ex*-boyfriend.

Stellen and I make good use of our time while we wait for the deputies to arrive. We need a distraction from the thoughts swirling in our minds, so we head off to work in the house.

I'm told that it's important to leave the heat on, even though he's not living here. Setting the furnace to a low temp keeps the pipes from freezing. Next we attempt to clean out the refrigerator. There's precious little food in there to begin with, but there's no point in letting it rot and stink up the whole place. We pack three grocery bags with perishables and some dry goods from the cupboards, and Stellen grabs two framed pictures from the wall in their sparsely furnished living room.

"I hear the cars. Should we meet them outside?" His youthful face is struggling to find courage.

"You load this stuff in the Jeep. I'll talk to the deputies." As I trudge out to the taxidermy shed, I cross my fingers inside my mittens. Hopefully, it will be only deputies, and no sheriff.

No such luck.

Sheriff Harper steps out of his vehicle, taps the button on his radio, and calls in. "10-8 at the Jablonski property." His jaw muscles flex. "Dispatch said there was a call about some new evidence. This your doing?"

The harsh tone of his voice hurts my heart, but I don't feel it's unwarranted. "Do you want me to talk to Deputy Johnson?" I peer over Erick's shoulder as his backup approaches.

Erick crosses his arms over his chest in that yummy way that makes his biceps bulge, which only pains me further. "No, Miss Moon. I'd like you to tell me exactly what you found. Or is this just a hunch?"

Ouch. Handing him the shard of taillight, I walk him through our discovery of the tire track and the specific tools that were missing from the shed.

"You say this hone has a nine-inch shank?"

"Yeah, that's what Stellen said. He's the one who organizes all the tools for his dad, so he knew exactly what was missing. When he showed me the picture of the hone, I thought it could be the murder weapon?"

Erick tilts his head, and my psychic senses finally deliver a useful message. He's impressed with my deduction, and it's difficult for him to keep from telling me. He's weakening.

"If the murder weapon was taken from this location, there's a chance the murder took place here and not on the mountain."

"That means it might not be Mr. Lee. Right?"

"I'm not at liberty to discuss an ongoing investigation with a civilian."

Yeesh! "Well, there's no blood in the taxidermy shed. But Stellen mentioned something he calls 'the grim reaper room,' and I didn't want to see it."

Erick's eyes widened, and he nods slowly. "It's a terrible nickname, but it would be the location where Mr. Jablonski processed the animals before mounting them. I'll have the deputies check into it." He turns to pass instructions to Deputy Johnson and I'm left standing in the snow like an abandoned Christmas tree in January.

Stellen waves from the car. I shrug and walk toward my Jeep.

As I yank open the door in a huff, the sheriff's voice calls out across the winter landscape.

"Thanks for calling this in, Moon."

"You're welcome, Erick." Before we were an item, my using his first name really got under his skin. Maybe I can soften him up by using a few of my old tricks.

He turns away to hide his smile, but I've revealed another crack in his icy shell.

CHAPTER 13

I BARELY RECOGNIZE my own bookstore when Stellen and I return from our investigation. Twiggy wasted no time in getting the inventory boxed up and moving the shelving to make way for the wedding festivities.

"Wow! This space is enormous. All those bookcases really make it seem a lot smaller."

Twiggy stomps out, crosses her arms, and fixes me with an impudent stare. "It's called creating a cozy atmosphere. People appreciate that when they're browsing for their next favorite read."

"I know I don't say it enough, but I really do appreciate everything you do for the bookshop. I'm sorry we had to upset the apple cart to make the bride happy, but she's my one and only father's fiancée, so I kind of feel like I need to make her happy."

A mischievous sparkle twinkles in Twiggy's eye. "Just wait till you see the dress. You're going to make a whole lot of people happy." She cackles all the way back to her rolly office chair.

"Let's head upstairs. How do you feel about ordering pizza for dinner?"

Stellen grins. "I'm never gonna say no to pizza."

Chuckling, I place the call and check the apartment to see if there's any additional evidence coming in from my furry informant.

"I'm gonna give my dad a quick call. Here's some cash. Will you pay for the pizza when they get here?"

Stellen retrieves the bills from the coffee table. "I think this is too much. How much did you want to tip?"

"You decide. And keep whatever is left."

He gulps loudly. "Thanks."

"Let's call it your allowance. I'm sure there'll be plenty of opportunities for you to pitch in while we're all trying to get ready for this wedding. You'll earn it twice over before the end of the week."

He nods. "No problem. I'm happy to help."

This cooperative attitude is refreshing. Having to deal with a stubborn Ghost-ma, a curmudgeonly alchemist, and an opinionated volunteer employee has conditioned me to expect resistance at my every suggestion. This kid is a real keeper.

"Hey, Dad, I was wondering— Sure. Right now? Got it. Be right there." I end the call and update my roommate. "Save me a slice. Apparently the bride needs to speak to me right away."

Stellen smiles and his face transforms into an impish grin. "Sure. I'll save you a *slice*."

Rolling my eyes and shaking my head, I don my winter coat and hustle over to wedding central.

The elevator doors glide open, and the look on my father's face is everything.

"Um, you look a little overwhelmed. How can I help?"

As I step into the penthouse, the muffled sobs from the back bedroom are audible. I lean toward my father and whisper, "Is everything all right? Did you guys have a fight?"

He pours us each a shot of whiskey and refuses to answer until we've downed the golden-amber liquid.

He wipes the corner of his mouth with the back of his hand. "Don't tell Mom. You know how she thinks anyone who drinks under pressure is an alcoholic."

His concise summary of Isadora Duncan's Alcoholics Anonymous-based judgment brings an instant chuckle. "Don't worry. I'm constantly having to tell her how I support her struggle and am glad to know she found a path to sobriety, but that since I'm not an alcoholic, I'm allowed to have wine in the apartment."

My father smiles, but his sharp inhale indicates more to this story.

I jut my thumb toward the continued weeping. "What's going on?"

"She just got a call from her mother. Her dad was

loading the suitcases into the car and suffered a heart attack. Amaryllis is pretty broken up about it. They'll know more tomorrow, but it could mean that her folks won't be able to attend the wedding."

"She's close to them?"

Jacob nods. "Yeah, they're one of those rare families that all get along and respect each other. Her father encouraged her to follow her dreams, and her mom approved of all of her decisions."

My father and I share the same startled expression before a wave of guilt washes over his features.

"Don't look like that, Dad. We both have baggage and we're doing everything we can to build a better relationship moving forward."

He refills our shot glasses. "I can't tell you what it means to me that you let me be a part of your life. I can't change the past, but I'm not gonna take a chance on messing up the future."

We clink our shot jiggers and round two goes down the hatch. A double-tap of the empty glasses on the countertop ends the ritual.

"I'll tell you the same thing that I tell Grams. All of our choices brought us to where we are now. I'd certainly like to go back and change a few things, but what if that meant I didn't end up in Pin Cherry Harbor? That would be the true tragedy."

My father smiles at me. "And then you wouldn't have met Sheriff Harper, right?"

His comment knocks the grin right off my face. "Yeah, about that." I fill him in on the unfortunate events of Bond-marathon movie night and push my empty shooter toward the bottle.

He gives us each half a shot more and offers some advice. "I'm not going to tell you how to live your life, Mitzy, but honesty is the only thing that makes my relationship with Amaryllis work. She's a brilliant attorney and a genuinely wonderful human being. She obviously has her pick of the litter. Why she would choose an ex-con with daddy issues and an interfering ghost for a mother-in-law is beyond me. The important thing is she knows everything about me, and she chose me anyway. You're selling yourself short if you don't give Erick the same opportunity."

Maybe it's the booze, or maybe my dad is actually making some sense, but I'm starting to consider the genuine possibility of having to let my guard all the way down. "I'll take it under advisement. I'm sure you didn't call me over here to endure the tale of my sorry love life. What does she need?"

He sighs and places both hands on the black granite countertop. "She needs her father to heal miraculously and arrive on our doorstep before the wedding, but since neither of us possess that kind of mojo, I was sort of hoping you'd try on your bridesmaid's dress and look at her hairstyle photos." His voice falters at the end and he swallows loudly.

"So you called me over here to be a sacrificial lamb? Real nice, Duncan."

He smiles sheepishly. "I'll definitely owe you one, world's best daughter."

I roll my eyes dramatically for his benefit. "Oh brother." Patting him on the shoulder, I shuffle down the hallway toward an uncertain fate. I ease the door open and lower my voice as I offer myself up. "Amaryllis? I don't want to intrude, but Dad thought I might be able to—"

Her tear-streaked face turns, and she grabs a handful of tissues. After an alarmingly forceful nose blowing, she wipes her eyes and pushes her hair back from her face. "Thank you, Mitzy. I'm sure my pops will be fine, and that's the most important part. It just breaks my heart to have him miss the wedding, you know?"

I really don't, but now is not the time to discuss my orphan-esque frame of reference and my difficulty in assimilating into family life. "I do. I was wondering if maybe you'd like to take your mind off things for a little while? Maybe I could try on the dress and you can decide what you want to do with my hair?" Fear coils around my spine as I offer these insane options.

"That's brilliant. I really appreciate the offer. It will definitely help to take my mind off things. Sitting here, crying and waiting for my phone to ring with an update is making me a nervous wreck." As she bustles into her closet, her voice carries an upbeat tone. "Let me grab the dress, and you can change in the bathroom if you're shy." She steps out with a beautiful garment bag and passes it to me.

"I'll just hop in there and get changed."

She rubs her hands together eagerly. "I can't wait to see you in it. It'll be perfect with your coloring." She leans over the bedside table and rifles through a stack of magazines. "You go change, and I'll find the pages I marked for possible hairdos. This is such fun. I'll grab a bottle of the wedding champagne and a couple glasses. No fitting is complete without bubbly! Thank you so much for coming over."

I step into the luxurious bathroom, close the door, and marvel at the classy appointments. Beautiful marble countertops, a double sink, a massive soaking tub, and a walk-in shower. My father may have temporarily turned his back on the Duncan fortune, but it seems as though he's coming back around.

Stripping off my winter layers, I toss everything to the floor. However, the pile of refuse looks out of place in such a fancy room. I'm compelled to fold all my clothes and place them in a neat stack between the sinks.

Unzipping the garment bag, I suck in a quick breath when I see the gorgeous red velvet dress. It's breathtaking. A fabulously ruched gown, with an off-the-shoulder neckline, a bow-back, and white faux-fur trim. A quick peek at the tag reveals it's a Badgley Mischka Couture creation. Ghost-ma would be thrilled. This promises to be quite the winter wonderland affair.

Removing the dress from the bag, I twirl it back and forth on the hanger. The overall look of the dress has a bit of a Victorian flair, and there's matching white faux-fur trim all around the bottom of the mermaid silhouette skirt. I unzip the dress and try it on.

The emphasis is on *try*. Because, despite the fully functioning zipper, there is no way in all of Christmastown that this dress is going to fit over my hips.

Before giving up completely, I attempt to put the whole contraption over my head. This results in half of a success. The top half. The waistline of the gown is too narrow, and the zipper refuses to come anywhere near closing over my ample backside.

Pacing in front of the mirror, I look a bit like a holiday tree skirt gone wrong. The last thing Amaryllis needs right now is another problem, but if I don't show her the dress, she'll think I don't approve.

Tossing my pride straight into the waste bin, I open the door and attempt a bit of comedy. "Well, you were right about the color. It definitely brings out the red in my cheeks."

Amaryllis looks up from the stack of magazines she's madly leafing through. Her initial expression of disappointment quickly transforms to mirth. "Oh dear. I'm so sorry! I didn't know your size. You look like such a tiny thing. I guess I underestimated those Duncan hips."

For a split second I'm offended, but then I realize she's complimenting a trait I share with my grandmother—and she did refer to me as a "tiny thing." "I always forget that you knew Isadora. You'll have to tell me what she was like before she got sick. I'm sure you dealt with her on more than one occasion. It seems her and Cal never quite got over each other."

Amaryllis clutches her stomach and stifles a guffaw. "Understatement of the century! Not that Isadora got over any of her ex-husbands, but she and Cal were such a pair. She definitely passed on her feisty streak. You and Jacob are a couple of tough customers."

I grab the edges of my hopelessly unzipped skirt and feign a curtsy. "I represent that remark."

We both laugh and she crosses the room to see how dire my situation truly is.

"Hmmmm." She sets down her crystal flute and taps her pearlescent fingernail on her bottom lip. Her head tilts back and forth as she surveys the catastrophe. "Try sucking in your stomach."

I oblige her request, and she tugs mercilessly on the zipper.

"It really is the hips, isn't it?"

I nod. "Unfortunately, I can't suck those in."

"No, of course not. You're perfect just the way you are. I'm the one who got the wrong size dress. There's just no time to replace it. I had to order it from a dressmaker in Chicago."

When she mentions dressmaker, I get a lovely idea. "Silas recently introduced me to a tailor in Broken Rock. Maybe he can make this work somehow."

Amaryllis throws her arms around me, and her icy hands send chills across my exposed back. "That's perfect! You take the dress home with you and get in touch with this tailor. Maybe he makes house calls. I'm sure he can figure something out. Perfect! Now that we've taken care of that, let's get down to business with this hairstyle."

Time loses all meaning as I sip champagne and watch Amaryllis page through magazine after magazine, folding corners over on a variety of hairdos that will never see the light of day on my head. Eventually my savior, I mean my dad, opens the door and offers a reprieve. "I was going to see if you girls wanted me to order— Wow, Mitzy. Is that how the dress is supposed to look?"

Crossing my arms over the velvet disaster, I narrow my gaze. "Do not test me."

His eyes widen, and he nods firmly. "Understood. Pizza, Chinese, or burgers?"

Amaryllis clutches my arm. "You decide. I'm too stressed out to think about food."

I wish I could say that I can relate to that concept in even a small way, but stress has the exact opposite effect on me. "Stellen and I have a pizza en route, but I'll call and have him bring it over. So, let's add some burgers, fries, and pin cherry pie à la mode to that, and we'll have a feast."

My father smiles and flashes his eyebrows. "That's my girl."

Amaryllis presses a hand to her chest. "Just get a cup of soup for me, Jacob. I have no appetite."

He nods, slips out of the room, and softly closes the door.

I hop off the bed and stride toward the bathroom. "No appetite. What a concept."

Her laughter follows me as I change back into my comfortable, zip-able clothes.

Stellen brings the pizza over and the four of us settle in for the evening. My dad attempts to get board games started, but Stellen and I insist on a movie marathon.

Since we're between holidays, we all agree on appropriately themed selections. We allow each person one choice.

Amaryllis chooses *Serendipity*. A solid pick.

My father goes with *Home Alone*, which technically only qualifies as a holiday movie because of the set decoration. If you ask me, it's more of a heist-gone-wrong/action film.

Stellen comes out of left field with a surprise pick of Bing Crosby's *White Christmas*.

"You've got some serious filmographic knowledge, buddy." I pat him on the back and he blushes.

"Not really. That one was my mom's favorite."

"Now it's your turn, Mitzy." My dad holds the remote firmly, poised to add my selection to the playlist.

"I have way too many favorite holiday movies to pick just one!"

"You're about to lose your right to choose. I'll give

you five seconds before I give your choice to Stellen." Jacob grins and gives my sidekick a "bro" nod.

"Fine, if you're going to be an absolute Grinch—"

My dad leans forward. "Is that your pick?"

"Absolutely not. My pick is *Elf*."

Stellen pumps his fist and Amaryllis gives a little "yes" as Dad types my selection into the search bar.

As I scan the faces illuminated by the light of the large-screen TV, my heart nearly bursts. This is what family should feel like. Acceptance. Support. Shared memories.

Amaryllis doesn't even stay awake long enough to make it to her pick, and as my broad-shouldered father scoops her up from the couch, he glances at his remaining guests. "Hey, you two wanna sleepover? I'm sure I can rustle up some snacks, and maybe we can think of a few more movies for the queue. What d'you say?"

I exchange a shrug with Stellen. "We don't have any other plans. Let's do it!"

He smiles but adds, "I just have to be at the clinic by eleven. Doc Ledo's going to let me observe a C-section on a basset hound."

Tossing a pillow at him, I laugh as he ducks out of the way. "You and I have very different ideas of entertainment, kid."

He snickers and tosses the pillow back.

I don't know how long Silas can keep Child Protective Services at bay, but I sure am enjoying my attempt to pay it forward.

CHAPTER 14

THE INSISTENT BUZZ of my cell phone yanks me out of my sorry excuse for dreamland and I reach toward the bedside table. Problem is, I'm not in my bed.

Instead of a wooden structure, my hand meets with thin air and I flop off the couch with a thud.

Stellen pops up from his pile of pillows on the floor. "Are you okay? Did you fall?"

"If there's one thing you should know about me, it's that I'm not a morning person. Now help me find my phone."

"On it."

We riffle through empty bags of chips, crisps, and crackers, but the phone is not on the coffee table.

"It's coming from your coat."

"Right!" I dive for the winter-wear-covered ottoman and dig into the pocket of my puffy jacket. "Silas. What would possess you to call at this hour?"

Unsurprisingly, he harrumphs and informs me that it is nearly nine in the morning.

"Point taken. Please continue. Stellen? Yeah, he's here. Done. Let me put it on speakerphone." I tap the speaker button and set the phone on the coffee table.

"Good morning, Mr. Jablonski. Did you sleep well?" Silas patiently awaits a response.

Stellen looks at me and scrunches up his face in confusion.

I wave my hand in a circular motion, trying to show that he has to go through the motions to get to the actual news. Somehow he understands.

"Good morning, Mr. Willoughby. I slept well. And you?"

I can almost hear Silas grinning on the other end of the phone. "A fine set of manners, young man. I apologize for disturbing you so early."

Rude. He didn't apologize for disturbing *me* so early.

"I've completed my examination of your father's estate. It pains me to report that he bore the burden of enormous debt. I'm sure you're aware of the high cost of medical bills surrounding your mother's illness."

Stellen nods. "Yeah. He complained about that a lot."

"Please do not infer this to be insensitive, but he had good reason. He had taken a second mortgage on the property and leveraged his accounts receivables to secure additional loans. In a word, your father was bankrupt."

Stellen sighs and shakes his head. "I wish he would've let me get a job. I don't think helping him with the taxidermy stuff really added anything to our bottom line."

"Perhaps we may never know the answer, but those critically endangered mounts that were stolen would have gone a long way toward pushing your father closer to being in the black."

"But we don't know who took them. What are we gonna do now?"

"Perhaps Mizithra can be of some assistance in locating them. Is it your intention for the Duncan-Moon Philanthropic Foundation to clear the Jablonski debts?"

I open my mouth to answer, but Stellen shakes his head vigorously. "No. No way. None of this is your fault. I want to sell the place. Any of the mounts that don't belong to clients, you can sell at auction, and you can list the property with a local realtor, or whatever."

My heart breaks a little, and I lean toward him. "Stellen, are you sure you want to do that? What about—your mom?"

He takes a deep breath and stares at the floor. "I have to move on. If I hang onto the house just because of the memories, what will it prove? I still want to go to veterinary school, and there's no guarantee that I would get to do my internship in Pin Cherry. I may as well sell the property now, rather than have you waste a bunch of your money trying to put out this dumpster fire of a situation."

I press my lips together firmly and nod my head. "I understand. It's your decision."

Silas clears his throat. "I shall begin the process. However, I believe it serves all of our interests to find the missing mounts."

"I agree. We'll get back to the bookshop and take another look at the murd—3 x 5 cards. You know, see if we're missing some connection."

Silas makes an odd sound. A combination between a groan and a squeak of surprise. "I was under the impression that my call had awakened you. How is it that you are not at the bookshop?"

"Oh, we're across the alley, at Dad's. I came over for some wedding stuff last night, and Dad asked me to stay for dinner. So, Stellen joined us and we had a holiday movie marathon."

Silas chuckles. "Most excellent. I shall be in touch regarding the progress of listing the property."

"Thanks. We'll check in later." I end the call and rub the sleep from my eyes.

"Let's grab our stuff and slip out. Are you all right with Fruity Puffs for breakfast?"

He grins as he places the throw pillows back on the sofa. "I prefer it."

"That's what I'm talking about."

. . .

After I drop Stellen at the animal hospital, my conscience and my mood ring stab me simultaneously. The handsome face of Sheriff Harper swirls within the black cabochon.

"Fine. Message received."

Am I ready for this? Let's see . . .

Big girl pants: check.

Heart on sleeve: check.

Terrified beyond reasonable doubt: check.

I drive to the sheriff's anyway and park on Main Street.

The station has returned to its normal, uninhabited state. The bullpen is empty, and Deputy Baird/Furious Monkeys is busily playing the app on her phone. All traces of tipsters and complainants have vanished.

"Good morning. What level are you on now?"

"I hit 225 this morning. It unlocks a whole new jungle and molten-lava-filled coconuts." Her eyes never leave the screen, but a smile briefly touches her lips.

"Nice work. Is he in?"

She nods, and if not for my extrasensory perception, I never would've noticed the concern that seeps from her aura.

Hurrying through the bullpen, I take a deep breath and step into his office.

His head whips up from the stack of papers that moments before held all of his attention. The initial smile is warm, but then he seems to remember that we're fighting. His jaw clenches and he leans back in his chair. "What brings you in, Moon?"

Taking a seat that wasn't offered, I paste on a weak smile. "I could say I'm here to get some information about the murder weapon, but that would be a lie, and I feel like our relationship is at the point where we should be honest with each other."

The tossing of his words back in his face brings an actual smile to his gorgeous full lips. "I see. So let me ask you again, why are you here?"

"May I close the door?"

The heat that races through his eyes sends my tummy into a tingly swirl. He picks up a pen, looks around, and sets it back on the desk. "Sure. I guess."

I slowly close the door and turn the lock. I'm unable to prevent the refrain from the Kenny Rogers' song from shooting through my head, but this is no time for jokes.

Returning to my seat, I take a ragged breath. "I need to tell you something. I know I should've told you sooner, and that's on me. And I know it sounds like an excuse, but it's not. It's not that I don't trust you, it's just kind of out there, and it scared me."

The crack in my voice brings down his shields. He leans forward, walks his fingers across the desk, and turns up his palm.

Looking at his hand, I smile. "I can hold your hand in a minute, but if I touch you right now I'm going to start crying, and totally lose my nerve."

He nods. "The hand's not going anywhere. What do you need to tell me, Moon?"

"I can see ghosts."

He chews his bottom lip and nods. "So, Isadora really is haunting the bookshop?"

"I don't think she'd call it haunting. She's managing her afterlife existence, while remaining at the bookshop."

He chuckles. "That sounds like something she'd say."

My throat tightens and I wish I could stop there. "It's not just Isadora. I see other ghosts too."

He nods, but I can sense his nervousness growing. That's all I can say today. If I tell him anything else, it will be too much. No point in giving him a drink from a fire hose on day one. I'll just leave it as *Sixth Sense* as possible for now, and maybe there'll be an opportunity in the future to mention the rest of my messed-up deal.

"Was there anything else?"

I gulp down some air. "To be perfectly honest, there is. But would it be all right to focus on the seeing ghosts thing today and you stop hating me?"

Before I have a chance to exhale, he is out of his chair and rounding the desk. He reaches down, scoops me close, and snuggles his face into my hair. "I could never hate you. Never. I was hurt, and it upset me that you didn't trust me. But there was never even a split second where I hated you."

I melt into his chest and wonder how long he'll let me stay in his arms.

A bang against the door, a mumbled curse, and a firm knock, answer the question for me.

Erick pulls away slightly and turns toward the door. "Who is it?"

"Deputy Paulsen. We brought that mechanic in for questioning."

"Thank you, Deputy. I'll be right out."

She mumbles something under her breath, and I hear her little feet stomp away.

"I guess I better get out of here."

Erick gives me a crooked grin. "Not quite yet." His warm lips meet mine, and the joy of acceptance floods over me as we kiss and make up.

Erick is the first to let the real world creep back in. "I better go talk to this witness. Should I stop by later?"

Ignoring my racing heart is impossible, but I can manage to get my breathing under control before I reply. "Sure. I just have to take care of some wedding stuff for Amaryllis, and *not* forget to pick up Stellen from the animal hospital, but other than that I have zero plans."

He chuckles and lets his hands linger on my waist. "Next time, don't wait so long to admit you were wrong."

My eyebrows hike upward and my mouth hangs open in speechless awe.

He leans in and kisses me softly. "You can tell me anything, Moon. Never forget that."

Pulling myself together, I nod slowly. "I'm working on it. Please be patient during construction. We are making a better Mitzy for you."

He smooths the hair back from my face and pulls away with regret. "See you later."

"Yeah. Sounds good, Sheriff."

He chuckles as he unlocks the door.

"Oh, wait. There's one more thing."

He turns and flashes me that irresistible crooked grin. "Oh yeah? And what would that be?"

I reach out a hand to steady myself on his old metal desk and my knees go all wiggly jiggly. "Would you come to my dad's wedding with me?"

His expression turns from playful to serious in a flash. "Twiggy didn't tell you?"

"Would it surprise you to know that she tells me almost nothing?"

He shakes his head and inhales sharply. "She asked me to run security for the Rare Books Loft. Apparently it has to be open during the ceremony and reception, and she doesn't want any riffraff making it upstairs."

I pull my hand from the desk and place it firmly on my curvy hip. "She did what? She hired my boyfriend to work at my dad's wedding?"

Tilting his head, he shrugs one shoulder. "To be fair, I think she was worried you'd be too stubborn to apologize, and she was attempting to force us into the same room."

A smile breaks through my frown. "Yeah, that definitely checks out. Well, you can tell her you're no longer working the wedding, since—"

He interrupts my rant with a muscular arm around my waist. "Because I'm working something else?"

My knees threaten to abandon me. "Because you are officially attending as my plus one." My voice goes up at least an octave and my eyelids are fluttering spastically.

He laughs heartily and exits the office.

I take a deep breath, smooth my hair, and walk out as though I wasn't just making out with the sheriff in his office.

Sadly, my acting isn't that great.

All heads turn in the bullpen, and deputies Johnson and Gilbert exchange unnecessary smirks.

Hustling out of the station, I jump into the Jeep and call Mr. Gustafson.

"Hello, it's Mitzy Moon."

He gushes about how wonderful it was to meet Isadora's granddaughter, and asks a series of rapid-fire questions about the suit, which I cannot answer.

"Actually, I was kind of hoping you might make a house call. I have a bridesmaid's dress that urgently needs to be altered, but I just don't have time to drive to Broken Rock this afternoon. I have to pick up my ward from his apprenticeship."

As he checks his day planner and mumbles various options, I chuckle inwardly at the grouping of words that just came out of my mouth. I really do sound a little like Bruce Wayne.

"Two o'clock? That would be perfect. And no pressure, but I'm going to need a miracle."

His laughter is light and airy, and he assures me he's never met an alteration he can't master.

Poor man. The hips of Mitzy Moon may be the end of his winning streak.

CHAPTER 15

Cut to —

"So, Mr. Gustafson took a million measurements and scooped the dress into his arms as though he was cradling a newborn babe, and assured me he'd have the dress back in my hands in time for the wedding."

Amaryllis wipes a hand across her brow and exhales loudly. "Whew, that is a load off my plate. Thank you so much for handling that. In fact, you're doing so wonderfully, I was hoping you might stop by the patisserie and make a couple of changes to my cake order."

This maid of honor gig is way harder than I anticipated. "Sure. No problem." Maybe I should make a recording on my phone with this patented answer that seems to fall out of my mouth every time my almost-stepmother makes a request.

"Oh, I almost forgot, Jacob and I wanted to talk to

you about something." She presses her hands to her mouth and squeezes her shoulders up in excitement.

For some reason my mood ring tingles briefly, but no image appears. A sense of unease settles over me, and I sincerely hope she's not about to tell me she's pregnant. Not that I have anything against her and my father having a family, but they will probably ask me to babysit, and I'm absolutely the worst with screaming infants. "Sure. No problem."

She ushers me to the living room and calls for Jacob to join us.

They snuggle together on the loveseat, and I fiddle with the zipper pull on one of her many throw pillows, as I struggle to find a comfortable position on the sofa.

"Your father and I have been talking." She gazes lovingly at my dad and he grips her small hand in his large one and gives it a gentle squeeze.

"By the way, I promise I wasn't eavesdropping, I was just coming out to make coffee, and I overheard."

My mind is racing, and I have no idea what she's talking about.

My father picks up the baton. "Amaryllis and I would like to buy the Jablonski property. I think we can convert it into a unique halfway house, and possibly a career-retraining center. Regardless, I know we can make great use of the property to support the restorative justice program."

"Oh, well, that's great. Silas will be thrilled to

learn that he sold the property before he even listed it."

They chuckle uncomfortably and exchange an unreadable glance.

"Why are you two so nervous? There's more isn't there?"

Amaryllis nods. "I want you to know that we would never dream of replacing you. You're Jacob's one-and-only daughter, and you're the second most important person in my life right now. I'm so looking forward to all of us being a family."

On the surface her comment seems positive, but why are the hairs on the back of my neck standing on end. "Yeah, I'm looking forward to us being a family too. I'm still waiting for the other shoe to drop, though."

My father chews his bottom lip, fidgets in his seat, and swallows audibly. "Everything Amaryllis said is exactly how I feel. Having you in my life and building our relationship is very important to me. I don't want you to think of this as anything that will take away from our bond."

I can't take it anymore. I toss the pillow onto the sofa next to me and lean forward. "Look, if you guys are having a baby, I'll deal with it. I'm not great with kids, but I'll figure out a way to get better. I'm not against having a halfling, or whatever, in our lives. But spill it. The suspense is killing me!"

Amaryllis throws one hand over her mouth and the other over her abdomen. My dad's mouth moves in a variety of interesting ways, but makes no audible sound.

Shrugging my shoulders, I lean back and wait for them to fill in the blanks.

She slowly peels her fingers away from her mouth and smiles. "I actually had a series of fibrous cysts removed when I was in my late twenties. I'm unable to have children of my own."

My face flushes a hideous shade of crimson. "I'm so sorry. That was so insensitive. The tension just got to me. Whatever your news is, I promise I'm happy about it."

Jacob slips an arm around her shoulders and smiles. "I'm glad to hear that, because we've decided to adopt Stellen."

Tears burst out of my eyes before I can say a single word.

Amaryllis lurches forward in a panic. "Oh dear, don't be upset, Mitzy. We promise it won't—"

I wave my hands frantically. "No. No. I'm not upset. These are happy tears. I was so worried about what would happen to him when the temporary custody ended. What kind of foster family he'd end up with? He's such a good kid, and he's had such a tough life. I just wanted him to catch a break, you know?"

Jacob and Amaryllis nod in unison. "That's exactly how we felt. We know he graduates in the spring, but we really want to make him a part of our family, and pay for his college, and whatever he needs."

All three of us are crying now. Even my stoic father has to wipe an errant tear from his square jaw.

"All right. Now that that's settled, I'm going to go pick up my brother from his job, and maybe we can all go out to dinner to celebrate?"

Amaryllis beams and my father bobs his head in support. "That's a great idea, Mitzy. Once again, world's best daughter."

As I step into the elevator, I suddenly remember that I already made plans with Erick. "Can Erick come? I'm not trying to be weird, but we just kinda made up today, and I was supposed to get together with him tonight—"

My dad's firm hand stops the elevator door from closing, and he grins. "We did say it was a family dinner, didn't we?"

My skin turns an unbecoming shade of red for the second time. "Easy, Dad. We're barely making it work as boyfriend/girlfriend. Let's not get the donkey ahead of the cart, or is it the cart ahead of the donkey?"

He pulls his hand away and his laughter is the last thing I hear as the doors press closed.

Despite being able to keep my psychic powers a secret, I'm actually kind of terrible at keeping my mouth shut about surprises. It's going to take every ounce of willpower I don't possess to keep me from blurting out the adoption news to Stellen. The best thing I can do is to get him talking about his day at work. Maybe then I'll never have a chance to accidentally spill the beans.

"Hey, little— Stellen." Strike one.

He hops in the Jeep and tosses me a teasing side-eye. "I'm almost as tall as you. I don't think you should refer to me as little Stellen."

My forced laughter hurts my own ears. "Yeah, right? How was your day?"

The entire drive home is occupied with detailed explanations of canine C-sections and newborn basset hounds. It's not exactly my cup of tea, but it absolutely keeps me from making any more slip-ups.

"We're going out to dinner tonight. So I don't know if you need a shower or anything. I kind of had conflicting engagements, so I scooped them all together."

He tilts his head. "Wait, did you and Erick make up?"

"Wow. That's some solid reading between the lines, bro." I'm counting that as strike two, even though he thinks I'm using "bro" as if I'm a cool kid.

"Sweet. I'll get changed and hang out with Pyewacket until dinner."

"Cool. I'll find Grams and have her pick out my outfit. She lives for that."

Stellen coughs and nearly chokes. "Good one."

I furrow my brow and stare at him for a moment. "Oh, right. Because she's dead. I wish I could say I meant it that way."

He heads off to take care of personal hygiene, and I hike up to the third floor of the printing museum.

Grams is trailing the ethereal fingers of one hand down Pyewacket's back and with the other she's fanning herself with a piece of paper.

"I didn't know ghosts got hot flashes. Everything all right?"

Her sparkling eyes drift lazily across the room and she grins stupidly. "I got a response to one of my query letters."

"By the way you're fanning yourself, I'd have to say it's not a rejection."

She drops the page, and it floats lazily toward the desk's surface. She zips over to me and she's positively glowing. "It's not. They want to see the first three chapters." Her glow sputters and she collapses into horizontal repose.

"That's good, isn't it? Why are you draping yourself across an invisible fainting couch?"

She sighs heavily and clutches her pearls. "They want something called a PDF. I've written everything longhand. I've written it all longhand, with a quill pen!" She rockets up to the ceiling and swirls around in a tizzy.

"Calm down, Emily Brontë. I'm sure Stellen can type it up in no time. He probably learned how to make PDF files when he was six. We'll get it handled, don't worry."

She throws glimmering limbs around me, and her energy pulses with gratitude. "I don't know what

I'd do without you, Mitzy. You're absolutely amazing."

"Careful, I may get full of myself, like some of my relatives."

She pulls back with a squeak. "Why you little—"

I turn tail and run down the stairs, taking them two at a time. For your information, it is impossible to outrun a ghost.

By the time I hit the first floor, she's already waiting for me with a bejeweled fist on each hip. "What's your plan now, smarty-pants?"

The fear in my eyes vanishes as I realize I hold the trump card. "If you promise to let this simmer until after the wedding, I'll tell you an enormous secret."

She practically drools. "You have yourself a deal, sweetie. Now, dish."

"Jacob and Amaryllis are going to adopt Stellen."

Her mouth moves, but the sound that reaches my ears is not her voice.

"They are? For reals?"

Strike three! I'm out.

I rush forward, and Ghost-ma spins on her axis. "Stellen!" We shout in unison.

He steps toward us. "Are you serious? Did they say that? That exact thing?"

I cover my face with my hand and flail my head in shame. "Can you at least pretend to be surprised at dinner? I'm sure I wasn't supposed to let the cat out of the bag."

"Ree-OW!" A warning punctuated by a threat.

The three of us share a good long laugh.

Stellen crouches and scratches between Pyewacket's tufted ears. "Don't worry, I won't let anyone put you in a bag." He looks up at me. "Did they mean like to just foster me, or were they legally going to adopt me?"

"They said adopt. But if you don't want them to—"

He rockets to his feet. "No. I do. It's just— So, you'll be my sister?"

"Big sister."

He smiles. "That's pretty lit."

"Show me your surprised face, little brother."

He widens his eyes and lets his jaw drop open foolishly.

Grams and I have a giggle fit. "That's next level. Let's dial it back about fifteen percent at dinner, and I think we can fool everyone."

"No problem, *sis*."

I roll my eyes. "Great. The list of my tormentors grows."

Grams and I head up to the apartment to fight over wardrobe, and Pyewacket curls up on one of the oak reading tables next to Stellen and an enormous reference book.

Unless my eyes deceive me, Stellen is studying feline anatomy, and Pyewacket is actually letting the boy stretch out his powerful cat-limbs and feel the joints and ligament attachment points. I must be dreaming.

Dinner goes off without a hitch, and Stellen's impressive performance wins the night.

Erick offers me a ride back to the bookshop. Jacob and Amaryllis invite Stellen to ride with them, so they can get better acquainted and discuss how he'd like to furnish his new room.

All is quiet back at the Bell, Book & Candle, and Erick and I take advantage of the alone time. We're rather busy canoodling on the couch when Grams bursts through the bookcase wall to announce she can't find Pyewacket.

I jump backward and embarrassment floods over me.

Erick sits very still and narrows his gaze. "Anything you'd like to tell me, Moon?"

"Yes. Yes, there is." I stand and walk toward the spot where Grams is hovering.

"Myrtle Isadora Johnson Linder Duncan Willamet Rogers, I'd like you to meet my boyfriend."

She curtsies and gushes about how wonderful he is. Thankfully, he can't see or hear any of that.

"She says it's nice to meet you." I gesture for him to walk toward me, and he steps forward with considerable trepidation coursing through his veins.

As he gets closer, I see the ghost-chills raise the flesh on his arms in tiny bumps.

"Do you feel that chill?"

He nods robotically.

"That's her." I wave my arm in a grandiose arc. "Erick Harper, please meet Ghost-ma."

He chuckles in spite of the tension. "Ghost-ma. That's clever."

"Thanks, I try."

"Nice to meet your ghost, Isadora." He offers a hand and Grams unwittingly grabs it and pumps out an over-eager greeting.

Erick jumps back and shakes his hand as though a rattler bit him. "Whoa! That's going to take some getting used to. Maybe warn me next time, okay?"

Grams prattles on about how he'll get used to it if he spends more time . . . blah, blah, blah.

I choose not to translate any of the rant. "Now that we're all acquainted, I'm sure you can see we were busy, Grams."

She vanishes in a huff, but the mood is lost.

The whole exchange proves too much for my virgin-to-the-paranormal boyfriend.

Erick retrieves his coat and runs a hand through his lovely loose blond bangs. "I better head out. I've got three more witnesses to question tomorrow, and two deputies combing through vehicle registration records for 1972 to 1985 truck models. Not to mention the long list of tire sales receipts. I'm anxious to see if any of those purchases match up with the trucks. If the taillight and the tires are connected to the same vehicle, that should point us toward the person or persons who broke into the taxidermy shed."

"Do you think there's a connection? Between Jablonski's murder and the theft?"

"Right now, we're treating them as separate crimes. Mr. Lee's fingerprints were all over that screwdriver the deputies located on the mountain, but it was from his toolbox. It stands to reason that the attacker would've worn gloves, so we'll need more to secure a case against him. But once we find out who's responsible for the theft, we may adjust our theory and our list of suspects."

"I don't have any wedding duties tomorrow, so hopefully I can lend a hand in the investigation?" I hate that my question comes out as more of a plea than a statement.

He slips an arm around my waist and pulls me close. "Can she hear me if I whisper? Nod once for yes and cough for no."

I clear my throat with a short cough. Even though I can't see her, she's probably eavesdropping, but he doesn't need to know that.

"Glad you're back on my team, Moon. I'm better at my job when you're around." He kisses my cheek softly, and as he pulls his lips away, my skin misses the warmth of his touch.

Grams pops into my visible spectrum and swirls up toward the ceiling. "I heard nothing. I saw nothing."

Her lies release an uncontrollable giggle-gulp in my throat.

Erick arches an eyebrow in concern.

"Don't worry, it's the ghost comedian, not you."

He shakes his head. "One day at a time, right? Don't get me wrong, I'm happy to be in the know, but I'm still a little unsettled to be in the inner circle."

I bat my eyelashes and grin. "We're happy to help you get settled."

My extrasensory perceptions catch a flash of desire, but he does the right thing and walks out of my apartment.

That man is too good for his own good.

CHAPTER 16

When the doorbell sounds announcing a visitor at the alleyway door, my heart skips a beat. I roll out of bed, shove my feet into my slippers, and throw a blanket around my shoulders, because I have no idea what I've done with my robe.

Turning off the alarm, I press one hand to the door and call out, "Erick? Is that you?"

The amused snicker of my new little brother deflates my expectations. "It's just me, Mitzy, and a half-frozen feline."

I shove the door open and Pyewacket stumbles through, followed by Stellen.

"Pyewacket, what were you doing outside? This is the serious heart of winter, son."

He turns his head, and his mouth opens, but he doesn't issue his usual snarky admonishing.

"Hey, what's wrong?" I kneel next to my fur baby

and hear his rough breathing. “He’s not breathing right. Should we take him to Doc Ledo?”

Stellen dives to my aid, running his hands over the cat and pressing his ear close to the caracal’s chest. “There’s a bloody discharge coming from his nose and his breathing is labored.”

Despite his condition, Pyewacket struggles to groan.

Continuing his examination, Stellen announces, “There’s something lodged in his throat.”

My chest constricts, and I blink hard to fight back the tears. “I’ll get the Jeep. You get a blanket.”

He grips my arm. “I don’t think there’s time.”

I gasp and press a hand to my mouth.

He gently strokes Pyewacket’s fur and whispers, “I can help you, buddy. Please don’t bite me.”

By way of agreement, Pyewacket lays his head back and closes his eyes.

Stellen expertly traces the feline’s esophagus, places a thumb in between his molars, and holds the dangerous jaw open wide. He reaches one finger in and carefully scoops deep into the animal’s throat.

To Pyewacket’s credit, he coughs and chokes, but he does not snap his dangerous fangs closed on his rescuer’s hand.

Stellen slowly withdraws the finger and then grips something between the forefinger and thumb. He extracts the item so delicately I forget he’s a sixteen-year-old apprentice, and not a fully licensed vet.

He stares at the object and looks up at me in wonderment. "It's a key. I think it's the key to my dad's desk."

I exhale the breath I didn't realize I was holding. "Put it in your pocket, and wrap this around Pye." Pulling the blanket from my shoulders, I toss it at him. "Give me two minutes to change and we're taking him to the hospital."

He nods in agreement. "Absolutely. Doc Ledo will need to make sure there's no serious damage to the esophagus."

I race upstairs with a speed that would make Usain Bolt jealous, whipping off my flannel pajamas as I go. In less than two minutes, I'm back downstairs fully dressed, keys in hand. "Let's hit it."

Stellen is already cradling Pye in his arms.

We hurry to the Jeep and I break all land-speed records as I race to the animal hospital.

Doc Ledo is manning the front desk, and when he sees Stellen rush in with a furry blanket-wrapped bundle, he rolls his wheelchair away from the counter and heads to one of the surgical rooms.

Stellen sounds like every paramedic on every hospital drama I've ever watched as he calls out vital statistics to the doctor as we hurry into the room.

He places my precious Pye on the table while Doc Ledo flips on lights and unwraps his instruments.

"You're sure you successfully removed the obstruction?"

"Yes, sir. I performed a finger sweep and removed it slowly to prevent any additional tissue damage."

"Good work." Doc Ledo gently strokes Pyewacket's head. "Look, buddy, you gotta be more careful with your lives. I think this brings your count down to five. I'm going to put you under, so I can run this scope down your throat. You won't feel a thing, and I promise to send you home by the end of the day."

Pyewacket slowly blinks his eyes, and even the casual observer would have to admit he understands what the doctor is telling him.

Ledo makes the injection and waits a moment for the sedative to kick in before passing instructions to his assistant.

"Turn on the monitor and hold the jaw securely while I feed the camera."

"Yes, sir."

Doc Ledo carefully threads the tiny camera down Pyewacket's throat and three pairs of eyes lock onto the monitor as we observe the key's damage.

"Was it a standard key?"

Stellen reaches into his pocket and shows the doctor. "It's more of a small skeleton key. I think it's the key to my dad's desk."

Doc Ledo finishes his examination of the esophagus and carefully retracts the camera. "Looks like superficial scratches, resulting in the blood you observed dried around the nasal cavity. No punctures. No serious lacerations." He lays the camera on a piece of blue surgical paper and removes his gloves.

Stellen closes Pyewacket's mouth and strokes his head.

"Excellent job, Stellen. That was quick thinking. You're going to make a wonderful veterinarian."

I step forward and stroke the soft fur under Pyewacket's chin. "Don't you ever scare me like that again, do you hear me, Robin Pyewacket Goodfellow?"

Stellen slips the key back in his pocket and gives me a minute with my furry companion.

He and Doc Ledo confer quietly on the far side of the surgical suite.

"What time should I come back to pick him up, Doc?"

He runs his finger down the chart and checks his watch. "We're open until 6:00 today. Why don't you come back just before closing? That'll give us time to let the sedative wear off and observe him for any difficulties eating or drinking."

"Take good care of him, all right, Stellen?"

"Hey, do you mind if we run out to my place real quick?"

"Sure, we can head out there. I'll bring you back after that errand and some breakfast. Sound good?"

He nods and checks out with Doc Ledo.

On the drive out to the Jablonski place, my mood ring sends an icy alert circling around my finger. An image of the key swirls within the black mists. "Is that key to the desk in the taxidermy shed?"

Stellen shakes his head. "No. That's what makes

me suspicious. It's the key to the desk in his room. I don't even know where he kept it. Pyewacket would've had to get all the way out to the property somehow. I'll check the pads of his feet for frostbite when I get back to the clinic."

"If he took that big a risk to get the key, it has to be important. I've never known Pye to bring me useless clues."

He rubs the key between his thumb and forefinger and his gaze trails out the window. As we pull down the driveway, fresh police tape cordons off the area under the tree and the entrance to the taxidermy shed. The house looks to be fair game. "I'll leave the car running, since this is just a quick trip. At least we'll have somewhere to warm up."

He nods and we head into the house.

Only one of the drawers on the desk is locked. Stellen employs the key, and we search through the contents together. Three folders containing birth certificates, a marriage certificate, a death certificate, and other important papers are the first things we encounter. But at the bottom of the drawer lies a journal.

Stellen pulls it out and runs his finger over the monogram. "Here. I don't think I can—"

"Understood." I take the journal and hold it in both hands. "Are you sure you want me to read it?"

He stands and walks toward the door. "I'm gonna go to the taxi shed and— I mean, maybe I'll just wait in the car. Go ahead and read some stuff, but I don't think I want to know."

"All right. If you change your mind, I'm happy to tell you what I find, or you might decide to read it yourself."

He shakes his head and hurries out of the house.

Any true fan of film and television knows that the important stuff is always written on the last few pages. While my curiosity yearns to devour the entire journal cover to cover, I'm hoping to find something useful in Mr. Jablonski's final entry.

Shockingly this movie trope does not disappoint.

And, BONUS! A folded piece of paper flutters toward the floor when I flip to the last page.

Retrieving the item, I gasp. "The page from the ledger!" Unfolding the sheet, I scan it carefully. No surprises . . . except—

A doodle in the margin catches my eye. "I wish he knew how much I missed you, Cryssie."

The thief didn't take the page to cover his or her tracks, Mr. Jablonski tore it out and secreted it away to hide his pain from his only son.

Tucking the page into the back of the journal, I hope that someday Stellen will feel safe enough to read these entries and come to a better understanding of his father's battle with love and duty. For now, I'll peruse this last entry to see if there is anything pertinent to the investigation.

December 25th

The holidays are always the hardest. I miss Crystal more than the boy will ever know. I'm doing my best to provide for him. Every day is such a struggle. I had hoped my work on the educational mounts of the endangered species would provide a means to send him to college, but today's discovery is just another nail in my coffin.

A chill runs down my spine as the eerie truth of his prediction rings in my head.

When I was going through the paperwork from the client, I noticed the same faint ink smudge on every one of the signatures from the U.S. Fish and Wildlife approval letters. Forgeries. Every one of 'em. These people are dealing in black-market animal trafficking, and now they pulled me into their web. I'll take the evidence to the sheriff tomorrow after the snocross, but there's almost no chance I come out of this unscathed. Just another way for me to let the boy down. He deserves better.

Letting the journal flop closed, I exhale sharply and get to my feet. This journal entry clearly points a finger at the traffickers and possibly takes Mr. Lee off the suspect list. I have to tell Stellen about this. He's the only one who might remember anything about the people that brought in those jobs.

"Is my boy all right?"

I'm not gonna lie, despite my now extensive experience with afterlife entities, I pee a little.

As I gaze at the floating apparition in the doorway, the brown curls and the loving green eyes are unmistakable. "Crystal?"

She surges toward me. "You can see me?"

I offer a tentative smile. "And hear you. You're Stellen's mom, right?"

Her aura glows like that of an angel, and she sighs with relief. "You know Stellen? I haven't seen him in the house for several days. I was so worried."

Since I find myself in a good news/bad news situation, I opt to start with the good news. "He's totally safe. He's been staying with me and I got him a job at the animal hospital with Doc Ledo."

"Oh, that's fantastic. I just hope Stanley can find a way to pay for college. I know he's been struggling with that."

"Crystal, I have some bad news too."

Her energy darkens as though someone is turning down the wick in an old-fashioned oil lamp. "Is it about Stanley? He's so hard on that boy. Did they have a fight? Is that why Stellen is staying with you?" She floats closer and stares at me with intense motherly concern. "Who are you?"

"First of all, let me introduce myself. I'm Mitzy Moon, Isadora Duncan's granddaughter. I inherited the bookshop on Main Street."

"Oh, I didn't know Isadora very well, only by reputation. She was a bit of a firebrand, if I remember correctly."

Covering my mouth with one hand, I chuckle. "That is accurate."

"But why is Stellen staying with you?"

"That's the bad news bit. Mr. Jablonski was murdered Friday night."

Her green eyes shift to darkest black and a serious avenging angel vibe fills the room. "Murdered? My Stanley? Who would do such a thing?"

"Take it easy, Crystal. We're investigating it. I lost my mom when I was young and I had to suffer through a series of mostly terrible foster homes, so when I heard the news about Stan, I came out here to offer Stellen a safe haven."

Her dark cloud immediately shifts to a warmer hue. "Thank you. But what happens now? He's all alone in the world . . . My sweet baby."

"The sheriff and I are investigating the murder, but in the meantime my father has offered to adopt Stellen and pay for his schooling."

I instantly recognize the sparkle of phantom tears as she clutches her chest and smiles. "Veterinary school? He's going to be a veterinarian?"

"If you ask me, he already is. He saved my caracal's life just this morning." She swirls around with the joy of a carousel horse and smiles at me with so much love it nearly breaks my heart. "Oh, my stellar Stellen! I always knew he was special. It broke my heart to have to leave before I got to see him grow up."

"Well, you did everything right, Crystal. He's a kind, thoughtful, generous boy, with a great sense of humor. My father and his new wife will take great care of him, and I promise you, I'll never let anything bad happen to him."

The apparition flickers, and a warm glow spreads out from her heart. "What's happening? I feel—"

Not that I'm an expert, but I've got more experience than your average human. "I think you're crossing over, Crystal. I think your love for Stellen and your powerful bond of responsibility kept you here."

The sparkles are growing more transparent. "Stanley was so broken after I passed away. As the cancer consumed me, I could see him losing a little more of himself each day. I just couldn't leave Stellen alone. He needed a mother's love."

"And you gave it to him. He told me about you. It was your visits that got him through the darkest days. But it's time for you to release your hold. To let him go, and for you to find the happiness you deserve on the other side of the veil."

She's barely more than a golden haze, and her voice echoes from the ether. "You'll tell him I love him? Can you keep him safe?"

"Absolutely. Rest in peace, Crystal."

And she's gone.

The silence in the room is heavy and final. Part of

me feels relief that she's no longer trapped between the worlds, but a little part of me feels sadness for Stellen—that he won't see her again.

Tucking the journal under my arm, I wipe my tears and march downstairs to share the wonderful news with my ward.

A foul frigid wind has picked up speed while I was indoors, and as soon as I open the front door, loose snow swirls violently around me, obscuring my vision.

Ducking my head, and pulling my coat tight around my neck, I run for the Jeep.

And I keep running.

And as the gust of wind abates, I turn 360 degrees and stop in a trance of confusion.

"Where's the Jeep?"

CHAPTER 17

THE RING ON MY LEFT HAND BURNS, but I'm in no mood to risk frostbite and take off my mitten. No need. A clairvoyant mini-movie impacts me like a giant snowball.

The hairs on the back of my neck tingle. I see a large black SUV. It stops in front of the taxidermy shed, but the occupants must see the police tape. They stomp on the accelerator and spray a rooster tail of snow as they spin the vehicle around and tear back down the driveway.

Unfortunately, the commotion grabbed Stellen's attention, and he hopped in the driver's seat of my vehicle and gave chase.

Perfect! Not more than thirty seconds ago I promised his mother's ghost that I would take care of him and that nothing bad would happen, and now he's in pursuit of some suspected murderers!

Pulling out my phone, I dial the sheriff's station.

"Please put me through to Sheriff Harper. It's urgent!"

The next voice I hear is Erick's, and I relay the events as though I witnessed them firsthand rather than psychically.

He promises to head out to the property immediately and wants me to wait inside where it's warmer.

"Copy that."

I end the call and instantly disobey his orders.

First stop the wounded pine tree. I risk pulling off my mitten and lay my hand against the scar, in hopes of a message. Unfortunately, the worry over Stellen's safety has flipped my powers into the off position.

Fine. Sheriff Harper wins. I'll wait inside.

Maybe I better call Silas and see if he has any ideas.

I re-enter the Jablonski home, lay my phone on the kitchen counter, and place the call via speakerphone, while I brew some coffee.

"Good morning, Mizithra. How may I be of assistance?"

"I've already called the sheriff, but Stellen took my Jeep and is in pursuit of possibly the murderer and maybe an illegal animal trafficker. Assuming they're one and the same."

Silas harrumphs. "That young man is too industrious. I must say, I do hope he's unsuccessful."

"What? You're wishing him ill?"

"Not at all. I am simply of the mind that catching his quarry would be the worst outcome."

"Oh, I agree." I sip my java and ponder. "What should we do?"

"I am perusing a new title that Twiggy acquired. It is extremely enlightening. I may temporarily shelve it next to *Saducismus Triumphatus*, while I complete my research. Does that suit you?"

"Sure. I don't care where you put the book, Silas. What are we going to do about Stellen?"

Holding the warm mug of coffee in both hands, to soak up as much heat as possible, I take another gulp as I wait for Silas to reply.

A second call beeps in. "Erick is calling. I've got to go."

Without waiting for Silas to acknowledge, I end his call and accept Erick's. "It's Mitzy. What's wrong?"

"In the grand scheme of things, I have to say it's more right than wrong."

"There's no time for riddles, Harper. What's going on?"

"Stellen lost control of the vehicle and slid off the road by that dilapidated silo. He's fine. Your Jeep is fine. But whoever was in the late model Escalade got away."

I breathe a huge sigh of relief. "Is there more?"

Erick chuckles. "Is that a hunch?"

"Seriously!" I nearly spill my coffee as I make an impatient gesticulation.

"Yeah, there's more. He followed them long enough to get a license plate. I have Deputy Gilbert on that, and Johnson is on his way out with the tow truck. Stellen's with me, and we're coming to pick you up."

"That's a relief."

Ending the call, I gulp down a little more coffee and wash out the mug. I know Crystal crossed over, but it feels wrong to leave a dirty dish in such a kind woman's home.

Peering out the front window, I see the cruiser rolling down the drive. I run outside and hop in the passenger seat. Stellen's in the back, and I take advantage of the situation. "Did you arrest him for joyriding, Sheriff?"

Stellen squeaks out a protest.

Erick laughs. "Not at all. I deputized him."

"Rude." I click my tongue and cross my arms.

Stellen leans forward and grips his fingers through the grate dividing the rear of the vehicle from the front. "Do you think those were the murderers?"

Erick chews his lip, deep in thought, so I field the question.

"I think they're connected to the animal trafficking. I know you said you didn't want to read your dad's journal, but I think you'll want to know that he figured out the U.S. Fish and Wildlife Service letters were forged. Whoever hired him to mount those critically endangered species was definitely running a black-market operation. He was going to bring the evidence to the sheriff, but died before he had a chance. Maybe they killed him, but I don't think they stole the mounts. If they did, they'd have no reason to come back. Right?"

Erick nods and rubs a thumb along his jaw. "Makes sense. If they killed Stan and stole the mounts, why return to the scene of the crime?"

Stellen's fingers slip out of the grating and he leans back. "It wasn't the same vehicle. That Escalade was a 2020 model and had current year tires. The taillight and the track by the tree—that's from an older truck. I'm certain."

Harper taps his thumb on the steering wheel. "As soon as Gilbert runs those plates, we'll bring 'em in. For now, let me get the two of you safely back to the bookshop. Johnson will have the tow truck drop your Jeep off in no time."

He stops the cruiser by the front of the store.

I hop out with the journal and open the rear door for Stellen. "Erick, this is Stan's journal. The last entry mentions the traffickers and there's a page from his ledger folded up in the back that shows the details of the jobs. I think we'd like the journal back though. Can you make sure nothing happens to it?"

Erick respectfully takes the journal, ducks down, and looks at Stellen. "I'll make sure that we only use what's necessary to shut these traffickers down. You have my word."

Stellen nods stiffly, and we step into the bookshop as the sheriff drives away.

The interior of the store is a flurry of activity, but

it isn't the wedding preparation that catches my attention.

"I told you once, kid. She ain't here." Twiggy's voice carries the weight of authority with a sharp edge.

"Look, biker chick, I have to talk to Mitzy. She'll know what to do."

Before Twiggy can body slam our visitor, I round the corner and wave my hands as though they're white flags. "Take it down a notch, everyone. I'm here. How can I help?"

Bristol spins toward me, her face a mask of concern and admiration.

Twiggy sniffs, shakes her grey pixie cut, and stomps into the back room.

"Mitzy! Who's the old bag? I was trying to tell her how important—"

Eager to protect this girl from Twiggy's wrath. I hasten to change the subject. "Let's not rehash it, Bristol. I'm here now. Did you need something?"

Stellen leans in and whispers, "I'll see if Twiggy can take me to the clinic."

"Good idea. I'll pick you and Pyewacket up later."

Bristol's mouth tightens into a fine line, and her eyes widen. "Is Pyewacket okay? He's part of the team, right? Will you even be able to solve this case without him?"

Ignoring her boisterous fangirl rant, I attempt to

drag her back on track. "Is there something I can do for you?"

"Yeah. Right. Crank didn't think I should tell you, but we haven't seen Eli since Saturday morning. He was acting super bajiggity at the race, and then he ghosted us."

It pleases me that I know bajiggity means nervous, upset, and anxious. I dive right in. "What kind of vehicle does he drive?"

She scrunches up her mouth and shrugs. "Some old '79 truck. I don't know. We call it the POC on wheels."

"And which one of you overheard coach Jablonski tendering his resignation from the Trey Lee team?"

She flicks the stud in her tongue back and forth over her lower teeth and her eyes dart up and to the left. "Well, I think AJ is the one who told Crank, and then Crank told me, but he didn't want me to tell you. But I told him that if you were gonna solve the case, you needed help—"

"So AJ overheard the conversation?"

"Maybe. Him and Eli are tight. Like, it's the four of us, but it's the two of them and then the four of us."

"So maybe Eli overheard the conversation?"

"Sure. Could be."

I slide my phone out and tap Erick's number as I toss her one more question. "And where does Eli live?"

She gives me the address, and as soon as Erick gets on the phone I fill him in. “I think if you check vehicle registration you’ll find that Eli McGrail drives a 1979 Ford pickup. And if you send a deputy over to his address at County Road 13 Box number 425, you’ll also find that truck has a broken taillight. And more than likely there will be some critically endangered species mounts stashed in his garage.”

Erick sighs loudly and comments about my uncanny hunches before he ends the call to follow up on my lead.

“Bristol, if Coach Jablonski switched to team Priest, what would that mean for Eli?”

“Um, like, Eli is the number three seed, you know? So even though he doesn’t win, he podiums at almost every race and makes some decent coin. Know what I mean?”

“I think I do. But what would happen if Freddy Priest got a coach like Jawbone?”

“Pretty likely that he’d jump from number four seed to at least number two in a couple of races. Jawbone was just that good. A magician.”

“So that would push Eli off the podium, most likely permanently, right?”

“For sure. Plus Eli’s hella moody. Once he starts losing, he gets super down. He might even drop out of the top ten. He’d lose his sponsors . . . It’d be major.”

“Thanks, Bristol. You did the right thing by

coming to me. I'll let Twiggy know, and thanks for the information."

She bobs her head and the little pom-poms at the end of the arms of her jester hat bounce up and down. "No doubt. No doubt. So, you think you got this one figured?"

I nod my head sadly. "Unfortunately, I think so."

"Sweet. I'll head out and let you wrap things up, you know?" She bows her head a couple more times. "If it's not too much trouble, like, can you mention to the paper, or whatever, how I helped?"

"If anyone asks to interview me, I will absolutely mention your help."

"Sweet. I'll put that in the blog."

"Great. Well, I better get going. I've got some stuff to finish before I pick up Pyewacket."

She stops in her tracks and turns. "Oh, right. Is he gonna be okay? Was he, like, hurt in the line of duty?"

It takes a powerful amount of self-restraint to keep from rolling my eyes. "In a manner of speaking, yes. He delivered a key piece of evidence though." The secret pun amuses me.

Bristol makes a little fist and pulls it down as she lifts her knee. "Sweet. That cat rules." She waves and stalks out the front door.

Fan clubs. Stepbrothers. Stepmothers. What is happening in my life?

CHAPTER 18

SOMETIMES THE QUIET before the storm is more unsettling than the storm itself. I swallow all of my theories and hypotheses and run out the front door toward the station. Once inside, I find there's no deputy at the front desk, and the bullpen is empty. Marching through the silence, I pause in Erick's doorway.

He looks up and shakes his head. "You were right about everything. I don't know how you do it, Moon? Paulsen ended up taking the call, and she's bringing McGrail in now. Gilbert and Johnson had to run that black SUV off the road, and one of the occupants pulled a gun. Johnson was able to de-escalate the situation and bring the perpetrators into custody without having to fire his weapon. That's always a good day, as far as I'm concerned."

Sinking onto one of the uncomfortable wooden

chairs, I cross my legs and make little circles with my foot. "Eli just turned eighteen, right?"

"Yeah, why?"

"I guess it doesn't matter. I mean, he killed someone."

Erick leans forward. "Who told you that?"

"What do you mean?"

"Well, Paulsen said he started confessing as soon as she put him in handcuffs, and despite the fact that she read him his Miranda warning, he wouldn't shut up. But how do you know?"

"It's a long story. Honestly, I'm not trying to hide anything. I never really suspected Mr. Lee, and the body dump theory didn't ring true for me. Even if there wasn't much blood, moving a body across the snow . . . I just couldn't figure out how the killer did it."

He leans back and taps the eraser of his pencil on the desk. "They groom the tracks every morning before the event. So if the plow driver didn't see the blood, it could have easily been scraped to the side. That part never concerned me. The precision of the wound was what made Mr. Lee such a strong suspect."

"True. Do you think Eli knew what he was doing?"

Paulsen's gruff voice echoes down the hallway as she yanks her prisoner toward Interrogation Room Two.

Erick glances across the desk and tilts his head. "Looks like we're about to find out."

She sticks her head in the doorway. "He's all yours, Sheriff. Shouldn't be too difficult to get him to sign a confession. He's been runnin' his mouth since I threw him in the back of the cruiser."

"Thanks, Paulsen. Can you follow up with Johnson and Gilbert? They might need some help with those traffickers and the warrant."

"10-4."

He walks around the desk, sighs, and heads across the hallway to question the suspect.

I take a beat before slipping into the observation room.

Eli is a disaster. His dark hair is greasy and unkempt, purple-black bags hang beneath his sunken eyes, and his sallow skin screams insomnia. The only thing more heartbreaking than his appearance is his story.

Sheriff Harper presses record on the device and begins the interview. "Please state your name."

The young man's hands shake, and he digs nervously at invisible dirt under his fingernails. "Elijah McGrail."

Once the particulars are on the record, the interrogation begins in earnest. "Mr. McGrail, did you kill Stanley Jablonski?"

"I guess. I don't know what happened. I was up in the pit tent, tweaking some settings on my sled.

They were arguing so loud, I couldn't ignore it, you know?"

Erick nods.

"Then Jawbone got on his sled and took off, and Lee's dad stormed out." He stops and rubs his throat with his left hand. "Can I get some water, man?"

Harper places the request over the radio, and Paulsen delivers a cup of agua.

"Anything else, Sheriff? Is he trying to lawyer up?"

Erick slides the cup of water toward the prisoner. "He's declined to have counsel present. Thanks, Paulsen."

She shrugs at the dismissive tone, but exits the interrogation room.

Eli drains the cup of water in one go. "I didn't mean to kill him."

The sheriff leans forward. "Eli, you took a screwdriver from Mr. Lee's toolbox. That indicates premeditation. Crimes of passion and weapons of opportunity go out the window when evidence of a plan is uncovered. Trying to frame Mr. Lee is evidence of a plan."

"Well, they were arguing, you know? I . . . I just can't afford to lose. My dad's out of work, my mom's homebound . . . My prize money was keeping us afloat. If Jawbone coaches Freddy Priest, I'm screwed. If I lose my sponsors, we lose everything."

The word "sponsors" tickles something in my memory, and I activate a psychic instant replay. The helmet. When I first met Eli, I noticed his helmet was covered with sponsor emblems, but now that I can slow down the image and focus on each one, a new detail emerges. A World Wildlife Fund sticker and two PETA decals. Eli is an animal rights activist.

Erick presses to get the interrogation back on track. "Tell me what happened after you picked up the screwdriver."

Eli's eyes seem to glaze over as he relives the events of Friday night. He waited until Jawbone parked his sled at the bottom of the drag tracks and started his inspection on foot.

"He had his helmet on, so he didn't hear me walking up behind him. As I got closer, I realized what a big guy he was. I figured he'd turn and see me. I thought he might kill me. I feared for my life."

"Mr. McGrail, I believe it's dishonest to admit to premeditation of murder and then try to blame the victim for the crime. Please continue describing the events that occurred after you approached Mr. Jablonski on the drag track."

Eli wrings his hands and struggles to get the last drops of liquid from the bottom of the cup. "I panicked. Like I said, I thought he might turn and try something, you know? So I just held up the screwdriver and lunged at him. It slipped in right under the back of the helmet and . . ."

The sheriff draws out the last few details, and Eli admits to shoving Jablonski off the side of the track, cleaning up any blood from the snow, and making sure the body was well covered. He also admits to moving Jablonski's sled into the tent and placing the murder weapon back into Mr. Lee's toolbox. He claims it wasn't to create a frame up, but Sheriff Harper doesn't seem to buy what he's selling.

"One last thing." Erick sighs and leans back. "Why break into the taxidermy shed?"

Eli's jaw clenches and I can feel waves of righteous indignation roll off him. "I always hated that he stuffed those poor animals. After Jawbone's body was discovered, I panicked. I thought if I staged a break-in it would muddy the waters. And, like, as soon as I saw the condor and stuff . . . I couldn't let anyone profit off them, you know?"

Sheriff Harper shakes his head. "Mr. McGrail, I'm placing you under arrest on suspicion of first-degree murder." Erick offers him another opportunity to call an attorney, but Eli refuses. Part of him continues to defend his actions as some form of self-defense, while the other half begs to be punished for a crime he can't believe he committed.

The satisfaction of catching the killer is missing for me. Eli is only a couple of years older than Stellen. I don't want to let myself think about it.

Life is full of disparity. I'm sorry he put himself in that situation, and that actions have consequences, and too often people seem to forget that.

Erick hands off the prisoner to Paulsen and she marches him back to the holding cells.

The handle on the observation room door twists,

and the handsome sheriff steps through. "What a sad story, eh?"

I nod my agreement and sigh. "It's always hard when the bad guy isn't all that bad."

"Yeah. Misguided. Suffering from poor judgment. But definitely not malevolent. Makes me double glad you and your dad stepped in to help Stellen. It's about the best we could have hoped for in a pretty terrible situation."

I hold out my hand and wiggle my fingers.

Erick steps forward, takes my hand, and pulls me close. "Thanks for your help on the case."

"That's what I do. What about the traffickers?"

"That's gonna take some unraveling. We're waiting on a second, more inclusive warrant, but Johnson said initial inspection of the property revealed several more animals, and a ton of cash. We're hoping to scare them into testifying against the rest of the ring. Obviously they didn't pull a hawksbill sea turtle out of the great lake. Someone's getting these animals into the country, and into their hands. I'm happy to shut down this end of the operation, but I'd be much happier to destroy the entire thing."

"Yeah, that would be fantastic. Hey, what's the update on Trey? I heard he could possibly have been paralyzed or suffered brain damage? Is that true?"

He pushes me away slightly and smiles down at me. "Oh, you heard that, did you? Do you happen to remember where you were or who you heard that from, Miss Moon?"

Gulp. "I plead the fifth."

He squeezes me close and kisses me firmly. "You may need more than amendments to protect you."

Tingles from head to toe. Weak knees. Inability to catch a breath.

He whispers in my ear. "Sounds like your *ward* is moving into new digs across the alley. Does that mean you'll be all by your lonesome in that apartment?"

And I'm dead.

His strong arms keep me from melting into a puddle of love-struck goo.

"I have to focus on this wedding. Don't try to distract me, or whatever."

"Fair enough. But the wedding will be over and done with Thursday night. You'd better start working on a new set of excuses."

"I just remembered, I have a dress fitting." Pulling away unceremoniously, I rush out of the observation room and steady myself on the wall.

There had better be some real-life magic in New Year's resolutions, because I'm running out of ways to resist that utterly irresistible man.

Running back toward my bookshop, I wish I had a dress fitting. The probability of Mr. Gustafson having the necessary magicks to squeeze these hips into that piece of couture is low. I best run over to wedding central and see if there's anything I can do for the bride. When the elevator doors open on the first floor, my new stepbrother looks as shocked to see me as I am to see him.

"Hey, I was just coming to your place."

I take a magnanimous bow. "Great minds think alike. What d'you need, buddy?"

He chews mercilessly on the edge of his fingernail and steps into the marble elevator lobby. "Um, do you think that . . . Would it be weird . . .?"

Finally, my resurrected psychic senses and my mood ring unite. I gaze down at the tingling image and grab the clairsentient message from thin air. "Would you like to go visit Trey Lee in the hospital?"

For a moment his face is blank of all expression, and then he tilts his head. "Cool trick. Can you teach me?"

"It's hardly a trick, young man." We share a little chuckle, and for a moment I have a glimpse of what it must be like to be Silas Willoughby. "Seriously, do you want to go?"

"Yeah. If you think it's okay."

"It's fine. Follow me to the Moonmobile."

I hear him snickering behind me as we cross the lobby of the empty foundation, now closed for the holidays.

My ring tingles warmly on my left hand, and I flick my eyes over in time to catch a glimpse of Crystal floating in the glassy mists as we load into the Jeep. Deep breaths. Deep breaths. "Hey, something happened out at your house, you know, when you took off in my vehicle."

He looks down at his feet. "Sorry about that. It was a stupid thing to do. I'm glad your Jeep wasn't trashed."

This amazing kid never ceases to amaze. "No sweat. That's not what I was talking about. When you left me alone to read the journal . . . she appeared."

His head whip pans my direction, and his expression is a heartbreaking mashup of hope and loss. "I missed seeing my mom? Can we go back out there? Do you think she'd appear again?"

Shaking my head, I struggle to stuff the emotions and speak. "I don't think she'll be making any more visits. She finally crossed over."

He chokes on his emotions and wipes his nose with the back of his hand. "Why?"

"I told her about your father's death and our friendship, and the adoption. She seemed so happy that you were surrounded by people who cared about you."

"But I don't want her to cross over. I have so much to tell her."

"She had a message for you too."

His tear-streaked face turns toward me, and I have to pull to the side of the street. "I told her about your apprenticeship and plans for vet school, and how you saved Pye. She called you her stellar Stellen. She said she always knew you were special." My fight with my own tears fails, and I take a minute to steady my voice. "Most importantly, she said it broke her heart to have to leave before she got to see you grow up. I think my update brought her the comfort she needed to get closure."

He sobs into his hands and sniffles. "I miss her so much."

"I understand. I'll tell you what Silas told me. We have to speak the names of the dead. If we stop talking about them, that's when they're truly forgotten. As long as you remember Crystal and tell her stories, she'll live on through you. It's hard, and some days it really sucks, but you're strong, like me. We'll get through it together, all right, Bro-seph?"

My Jack Black reference tickles his funny bone, and he smiles through the tears. "Thanks for telling me." He exhales loudly and presses his hands on his thighs. "Crystal was the best mom. The best, you know?"

"I know." Reaching over, I place my hand on his and give him a reassuring squeeze. I pull back onto Gunnison and continue toward the hospital.

"Tomorrow's the big wedding, right?"

And I thought I had cornered the market on "left field" questions. I let the question hang for a moment. "Yeah. I'm thrilled for my dad. He's been through a lot."

Stellen draws a tic-tac-toe on the frost inside the window. "Seems like Amaryllis really cares about him. Some people are just lucky in love, you know?"

Oh, the days of teenage angst. So near, and yet so far. "Don't worry, bro. High school is the last place on earth you should worry about fitting in. You're destined to be a great-looking guy, and you already have a heart of gold. That's a pretty irresistible combination."

His finger delicately connects the diagonal row of "Xs" and he smirks. "Like Sheriff Harper?"

Unexpectedly blushing a deep scarlet, I clear my throat and briefly choke. "Mind your own business. How can you already be this good at being an annoying little brother?"

He shrugs. "I got skills."

We struggle to stifle our giggles and strike the appropriate mood as we stroll into the hospital to request directions to Trey's room.

Outside the door of the private recovery room, Stellen and I exchange a shrug. Mr. Lee is asleep in a chair next to the bed, and Mrs. Lee is whispering softly into her phone.

Stellen shakes his head. "I don't want to interrupt."

"Hey, the worst they can say is no. I'll handle it." Knocking softly on the door, I offer a friendly smile through the narrow pane of glass.

Mrs. Lee fumbles with her phone, ends the call, and walks toward the door. "Hi, are you friends of Trey?"

I smile and offer my hand. "I'm Mitzy Moon, and this is Stellen Jablonski."

The color drains from her face and she tilts her

head in that all-too-predictable way. "Oh dear, I'm so sorry for your loss."

Stellen swallows and struggles to find his voice. "Thanks. My dad was really proud of Trey. I just wanted to see if he was okay."

She waves us in, and we stand awkwardly at the end of the boy's bed.

"My husband's been here twenty-four hours a day since the accident. Well, except—Never mind."

Gently placing my hand on her arm, I offer a bit of good news. "They've arrested Eli McGrail for Stan Jablonski's murder. I'm so sorry Mr. Lee was ever a suspect."

She breathes a tremendous sigh of relief and tears leak from the corners of her eyes. "Thank God." She looks over at Stellen and leans toward me to whisper, "What's going to happen to him? I remember when his mother passed away. He's all alone, isn't he?"

I give her a brief recap of the best-case-scenario outcome for Stellen. She's pleased with the news.

"Two days ago, the doctor told us Trey had suffered a serious spinal injury. He said the helmet had protected him from any brain damage, but the prognosis for him ever walking again was in the single digits."

Pressing my hand to my heart, I exhale as Stellen moves closer to the sleeping boy.

"The lawyer from the hospital came and wanted us to sign a bunch of papers. Such a strange little man and so bossy."

The hairs on the back of my neck tingle. "He came to your hospital room?"

"He gave me a huge stack of papers and waved us outside to review them. For some reason, I didn't feel like I could say no to him."

My heart is already swelling with gratitude, because, psychic or not, I am predicting the end of her story.

"When we came back in, he actually had his hands on Trey. My husband was furious. The man completely ignored us. He collected the papers and disappeared. Don't you think that's strange?"

"Very strange. And how is Trey doing today?"

She rubs her hand across her forehead and sighs. "The doctors can't explain it. They came in to run the usual tests, and Trey moved his feet." Mrs. Lee covers her mouth with her hand, and I pat her back reassuringly.

"That's wonderful. I'm sure he'll make a full recovery."

She nods and smiles. "I know. At first the doctor was speechless, but eventually he said the same thing. Just that miraculous healing thing that kids have, I guess. I'm not going to ask any questions. If Trey couldn't race, I have no—"

Trey opens his eyes and looks up at Stellen. "Hey, man. What's up?"

Stellen shrugs and looks at the floor. "Just making sure you're gonna get back on your sled, you know?"

Trey smiles, but is unable to nod his head in the

cervical brace. "Tell your dad not to worry. I'll be back next season, and I'm gonna win the championship for him."

Stellen nibbles his fingernail and nods. "Totally, dude. Totally." His tender green eyes search me out, and I answer with a subtle nod.

"Thank you for taking the time to see us, Mrs. Lee. Stellen and I really should get going."

She sniffles and smiles at Stellen. "Thank you for stopping by. He's on a lot of medication, but I'll make sure to remind him you were here."

We smile politely and make our way out.

As we drive back to Stellen's new home, he places a tentative hand on my shoulder. "Thanks. I don't know why, but somehow it makes me feel better to know that he's going to be okay."

I wish I could tell him the role I suspect Silas Willoughby played in the boy's recovery, but that's not my secret to tell. "Me too. Me too."

CHAPTER 19

THE BOOKSHOP HAS BEEN TRANSFORMED into a magical fantasy. All the oak tables are carefully repositioned down the curving arms of the mezzanine and camouflaged with layers of white tulle and shimmering fairy lights. Despite Twiggy's endless protestations, Amaryllis and I eventually convinced her to give in to the wedding juggernaut. Crisp rows of seating fill the first floor, and the small dais, which we use for fundraisers and author events, has been completely transformed with a delicate snowflake-and-fairy-light-encrusted archway and mountains of fake snow.

My film school experience actually came in handy when it was time to devise a method of delivering an indoor cascade of snowflakes following the completion of the vows. Stellen used his father's huge network of suppliers to procure the realistic-looking plastic snowflakes and helped me wire the fancy delivery tubes to the ceiling. My natural clumsiness would have certainly ended with my death or severe injury, whereas the nimble young lad scurried up ladders and balanced precariously three stories in the air, with no sign of fear. Miraculously, everything was in place in time for the rehearsal.

To be clear, the rehearsal was not without its hiccups.

Grams was entirely unwilling to abide by the rules I'd set, and she kept popping in to weep uncontrollably at the most inconvenient times. Stellen's poker face is improving, but he's still rather excited by his ability to see ghosts, and his frequent outbursts and pointing derailed the proceedings multiple times. The confused justice of the peace simply chalked it up to the young man's grief.

However, the day has finally dawned and my newly adopted brother and I are eager to fulfill our roles. I as the plucky maid of honor, and he as my father's best man.

The bride and groom planned their post-nuptial march to wend through the faux snowfall indoors, down the aisle, and out the front door of the bookshop, where they will likely be met with genuine snowfall as they make their way to the reception area behind the bookshop. Hundreds of twinkling lights line the pathway and surround the eating area and dance floor. Propane heaters were trucked in from as far away as Grand Falls to make sure the attendees stay above freezing despite the predicted subzero temperatures.

While the prospect of my father's wedding is, of course, an exciting event, the piece I'm truly looking forward to comes at the reception. I'm told that each and every citizen of Pin Cherry Harbor traditionally purchases their own supply of fireworks, and at midnight everyone lights their horde simultaneously. The dark sky becomes a beautiful cacophony of lights, and the scene warms hearts and souls across the northland.

Time to start the official wedding day. Now that Stellen has moved into the spare room at the penthouse, I opted for the settee and gave Amaryllis my bed so she and my father could spend the pre-wedding night apart. However, Pyewacket is taking far more room than he's entitled to, and the crick in my back wakes me up sooner than I'd like.

"Amaryllis?" My voice is barely more than a whisper. Pyewacket stretches out one of his large tan paws to cover my mouth, in what he'd like to pretend is an accident.

"Oh my gosh, I'm so glad you're finally awake. I've been lying here for at least two hours." Amaryllis flicks back the heavy down comforter and sits upright. "Should we grab some breakfast before we start the massive effort of whipping this—" she jumps up and gestures comically to her ratty flannel pajamas "—into shape?"

Slipping out from under the weight of a lazy half-wild caracal, I yawn and stretch. "You look amazing, as usual. But I absolutely need breakfast, and at least a gallon of coffee."

I take a quick turn in the bathroom and get dressed while Amaryllis washes and moisturizes her face like a grownup.

The diner is more than half full, and Tally's daughter is helping her mother take care of the flood of tourons who are visiting the great lake over the holidays. "Hi, ladies. I'll be right over with your coffee. I'm sure Odell already has your breakfasts on the grill."

We both nod our thanks and my clairsentience picks up on a wave of nerves from my tablemate. "Everything all right? Just normal nerves, or is there something else going on?"

"Just worried about the ceremony. My father is recovering surprisingly well from his heart attack, but he's not able to travel. Which is fine. I'd much rather have him well than risk his health for a short walk down the aisle. But—"

"I'm sure Silas would be honored to stand in, if you're all right with that."

Her hands shoot across the table. She grips my fingers and squeezes them so tightly a small squeak escapes my mouth as I ask, "Do you want me to ask him for you?"

"Would you? I know you keep telling me what a sweet old man he is, but every time I think about asking him, all I can picture is his disappointed face during my second year in law school when I got a 'B-' on my history of torte law brief." Her nervous laughter reddens her cheeks.

"I keep forgetting that he was one of your professors. You poor thing. Trust me, I've been on the receiving end of that look many times. I won't say I'm immune to it, but I'm happy to endure it for someone else's benefit. Especially you." I squeeze her hand and an enormous sigh of relief escapes her lips as she leans back against the red-vinyl bench seat.

"Well, that's a load off. I think I might actually be able to eat my breakfast now."

Right on time, Tally approaches the table with our food. She starts to push a plate in front of me, but stops halfway to the table. "Wait? You both— I never realized!"

Amaryllis and I exchange a shrug.

Tally sets our plates on the table and an entire *Three Stooges* sequence plays out.

I look at her plate.

She looks at my plate.

Tally looks back and forth between the two of us, until finally our eyes meet and the three of us laugh heartily.

I wave to Odell through the orders-up window, and he gives me a quick spatula salute before he continues filling orders.

Amaryllis holds up her coffee cup. "Cheers to the chorizo sisters!"

I pick up my mug, clink it against hers, and let the warmth of family fill my heart.

Back at the apartment, Grams is insisting on helping Amaryllis with her hair. After at least fifteen minutes of playing otherworld interpreter, I manage to convince Grams that having the wedding at the bookshop is her win for the year, and she should be ecstatic that Amaryllis has a trusted stylist showing up at two o'clock to create the hairstyle of the bride's dreams. Grams vanishes with a loud, self-indulgent pop, and I spend another ten minutes reassuring Amaryllis that she made the right choice and the motto is absolutely, "Her day, her way."

Caterers, florists, cake creators, and general delivery personnel are scurrying in and out of the bookshop all day.

However, my volunteer employee, Twiggy, is one hundred percent in control of all the main-floor shenanigans.

When my father makes an unscheduled visit, Twiggy's half-panicked voice crackles over the intercom. "Hey, kid, your dad's here, and I'm not letting him upstairs for the life of me. So you better get down here before I hafta put him in a chokehold."

Amaryllis laughs so hard she snorts. "I don't believe in superstitions, Mitzy. If it's important, he can come upstairs."

I throw my hands in the air as though it's an old-fashioned stickup. "No way! There were a lot of things I didn't believe in before I came to Pin Cherry, and I've discovered that most of them actually exist. So I'm not going to push my luck on this important day. I'll go take care of this, and under no circumstances will I allow him to come upstairs. Besides, your stylist will be here any minute."

She smiles proudly and winks. "I'm not even married yet, and you're the best stepdaughter anyone could ever ask for."

A ball of emotion clogs my throat. I can't keep images of my mother from popping into my head.

Amaryllis must be able to read my face as clear as a street sign, because she hops up from the scalloped-back chair and hurries to my side. "I'm sorry. I know today is hard for you. I wasn't trying to flaunt it or anything. I just want you to know how special I think you are, and how grateful I am to be part of your and your father's life."

Her kindness only forces a fresh flood of emotion, and I have to swipe salty drops from my cheeks. "It's fine. I'm super happy for you and Dad. My mother was definitely taken from me too soon, but that doesn't mean I don't want you and Jacob to be happy. You've changed his life. I can see, and sense, how much he loves you." Before I can prepare myself, she throws her arms around me and squeezes me in a bear hug.

"Thank you, Mitzy. Thank you for saying that."

I struggle to free myself from the cage of emotions. "I better get downstairs. I'm pretty sure Twiggy could take Dad, but I don't think we want to see that match on this day."

Amaryllis's tinkling laughter trails behind me and is finally cut off as the bookcase door slides closed.

At the bottom of the spiral staircase, my father is nose to nose with Twiggy.

"Easy, Dad. It's bad luck for you to see the bride on the wedding day. Just tell me what you need, and I'll take care of everything."

He rakes a nervous hand through his hair and his breath is coming in quick gasps. "I lost the ring. I picked it up from the jewelers last week, before they closed for the holidays, and I must've left it in the pocket of my pants. Maybe it fell out . . . I don't know! I can't find it anywhere."

"I bet I know someone who can find it." I give my father a huge over-obvious wink as I wiggle a finger back toward myself.

He sighs with relief. "Right. Get yourself over to my apartment tout de suite."

I step over the chain at the bottom of the stairs and scowl at Twiggy. "You have to unhook that. You can't expect Amaryllis to step over the "No Admittance" chain in a wedding gown."

Twiggy crosses her arms and kicks the toe of her biker boot on the bottom step. "As soon as the security gets here. I'll unhook the chain."

I gasp. "He's my boyfriend, not a gun for hire!"

She shrugs silently, turns my shoulders toward my father, and gives me a gentle shove.

Grumbling under my breath all the way across the alley, I can't ignore my father's chuckling.

"Don't worry, Mitzy, she's messing with you. I'm sure it's one of the other deputies. Indignantly jumping to conclusions is an unfortunate Duncan trait. I apologize for passing it on to you. But allow me to pass on a little wisdom, too. There are a great many things in this life that are out of your control. What other people think about you is absolutely one of them. I'm sure you want to protect yourself from the pain of losing someone you love, but keeping Erick at arms' length and refusing to trust him with the *whole* truth, will turn out to be a self-fulfilling prophecy. You're right in thinking he might not understand the psychic thing. But if you don't give him a chance, you'll always wonder what could have been."

There's a raw pain in my father's eyes, and I know he's thinking about the time he came to Arizona and saw my mother and me enjoying an ice cream. He chose to walk away that day. He thought I'd be better off without him. Who knows what would've happened if he had joined us instead of disappearing from our lives? Maybe this is my ice-cream-shop moment with Erick. If I don't trust him . . . if I don't walk over there, sit down, and ask to share his ice cream, I could drive away the one person I truly let myself care about since my mom died. "I hear what you're saying, Dad. I'll take it under advisement. Now, let's find that ring."

The immediate gratification of using my psychic powers to find something that means so much to my father, in less than three minutes, gives me a lovely boost of confidence. "You're welcome."

He squeezes me and lifts me up off the ground. "Have I told you that you are literally the best daughter in the entire world?"

"Oh, sorry. I didn't mean to interrupt."

My father drops me on the floor and both of our heads turn toward Stellen. "You didn't interrupt anything, little brother."

He blushes and looks away. "Mr. Duncan, are you sure you want me to be in the wedding party?"

Jacob strides across the tiger-maple flooring and puts a hand on the boy's shoulder. "First of all, I'd like you to call me Jacob. And I said it before, but I'll say it again, I'm honored to have you stand beside me on such an important day. You're a strong kid, and the fact you're the only other person I know who can see ghosts is a clear sign that you were meant to be part of this family." He slips his arm around the boy's shoulder and turns toward me. "What is it that you always say, Mitzy? The family of our choosing?"

I nod and join them in an impromptu family hug. "All right, boys. Let's make sure Amaryllis has the most perfect wedding in history, deal?"

They both nod, and we all put our hands in a circle like a small sports team. "Best wedding ever, on three. One. Two. Three!" We throw our hands up in the air and laugh.

"I better get back. It's going to take a small army and a large shoehorn to get me into that bridesmaid's dress."

Stellen snickers, exactly as I imagine a real baby brother would, and I punch him playfully on the shoulder before running to the elevator.

CHAPTER 20

Twiggy hands me a garment bag and I glare at her as I struggle over the chain and start up the circular staircase.

"Good luck with the dress, doll. Let me know if you need any safety pins or duct tape." She cackles happily as she struts over to check the florist's credentials.

When the secret door to the apartment slides open, Amaryllis calls from the bathroom. "Jacob, is that you?"

"Nope. It's only me."

"Everything okay?"

"Absolutely perfect. Do I put on my dress now, or is it better to wait till after the hairdo?"

The stylist steps out of the bathroom, takes a sip of bubbly, and sizes me up. "Hair first. We're probably going to need a lot of product, and I'd hate to get anything on the dress."

"Copy that." The hours disappear as we primp and bobby pin, and apply more layers of makeup than I've worn in my entire life. When the moment finally comes to cross my fingers and wedge into the dress, both Amaryllis and I are speechless.

"It fits you like a glove!" She blinks her false eyelashes and claps her hands.

I turn in front of the mirror and adjust the faux-fur trim on my shoulders.

"This can't possibly be the same dress?"

Amaryllis whistles. "Enjoy the win, Mitzy. And you might want another mimosa. I regret to inform you, I lost the shoe battle with your grandmother."

I roll my eyes and search the room, but Grams has cleverly hidden. "Do I even want to know?"

She leads me into the closet and reveals a strappy pair of silver heels somewhere in the four- to five-inch range. My fur-trimmed shoulders sag, and Amaryllis gives me an encouraging pat on the back. "You only have to wear them for the ceremony. If you change into high-tops for the reception, I'll never tell."

I laugh too loud and too long. "You severely underestimate the machinations of a vengeful fashion diva."

Once again, the flurry of activity swallows time, and before I can adequately admire the magical alterations of Mr. Gustafson, the music swells and I'm walking across the Rare Books Loft in my perfectly fitted gown.

The white fur hugs my shoulders, and I'm

grateful I didn't finish my mimosa as I circle down the wrought-iron steps and all eyes turn. Thankfully the chain is unhooked at the bottom, and Deputy Johnson is the actual security guard.

As I stride down the aisle toward the glittering archway, a familiar face catches my eye.

Erick makes a point of looking me up and down before nodding his heartfelt approval.

My cheeks flush to match my dress as I join my father on stage.

The tune shifts from "Winter Wonderland" to the traditional bride's march. Although I helped her into her gown, and observed the three hours of preparation, when Amaryllis stops at the top of the staircase, I gasp along with the rest of the guests.

Her auburn curls cascade down her back, and a sparkling winter princess's tiara sits atop her head like a delicate ice sculpture. The crown is festooned with holly berries, pine sprigs, and snowdrops. Her gorgeous bell-sleeved gown sparkles in the intimate lighting, and I can barely tear my eyes away from her descent in time to see my father brush a tear from his cheek.

The "I dos" are said, and the groom kisses the bride. Mr. and Mrs. Duncan descend the stage under a cascade of lightly falling snowflakes.

Guests ooh and ahh.

The happy couple stops behind the last row, so Twiggy can help the bride into her stunning white faux-fur cloak. They proceed to the outdoor reception area, and Stellen, handsome beyond his years in his white tuxedo and red bowtie, offers me his elbow.

We march out to the cheers and celebration of the crowd, who soon join us outdoors.

I help myself to the signature cocktail of brandy-infused mulled cider, and unabashedly take my seat at the head table. Food first, dancing later.

The seared elk medallions with garlic mashed potatoes and roasted root vegetables are spectacular.

The five-tier chocolate wedding cake brushed with Chambord liqueur and filled with dark chocolate ganache and raspberry preserves is divine.

And the propane heaters are life saving.

When it's time for the bride to throw her bouquet, Stellen nearly drags me out to the dance floor to join the growing group of single ladies.

I ease my way toward the back of the crowd, sincerely hoping that more eager, more coordinated women win the evening.

Amaryllis turns her back to us and, as her beautiful poinsettia, snowdrop, and pinecone bouquet floats through the air, I see the expectant faces of the women around me tracking its motion.

A tall blonde in the front row looks to be in perfect position, but at the last moment the bouquet takes a sharp turn and practically forces itself into my hands.

I immediately suspect Grams, and my eyes shoot up to the apartment windows.

She's whirling with glee like a mad dervish, but

she can't leave the apartment. I suppose that places her in the clear.

Awkwardly clutching the birch bark-wrapped bouquet grip, I smile my apologies to the disappointed faces around me.

The crowd parts to reveal the self-satisfied smirk of my mentor. His role as surrogate father of the bride may not have won him any awards, but his transmutation of the elements that altered the bouquet's trajectory will earn him high praise from my interfering Ghost-ma.

The music swells for the bride's first dance, and I scurry toward the sidelines.

The dapper Erick Harper intercepts my escape, twirls me back onto the dance floor, and winks at Stellen.

My conniving little stepbrother is enjoying a hearty chuckle and a second piece of cake.

"You know I'm a terrible dancer, Erick."

He twirls me out, spins me back, and dips me. "And you know—I'm not."

As he plants a memorable kiss on my lips, I drop the bouquet and possibly lose consciousness for a second.

Without missing a beat, he swoops me back to my feet with one hand and scoops up the floral arrangement with the other.

"I hope you believe in tradition, Moon." He offers me the bouquet.

I open my mouth to protest, but the sight of

Deputy Johnson grooving at the edge of the dance floor sends a sharp shock up my spine.

"Mitzy, are you okay?"

Peeling my eyes away from the wandering deputy, I stare blankly at Erick as the mood ring on my left hand burns with an unholy fire. "I have to find Silas."

Hiking up the skirts of my magnificent dress, I tempt fate and run in heels.

As though he senses the disturbance, Silas meets me at the edge of the dance floor and offers his elbow. "What has transpired?"

"I'm not sure. I saw Deputy Johnson standing at the edge of the dance floor, instead of guarding the Rare Books Loft." I lift my mood-ringed finger and shrug.

My mentor's bushy eyebrows arch, and he increases the pace. For a man who looks to be in his late seventies or early eighties, there's a strength that lurks beneath the surface.

We round the corner and rush inside. Unsurprisingly, he reaches the top of the spiral stairs before me and calls down, "Mitzy, did you move *Loca Sine Lumine, Loca Sine Lege*?"

"Is that the book that just came in? The one about places without light or laws?"

A worried sigh is his only reply.

When I reach the top stair my eyes dart toward the candle handle, and the shelf where the new book should be resting. "It's gone!"

"Indeed." He smooths his mustache with a thumb and forefinger. "There's nothing that can be done tonight. We must return to the festivities, properly admonish Deputy Johnson, and allow your father and his new bride to enjoy their evening."

"I know the book was rare, and I'm sure valuable, but is it dangerous?"

Silas takes my hand and pats it with fatherly patience. "Anything can be dangerous in the wrong hands, my dear. Let us return to the party. If I'm not mistaken, you left a very confused sheriff alone on the dance floor, holding a bouquet of flowers."

My eyes widen, and I stifle a giggle. "I'll blame it on Ghost-ma. He wanted to be in the inner circle, right?"

We both wait with bated breath, but no apparition rockets through the wall.

Silas's cheeks redden, and his round belly shakes with laughter. "You're fortunate she is otherwise occupied with her observation of the reception."

We return to the dance floor, where Erick is already dressing down Deputy Johnson for his dereliction of duty.

The young rookie shuffles back toward the bookshop, and I slip in to make my apologies.

Sheriff Harper cocks his head to the side and scrunches up his face. "If you keep running out on me when I'm using my best moves, I'm going to get a complex."

"Sorry. Ghost business." I jerk a thumb toward the windows. "It won't happen again—tonight."

He waves to Stellen, who raises the bouquet as though it is a glass of champagne, and the young man offers me a brotherly wink.

Erick smiles. "I gave it to him for safekeeping. Can we finish our dance?"

Before I can offer up my prepared litany of excuses, the clock strikes midnight and almost-Canada bursts to life with a flurry of fireworks and cheers.

Watching the reflection of sparkly explosions in Erick's deep-blue eyes holds me in a trance.

If I had words, I wouldn't know what to do with them.

This moment, this feeling, this is me—living my best life.

End of Book 11

A NOTE FROM TRIXIE

Thank you to each and every one of you! Another case solved! I'll keep writing them if you keep reading . . .

The best part of "living" in Pin Cherry Harbor continues to be feedback from my early readers. Thank you to my alpha readers/cheerleaders, Angel and Michael. HUGE thanks to my fantastic beta readers who continue to give me extremely useful and honest feedback: Veronica McIntyre and Nadine Peterse-Vrijhof. And big "small town" hugs to the world's best ARC Team – Trixie's Mystery ARC Detectives!

Another thing I'm truly grateful for is my editor, Philip Newey. Thank you for the elegant "fluttering page" solution. I'd also like to give some heartfelt thanks to Brooke for her tireless proofreading! Any errors are my own, as my outdated version of Word insists on showing me only what it likes and when it feels so moved.

FUN FACT: I have actually driven a snowmobile across a frozen lake!

My favorite quote from this case: "Poor man. The hips of Mitzy Moon may be the end of his winning streak." ~ Mitzy

I'm currently writing book thirteen in the Mitzy Moon Mysteries series, and I think I may just live in Pin Cherry Harbor forever. Mitzy, Grams, and Pyewacket got into plenty of trouble in book one, *Fries and Alibis*. But I'd have to say that book three, *Wings and Broken Things*, is when most readers say the series becomes unputdownable.

I hope you'll continue to hang out with us.

Trixie Silvertale (December 2020)

PARANORMAL COZY MYSTERY

Hearts & Dark Arts

TRIXIE SILVERTALE

CHAPTER 1

Have you ever closed your eyes and imagined what your future might be like? I have. There were many times I tried to lessen the sting of life as a foster kid by dreaming about seeing my name in lights. "Mitzy Moon's directorial debut . . ."

Spoiler alert.

Life as a film-school dropout and a practically penniless barista took a shockingly different turn. However, today, as I inch forward in the line of parents picking up students in front of the high school, I can't help but reflect on the way Silas Willoughby changed my entire existence.

What the—?

A tall man in an expensive-looking charcoal trench coat strides by with a perfectly coiffed black chow chow on a golden leash.

Weird. Where was I?

Right. Back in Sedona, Arizona, when I opened

my decrepit door to discover a wizened old man hunched in my hallway, time seemed to slow down. His bulbous nose twitched and he harrumphed into his thick grey mustache with, what I can now state with certainty was, disdain.

He had balanced an ancient leather briefcase against the wall and rummaged through the contents while my hangover head pounded and words escaped me. His gnarled hand grasped a bulging manila envelope and he cleared his throat—three times, if memory serves. His saggy cheeks flapped unceremoniously and he announced, "I'm looking for Mizithra Achelois Moon." A gust of pipe smoke and *eau de* denture cream had wafted toward me on the tail of his inquest.

Wait! Is that a mastiff? A plump woman in a red velvet cape is sashaying—true story—past my Jeep with a drooling brindle mastiff on a thick diamond-encrusted chain.

Geez!

Back to my reminiscing about Silas . . . I stared at him in surprise, flavored with a pinch of gut-churning horror. The last time someone had come to the door and slaughtered the pronunciation of my full, legal name, they followed up by informing my babysitter that a commuter train had killed my mother.

I think I nodded; I don't actually remember that part.

He handed me the large envelope and said, "I'm sorry for your loss," before shuffling away.

Hold on a minute! Blonde twin girls with beribboned pigtails and matching Chihuahuas on red leashes? What is going on at this high school?

The current disorientation is similar to the feelings that flooded over me when I looked inside that fateful pouch and found a will, a lot of cash, and a key.

The contents transformed my life—for the better—and filled my heart with love, revealed a secret family, and most of all gave me the gift of gratitude.

And now, thanks to the sometimes cruel/sometimes kind hand of fate, I have the opportunity to push the kindness angle and make a difference in another orphan's life.

The high school student I'm collecting is neither my child nor my actual brother, but, since my father and his new wife recently adopted the boy, I've been making the best of having a stepbrother.

Stellen is a shy, handsome boy who dreams of being a veterinarian. He's still discovering who he is, and his place in the world, but since we stumbled upon the fact that he's the only other person I know who can see ghosts, we have a special bond. He can't communicate with them, like me, but simply knowing that someone else can see them has helped me feel a little less like a freak.

I finally reach the front of the queue, but there's no Stellen.

Lowering the window of my Jeep, I call out to a

group of students loitering near the pickup zone. "Hey, any of you seen Stellen Jablonski?"

The girls giggle, and one of the boys calls out, "The woodchuck stuffer?"

Ignoring his reference to Stellen's late father's profession as a taxidermist, I employ my psychic powers to put the wiseacre in his place. "Look, you're already failing geometry, maybe you should avoid failing at life too, and try to be a little less of a jerk. Have you seen him or not?"

The boy's eyes nearly pop out of his head, and the surrounding whispers easily shift to the new hot topic.

"He's in the gym."

"Thank you." And that's what we call manners, kid.

I pull out of line, circle back toward the lot, and park. It's highly out of character for Stellen to be somewhere other than exactly where he's supposed to be. Unlike many of his peers, he's a respectful teenager, with a sense of responsibility and gratitude. If he's in the gymnasium, there's a good reason.

The brisk late-winter temperatures in almost-Canada force me to tug my stocking cap down over my snow-white hair and shove my hands into the pockets of my puffy jacket. Luckily, a petite woman in blue is exiting the building with a rotund basset hound trailing her when I get to the doors, and I'm able to slip inside without exposing my bare hands.

My fault for leaving the house without mittens and thinking I'd be safe inside my vehicle.

A huge sandwich board wrapped in repurposed flashing red Christmas lights reads: *Welcome to Cupid's Pet Invention Convention.*

Aha! Things are starting to slide into place. Stellen is obsessed with animals. To further his goal of becoming a veterinarian, he's already working after school as a part-time apprentice at the local animal hospital.

Inside the garishly lit gymnasium, a buzz of untamed activity echoes from the polished wooden floor to the ultra-high ceiling.

A plethora of booths are in an array of readiness. Some are completely constructed, while others are still being unpacked from shipping crates. A handful of interesting inventions are displayed in those that are complete, while many others are only partially constructed and resemble medieval torture devices.

Wandering up and down the aisles, I finally spot my little brother. He's hard at work unpacking the final pieces of a small but intriguing device, and at first I think his cheeks are flushed from the effort. Then I catch sight of *her*.

A tiny, elfin-like creature, with lavender hair, violet eyes, steampunk attire, and a wholly anime vibe. The assortment of buckles, straps, and gears connecting her garments boggles the mind.

"Hey, Stellen, I didn't see you out at the pickup zone."

The color drains from his face. "Oh. Right. Sorry. I— I was— I forgot to text."

Hopefully, my easy laughter will lighten his burden of guilt. "No worries, bro. What's going on here?" I gesture to the contraption beside him.

His cheeks flush a fresh shade of crimson, but it's the cartoon girl who responds.

"Stellen is helping me set up my exhibit. Isn't he just the best? Of course, I could've put it together myself. I built it. But it's, like, super nice to have help. You know?"

My experience with this age range of human has taught me that "you know" is rhetorical, so I stifle a reply.

She continues with barely a breath. "But if he needs to get home, or whatevs, I can finish by myself."

Stellen's big green eyes plead for assistance.

"Not at all. I'll let Doc Ledo know that you're working the convention floor. I'm sure he can hold things down at the clinic for one afternoon."

He brushes his brown curls back and smiles gratefully. "Um, that's okay. I already texted him."

Kicking out a hip, I plant a fist on my curves and tilt my head. "Oh, I see. So in the order of importance, your own sister falls below the local veterinarian?"

The lavender creature laughs lightly, and I can't help giggling along for the ride.

She bats her beautifully applied false eyelashes and her gaze sparkles. "I'm Yolo. Nice to meet you."

"Nice to meet you. I'm Mitzy Moon, Stellen's stepsister. What's your invention?"

Her energy shifts up a few frequencies, and my psychic senses tingle in anticipation.

"I'm super excited about it. It's a pet aura photography booth. People place their pet inside, and then it takes an aura photo, and I can interpret it for them. It shows a lot about the animal's temperament, but also it can show areas for further investigation—like, medically."

"You have my attention." Smiling, I point to the machine. "How does it work?"

She purses her tiny heart-shaped mouth and gives three rapid whistles. A small dog appears from nowhere, wagging his tightly curled tail.

"This is Bricklin. He's a basenji. He'd be happy to demonstrate." She leans down and places her hands on the knees of her jodhpurs as she coos to the beast in a sugary baby voice. "Wouldn't you like to demonstrate? Wouldn't you? You're such a good boy."

The russet-and-white dog prances into the invention's tunnel like Anubis guiding a soul into the underworld.

Yolo steps forward and draws the thick black curtains closed. Her hands fly over the keys of her laptop and there's a momentary flash of light from within the tunnel.

She pulls back the drapes, and Bricklin struts out as though he himself invented the machine.

"Wait for your reading, Bricklin."

The little pup sits patiently, while both his sharp, pointed ears track every sound in the vast space.

"Step over to my screen, Mitzy. I don't want to waste the photo paper, so I selected 'No Print' for this one."

Smart, friendly, and ecologically aware. What a lovely match for my sweet, strange stepbrother.

She makes room for me in front of the screen, and I stare at the image. In the photo, the air around Bricklin seems to glow with a variety of colors.

"This yellow band directly around his physical being indicates happiness or satisfaction in his lifestyle. This blue area here shows intelligence and a higher than average aptitude for understanding human communication." Her fingers move to the left side of the image. "These bits of red and purple here indicate his various joys. Purple generally shows a love of outdoor activity, while red indicates a need for closeness and affection. He's just getting over some nastiness from eating a poisoned mouse, so this dark brown streak here on the left side means he's not completely well." She bends and pats Bricklin's head. "A few more days of rest and then back to walkies."

The pup wiggles with suppressed energy and licks her hand.

"That's impressive. Did you build the contraption first and then learn how to interpret the pictures or the other way around?"

She tilts her round face up at me and twists one of the piecey chunks of her lavender hair around her finger as she ponders my question. "Not to be weird, but I've sort of always been able to see auras with the naked eye, but only on animals. I started researching it about four years ago, and that's when I got the idea for the Tunnel of Truth."

I nod my head and give a little whistle. "Great name."

She hops up and bounces on her tiptoes for a moment. "I know, right?"

"I better let you finish setting up your booth." Turning to my utterly entranced brother, I offer him an easy out. "Are you ready to go? Or do you want to text me later when you need a ride?"

His Adam's apple struggles mightily, but he finally forces out a few words. "Can I text you?"

"No problem. I've got a bunch of errands to run, so you just fire off a pickup request, and your personal Uber will be here in five to ten minutes."

He blushes and looks at the floor. "Thanks, Mitzy."

I stride past, pat him firmly on the back, and stop in mid-stride. "Wait, is her name actually Yolo? Like, You Only Live Once?"

He leans toward my shoulder and whispers, "Her full name is Yolonda Olson, but she doesn't like it, so . . ."

Giving him a friendly elbow in the side, I nod. “Hey, let’s not forget, you’re talking to Mizithra, goddess of Greek cheese. You don’t have to tell me about nicknames.”

“Nice to meet you, Yolo. Good luck with the convention.” I call over my shoulder.

“Thanks, Mitzy. I hope you’ll come back during the show. You can bring your cat.”

Quite the observant little pixie. The feline hairs on my skinny jeans must’ve given me away.

“Thanks for the offer, but that would not end well.” Waving, I thread my way through the abandoned packing bubbles, carpet remnants, and wads of discarded gaffer’s tape with a sly grin on my face.

I believe Stellen has a Valentine’s crush.

CHAPTER 2

There's a hint of spring in the air. Despite the frigid temperatures and the layer of snow still blanketing the ground, the sun has a warmer hue. It's hard to describe when I noticed the phenomenon. Growing up in the Southwest, with sunny days most of the year, I never noticed the way light changes with the seasons. Now that I've spent more than a year as far north as I've ever been, I can see the subtle shifts from grey to hints of yellow, to the deep golds of summer. The bleak winter sun is warming, and I can't wait to ditch all the layers of cold-weather gear needed to keep me alive at this latitude.

Stepping inside the Bell, Book & Candle Bookshop, left to me by my late grandmother, the scent of worlds and possibilities envelops me. Books are truly a gift. Before I can wax poetic and spin dreamily in the dust motes floating down from the tin-plated ceiling, my volunteer employee stomps out of the back room, plants her biker boots directly in my path, and scowls.

"Are you going to tell me what I did wrong, Twiggy? Or do I have to guess?"

She shakes her head and flicks the short bangs of her grey pixie cut to the side. "Believe it or not, doll, you didn't cause this problem."

"Care to share?"

"Since the most recent book theft, I've added some additional security to the Rare Books Loft."

I wish I could tell you that I was able to stop myself from rolling my eyes, but I can't. "Oh brother."

The aptly named Rare Books Loft contains valuable arcane texts, occult tomes, and some one-of-a-kind volumes never translated into English. My grandmother collected the wealth of information with the help of her lawyer and secret alchemist, Silas Willoughby. The same man who delivered the news of my inheritance to Arizona. Prior to our latest theft, a simple chain and a "No Admittance" sign at the bottom of the staircase provided all the security we needed. However, this second robbery has clearly prompted Twiggy to take decisive action.

"Do I even want to know?"

"You tell me, kid. If you trigger the alarm, do you want to know how to shut it off? Or do you want to have to call me and see if I'm feeling generous?"

Shrugging my shoulders, I exhale loudly. "I want to know."

She shoves one hand in the pocket of her dungarees and gestures for me to follow with the other. "That's what I figured. This hook is now fitted with a pressure-sensitive insert. When it's unclipped a thirty-second clock starts ticking, and if the hook isn't replaced within that window, an alarm sounds and automatically sends me a text."

I frown and cross my arms over my chest. "You're serious? You already monitor that chain like a possessed nun at a parochial school. I think the only reason you put in the pressure-sensitive thingy is to double down on enforcing your policies. What if the thief re-hooks the chain behind them?"

She shakes her head. "Come on. No one does that in the middle of a robbery. Only the people who know the rules will hook the chain up properly."

Letting my arms fall limply to my sides, I halfheartedly nod in agreement. "I've gotta say, for a town that shuns technology with as much effort as Pin Cherry Harbor, it's a rather impressive system. Did you have to fly somebody in from the big city?"

Refusing to answer, she instead unhooks the chain and lets it drop. The clock ticks down, and the ear-splitting alarm shatters the silence.

I cover my ears and shake my head. "All right, all right! I get it. Shut it off."

Twiggy smirks and tilts her head. "Oh, so you *do* want to know how to shut it off?"

With my hands still clasped over my ears, I nod furiously. "Yes! Now, please."

She strides past me and turns into the back room.

Next to the ancient computer on our small built-in desk sits a tiny keypad with an LCD screen. Typing in a code, she presses enter, and the horrific cacophony of beeps and sirens ends. She drops onto her rolly office chair, turns toward her computer, and opens the weekly orders document.

"Um, are you going to give me that code?"

She turns slowly in the chair and looks up at me. "You're the psychic. I thought you'd already know."

And this is why I'm so hesitant to tell people about my special gifts. "That's not how it works, and you know it."

Twiggy recites the code and insists that I promise not to write it down. "Commit it to memory, kid. There's no point having a secret code written down where anyone can find it."

"Understood."

Returning to the wrought-iron spiral staircase, I step onto the second tread and hook the chain up behind me as quickly as possible. I still feel rather confident that Twiggy chose this method of security as a way to punish me for all the times I defiantly left this chain unhooked.

The oak reading tables in the Rare Books Loft have been freshly polished, and the brass lamps with their green-glass shades are each carefully aligned in the upper left-hand corner of their respective desks. Before walking across the plush Persian carpets to my apartment's secret door, I turn and lean against the thick curved banister that reaches out in two directions like arms encircling the first floor in a loving embrace.

It's hard to imagine the number of volumes contained within this three-story bookshop, but the architectural decision to leave this lovely mezzanine in place was a solid choice. The light filtering through the 6 x 6 windows creates a cozy, inviting ambience on the first floor and, on the rare occasions when we have customers, I'm sure they appreciate it.

As I approach the candle sconce that serves as the secret handle to open the sliding bookcase door to my swanky apartment, my heart sinks a little. The book—priceless according to my mentor Silas—that used to sit on the adjacent shelf was stolen during my father's wedding reception. Twiggy had been searching for the new acquisition, *Loca Sine Lumine, Loca Sine Lege*, for years. The book contains cryptic spells and rituals dealing with things like necromancy, séances, and other interactions with the darker side of magic. The title, loosely translated, means "Paths without light, paths without laws." Not the kind of thing that should fall into the wrong hands.

Mr. Willoughby is not a practitioner of magic, and under no circumstances would he refer to himself as a wizard. He is an alchemist and studies the transmutation of matter. However, this missing tome sounds very much like a practitioner's guide to the dark arts.

Pulling the candle handle, I wait for the bookcase to slide open.

Grams rockets out of the closet. “Mitzy! I thought you’d never get back.”

The late Myrtle Isadora is not as dead as everyone thinks. Her spirit was tethered to the bookshop, with the help of our resident alchemist, and we’ve had a riot getting to know each other. Since I’m the only human who can see and hear her, I play a vital role in her afterlife. “What’s on your mind, Grams?”

“Where is Erick taking you for Valentine’s Day?”

“What?”

She tilts her shimmering head. “Is it a hearing thing, or an understanding thing, sweetie?”

“I heard you. I just— What day is Valentine’s Day?”

Ghost-ma throws her ethereal arms in the air. “How can a girl dating a gorgeous, kindhearted man like Sheriff Too-Hot-To-Handle not know that Valentine’s Day is next week?”

“Simple. This girl isn’t in the habit of being in serious relationships, and, in the past, I’ve made quite a point of not celebrating the holiday of love. I’ve been to anti-Valentine’s celebrations, I’ve been to February the thirteenth Galentine’s celebrations, and embraced pretty much any and every way one could avoid admitting to being single during this sappy, love-soaked time of the year.”

Grams dramatically swishes the silk-and-tulle

skirt of her burgundy Marchesa burial gown and clutches at one of her many strands of pearls. "Well, you better get on board! Because Valentine's Day is my favorite holiday, and I'm working on a special outfit for you."

Now it's my turn to throw my arms in the air. "Why does that not surprise me? Imagine someone with five ex-husbands buying into a holiday based on the fantasy of true love." My sarcastic tone carries more sting than I intend.

Her ghostly eyes sparkle with indignation and she zooms down to eye level. "You listen to me, young lady. True love is not a fantasy. That handsome sheriff of yours is a good-hearted man from the top of his beautiful blond head to the bottom of his, what I'm sure are perfectly shaped, feet."

The reference tickles my funny bone, and I burst into a fit of giggles. "I think you're the only person I know who would describe feet as 'perfectly shaped.' Is that even a thing? Are you losing your ghost mind?"

She swirls up to the ceiling in a fit of ghost fury. "Well, I never!"

"Oh, Myrtle Isadora Johnson Linder Duncan Willamet Rogers, I think we both know that you did. At least five times!"

The familiar gibe dissipates her anger, and she floats down to embrace me. Her ability to take corporeal form, at will, has greatly improved since our first meeting, but there's still a lingering strangeness about the sensation of being wrapped in someone else's energy.

"Ree-ooooow." The furry fiend has returned, and it sounds like he doesn't have time for gooey emotions.

My half-wild tan caracal appears out of nowhere, as per usual, and his black-tufted ears flick back and forth with irritation.

"Good afternoon, Pyewacket. To what do we owe this pleasure?"

Completely ignoring my attempt at communication, he struts past, brushing my leg with an aloof, accidental hip check, before leaping onto my four-poster bed for his late-afternoon nap. Circling three times, he drops into the down comforter and lays a paw over his eyes, as though he can't bear to be disturbed by our antics.

Fine, two can play the ignore me game. "Oh, did I mention I have some hot gossip?"

Grams swirls toward me, rubbing her phantom hands together eagerly. "Dish!"

"Stellen has a crush!"

She nods and taps a ring-ensconced finger on her coral lip. "Finally! That boy just needs a little boost of confidence. He's handsome, intelligent, and clearly has good taste."

"Are you saying that because he can see you?"

She snickers. "Maybe. Tell me all about the girl, or boy, no judgment."

"It's a girl, and she looks like she stepped straight

out of a Japanese anime. She's a lovely, tiny waif, with lavender hair and fantastically complicated clothing."

Grams places a fist on her ample hip and wags her head back and forth. "Now, now, Mitzy. Never underestimate the power of the right amount of junk in the trunk."

I shake my well-stocked caboose in her general direction, and we collapse in a fit of giggles.

"Did you get to talk to her? Is she one of those vapid mean girls?"

"Not at all! She's brilliant. She invented an aura photography machine for pets, and I think she might be a little psychic or something. She also interprets the photographs for the pet owners."

Ghost-ma zooms toward the sleeping Pyewacket and dares to disturb his slumber. "Do you think you could get an aura photograph of Mr. Cuddlekins? Oh, that would be divine!"

"I guess." Chewing my bottom lip, I run through several montages of me attempting to transport a wildcat into a gymnasium full of people and defenseless animals. None of the scenarios ends well. "I'm not sure it would be entirely safe. You know how Pyewacket can be."

She indulgently strokes his head. "Nonsense. He's a perfect angel. Just explain the process to him and I'm sure he'll come along without complaint."

Yeesh! This woman has no better understanding

of her spoiled feline in the afterlife than she did when she was alive.

"I heard that."

Holding up my finger, I shake it sternly in her direction. "You know the rules. No thought-dropping. If these lips aren't moving—"

She scoffs and crosses her arms. "You have to give it a shot. Pretty please?"

I kneel next to the bed and proceed to explain the aura photography tunnel, the lovely pixie girl, and Stellen's obsession with both the girl and her technology.

"Reeeee-ow." A warning.

Tilting my head to Grams, I have to disagree with her positive attitude. "That distinctly sounded like a protest. Maybe when the convention is over, she can bring the tunnel here? I'd be happy to pay her for a private photo session."

Myrtle Isadora shakes her head with disappointment.

"Will that meet with your approval, Pye?"

He lowers his eyelids lazily and chooses to pretend I do not exist, rather than deign to reply.

Before Grams and I can get into any additional debate, my phone pings with a text from Stellen. "We'll table this discussion. Looks like it's time for me to go pick up Stellen and see if I can casually invite Yolo to join us for breakfast tomorrow before the convention."

Grams nods and follows me out of the apartment

and down the circular staircase. "Good thinking. I like where your head's at. The boy is shy, but he has potential. Just needs a little push in the right direction. And I think you're the girl to give him that push."

There's no need for me to say my "oh brother" out loud; she hears it loud and clear.

The parking lot at the high school is nearly empty by the time I arrive, and I can only imagine that Stellen needlessly strung out the set up in order to spend additional precious moments with Yolo.

There are only a handful of inventors left inside the gymnasium.

"Yolo, do you need a ride too?"

She shakes her head. "Thanks, but no. I drove my Hyundai Tucson here, with all my gear."

"Of course. That makes sense." I nod and smile. "I'm not sure what time you have to get here tomorrow morning to finish setting up, but would you like to have breakfast with Stellen and me at the diner before the convention?"

She shakes her elfin head slowly and blinks her large round eyes before answering. "Normally, I'd say yes, but I'm pretty nervous about the convention. There's a ton of prize money at stake, and I think I'd feel better if I, like, just come straight here in the morning and test my equipment one more time before they open the exhibits to the public, you know?"

Stellen jumps to her rescue. "Yeah, totally. That's a good call. I can bring you something."

Her cheeks flush, and she bats her glorious eyelashes. "That would be sweet. I love cinnamon sticky buns."

He gulps audibly. "Yeah. Also, do I. Cinnamon."

Oh, the poor sweet child. "No problem, Yolo. I'll make sure we're here before they open the doors, and you can enjoy your cinnamon roll after you test the tunnel. Sound good?"

She smiles, winks, and gives three sharp whistles. Bricklin once again appears from nowhere, and the four of us walk out together.

My psychic senses are tingling madly with the nervous anticipation rolling off my stepbrother like the shock waves from an EMP. We part company in the parking lot, and Stellen and I head home.

Pausing in the alleyway between my bookshop and my father's restorative justice foundation, and the penthouse where Stellen now lives, I make one last suggestion. "Did you want to come in and order pizza?"

"I better not. Amaryllis sent a text and said she was keeping a plate of dinner warm for me. I don't want to seem ungrateful."

Placing a hand on his shoulder, I give him a squeeze. "Don't worry, you never seem ungrateful, and I think you're making the right choice. What time do you want to meet for breakfast?"

"The exhibits open at nine, and I'm sure Yolo

will be there by seven . . . If we show up by 8:15, that should give her enough time to test her equipment, and enjoy her cinnamon roll, before the crowds swarm in."

"So meet me back here at 7:45?"

His eyes scan back and forth as he does the math. "Will that give us enough time to eat our breakfast and drive to the high school?"

I chuckle as I pull my hand back and head toward the metal alleyway door. "You've seen me eat, right?"

His snicker serves as the only reply as he disappears into my father's building.

Look at me. Not only am I turning out to be an amazing big sister, but I also seem to have a bit of skill in the matchmaking arena.

CHAPTER 3

Walking in to Myrtle's Diner, named after my grandmother and operated by her first husband, never ceases to provide comfort. A familiar touchstone like this is something I never had growing up in foster care. The idea of dining in a place filled with people who know and care about me is one of the many things I've learned to love about Pin Cherry.

My surrogate grandfather, Odell, offers me his standard spatula salute through the red-Formica-trimmed orders-up window, and Stellen and I slide into our regular booth.

Tally, the best waitress on the shores of our great lake, shows up with a steaming cup of coffee for me, and a lovely mug of hot cocoa with tiny marshmallows for Stellen. "How's everything going over at my big brother's animal hospital?"

Stellen eagerly reaches for the mug of cocoa, but

politely replies before gulping it down. "Doc Ledo is the best. I'm not sure how I can ever repay him for all the stuff he's teaching me. It's pretty lit."

Tally nods her tightly bound flame-red bun, but raises an eyebrow in my direction.

"It means great, or cool, or awesome. Something in that vicinity."

My interpretation draws a chuckle from our server, and she shakes her head as she moves on to help other patrons.

"So what's the story with Yolo?"

Stellen's cheeks instantly flush the color of puppy love, and he swallows with difficulty. "I don't know. She's cool, or whatever."

"Do you like her?"

He unwraps his silverware, fumbles the napkin, and drops his fork.

I lean toward him and whisper, "Hey, it's me. You don't have to be nervous. I'm not going to tell her what you say."

My clairsentience picks up on an instant wave of relief washing over him.

"Yeah, sorry. The kids at school—"

"Oh, you don't have to tell me. Kids at school are the worst."

He nods. "Right?"

Before I can pose my question a second time, Odell shows up with a clean fork and slides our breakfasts onto the table. I receive the scrambled eggs with chorizo, the side of golden-brown home fries, and the bottle of Tabasco that serve as my standard delicious breakfast, while Stellen gets the french toast of his dreams.

"Thanks, Odell. You really are a magician back there." I inhale the fabulous aromas.

He nods. "Good to see you two out and about. You headed over to the convention?"

These seemingly prescient comments used to freak me out when I first arrived in town, but now that I'm a "local" I have a grasp of how fast news travels in a small town. "As a matter of fact, we are. We wanted to take a cinnamon sticky bun to-go, for a friend of Stellen's. Can you make that happen?"

The deep creases around his eyes crinkle as he smiles and looks from my full plate to me, and back. "So how much time d'you figure I got? Three minutes?" He raps his knuckles twice on the table and chuckles as he saunters back into the kitchen.

As you can see, my reputation precedes me.

Stellen gulps down a few bites and pauses. "Thanks for not saying girlfriend, or something."

"Hey, I can keep a secret. Plus, I'm a cool big sister. Remember?"

He stops with a forkful of syrupy french toast halfway to his mouth and chokes on his own laughter. "Right. If I do forget, I'm pretty sure you'll remind me."

"Rude."

We share a round of snickers and gobble down our scrumptious morning meal.

While I collect our plates and take them to the dish bin tucked behind the counter, Tally walks over to Stellen with a plastic bag holding a small to-go box.

"I'm not sure if it will stay warm all the way to the high school in this weather, but I warmed it up for you just in case."

"Thank you, ma'am."

Her cheeks nearly match the shade of her hair. "Well, aren't you the sweetest thing?"

He takes the bag, and we hop into the Jeep to deliver his first thoughtful boyfriend gift.

If possible, the gymnasium seems even busier this morning than it was last night. Cupid's entire Pet Invention Convention is buzzing like a massive beehive.

Stellen leads the way to Yolo's booth. But when she catches sight of him, her expression is one of frenzied panic, rather than welcome.

He hurries to her side.

I arrive in time to catch the bagged cinnamon roll as Stellen tosses it aside and dives into the Tunnel of Truth.

"Can someone catch me up?"

Yolo turns, and her hands gesture frenetically as she speaks. "Everything was fine when I got here this morning. I ran the tests. I even tested the printer.

Bricklin was an absolute angel. Like, for reals, it couldn't have gone better."

My assumption is that this story of perfection is not going to end well.

She leans down, and the layered, full bustle on today's deep-purple steampunk overcoat brushes me back a stride. "Can you see it? I'm sure it's the photocathode," she calls to Stellen.

He mumbles a reply from inside the tunnel, but it's not the answer she was looking for.

She stands and runs a finger under each of her eyes while she struggles to blink back tears. "This is unbelievable. I've been working on this invention for, literally, years. And here it is, the most important day of my life, and . . . total meltdown. I could've won, like, thousands of dollars for my invention or school or whatevs. How is this my life right now?"

My suspicion of catastrophe—confirmed. Something's gone wrong with her wonderful invention, and panic has ensued. Time to test little brother's skills. "Hey, Stellen? Can you fix it?"

He slides out with a hopeful glint in his eyes. "I can fix anything. Tools and other stuff would break around my dad's shop all the time, including his truck, and I always figured it out. But Yolo's invention is on the demonstration list for today. I just don't know if I can fix it in time for the judging."

I kneel next to him and fish around in the pocket of my puffy coat. "Tell you what, you take these and all of this." I hand him the keys to the Jeep and a wad of cash. "And I'll see what the Duncan-Moon Philanthropic Foundation can do to influence the judges. Not in a cheating way, just in a 'hey, can we move this invention to tomorrow's list' kind of way."

Yolo grips my arm with surprising firmness for such an airy-looking creature. "Are you serious? You can do that? Oh, my gosh! Oh, my gosh! You're like a fairy godmother! If you can do that, I know Stellen and I can fix it. I built it once, we can rebuild it. Right?"

I get to my feet and pat her on the back as the theme from the Six Million Dollar Man races through my head. *A man barely alive . . . we can rebuild him . . .* "Let's all take a deep breath. Speaking for myself, I function much better when I'm calm and focused. So you two get this thing working, and I'll grease some palms. Again, not in a cheating way."

The sweet little anime waif actually giggles for a moment. "Thank you, Mitzy. Stellen was right about you. You are, legit, the best."

Taking a moment for a mock curtsy, I accept her compliment and stride off to throw my weight, and my cash, around the convention.

The presence of Pin Cherry Harbor's mayor is a solid clue to the whereabouts of the bigwigs. He's surrounded by a handful of brainy-looking men and women dressed in business attire and carrying clipboards. Of course there are clipboards! After all, Pin Cherry Harbor is the town that tech forgot. We have credit card slidey machines, passbooks at the bank, and, with very few exceptions, cash is king at all local establishments.

"Good morning, Mr. Mayor. This looks like a wonderful convention."

The advantage of being one of two people in town with naturally bone-white hair and what I'd like to think are intelligent grey eyes, the mayor instantly recognizes my lineage. "Miss Moon! How good of you to come. Is the Duncan-Moon Foundation sponsoring this event?"

The event promoters and judges immediately turn toward the whiff of money. "Not yet, Mr. Mayor, but that's what I'd like to speak to you about. Do you know who's in charge?"

The mayor slides an arm around my shoulders as though we're old friends and offers me up to the PIC powers-that-be. "Mr. and Mrs. Cupid, I'd like you to meet Mitzy Moon, founder and president of the Duncan-Moon Philanthropic Foundation. Miss Moon has done some wonderful things for our community, including some invaluable scholarships at this very high school."

Hands are shoved in my direction, and I shake them like the dancing monkey I've become. Fortunately, it's all to support a good cause, and that's reason enough for me. "I was hoping we could discuss a slight change in the schedule. I'm happy to add a Duncan-Moon Foundation prize to the list and cover any expenses that might be incurred as a result of the adjustment."

Lucky for me, I have more than the basic five senses at my disposal. Their initial hesitation vanishes when I offer to foot the bill.

Mrs. Cupid steps forward and smiles, not in a comforting way. It seems like the way Cruella de Vil would've smiled when *101 Dalmatians* were delivered to her creepy mansion.

"Ms. Moon, we will certainly accommodate a schedule shift if we are able. What did you have in mind?"

"I was hoping that we could shift one of the inventors scheduled to demonstrate today over to tomorrow. I know it's a strange request, but if there's an inventor who's scheduled to demonstrate tomorrow and would be willing to trade places, I'd happily compensate them for the irregularity."

She crosses her arms and nods. "I see. Do you have a vested interest in this invention?"

"Oh, absolutely not. Just want to make sure everyone gets the opportunity they came here for."

The hairs on the back of my neck tingle, and I suddenly have a strong dislike for the wife.

"It's rather late in the competition to make those kinds of adjustments, Ms. Moon. Inventors are required to select their day for demonstration when they sign up. There are advantages to being in the first round of judging today, and advantages to participating in the final round tomorrow. It hardly seems fair to force someone to demonstrate ahead of their planned schedule."

Yep. Definitely don't like her.

Mr. Cupid clears his throat and attempts to assert his authority. "Well, to be fair, Fiona, if one of tomorrow's scheduled demonstrators would willingly swap, there's nothing in the rulebook to specifically prohibit such a change."

This guy is on his way to becoming my new best friend. "This is what I'm saying, Mr. Cupid. A completely voluntary trade. And I'm sure the Duncan-Moon Foundation would be more than willing to add a five thousand dollar donation to the top prize."

Fiona's standoffish vibe begins to weaken as her husband grips my hand firmly and thumps me on the back. "Call me Wibb, please. That is quite a generous offer. The current top prize is only three thousand dollars. We wouldn't have time to change the banners, or mention your sponsorship in the radio ads—"

I wave both of my hands in surrender. "Oh no, Wibb, you misunderstand. The Duncan-Moon Foundation doesn't need any publicity from this. In fact, it can be an anonymous donation, if you like. How do we go about finding someone willing to swap places?"

Two of the nameless judges who were orbiting our conversation lean in eagerly.

"Looks like these two might have an idea, Wibb." I keep using his name, like a Tony Robbins acolyte, and point to the eavesdroppers.

He smiles warmly, and his ruddy cheeks tug into a massive grin. "What are you guys thinking?"

The female judge sweeps her bangs to the side. "I

heard the man with the reptile display mention that two of his heaters were broken, and he was quite concerned about his exhibits surviving in these cold temperatures. He seemed very upset about having to stay another day, being short on equipment and all."

Wibb pats her so hard on the back her glasses are nearly ejected from her face. She coughs a little, and I link my arm through Wibb's elbow. "Let's go have a talk with that gentleman."

Fiona trails behind us, emitting a mixture of jealousy and suspicion.

I'm not sure what I've done to earn such distrust from her, but this epic performance I'm putting on is not for my benefit. If I can buy another day for Yolo and Stellen, the reward of knowing that I'm the world's best big sister, and an honorary St. Valentine, will be enough.

As we approach the reptile booth, I remember my gut-twisting discomfort around snakes. I want to land on this man's good side, so I better put on a Meryl Streep-level performance.

Wibb takes the lead. "Mr. Thompson? Excuse me, Mr. Thompson, a word?" A small, pale man with a pencil-thin red mustache and wisp of red combover approaches with the smooth, silent glide of, dare I say, a serpent.

"Mr. Thompson, we're in a bit of a situation and need to move one of tomorrow's demonstrations to this afternoon. Would you be willing to take an earlier slot?"

Mr. Thompson exhales loudly. "Oh, my prayers have been answered. I've already lost two heating mats, and this morning a third one went out. I can't combine some of these species, and I'm running out of options. I would love to do my demonstration this afternoon, and if it would be all right, pack up and head for warmer climes as soon as I'm done."

Wibb pats the man heartily on the back. "Absolutely. Good man, Mr. Thompson. We'll put you at the top of the schedule this afternoon, and, as you know, you need not be present to win. You've helped us out of such a bind, my good man."

The snake wrangler is so overjoyed, offering him any additional compensation seems like offering a satisfied diner a second dessert.

Since Wibb doesn't mention my offer of cash, I keep my mouth shut and avert my gaze from the tanks of slithery things. Nod and smile, as my mother taught me.

Wibb scoops me back into the aisle and we march toward a sequestered meeting room. Once inside, Fiona produces a contract more rapidly than a sleight-of-hand magician. "Ms. Moon, if you're serious about making your prize-money donation, we would need to have that in writing, and we would need to speak to the treasurer of your philanthropic foundation."

"Of course. I was absolutely serious. Let me just make a quick call to the treasurer. And I'll sign whatever papers you need." I better wait until after the financial transaction to push my Yolo agenda.

Wibb for the win. "Oh, Miss Moon, who was the inventor we need to move to tomorrow's schedule? The one we're swapping with Mr. Thompson?"

I plaster on a huge smile and pat *him* on the back. "Thank you for keeping us on track, Wibb. The inventor we're rescheduling for Mr. Thompson's slot would be Yolonda Olson."

The snarly expression and aggressive energy rolling off Fiona make me wonder if she's the one who sabotaged the machine.

No time to worry about that; Wibb has already produced his clipboard and made the necessary switcheroo. "There we go. All taken care of, Miss Moon. Thanks again for bringing this matter to our attention and being such a generous supporter of pet inventions."

"It's my pleasure. Now let me just make that quick phone call, and we'll get this paperwork signed."

I'm not looking forward to explaining this most recent act of generosity to my *treasurer*, Silas Willoughby, but the call goes much smoother than expected, and he agrees to deliver a check in the winner's name to the convention the following day.

Fiona seems less pleased than I would've expected, but Wibb is all back pats and attaboys.

Ignoring the scrooge, I extend a warm invitation to my co-conspirator. "Wibb, would you care to accompany me to Miss Olson's booth and give her the good news?" This enormous smile is gonna give me cheek cramps!

He taps his clipboard and broadens his grin. "Wonderful idea. Just wonderful."

CHAPTER 4

Back at the Tunnel of Truth, my amazing news goes over like a lead balloon. To her credit, Yolo puts on a brave face and graciously thanks the event organizers. But, once they shuffle off to attend to other convention business, she collapses cross-legged on the floor and shoves chunks of cinnamon roll into her mouth.

Finally, something I have in common with this rare creature—stress eating. "What's wrong? I thought the extra day would give you the time you needed?"

She looks up, and her huge violet eyes brim with tears. "I can't thank you enough for whatever you did. If we didn't live way past where Jesus lost his sandals, I'm sure that a day would've been enough time. But Stellen and I confirmed it was the photocathode that was damaged. It looks like there are micropipe defects in the silicon carbide wafers."

Her scientific mumbo-jumbo is meaningless to me, but my extrasensory perceptions tell me everything I need to know. "Don't give up hope, all right? Stellen can be surprisingly clever. If he thinks he can fix this thing, I'd put my money on him."

She draws a ragged breath and licks some sticky caramel sauce from her fingers. "I hope you're right. He said he knew a guy that has everything. I just wasn't sure if *everything* included a photocathode though, you know?"

I take a seat on the floor next to her. "Well, it looks like you're stuck with me until Stellen gets back with the part. Is there anything I can do to help?"

She smiles and winks. "Do you know how to prevent pre-avalanche reverse-bias point failures in epitaxially-grown pn junction devices?"

Shaking my head, I raise my hands in surrender. "I don't even know how to spell most of the words you just said. Why don't we take this opportunity to walk around the rest of the convention and check out the competition?"

Her smile wavers and her eyes dart toward the disassembled tunnel. "There's a lotta proprietary stuff here. I'm kind of afraid to leave it unprotected. You go ahead and walk around. I'll stay here with Bricklin."

I nod my head as though I'm in agreement. "Great plan, except for the fact that I have no idea what qualifies as competition. Let me see if I can call in a favor." Leaving her on the floor to finish her cinnamon roll, I call my boyfriend. "Good morning, Sheriff Harper."

Without missing a beat, he asks me who's dead.

"Hey, I could be calling to make conversation, not to report a crime. You don't know."

His warm laughter makes my skin tingle, and I hope he buys what I'm selling. "Do you have a few minutes to stop by the high school?"

He makes no objection, so I continue.

"Stellen and his friend have an invention on display at this pet expo thingy, and something malfunctioned on it this morning, so they had to disassemble it. She's nervous about leaving her proprietary technology unprotected—"

He jumps to the conclusion before I can complete my sales pitch.

"Well, no. You're right, it's not *technically* a crime scene, but someone could've tampered with it. I was hoping your well-trained eye would be able to put her fears to rest about possible sabotage."

Whether it was my convincing argument or his hidden need to see me, he agrees to come to our collective rescue. Ending the call, I slip the phone in my pocket and mentally pat myself on the back. Still got it, girl.

I distract myself from the anticipation of Erick's arrival by playing a subdued game of fetch with Bricklin.

When Sheriff Harper arrives, I allow my inner

film student a slow dolly shot with a push in at the last minute.

Erick's blond locks are slicked in place with his favorite pomade, and he's wearing that uniform like a runway model at Paris Fashion Week. The way his jacket hangs open to reveal that row of buttons leading down—

"Is that him?" Yolo elbows me and nods toward the approaching badge.

I cough to cleverly disguise my open mouth. "Yep. Here comes the law. Wait, who's trailing him?" He has a deputy who barely looks old enough to shave in tow.

Sheriff Harper's warm smile melts my insides. "Mitzy Moon, meet Deputy Candy."

Shaking the man-child's hand, I can't stop myself from blurting, "Candy? Like, C - A - N - D - Y?"

The youthful deputy nods and exhales loudly. "Thanks for not rhyming it with something or making a porn star joke."

His candor catches me off guard, and I have to cover my mouth to keep from hooting with laughter. "You're quick on your feet, Candy. That's going to come in handy—" Gulp. "I didn't mean to make a rhyme. That was totally accidental. It's just— Quick thinking is useful in this town."

Erick chuckles. "Good save, Moon." He gestures to the under-construction machinery behind me. "Is this the invention?"

I jerk a thumb toward Erick and wink at the

rookie. "See what I mean. You can learn a lot from this guy."

The deputy nods, but refuses to take the bait. "I've been reading through a lot of the old case files, Miss Moon. Seems like I may be able to learn quite a bit from you as well." An easy grin graces his boyish face.

Is he flirting with me? Was that flirty? Right in front of my boyfriend? Awful brave for a newbie. "Flattery will get you everywhere," I joke, and gesture for Yolo to join me for introductions to the officers. "So, this is her invention. She and Stellen are in the middle of repairing it. Would it be all right if she and I walk the convention floor while you two poke around for potential clues? There's a lot of prize money at stake, so sabotage isn't impossible."

Erick nods.

Yolo squeezes my arm. "Can you tell them not to touch anything?"

"Also, it would be great if you can conduct your investigation without actually moving any of the parts. It's a pretty complicated machine, and they have to get it back together and ready for demonstration by tomorrow's round of the competition."

"10-4," says the new deputy.

Erick leans toward me and whispers, "So basically, you called us over here to serve as private security, while you snoop around for possible sabotage suspects?"

I let out a low whistle and quickly kiss him on the

cheek for distractionary purposes. "Nothing gets by you, Sheriff."

I'd like to tell you that I'm hanging on Yolo's every word as we wander down the rows of invention-filled booths, but my mundane sense of hearing is off-line due to the amount of focus I'm pouring into potential psychic signals. That, and I'm madly rubbing the ancient magicked mood ring on my left hand, silently begging for assistance.

"Mitzy? Mitzy, are you in there?"

I stare at the purple-haired being before me and blink. "Oops. What did I miss?"

She puts a delicate hand over her mouth and giggles softly. "Probably, like, everything. We should get back to the booth. Maybe Stellen found the part and needs my help."

"Copy that. I don't want to abuse the sheriff's goodwill."

As we thread our way through the increasingly thick crowds, Yolo delves into my personal life. "Are you really dating the sheriff?"

"Mmhmm."

She bites her bottom lip for a moment. "He's totally hot, but you seem like a rule breaker. From some of the stuff Stellen said."

Note to self: double-check the stories little brother is spreading around town. "I don't think of it as breaking, more of a bending or stretching."

She chokes on her own laughter. "I'm definitely

going to use that line next time I get called into Principal Puig's office."

"You should know, the principal and I are old friends. Next time you're in there, just drop my name, and you should leave with no detention and possibly even a pat on the back."

She laughs out loud and struggles to catch her breath.

We round the corner, and she spies Stellen standing in her booth chatting with Erick. "He's back." She takes off like a gazelle across the Serengeti, and I stroll casually behind like the king of the jungle. Mentally, I had to close that analogy loop for myself.

Stellen catches sight of the approaching lavender streak and waves an object as he smiles broadly.

Even non-inventors like me can guess that he found a replacement photocathode. The two super nerds dive into the tunnel and begin work on the critical repair.

Erick turns to his deputy. "Go ahead and make a pass through the convention center. Be obvious, greet folks, and, in general, make your presence known."

"10-4." Deputy Candy marches off with his thumbs hooked behind his Sam brown.

"He looks a little like a kid at Halloween. How old is that guy?"

"If I tell you he had to have his parents sign a waiver so he could enter the academy, will you promise it stays between us?"

I pinch my lips together firmly and my eyes widen.

Erick chuckles. "He graduated from high school when he was fourteen, college at seventeen, and told his parents he wanted to take all of that brainpower into law enforcement."

"So how did he end up in Pin Cherry?"

"He's one of the smartest recruits ever to complete the program. Highest score in history on the written exam. He lacks a little on the physical strength scale, but his real deficit is common sense—life experience. I think they were hoping to put his brain to use, but keep his body safe by placing him in a less densely populated county for a year or two."

"Well, I scored top marks in common sense, so if you want me to break him in, just let me know."

Erick hooks a finger through my belt loop and pulls me alarmingly close in such a public place. His delicious woodsy-citrus scent threatens to end me, and his lips are so close I can feel his breath as he whispers, "And miss out on all the fun we have working cases together?"

My heart is stuttering like a metronome gone wrong, and breathing is a real struggle. "Erick, there are children present."

He steps back and releases his hold on me, but the fire in his eyes is not diminished. "Do you have plans tonight?"

My heart is beating so loudly, I'm sure everyone within a ten-foot radius can hear. "Me, no. Why?"

The attempt to keep my tone casual fails completely, as each word I utter goes up nearly an octave.

He flashes me a crooked grin. "Can I take you out to dinner? Or would you prefer I grab some takeout and we stay *in*?"

"Um, I mean, you know I'm not totally *alone* at the bookshop."

His recent acquisition of the knowledge that I live with a ghost bubbles to the surface and quenches the fire in his eyes. "Can you lock her out of the apartment?"

Laughter erupts from me so abruptly that I have absolutely no control. Once I catch my breath, I wave my hand and shake my head. "You knew my grandmother when she was alive, right?"

He nods.

"Then I think you know exactly how easy it is to tell her what to do."

He sighs. "Well, I can't exactly invite you over to my place."

For those of you who've forgotten, Erick bought his mother a house after he returned from his second tour in Afghanistan. He lives in the house with her. So, technically, he lives with his mom, but only because he is a wonderful son who wants to repay her for all the sacrifices she made as a single mother. "Blerg. We can't go to your place, and we may or may not have otherworldly interruptions at my place. Where does that leave us?"

He shrugs. "Let's take our chances with Isadora.

Maybe you can strike up a deal. I can't afford to buy a love nest on a public servant's salary."

This time the laughter hits me so hard I snort. The mere thought of a love nest sends a flood of tingles washing over my body. I promised myself I would take things slow this time and not repeat the terrible relationship mistakes of my past. But if he keeps suggesting things like love nests . . . my resistance ain't that strong!

Lucky for me, Stellen and his super-genius friend, who is also a girl, interrupt my uncomfortable conversation with cheers and high-fives.

"It's fixed!" Stellen beams with a combination of pride and self-conscious embarrassment.

"Dude, you're a rock star! Where's Bricklin? Let's test this thing out."

Yolo purses her lips and emits the three sharp whistles that call her canine sidekick to the ready. As usual, Bricklin appears beside her, from who knows where, ready for his assignment.

She powers up the equipment, gestures for the dog to enter the tunnel, and pulls the thick curtains closed.

Erick steps closer to me and whispers, "What is this thing?"

"It takes pet aura photos. Then Yolo interprets the photos and helps pet owners get a better understanding of their animals."

He raises one eyebrow and shakes his head. "If you say so."

Yolo's beautiful hands flutter over her keyboard, and there's a brief flash of light behind the black curtain.

She glances toward me and smiles. "Looks like it worked."

I give her a thumbs up and offer a congratulatory smile to my stepbrother.

Yolo returns to the tunnel and slides the curtains open.

A collective gasp rises from those gathered.

Stellen is the first to find his voice. "Where's Bricklin?"

Several heads nod their agreement with the question.

Yolo's violet eyes widen with fear. She struggles to issue the whistle, but no beautiful basenji appears.

Erick turns to me. "Is this part of the demonstration? Is the dog supposed to disappear? Is it kind of like a magic trick?"

I exhale softly. "No, to all of your questions. Something has gone horribly wrong."

He depresses a button on his radio and requests Deputy Candy to return to the booth immediately. Erick turns and pushes back the crowd. "We just need everyone to step back, please. And if you were here during the demonstration, please don't leave. I have a deputy coming over to take your statements."

A variety of questions echo through the crowd.

"What happened?"

"What's that machine supposed to do?"

"Did someone say a dog disappeared?"

I leave Erick to handle crowd control while I step over to the laptop. "Yolo, can you show me the picture that you just took?"

She wipes a tear from the corner of her eye and nods. She clicks open a folder and launches the app to display the saved image.

The dog is not in the photo. But something entirely unnerving is.

"Stellen. Come quick." The hairs on the back of my neck are standing on end.

He hurries to my side, and the instant he sees the image he squeaks with fright.

Yolo turns and looks at both of us. "What? What is it? Bricklin went in there for the photo. Something must've happened when the photocathode was activated. Maybe it's some kind of quantum acceleration?"

Stellen shakes his head slowly and swallows hard. "Yolo, this is gonna sound freaky. Please don't judge. There are two ghosts in the photo. I can see ghosts."

She looks back at the screen and scans for a hint of what Stellen reports.

Gripping his arm, I ask, "Two ghosts? I only see the girl."

He points to the center. "You don't see Bricklin? Right here?"

I shake my head. Apparently, I can't see animal ghosts. Weird. There's a conundrum for Silas. At least Stellen took the paranormal hit square in the chest this time and didn't drag me under the bus with him. When the inevitable screaming starts, I'll have to come up with a cover story for him.

She reaches out and grips Stellen's arm. "For reals? Ghosts? You can actually see spirit forms?"

He nods, and my extrasensory perception feels him bracing for the next heartbreaking blow.

She bounces on her tiptoes. "That is, like, the best thing ever!"

I can only imagine the confused expression gripping my face. She's not going to flip out? She's not going to point at him and yell, "Freak! Freak! Freak!" What is happening?

Stellen's jaw muscles loosen and he chews on a fingernail. "You're not freaked?"

Yolo bites her lip. "I'm a little freaked that Bricklin is a ghost. Is he dead?" Her voice catches and her eyes flood with emotion.

I offer the only consolation I have. "Let's assume the best for now. I'm no expert, but it looks like that ghost stole your dog—somehow. Maybe he's still alive, but trapped."

She shakes her head. "No way. You're telling me a ghost stole my dog. That's a lead, right?" Her big eyes look at me expectantly.

"It absolutely is." What am I saying?

Unable to release her hold on Stellen, she grips me with her other hand. "Does that mean you'll take the case?"

CHAPTER 5

Sheriff Harper radios Deputy Candy to meet him at the cruiser when he finishes taking statements. Then he grabs me by the elbow and leans deliciously close. "The bystanders were making a lot of noise, but I'm pretty sure I heard you say the word 'ghost' more than once. How about we march on outside and you fill me in?"

Swallowing my nerves, I turn to the adorable lovebirds and plaster on a smile. "Hey guys, I'm gonna look into a few things and get back to you as soon as I can. Are you all right if I leave you here?"

Stellen nods, and Yolo grips his arm for support. "We'll be okay. Thanks, Mitzy."

Erick hustles me outside and offers me a seat inside the patrol car. He hops into the driver's seat and cranks the heater. "So what did I just see? Where's that dog?"

Taking a deep breath, I shuffle through snippets

of how much I can reveal without risking my sanctum sanctorum. "So, you know how I can see ghosts?"

He nods.

"And how Stellen can see ghosts."

"Yeah, it's uncanny. Not sure I totally believe in ghosts, but what does that have to do with the disappearing dog?"

"When I looked at the photo that Yolo's machine took, I saw the ghost of a girl in the tunnel."

"Are you sure? A lot of these ghost lights in photos turn out to be hoaxes. Maybe her machine just had a glitch."

"It wasn't a blur or a flash. It was a fully formed girl in a poodle skirt and penny loafers wearing a sweater with a huge organza dahlia pinned on the left side. Her hair was light brown and pulled into a high ponytail, tied with a ribbon that matched the flower in her sweater. Oh, and she had a sweet pair of pink cat-eye glasses."

Erick angles away from me and eyes me suspiciously. "I've interviewed a lot of eyewitnesses in my day, Moon. Not one of them has had the ability to recall what they saw with such detail. You only looked at that photograph for a few seconds. How can you be so sure about the description?"

And here we reach my invisible line in the sand. "I have a super good memory. I told you that before. Anyway, when Stellen looked at the picture, he saw a second ghost."

He exhales and rolls his eyes. "If you're about to tell me it's a greaser in a black leather jacket with his thumbs in the air saying 'Hey,' we're done here."

"Not a human ghost. It was Bricklin. It was the ghost of the dog."

Erick leans forward and grabs the steering wheel with both hands. He bounces his forehead on the top of the wheel. "Hold on. You're telling me that a living dog walked into the tunnel and ten seconds later he's a ghost? That's not possible."

"Normally, I'd agree. But we all saw it happen."

He pushes himself back and takes a deep breath. "Well, some of us saw part of it, and some of us saw a whole lot more than others."

The tone of doubt in his voice pricks my protective bubble, and a little pain in my heart makes my chest constrict. "Are you saying you don't believe me?"

His shoulders sag. "Of course I believe you. I just don't believe *it*. I don't buy the whole dog ghost thing. Give me a chance to catch up, Moon." His bewildered smile eases my hurt. "I'm on your side. Just lagging behind the rest of the *Scooby Gang*."

His reference to one of my favorite cartoons brings a much needed round of laughter to the occupants of the patrol car.

Deputy Candy knocks on the window and waves.

The sudden noise intrudes on our moment.

"Looks like your new partner is here. I'm gonna check into this, and I'll have to get back to you."

Erick reaches across and gives my hand a squeeze. "Keep me posted, and ask the girl to disable the machine. I don't need any other pets disappearing while you're solving this case."

I return his affectionate grip and smile. "So you're officially calling it a case?"

He shakes his head and shrugs. "I don't know what to call it, Moon. But I'm looking forward to hearing all about it tonight."

A little shiver passes through me that has nothing to do with the temperature outside. "Copy that."

Stepping out of the vehicle, I nod politely to Deputy Candy, and he smiles a little too eagerly and for a little too long.

What is up with that kid? Doesn't he realize he's batting way out of his league? Not that I'm calling myself a straight-up Bo Derek 10, but I'm old enough to be his babysitter!

Once I'm safely inside the Jeep, I put my phone on speaker and call the almighty Silas. "Good morning, Mr. Willoughby. I have some disconcerting news and I'm definitely hoping you have ideas."

"Allow me to favor you with a brief update before you proceed. I just received word from Twiggy that she is off on a road trip to meet with several of her sources regarding the missing volume. It hasn't come up on any of the regular auction sites, but she knows some folks who deal outside the shelf, if you receive my meaning."

"Oh, I do. Can you meet me at the bookshop?"

"How soon?"

"Stellen and I just witnessed an aura photography tunnel take a photo that caused a dog to turn into a ghost. And that dog-ghost was then kidnapped by another, human, ghost. So you tell me."

Silas gasps with uncharacteristic shock. "I shall depart my residence immediately."

To the bookstore!

Hurrying in through the side door, I tempt fate by hopping over the "No Admittance" chain, and serendipity smiles upon me as I land clumsily, but intact, on the other side.

"Grams! Grams, we have an emergency. Get your ghost butt in here."

A burgundy streak rockets through the wall leading from the printing museum into the bookshop. "Did you say emergency?"

"Silas is on his way over, but it's a paranormal brain bender! We're definitely gonna need all the ghost help we can get."

She zips through the wall into the apartment, while I wait for the door to slide open like a civilized person.

"Don't judge what you don't understand, dear."

Taking a single finger, I point meaningfully toward my lips. "Don't comment on what's none of your business, woman."

She shrugs her designer-gown-clad shoulders. "Should I get the murder wall?"

"Yes, but it's not a murder. At least I hope it's not a murder."

Struggling to quell her excitement enough to take corporeal form, Ghost-ma is not making much progress with the rolling corkboard.

"Here, let me help."

Together, we get the board in place, and she hovers near the stack of 3 x 5 cards, pen in hand.

"Like I said, it's not a murder." I catch her up on the strange happenings at the invention convention, and she makes cards for Yolo, Stellen, Wibb, Fiona, and Bricklin.

Before we can delve too deeply into profiling an animal-stealing ghost, Silas arrives.

"Ah, I see you've begun assembling your list of suspects."

I scoff. "Not so much a list of suspects, as a list of people who were around at the time. The only suspect we have is a ghost. And I have no idea how to track her down."

Silas smooths his bushy grey mustache with a thumb and forefinger, and his jowls waggle as he nods his head. "A girl, you say?"

I repeat my description of the ghost, and Grams zooms in. "She sounds like she stepped right off the floor of a sock hop, sweetie. Either it was some kind of dress-up day, or she's been a ghost since the 1950s."

"I'll have Stellen and Yolo check the yearbooks. If she's been a ghost since the 1950s—"

Grams nods her head knowingly. "I've been able to learn several useful things in the short time since my earthly death. Imagine if someone had over seventy years to work on her skills. I'm not surprised she stole that dog. She's probably lonely as all get out!"

"Grams! I hardly think loneliness is a justification for dognapping and possible pet murder."

She checks her manicure and nods dismissively. "Of course, dear, I'm sure you're right."

"If we can't figure this out by tomorrow, Yolo won't be able to demonstrate her device for the competition. She'll lose her chance at all that prize money." I shake my head and sigh. "It really is a brilliant invention. I can't imagine what went wrong."

"Indeed." Silas steeples his fingers and bounces his chin on the tips of his pointers.

I feel a lesson brewing.

"Describe the events of this morning. Do not leave out anything. The subtlest tidbit could be the clue we need."

"You want me to use the psychic recall?"

He continues to bounce his chin methodically.

"All right, but let me call Stellen real quick and get him and Yolo on this yearbook assignment." After relaying the mission details to my stepbrother and confirming that they disabled the machine, I take two deep breaths and clear my mind. As I play through the events of the morning like a video clip, I pause and rewind as needed to give Silas as much detail as possible.

He draws a deep breath and harrumphs as he scans the 3 x 5 cards on the murder wall. "I believe we should add a card for this Deputy Candy you mentioned. I do not yet see his connection to the events you described, but he was at the venue."

"Add him to the board, Grams." I turn to Silas. "If being at the venue makes someone a suspect, there were hundreds of people in the gymnasium. Deputy Candy took statements from everyone that was gathered around the booth at the time, but it would've been simple to slip away unnoticed."

Silas nods. "Precisely."

"What do you mean? Do you think someone stole the dog, snuck it out of a crowded gymnasium, and then magically made ghost images appear in our photograph?"

"I do not." Silas scoffs at the very thought. "However, it seems more than plausible that the equipment could've suffered from malicious tampering, and the saboteur would've had no problem blending into the crowd."

The morning's sequence of events does not seem to fit with his hypothesis, but Silas and his wild theories will have to wait. My phone pings with a text notification. "Hold that thought. Looks like the junior sleuths have an update."

"found photo. 2 creepy. otw."

Silas leans forward and stares at the phone as

though it possesses strange powers. "What is it that you are interpreting? It appears to be a hybrid language."

"It's a text." My face cannot hide my shock and awe. "You speak a dozen languages and converse in Latin like it's normal, and you've never gotten a text?"

"I couldn't say. My mobile device is simply for placing the occasional phone call, when I am unable to properly converse face-to-face."

My eyes roll wildly of their own free will. "Let me see your phone!"

The ridiculous antique he pulls from his pocket nearly gives me a case of the vapors. "How old is that thing?"

"I can't recall. It works perfectly. Why replace it?"

"Remind me to never send you a text."

"I would have assumed that was understood, Mizithra. I prefer to speak to you in person, so that I may benefit from the subtleties of body language. And if that is impossible, the nuances of the human voice carry important information. Why would I have any interest in reading this mutated script from a small impersonal screen?"

"Why indeed." I permit myself a brief and satisfying chuckle before interpreting the message for my mentor. "It's a text from Stellen, and it sounds like he and Yolo not only located the yearbook containing the girl's image, but they've uncovered a creepy back story. If I know Stellen, he's found a way to temporarily borrow the yearbook from the school's library, and the two of them are on their way here to share their findings."

"Very well. I should like to peruse this annual book for myself."

CHAPTER 6

STELLEN'S VOICE CRACKLES eagerly over the intercom. "Is it all right if I bring Yolo up to the apartment?"

I hop up from the settee and tap the mother-of-pearl inlaid button on the left. "Come on up. Make sure you hook the chain behind you. Trust me, it's a whole *thing*!"

A moment later the bookcase door slides open, and the tiny purple pixie-girl gasps in amazement. "I love it!"

Stellen blushes with pride. "It's lit, right?"

She nods, and her large violet eyes sparkle as they enter the apartment.

"Welcome to headquarters, Yolo. Sit wherever you like. Silas is eager to get his hands on that yearbook. And, on that subject, how did the two of you get into the school library on a weekend?"

Yolo gazes towards Stellen with admiration.

"He's super good buddies with the janitor. I guess he goes in on weekends kind of a lot, to, like, study and stuff."

Stellen smiles and shrugs. "It's awesome, being the only one in there. It's less distracting, you know?"

"Good job, little bro. Connections are important in the world of super sleuthing. Where's the goods?"

He slips off his backpack, unzips the main compartment, and retrieves the book.

Silas accepts the yearbook and admires it with the genuine care of a true book lover.

Stellen steps toward the attorney/alchemist and asks, "Do you want me to show you the memorial page?"

The older man gazes up at the boy and his saggy jowls lift in a nostalgic grin. "Would you?"

Stellen flips to the back of the annual and points to a full-page spread.

I step over beside them and immediately recognize the face from the ghost image in the aura pic. The one in the old book is a black-and-white photo, but the horn-rimmed glasses, high ponytail, and similar outfit confirm the identity of our phantom. I read her name aloud. "Irene Tir. It says here she died in 1956 at something called a *Nikdäg*? What the heck is *Nikdäg*?"

Silas opens his mouth to give us one of his fastidious speeches, but Yolo beats him to the draw.

"Oh, it's a super-old-fashioned tradition, from Sweden or something. It's where the girls asked the guys out. There were, like, lists of available guys, and rules. I did a paper on it for my women's studies class last year. I take classes at the community college. I'll have enough credits for an AA by the time I graduate high school."

I open my mouth to respond, but my moment is stolen by another over-eager teen.

"That's how we met. Taking the extra classes and stuff." Stellen smiles down at his own feet.

"Well, you two might be late to the investigation game, but you're hittin' it out of the park so far." I tap my finger on the glossy page. "The dog in the picture with her looks very similar to Bricklin."

Yolo jumps up from her cross-legged spot on the floor. "I know, right? I'm sure it's a basenji. They started importing them to America in the 1940s, so it's totally possible. They can live up to twenty years under the right circumstances." She sniffles softly. "If they're not turned into ghosts." Her voice catches in her throat and she collapses onto the settee with a moan.

"Don't worry, Yolo. We're gonna figure this out. Right, Silas?"

He leans back in the over-stuffed chair and stares at the image of Irene Tir.

"Time is of the essence. The longer the dog's spirit wanders, the more difficult it will be to coax him back." He smooths his mustache with a thumb and forefinger. "We must uncover the cause of this young girl's demise. Mitzy, I believe it's up to you and your sheriff to ascertain if Irene has any living relatives in the area. Perhaps they know the story of this fateful *Nikdäg* night."

"Understood. I'll just run over to the station. You guys are welcome to hang out here. Maybe Stellen can introduce you to Pyewacket. Sound good?"

Stellen smiles. "Can I show her the printing museum too?"

My extrasensory perception easily translates "printing museum" to "Grams." "I suppose. But I hope it goes without saying, that anything that happens in the bookshop, stays in the bookshop." I tilt my head and raise an eyebrow knowingly.

Stellen is no idiot. He knows exactly what the look on my face means. "You got it."

Grabbing my coat, hat, and mittens, I skedaddle down the circular staircase and head to the sheriff's station.

Deputy Baird, also known as Furious Monkeys, is deep into her favorite phone app when I push through the front door and stomp the snow off my shoes. "Is he here?"

Without removing her eyes from the intense game she's playing on her cell, she nods her head toward the crooked wooden gate.

I push through, and, while I'm crossing the bullpen, Deputy Candy appears from the hallway between the sheriff's office and the interrogation rooms. "Hello again, Miss Moon. What brings you into the station?"

He's changed out of his uniform, and his tight T-shirt barely reaches the waistband of his low-slung jeans. I fight the urge to stare and mumble my answer. "Here to see the sheriff."

He grabs a file box from a desk and lifts it high into the air, to slide on top of the bookcase. Inevitably, his tiny T-shirt rides up, exposing his bare midriff.

Yes, I take a peek. Don't worry, he couldn't give Erick a run for his money if he had a thirty-second head start.

He tracks my line of sight and grins.

I inhale sharply and turn the other way.

"I have a few more boxes to put away, but I'll be free for coffee in about ten minutes."

His brazen invitation has me flustered. I'm not great on my feet when I'm flustered. So I'm going to ignore this whole exchange. Later, when the perfect response comes to mind, I'll log it away for my next encounter with this eighteen-year-old Lothario.

Thankfully, Erick is in his office and smiles when I walk in. "Have a seat, Moon."

"Quick update for you. The gh— What can I call it, so we both know what I'm talking about, but I don't sound insane?"

He leans back in his chair and rubs his left thumb along his jawline. "Let's just refer to it as the person. That should keep you safe, right?"

"Yup. The person in the photo is Irene Tir. She died in 1956, and she had a pet basenji."

He lets out a low whistle. "Impressive. There are

a few too many things that line up to call them all coincidences."

"This is what I'm saying." I lean forward and put on my best grin.

He sighs and hangs his head. "Uh oh, here comes the favor."

"You're not wrong." I take a pause and offer him a suggestive wink. "Can you tell me if any of Irene's relatives live in the area? We'd like to find out how she died, and what happened to the dog."

"Let me ask Paulsen."

My mouth opens and my shoulders droop.

He shrugs. "I know, I know, but she knows everyone. It's the fastest way to the answer you need. Sit tight."

I will not sit tight. I will sit loosely, and I will dislike every part of this solution.

He returns with the short, squat deputy Paulsen trailing him. Her face bears a permanent scowl, and her right hand rests on the grip of her gun. "What business do you have with the Tirs, Moon?"

When in doubt, lie it out. "My stepbrother, Stellen Jablonski, is doing some research and came across a memorial page in an old yearbook. He'd like to interview the family for additional details."

She raises one brow and eyes me suspiciously. "Yeah, the Tirs own a farm outside of Pin Cherry. Property's been in their family since the early 1900s. I think there's a Kevin or a Kent who lives out there now. Might be a great-great-grandson, or nephew. Not sure how much they'd know."

"Well, I appreciate the information. Thanks."

Her scowl softens minutely, but doesn't quite turn into a smile. She nods curtly and returns to wherever Erick found her.

He crosses his arms in that yummy way that makes his biceps bulge. "Anything else I can do for you?"

My cheeks flush and I can't keep from smiling. "You might want to ask Deputy Candy to stand down."

Erick's face scrunches up in confusion. "Stand down?"

"Yeah. He's coming on *real* strong. The kid does not take a hint."

He laughs a little too hard at my expense. "Look in the mirror, Moon. Can you blame him?"

The light-pink hue on my cheeks turns to a flaming crimson. "Thanks for nothing, Sheriff."

As I brush past him to squeeze out the door, he leans close and whispers, "See you tonight."

Tingles roll down my spine and my tummy goes all warm and gooey. Luckily, I have enough left in the tank to add a little extra wiggle to my waddle as I head out the front door.

Hustling back to the Bell, Book & Candle, I weigh the pros and cons of taking the teens with me to interrogate the Tir family. In the end, I have to admit that the anime-come-to-life Yolo is practically irresistible. If I bring her and Stellen along for the ride, it should soften up the family and help us get the facts we need much quicker. When those big, innocent eyes fill with tears . . . Decision made.

Silas has migrated to the Rare Books Loft and is researching possible explanations for Bricklin's disappearance, and Stellen and Yolo have returned from their tour. I bring the gang up to speed, and Yolo offers to drive out to the farmhouse.

Maybe growing up in almost-Canada makes one a more competent winter driver, but from my vantage point in the back seat, this excursion only serves to fill me with mounting dread. Yolo manages to keep her vehicle on the road, but only by the skin of her teeth. She's definitely driving over the speed limit, and if we hit even a small patch of ice near one of these four-way intersections, her last-minute break-stomp maneuver is going to fail miserably. I can only cross my fingers and hope we don't encounter a semi truck on a perpendicular trajectory.

Stellen seems cool as a cucumber. Either he is a far better actor than me, or he is legitimately UN-terrified.

By the time we reach the Tir farm, my nerves are a disaster and an unwelcome wave of carsickness is swirling in my gut.

Exiting the vehicle as quickly as possible, I plant my feet on terra firma and gulp in the fresh air.

Yolo places a hand on my shoulder. "You should

ride in front on the way home. I always get carsick when I'm sitting in back too."

Sure. I'll let her believe that's the reason. "What's the plan? We definitely can't tell them about ghosts or an aura photo machine gone wrong."

Stellen nods. "I think we should say it's for a school project. Maybe something about the history of Pin Cherry High School and remembering students who were taken too soon?" He shrugs his shoulders and looks toward the two of us for approval.

Yolo claps her delicate hands in a way that reminds me of Grams. "Yes. That's perfect. And I can mention the picture because I have a basenji too." She dabs at her eye. "I won't mention that he's missing right now."

"Great. Stick to the script. Nobody tries to be a hero. Get in. Get out. Got it?"

Stellen smirks. "No man left behind, and more stuff like that."

I roll my eyes. "Lead the way, smart aleck."

He chuckles, and the three of us mount the front steps, ring the bell, and cross our collective fingers.

CHAPTER 7

A MAN LOOKING ROUGHLY the same age as my dad opens the door and sizes up our motley crew. He rubs a hand across his thick salt-and-pepper beard, and eyes Yolo and her steampunk wardrobe suspiciously. "We don't support the high school drama club. You have a nice day."

She smiles and lifts on her tippy toes ever so slightly. "Oh, I completely understand. Are you Mr. Tir?"

The man shuffles backward an inch or two and raises his chin. "I'm Kent. Who's asking?"

"Oh, great. I'm Yolo Olson. My friend Stellen and I are writing an article for the school newspaper. Actually, a series of articles featuring students from the history of Pin Cherry Harbor High School—that were taken too soon. We're interviewing families, highlighting important events from each student's past, and trying to raise awareness about the wonderful people who made our school what it is today."

Wow! She's quick on her feet. Some part of her speech connects with him. He nods and scratches his beard thoughtfully. "So what brings you out here?"

"One of our articles features Irene Tir. She died in 1956, but we were hoping you, or someone in your family, might know something about the girl she was before she passed."

He snuffles and shrugs. "My wife's into all that genealogy stuff. Hold on." He turns and shouts down the narrow hallway of the farmhouse. "Monica? Monica, there's some people here about the family history?"

A woman about my height, with faded blonde hair tucked behind her ears, tentatively peeks over her husband's shoulder. "What's this about?"

Yolo repeats her brilliant speech, as Kent disappears into the bowels of the house. Fortunately, Monica takes the bait.

"Oh, I'd love to help you out. I think it's just great that you're working on a school project on the weekend. Come on in and have a seat at the kitchen table. I'll grab my laptop and the photo albums. I can certainly give you any information I have on Irene."

We follow her into the house and take a seat at her large kitchen table. Six old wooden chairs surround a white-legged table with a thick butcher-block top. Every piece of décor in the kitchen is an incarnation of pig. There are little piggy salt-and-pepper shakers, a rotund porcine cookie jar, and various wooden and porcelain versions of swine in chef's hats and/or aprons. This woman has a serious pig preoccupation.

The lady of the house returns with her laptop and three ancient photo albums. She slides a photo book toward each of us and smiles. "You can page through these, while I call up the genealogy information on my computer. I have this great software that tracks everything. I spent years requesting information from family members and making notes and new entries whenever something was submitted. I'm actually really happy you guys showed up today. It's a lot of work, you know? For me it's a hobby, but it's kind of nice for someone to actually want to look at it."

Yolo flashes her an enchanting smile. "I can't tell you how much this means, Mrs. Tir."

Monica blushes a little and glances toward the stove. "Can I offer you some hot chocolate, or maybe you kids drink coffee? I know a lot of kids your age do."

I smile at our hostess. "I think hot chocolate would be fine for all of us. Thank you very much."

"No trouble at all."

She pulls a saucepan from a cupboard and retrieves milk, baking chocolate, sugar, and several spices. At this point, it dawns on me she is going to make hot cocoa from scratch. Something that never would've occurred to a "packet girl" like me. "Oh gosh, Mrs. Tir, that looks like a lot of work. We're fine with water."

She brushes my comment away with a swipe of her hand. "Nonsense. It takes two minutes. You keep paging through those scrapbooks, and I'll have this ready in a jiffy."

Stellen glances at me and shrugs. I return the gesture and open my album. Yolo is the first to strike it rich. "Look! This is the picture from the memorial page in the yearbook." Her fingers trace over the other photos in the spread, with their edges carefully tucked into the red corner holders affixed to the black pages of the album. "These are, like, all of Irene. And there's some more of her dog, too."

Monica leaves her pan simmering on the stove and looks over Yolo's shoulder. "Oh, my goodness. Irene! Of course. What a sad story."

Yolo looks up eagerly. "Did you know her?"

Mrs. Tir's eyes widen. "How old do you think I am, dear?"

The purple pixie-girl blushes and bats her perfectly applied false lashes. "I'm so sorry. I didn't really think about it. Of course you didn't."

Monica puts a comforting hand on her shoulder. "Don't feel bad. When I was your age, I could never tell the age of adults. Anyone from thirty to seventy was all the same to me."

We all offer a compensatory chuckle.

Monica returns to the stove to give her concoction a stir and steps back toward the pictures. "I only remember Irene because of that dog. He's buried in the cemetery right next to her."

She has my attention. This story gets more interesting by the minute. "If you don't mind my asking, how did Irene die?"

"Gosh, aside from the infant deaths during the diphtheria outbreak in the early 1900s, hers was the saddest story I ever entered into the genealogy database. She was a sweet young thing, always helping, always making the extra effort. She was on the decoration committee for that year's *Nikdäg*. Do you know what that is?"

Yolo nods. "Yes, ma'am."

Monica smiles at her with motherly admiration. "Well, Irene had a wonderful idea to set up a spring-themed dance in the fall. You know how cold it gets around here in November, so she thought it would lift folks' spirits to dream of spring. She got a local farmer to donate a big batch of baby chicks, and she took it upon herself to dye them all Easter colors and set up a whole beautiful pink barn in the gymnasium. I'm sure it was magical. The black-and-white photos in the yearbook don't do it justice."

I'd love to interrupt and ask her to head in the direction of the point, but we're supposed to be writing the story of Irene's history, and we should consider all these minute details journalistic gold.

Monica presses her hand to her heart. "Well, as you can imagine, baby chicks don't like to be dyed pink, purple, and blue, so she got scratched several times. The doctor's report said a few of those scratches were awful deep. And the thing about baby chicks is that they poop as much as they eat. Pardon my French."

We all make gestures of absolution for Monica's harsh use of the word "poop," and she continues.

"And I'm not sure if you're aware, but their feces carry salmonella. Irene's folks had no idea that she had a compromised immune system. Now, most people can fight off salmonella in a day or two. I'm not saying it's pleasant, but you get over it, you know?"

We all nod.

"Poor little Irene. She didn't make it. She collapsed right in the middle of the gymnasium, under the mirror ball, during the last dance of the evening. The story I heard said she was in the arms of her true love."

Yolo leans forward and whispers, "Was it her dog?"

Monica pats her shoulder. "Oh, you truly are the sweetest. No, some boy or other. But that wasn't the end of the sad story."

Stellen is mesmerized by the tale and asks, "What happened next?"

"She was in the hospital fighting for her life, and at the same time her poor little pup took ill."

"What was wrong with him?"

"Turns out he had been fighting distemper for months. They died on the same day."

Yolo gasps and presses a hand to her mouth.

Stellen shakes his head. "How awful."

Monica shakes her head. "Isn't it just? The family buried the dog next to the girl, and there was a big write-up in the paper about the tragedy, and reminding everyone about the dangers of salmonella. Terrible. Just terrible."

We all nod solemnly.

"Irene was a photographer for the yearbook. She probably took half of the pictures in that 1956 yearbook. Can you imagine? To spend so much time and effort capturing memories for your class, and then you end up as one. Well, it's just the saddest thing."

Stellen and Yolo exchange tender glances, but there's something in the story that causes the mood ring on my left hand to burn with urgency. Looking down, I see a flash of an old camera swirling in the black mists trapped inside the cabochon. "Did you say she was a photographer?"

"Mmhmm." Monica steps over to the stove and pours the hot chocolate into four mugs. She passes them out and joins us at the table.

"Do you know what happened to her camera?" Blowing my cocoa, I take a careful drink of the steaming beverage.

Stellen's eyes lock onto me, and the deep emerald irises shimmer with understanding.

Mrs. Tir casually sips her cocoa, wipes her mouth, and shakes her head. "No idea. I would've loved to have something like that, or even one of her adorable poodle skirts. The girl really had an artistic eye."

My extrasensory perceptions pick up on a swelling panic coming from Stellen's side of the table. "Thank you so much for your time, and the hot chocolate. It was delicious. We really need to be going. Do you know if Irene has any other relatives in the area?"

Monica consults her genealogy chart. "Let's see, Irene had two sisters and two brothers. Looks like they've all passed. One sister never married, one brother lost two children. Oh, poor man! His wife died in childbirth. The other sister's line moved way, and . . . Well, that just leaves us. Kent had an older brother, but he passed away two years ago, whitewater rafting in the Colorado River. One of those bucket list things that ended up kicking the bucket. That's why I always tell Kent he's better off living a smaller life for a longer amount of time than reaching for the stars only to fall and cut his life short."

We all nod, thank her profusely for the information and the refreshments, and hightail it out the front door.

My new seating assignment in the front does little to quell my fears on the drive back to town.

From the back seat, Stellen offers his analysis.

"There's got to be some connection to the camera. Right?"

If I turn my head to look back at him, I will most certainly hurl. So I keep my eyes locked on the road ahead as I reply. "Yeah. I've been meaning to ask you: Where did you get that part?"

CHAPTER 8

THE SHORT WINTER days send the sun packing by 4:30 in the afternoon, so we'll have to visit Stellen's tinker tomorrow. According to my stepbrother, the photocathode replacement part came from an "ancient" man who deals exclusively in salvaged parts, and has a huge property south of Pin Cherry on the edge of town.

An icy wind rips across the great lake nestled in our harbor and swirls small tornadoes of snow into the air. Back in Arizona, when the desert winds would whip up the sand in this way, we called them dust devils; or massive ones were called haboobs. I'm sure the Eskimos have a similar name for what we're witnessing, but for now Stellen and I call it "freezing" as we regretfully exit the warm interior of Yolo's car to run for cover.

"I'd invite you over to hang out, but Erick is supposed to bring me dinner and let me sneak a peek at the statements Deputy Candy took from the bystanders today."

Stellen shrugs. "No sweat. I know you guys gotta hook up whenever you can."

"For at least the fiftieth time, we are not *hooking up*. We are casually dating and we'll see where things go."

He smirks and traces a heart shape in the snow. In the center, he draws MM + EH. "According to Amaryllis, the two of you spent, like, a week in Arizona. And one night after she downed her third or fourth glass of wine, she spilled that you shared a hotel room."

"You know what? You can file that under none of your business, buddy. Amaryllis doesn't know what she's talking about, and, plus, that's a whole 'nother story."

Stellen chuckles and flashes his eyebrows. "Oh, I'm sure it is."

"Has anyone ever told you what an annoying brother you are?"

For a moment the mirth drains from his eyes, and he swallows loudly. "Actually, no. I've never had a sister before."

Blerg. This kid knows how to win every conversation. If teasing me about my love life doesn't work, just yank one of my heartstrings until it breaks. "You win!"

Stellen scrunches up his face. "Win what? I'm

serious. I don't really know how to be a brother. Do I suck at it?"

Sighing in exasperation, I reach over to give his shoulder a squeeze. "Keep in mind, I have no idea what it's like to have a brother. But, as far as I'm concerned, you're crushing it, dude."

He laughs out loud and we part ways in the alley. He heads into my father's building for a lovely home-cooked meal in the penthouse, and I scurry into the bookshop, hoping Erick will be along shortly with some sustenance.

However, once inside I choose to reheat a mug of leftover coffee in the microwave, and tide myself over with a day-old doughnut.

"You really do have no concept of time, sweetie."

The sudden appearance of Grams results in a little spilling of my coffee and a momentary choking on my stale doughnut. "Grams! We agreed upon the slow, sparkly reentry. You can't just pop into existence and shout things at me. I have a delicate constitution."

This blatant falsehood initiates a burst of shared laughter.

"Why don't you head over to the diner for a proper meal?"

Painting my features in a portrait of innocence, I reply, "About that . . ."

Ghost-ma crosses her bejeweled limbs over her bosom and lifts one brow. "I smell a deal?"

"Nothing gets past you. Erick is bringing over

some dinner, and he specifically asks that we have privacy."

She zips down to eye level, and I'm certain that I can hear her non-existent heart beating faster. "Privacy? Really? Is tonight the night?"

"Grams! Not only is it none of your business, but I told you I want to take things slow. Now that he knows about you, I think he simply wanted some assurances that there won't be any eavesdropping or peeping ghosts."

"And what are you offering in return?"

I scan the room as though there's an audience to back me up. "Wow. Are you blackmailing me?"

She shrugs and adjusts one of her many diamond rings.

"Fine. In exchange for your complete and total absence from the apartment until tomorrow morning at 10:00 a.m., I will allow you to pick out a marginally sexy outfit for me to wear this evening."

She rockets up to the ceiling, clapping her hands maniacally. "Give me twenty minutes." She swoops into the closet I call *Sex and the City* meets *Confessions of a Shopaholic,* and her murmurs of glee give me cause for concern.

Meanwhile, I take the opportunity of her preoccupation to have a shower. The thick swirling steam and delicious eucalyptus body scrub clear my head and calm my nerves.

Wrapping one towel around my freshly scrubbed hair and one around my body, I go to work on makeup application. Next, I apply some product to my hair and attempt to use the round bristle brush to blow it out the way Grams taught me. It doesn't turn out great, but it's definitely better than the stocking-hat hair I was sporting pre-shower.

And now, like a lamb to the slaughter, I must join Grams in the closet.

"Do your worst."

She grins and points at the two options she's selected.

My eyes nearly pop out of my head as I scan the items placed on the padded mahogany bench in the center of the space. "You can't be serious?"

She swirls above the 1950s-style cocktail dress, pearls, and slip-on heels with fur trim and shrugs. "Don't blame a ghost for dreaming."

I approach the second option, which consists of a crossover cashmere sweater, black skinny jeans, and suede ankle boots with at least a four-inch heel. "I'll definitely be choosing option number two."

Her shimmering shoulders sag, and she begrudgingly returns the outfit from another era to its proper place in the closet.

"May I have a bit of privacy to get dressed?"

She blasts through the wall of the closet into the apartment. "Make it snappy. I want to get a good look at you before I'm banished."

Her flair for the dramatic never ceases to make me smile. The jeans are quite snug, but I'll chalk that up to the extra treats I snarfed during the holidays. The sweater fits perfectly, even if the neckline is a little plunge-y, and the warm purple hue reminds me of Yolo. The boots are more comfortable than they appear, and by the time I stride out of the closet and perform the requisite spins, I'm feeling pretty good about myself.

"And you should! You look fantastic. That color is divine on you. Erick is a lucky man."

I pantomime pushing her out of the apartment. "He's not going to be that lucky, so don't get your hopes up. I'll see you tomorrow morning at 10:00."

She exhales loudly. "Such a spoilsport." Her laughter lingers even after she disapparates.

BING. BONG. BING.

Let the date night begin! I rush down the stairs and catch the toe of my boot on the "No Admittance" chain as I attempt to climb over. My ankle gives a little, but I save myself from serious injury with a last-minute desperate lunge for the railing.

Twiggy has me terrified to unhook that chain, now that it's set to trigger a secondary alarm. The last thing I need is to launch my evening with Erick to the tune of sirens and bells.

"Who is it?" I ask coyly.

"It's the escort you requested, Miss. The service sent me."

Erick's hearty chuckle radiates through the steel alleyway door, and I push it open with one fist on my hip. "Hilarious."

He opens his mouth to issue a snappy reply, but then his eyes get real busy checking out my ensemble.

"You—that's definitely—nice outfit."

I grab the bag from his hand. "Nice outfit? That's where you landed?"

Turning, I strut into the back room to retrieve plates and utensils.

He follows me and mumbles something salacious under his breath.

"I'm sorry, I didn't quite catch that, Sheriff."

He sidles up next to me and pulls me deliciously close. "Oh, you will. I can promise you that."

My knees get wobbly, and I toy with the idea of calling for otherworldly backup.

"By the way, were you able to strike a deal with Isadora?"

"Mmhmm." I'm afraid that if I open my mouth, the drool will dribble down my chin. Instead, I busy myself collecting plates, forks, and napkins. "Did you want to eat down here, or in the apartment?"

"Here's fine. I brought some wine. We can have it with dinner, or we can drink it during the movie."

"We're watching a movie?"

He blushes and shrugs. "If you want. By the way, did you leave that love note in the snow for me?"

My face must show my utter confusion.

Erick grins. "The 'MM + EH' inside the heart."

I blow a raspberry and shake my head. "You can thank my dastardly little brother for that."

He smiles. "I always liked that kid."

I open the food and set the small bistro table with my mismatched plates and silverware. "Do you mind drinking wine out of water glasses? I used to have a couple of wineglasses, but sometimes the resident recovering-alcoholic ghost takes issue with my stemware choices."

"Not a problem." He loads up a plate with lasagna, roasted Broccolini, and cheesy garlic bread from the local Italian ristorante, Angelo and Vinci's.

Taking the seat opposite, I follow suit and dig into the scrumptious pasta.

Erick wipes his mouth with a paper napkin and eyes my sweater as he finishes swallowing. "That color looks really nice on you."

I wash down my cheesy garlic bread with a glug of Chianti and grin. "Oh, it's the color, is it?" I run my finger along the edge of the deep-V neckline and wink.

He snickers. "Careful, Moon. I'm afraid you might be writing checks you can't cash."

For some reason the reference tickles my funny bone, and I can hardly stop laughing.

"Wow. I didn't think it was that funny." He lifts an eyebrow.

Finally getting myself under control, I take a deep breath and explain. "Before I came to Pin Cherry, not only would that not have been funny, but I would've had no idea what you were talking about. But now that I'm a regular in the town that tech forgot, the idea of checks, in and of themselves, is hilarious."

He leans back and lays his napkin in his lap.

For a moment, I can't help but wish he were wearing one of Deputy Candy's tiny T-shirts.

"Did I lose you for a minute there?"

I shake my head and take another sip of wine to hide my smirk.

"So, before you came here, you never wrote a check? How would you pay your bills?"

"Great questions. To be clear, there were a lot of times I wasn't able to pay my bills, and when I did it was usually at the last minute or after it was already late, with cash at a window across the counter from a scowling middle-aged woman looking at me with sad judgey eyes."

He tilts his head, opens his mouth to speak, rethinks his approach, and starts the whole sequence over. "Let me get this straight, you didn't have a bank account?"

I exhale and hang my head. "I'm not sure I like your tone, Sheriff. But the truth is, there's not much call for a bank account that's simply going to have a zero balance or possibly a series of insufficient funds charges. To be honest, paying for everything in cash when I came to Pin Cherry wasn't that much of a change for me. The difference was, I actually had the cash."

He laughs heartily. "I'm not laughing at you, I promise. I'm sorry to ask, but it's gonna bother me if I don't. Did you take care of your outstanding debts once you got the inheritance?"

"Geez! What do you think? Between my dad and Silas, everything I do has to be above board."

He pushes his empty plate toward the middle of the table and narrows his gaze. "I don't think that's entirely true."

"Rude, but I suppose you're not wrong." I grab the open bottle of Chianti and strut my stuff up to the apartment.

Erick joins me on the settee and refills my glass.

"If I didn't know better, I'd say you're trying to get me drunk, Mr. Harper."

His cheeks flush an adorable shade of pink, and I can't stop myself from kissing him.

He leans back, clears his throat, and attempts to use his all-business voice. "Did you want to look at those eyewitness statements from the convention?"

I set my tumbler of wine on the coffee table, grip the placket of his button-down shirt, and pull close enough for him to smell the wine on my breath. "Not right now, Your Honor, but I reserve the right to examine that evidence later."

He chuckles and scoops his arms around me.

Canoodling, small talk, and somehow a second bottle of wine keep the evening interesting. To be clear, that second bottle of wine is all me—as in, all in my glass. I'm not sure if I'm keeping demons at bay or trying to weaken my own defenses . . .

As we slide past the witching hour into the wee

hours, Erick untangles himself from my arms and takes a deep breath. "My shift actually starts at 0600. Trust me when I tell you I don't want to leave. But it's never good to drive a vehicle or brandish a firearm when I'm sleep deprived."

Snuggling back into his embrace, I wish I had the courage to break my own rules. "Brandish a firearm? You're starting to sound like Paulsen."

He grins and kisses my forehead.

There it is. The official sign that *date night* is over, folks. For what it's worth, I appreciate his commitment to serve and protect, and I'm actually happy not to test my severely inebriated resolve.

"Do you mind if I swing by the station and have a look at those statements later?"

He slides his finger along the neckline of my crossover sweater, and I feel as though my skin is on fire. "We can do anything you want as long as you wear this sweater."

And I'm dead.

Struggling to find enough breath in my lungs to form words, I mumble something like "copy that."

He winks, presses the twisted ivy medallion that activates my sliding bookcase door from inside the apartment, and walks out.

The dim light from my apartment provides the perfect fade-to-black moment, as his excellent exit disappears into the darkness of the bookshop.

The bookcase slides closed, and I collapse onto the settee with a groan.

Before I can make plans to change into my pajamas, or fall into bed fully clothed, Pyewacket climbs onto my midriff and settles in.

"Hey, Mr. Cuddlekins, I'm absolutely not sleeping on this settee. Let me up, and you can hog the bed as usual."

Instead of responding or moving, Pye drops something on my chest.

The foreign object surprises me, and I sit up too rapidly.

My bossy caracal leaps to safety while I examine the item.

"A dog collar? Normally you're ahead of the curve, son. But we already know there's a dog missing. I'll log it into evidence, but I'm not sure you're giving us anything we didn't already know."

"Ree-ow." Soft but condescending.

As I lay the green dog collar on the coffee table, the heart-shaped tag clanks against the wood.

"I'm sure you're right, but I need a huge glass of water and I've got to get some sleep."

The ping of a text and the intrusion of Ghost-ma tie for first place in what wakes me up.

She whizzes around the room. "There's no sign of Sheriff Harper. What happened? Dish!"

Rubbing the sleep from my eyes, I cradle my head and reach for my phone. "Hold on, Chuck Woolery, let me see who's texting."

The message is from Stellen. Apparently Yolo has decided to withdraw from the competition, and he's helping her pack up the machine and the rest of her booth. I quickly fire back a "so sorry" and tell him to meet me at the bookshop when they're finished.

Grams places a fist on her curvy hip and chews the inside of her cheek. "Are you going to spill, or am I going to have to haunt you?"

"At least let me have a cup of coffee, woman."

She scoffs and vanishes. I take advantage of the reprieve to use the facilities, grab my thick robe, and stumble down to the coffeemaker.

Once I've poured my liquid alert, I have no more excuses.

"Dish. Now." Her glimmering eyes spark with potential retribution.

"All right. All right." I fill her in on the highlights of the evening, and my difficulty in watching Erick walk away.

She chuckles. "Well, partially difficult. Partially I'm sure it was rather entertaining. That man knows how to fill out a pair of jeans."

"Grams!"

She shrugs. "I'm dead, not buried!"

Despite my lack of sleep, or possibly because of it, the ghost joke gets me giggling until I'm struggling to breathe. "I better grab a quick breakfast at the diner before Stellen gets here. Seems like we're going to have a pretty full schedule today."

An air of sadness settles over Grams, and she floats lazily through the wall. "I sure do miss Odell."

"And he misses you, Grams. I know how close you were during that last year, before you died. Would you like me to give him a hug that's secretly from you?"

She hurtles back through the wall. "Would you?"

"Anything for you, Isadora."

"World's best granddaughter! I love you, Mitzy."

"I love you too, Grams."

CHAPTER 9

At the cozy local diner that serves as my home away from home, I deliver Grams' secret hug to Odell and slide onto the red-vinyl bench seat to enjoy a genuine cup of black gold. Traffic at the diner is surprisingly sparse. The convention attendees must've been up at the crack of dawn to enjoy their morning's repast.

I down my usual breakfast with unusual haste and rush back toward the bookshop as my phone pings with a text from Stellen.

"Here."

You have to hand it to the kid. He does not mince words. We load into the Jeep and he gives me directions to the tinker.

At some point, the route begins to feel familiar, and an unsettling swirl upsets my stomach. There is no helpful image in my mood ring, but as soon as I make the next left turn, my worst fears are realized.

The gypsy's shop—*Ania's Emporium.* If I never visit that store again in my lifetime, it will be too soon.

Stellen points. "See that chain-link fence up ahead on the left?"

"Yep."

"That's the junkyard. He has a bunch of stuff inside an old building in the middle, but if you pull up to the gate and press the intercom, he'll come out and let us in."

I turn my head and slouch down in my seat as we drive past the emporium, just in case Ania Karina Nowak is peeking out her front window, giving me the evil eye.

"Why are you acting so sketchy?"

Busted. "It's complicated. The short version is that her and Grams had a long-standing rivalry, and I didn't exactly 'heal old wounds' when I came on the scene."

He chuckles. "*It's complicated*. Classic."

Ignoring his attempt to goad me into revealing my secrets, I put down the driver's window and stretch to push the call button on the tinker's intercom.

"Tell him it's Stellen Jablonski. He knows me."

"Copy that."

"Who is it?"

I glance at Stellen and nod my head. "I'm with Stellen Jablonski. He says you know him."

"Sit tight."

Stellen nods. "Here he comes."

The tall, lanky man brings to mind one of those wobbly windsock people you see in front of car dealerships every weekend. His limbs seem to flail in uncooperative directions as he ambles toward us.

He tugs the flaps of his deer-stalker hat down and spits into the muddy snow as he flips the chain off the gate and swings it open.

Back in Arizona, they call that a cowboy lock. It means that the gate isn't actually locked, it just appears so to the uninformed "non-*vaquero*" passersby.

He waves me through and points confusingly.

Thankfully, Stellen interprets. "Drive straight ahead and park in front of the 'No Parking' sign."

Raising my eyebrows, I tilt my head comically. "Are you serious right now?"

He shrugs. "It's an inside joke with regulars. Trust me. Park by the sign."

I do as I'm told and, as we climb out of the Jeep, Stellen whispers, "Let me do the talking."

Stifling a chuckle, I follow orders.

"What can I do ya for, Jawbone Junior?"

Oh, I'm going to get some mileage out of that nickname later.

Stellen offers his hand, and he and the tinker exchange a friendly greeting. "The other day you did me a real big favor by finding that photocathode."

The tinker nods and rubs the wiry grey stubble on his chin. "Ain't got another one, if that's what you're after."

Stellen laughs amiably. "No. One was enough.

Thing is, I was wondering if you knew where it came from?"

The old-timer's milky eyes scan through the dim corners of his memory, and his tongue works between the crevices of his teeth as he searches for the requested information. "Seems to me that was all part of a whole lot I scooped up from the high school about twenty years ago. Maybe more."

"Was it a bunch of cameras?"

The old man smiles and smacks Stellen on the shoulder. "You always were a sharp cookie. Now that you mention it, I reckon it was maybe forty years ago. Bunch of old cameras; even some old rolls of film. Course the film was all ruined, but some of them cameras was in decent shape."

Stellen smiles and nods. "I bet they were. You wouldn't happen to have the camera that gave us that donor part, would you?"

The friendly old man instantly shifts to shrewd business owner. "I might, I might. What's she worth to you?" He lifts his chin and squints.

It takes every ounce of the self-control I don't possess to keep from blurting out an outrageous number.

Stellen is a far better negotiator. "I was thinking you might part with it for a ten spot."

"Pshaw. I'd be a fool to take less than fifty."

My little brother scoffs and shakes his head. "Fifty? I already paid you twenty-five for the photocathode. We both know that was the only valuable part in the whole thing. I'll give you fifteen for the camera."

A proud grin turns up one side of the man's wrinkled face and he slips an arm around Stellen's shoulders as we move indoors to complete the transaction.

The tinker disappears into a back room and, after at least five minutes of shuffling, banging, colorful language, and one serious sounding crash, he returns empty-handed. "Well, doesn't that just beat all. The wife has the camera. I forgot. I was in such a hurry for that thing the other day. I ran over to her place and snatched it out of her camera. Then I sold it to you without a second thought."

When the man says "over to her place," a slow burn tightens around my ring finger and I know the truth without looking.

Stellen turns to offer me the news, as though I'll be pleased. "Oh, his wife owns the tarot shop next door. Should we run over there and see if she'll sell us the camera?"

The tinker snuffles loudly. "She might, she might not, but you'll hafta wait till she gets back from her sister's."

"How soon will that be?" Stellen's shoulders sag.

"S'pose to be late tomorrow night. You come 'round the day after and see if you can strike a deal."

I smile and nod. Underneath my faceplate, I'm freaking out. The last time Silas and I confronted this woman, things got a little *Mortal Kombat*!

Stellen thanks the tinker and we say our goodbyes.

Once we're back inside the Jeep, I have to let little brother in on my big secret. "I can't get into the details, but I had a bit of a run-in with the gypsy, and there's also the historic feud with Grams. There's no way she'll sell me anything."

The tinker appears beside the vehicle, waving us on impatiently.

"You better drive out of here before he gets the Persuader."

I put the vehicle in gear and drive out of the gate. "The persuader?"

Stellen grins. "Yeah, that's what he calls his rifle."

"Wow, they're quite the power couple."

Driving past the tarot shop, I park out of sight. "Do you remember what Silas said? The longer we wait, the less likely it is we'll be able to bring Bricklin back to the land of the living."

Stellen nods. "A couple more days won't hurt, though. Right?"

Gripping the steering wheel with both hands, I take a deep breath and battle my conscience.

"What are you waiting for, Mitzy? Shouldn't we get back to the bookshop?"

"I'm going to level with you, pal. I wasn't always an heiress or an upstanding citizen. And don't think for one minute that I'm encouraging you to bend the rules."

He scrunches up his face and shrugs. "What are you talking about?"

"I'm going to go get the camera. Right now. I'll leave some money on the counter, so technically it's not stealing. Technically, it's just some light B&E."

"B and E?"

Sighing, I bend forward and hang my head in shame. "Breaking and entering. You can thank my foster brother Jarrell for teaching me how to pick locks and pockets, and run the occasional grift."

Stellen's eyes widen and he leans back in shock. "You were a criminal?"

"Not exactly. I was a suggestible girl with no parents and a desperate need to fit in. I'm not proud of it."

He grins and leans toward me. "Can you teach me how to pick locks?"

"Geez! This is exactly what I'm talking about. I'm not trying to glorify a life of crime. We need that camera. We need it now. I'm our best chance. You wait here, and if I'm not back in fifteen minutes, call Silas."

I grip the door handle, but the firm hand of my little brother on my right arm prevents my egress. "I'm coming with. You'll need a lookout."

"No way."

He smiles wickedly, and I already dislike the twinkle in his eyes. "Either I'm coming with, or I'm calling Jacob right now." The little extortionist pulls out his phone and twists it tauntingly.

"Fine. But you can absolutely never tell my dad about this."

The thrill of victory turns up the corners of his smart mouth. "Deal."

Pulling the vehicle farther off the road, I turn off the engine and slip the keys in my pocket.

We climb over the mountain of snow at the edge of the emporium's parking lot and slink along the tree line toward the entrance.

I have my lock pick and tension wrench at the ready by the time we reach the door.

Stellen wisely pulls out his phone and acts as a screen, while I drop to one knee and hastily push the pins to the shear line. Lucky for me it's a simple lock with no anti-picking devices, and the plug easily spins. "We're in."

Before pushing the door open, I issue a warning. "There are some chimes hanging up there. Grab them and make sure they don't go off when we slip in."

He nods and stretches up to silence the tinkling before it starts.

I ease the door closed behind us and exhale. "I'll check the back room, you check behind the counter. What am I looking for?"

"It should be a fairly large camera, probably black, but it could be tan. I never saw it, but from what I know about the types of devices that use those photocathodes, they're big."

"Well, that's something in our favor."

We head our separate directions and begin the hunt.

For some inexplicable reason, the theme song from *Mission Impossible* will not stop running through my head.

When I step through the beaded curtain, and of course there's a beaded curtain, I stand still and attempt to calm my nerves. If I can grab a sliver of focus, my extra senses could come in real handy right about now.

Stellen's quiet searching serves as a backdrop, and I follow my breath in and out until I locate that peaceful spot within.

Reaching out with all of my senses, I search for the camera.

The number of strange tingles unnerves me. There are too many magicked or cursed items in this place to allow my senses to lock onto a single one. However, once before I was able to use my mood ring like a divining rod. Let's see if today is my lucky day.

I hold my right hand above the miniature glass dome and beg for assistance.

Fortunately, my moody ring is feeling generous. As I move my left hand around the back room of the shop, the temperature of the ring shifts. I'm deep into a psychic game of hot or cold.

The intensity of the burning sensation peaks at the precise moment Stellen clacks through the beaded curtain.

"You found it!"

Lucky for me, he thought my weirdly extended arm was a completely natural gesture. I happen to be pointing right at the thing.

"That's the one? You're sure?"

He flips some levers, opens a panel, tilts the thing in a couple different directions, and nods. "This is it."

"Great. Let's get out of here." We head for the front door, but he grabs my jacket. "You said you'd leave some money."

"Right. Thanks for the reminder."

I step over to the counter next to the register and pull a wad of twenties out of my pocket. "Do you think a hundred dollars is enough?"

Stellen smirks. "It's more than enough for the camera, but I'm not sure it's enough for your guilty conscience."

Dropping the bills, I turn and scowl at him. "You're insufferable. Remember, this never happened."

He shrugs. "As long as you keep up your end of the deal and teach me how to pick locks."

I open my mouth to protest, but a strange wave of foreboding passes over me. "We need to get out of here. Now."

Outside the front door, I grab the back of his jacket. "Wait. Do the phone again."

With some difficulty, he tucks the large camera under his coat and once again screens me.

Pulling out my tools, I reengage the lock. It's not always necessary, but since we're trying to leave the place as we found it, apart from the missing camera and the found cash, I'd hate for someone to actually break in and steal something because I carelessly left the door unlocked.

"Done. Let's go."

We crouch low and hustle along the tree line.

Back in the Jeep, I flick the speakerphone on and call Silas.

"Good morning, Mr. Willoughby. There's been a development."

"Good morning, Mitzy. Is everyone all right?"

"Yeah. We went to that junkyard where Stellen got the photocathode, and it turns out the tinker is the husband of Ania Karina Nowak."

Silas harrumphs. "That is not the best news."

"It gets worse. He actually took the part from a camera she had in her shop."

"That is indeed worse. In all likelihood, the item itself was magicked in some way. Perhaps removing the part from the camera changed the curse, but it will be difficult to ascertain the original intent without that camera."

"And that's why I'm calling. We went into the store and got the camera."

"That seems unwise." Silence hangs between us, and finally Silas breaks it. "It is a mistake to underestimate Mrs. Nowak. A mistake I made once before, and will not make again."

Inhaling sharply, I head toward the truth. "She's out of town for a couple days."

Silas harrumphs. "Who was running her shop?"

"It wasn't exactly open." I glance at Stellen and squeeze my shoulders up toward my ears.

"And how did you obtain the camera?"

"You don't want to know the details. Plausible deniability, and all that."

Stellen tries to help. "She left money on the counter."

I can practically feel my phone frost over from the icy tone of Mr. Willoughby's reply. "The boy was with you? Mizithra Achelois Moon, this is a new low."

"I'm sorry! But we don't have two more days. If we're going to save Bricklin—"

"Trust me when I promise you that this topic is not closed. However, a deadly clock is ticking and my retribution must wait. I shall meet the two of you at the bookshop. We will need the missing part. Is it possible to obtain that piece from your young friend, Mr. Jablonski?"

Stellen blushes. "I'll text her right now. She might still have the machine in the back of her car, but otherwise she can totally take out the part and meet us at Mitzy's."

CHAPTER 10

WHEN I TURN from Main Street onto First Avenue, the presence of my mentor's 1908 Model T parked in front of my bookstore does not bring me comfort. I made a terrible decision. Part of me knew that all along. I deserve whatever detention Silas deems appropriate.

Stellen's phone pings. "It's Yolo. She'll be here in like two minutes. She's got the part."

As we walk up the alleyway toward the door, I offer another apology. "I never should've let you come in that store with me. In the future, when I make bad decisions, I'm going to make them alone. And don't try to blackmail me into including you in my trips to the dark side. Got it, Jawbone Junior?"

He laughs. "I'm not a kid, you know? I'm graduating in four months, and when I'm at college, there's not gonna be anyone but me to make decisions.

Maybe I'll screw up sometimes, but that's part of life. Right?"

Pulling the door open, I hold it and usher him inside. "Yes, it is. But learning from other people's bad decisions without having to make them yourself is an even better way to grow up."

His eyes twinkle, and he bites his bottom lip. "So what you're saying is, you can always be a good, *bad* example?"

I struggle to keep a stern threat in my gaze. "Just so you know, you're not too old for a swirly."

"Dude, that's disgusting." He unhooks the chain and marches up the circular staircase—laughing all the way.

As though she has psychic powers of her own, my phone instantly rings with a call from Twiggy. I tap the speaker icon while I race to hook the chain back up. "It's hooked. You said I had thirty seconds. Did the thing call you immediately?"

The sound of her cackle traveling through the phone warms my heart. "It's called coincidence, kid. Get over yourself."

"Hello to you too. To what do I owe this pleasure?"

"Got an update for you and Willoughby. Turns out, my guy didn't have the book. But he had a solid lead. Someone contacted him last week looking for hypothetical pricing information."

The hairs on the back of my neck tingle. "Please tell me it wasn't the gypsy."

Twiggy hoots and hollers. "If I didn't know better, doll, I'd say you're psychic." She guffaws at her own hilarious quip.

"Thanks for the update. I'll let Silas know. When will you be back?"

"You miss me already, eh?"

"Absolutely."

"I'll be back in a couple days. Anything I need to know?"

A sigh escapes. "As far as the bookshop, not a thing. But we might have a paranormal update for you by the time you return. See you soon."

"Back at you."

The line goes dead, and, for a minute, a soft knocking at the alleyway door pulls my attention away from the terrible news.

Before I reach the door, Stellen zips past me, pauses for a moment to catch his breath, and pushes open the door. "Hey. What's up?"

The lavender delight that is Yolo steps lightly across the threshold, bats her eyes, and smiles. "Not much. You got the camera?"

He nods. "Follow me."

Silas waits in the middle of the Rare Books Loft. He offers me a scathing glance and sets the camera on one of the oak reading tables. "Did you bring the part, Miss Olson?"

She retrieves the item from a pocket in her black frock coat and carefully opens the bubble wrap. "Here it is."

"Good. I shall require peace and quiet. The three of you may wait in the apartment, and I shall inform you of what I discover."

Stellen opens his mouth to speak, but I grip his arm firmly. "Come on, guys. Let's head into the apartment."

The bookcase door slides shut behind us, and Stellen immediately lists off five reasons why he should be helping Silas.

"I hear what you're saying, but he's very particular about how he works."

Stellen tilts his head and squeezes one eye partially closed. "How does a lawyer know so much about old books, old cameras, and disappearing dogs?"

Since I've already crossed the line with Silas once today, I choose my words carefully. "Mr. Willoughby is a conundrum. He is widely read, and apparently remembers everything he's ever perused. He has a lot of useful arcane knowledge. If anyone can figure out what's been done to that camera and if there's a way to reverse it, he's our man."

Yolo glances around the apartment and lunges for the coffee table. She grabs the green dog collar as though it's a life preserver in a stormy sea. "Where did you get this? The last place I saw it was in a storage box in my booth. I have to take it off —had to take it off—Bricklin before we demonstrate the Tunnel of Truth." She looks at me with a mixture of accusation and curiosity. "How did you get this?"

"You'd have to ask Pyewacket. He jumped on my chest and dropped it in the wee hours of the morning. I almost never know where he disappears to, and he seems to be able to come and go from the bookshop as he pleases."

Stellen jumps in. "Pye helps with the investigations. If he brought it to Mitzy, it's important."

She rubs the rough nylon and turns the heart-shaped tag over in her hand. "I'll bring you back, my little yodeler." She kisses the tag and slips the collar into her pocket.

Before he can protest, I shoot Stellen an "easy, buddy" look, and we all stare at the floor.

Yolo shifts her weight and inhales sharply. "Have you, like, got anything to eat?"

A girl after my own heart. "Why don't we head down to Myrtle's? Silas will give me a call when he's finished examining the camera."

She rubs her purple fingernails together with a rapid clickety-clack. "Sure. Sweet."

At the diner, we have time for a full, three-course meal.

Appetizer: malts.

Main course: burgers and fries.

Dessert: pin cherry pie à la mode.

The urge to keep checking my phone produces no results. Stellen busses our dishes, and I leave a huge tip.

The sun is creeping away for the evening as we trudge silently down the chilly street. The sky is clear and the icy wind is fierce, but sparkling stars are already grabbing up the real estate abandoned by their solar nemesis.

"What do you think is taking Mr. Willoughby so long?" Yolo hugs her arms around her tiny middle, making me wish I had offered her an extra jacket before we left the shop.

"He's very meticulous. If it's taking him longer than usual, it's not a bad sign. It means he's double-checking everything, you know?"

She nods, but I can tell she's on the verge of tears. Stopping to fake tie my tennis shoe, I rejoin the trio, but on Stellen's left. I give him a sisterly nudge toward the freezing girl.

He looks at me questioningly and shakes his head. I pantomime shivering and nod toward Yolo. His eyes widen with fear.

I nod encouragingly and stick out my tongue for good measure.

He finally takes the hint and musters up the courage to slip an arm around her shoulders. "Are you cold?"

She immediately curls into his side and shakes. "Freezing. Thanks for noticing."

His eyes shine, and my heart melts a little. Unfortunately, it took so long for him to catch a clue, we're already at the bookshop.

Opening the door, I let the couple squeeze through in front of me, still entwined.

They continue to the Rare Books Loft, while I secure the door behind us.

"Silas, are you here? We need an update."

The cantankerous old curmudgeon leans over the balcony, harrumphs, and smooths his mustache. "I have checked my calculations thrice."

More than one of the "first floor" occupants stifles a giggle.

He ignores us and continues. "The functionality of this device is most complex. I can assure you Ania Karina Nowak had nothing to do with this. I sense her mother's hand at work. Sadly, the woman is no longer with us, or I may have considered requesting her aid."

"Silas, you're talking in circles. Can we get the dog back or not?"

His jowls sag as he glowers at me from above. "Why don't the three of you join me, and we'll discuss our strategy."

Yolo looks at me questioningly, and I shrug. "That's as close to a yes as we're going to get. Let's go find out what we have to do."

Once we've all pulled chairs up to the table that holds the camera, Silas steeples his fingers and slowly bounces his chin on the tip of his pointers.

Little brother grows impatient, but I narrow my gaze and shake my head firmly in his direction. He shrugs and sighs helplessly.

"It is not a solution I am pondering. I am

weighing the consequences of sharing certain details with Miss Olson."

Stellen leans forward and begs her case. "You can trust Yolo. She won't say anything about ghosts, or whatever."

Silas nods slowly. "What I am about to share definitely lands on the side of *whatever*, my young friend. But more than that, there are risks. I am concerned that the young woman's constitution may be challenged."

Yolo leans forward and speaks in her own defense. "If you found even the slightest chance that we can bring Bricklin back, I'll do anything. Even, like, one percent of a sliver of hope is more than I have now. I get that it might not work. I get that I might never see him again. So, if you're going to say that it could all go wrong, and he'll be gone forever . . ."

I glance toward Silas and try to send him a mind picture, like he taught me so many months ago. The first image is of the ghost girl at the high school, the second is the memorial page photo in the yearbook. I'm hoping he understands my belief that the ghost plays some part in safely recovering the dog.

He glances at me, a faint smile curves the corners of his mouth, and he nods. "Very well. Success is not guaranteed, as you rightly assumed. I have reversed the functionality of the camera. The three of you will proceed to the high school this evening. Precisely at midnight, you will begin a séance."

Stellen and Yolo lock eyes. Thankfully, they don't interrupt.

"Mitzy will lead the séance. I will explain the details to her alone. If you are able to bring the ghost-dog into the circle, Stellen will take its photograph." Yolo opens her mouth to speak, but Silas holds up a hand. "Because only he can see the animal's ghost."

She nods and smiles at my brother.

"The key is to ground the spirit in this reality as soon as it's photographed." He pauses and his eyes drift to a faraway place. "If we had something that belonged to the dog before he was transmuted—"

Yolo can't contain herself. She pulls the collar out of her pocket and drops it on the table. "Will this work?"

"Reow." Can confirm.

Silas gazes at the dog collar, bobs his jowls, and turns toward the intrepid feline. "Robin Pyewacket Goodfellow, do I have you to thank for this trinket?"

Pye nods in a very human way, and slinks over to scratch his back against the alchemist's leg.

"The moment after Stellen takes the photograph will be critical. You must slip the collar around the dog's neck, whether or not he is fully corporeal. It is your only chance. One of one."

A tense quiet settles over us.

"Do you want me to break into the high school?" My voice wavers. On the heels of my earlier unsanctioned break-in, I'm finding it hard to believe that he's about to send me on another.

Stellen interrupts. "I have a key."

Three heads whip pan toward my bro. "You have a key? To your high school? How in the world did you get a key?" My mouth hangs open in awe.

"I'm *really* good friends with the janitor. He had a pet turtle that passed away last year, and I mounted it for him. He was super grateful, and he knows I like to study after hours."

Silas claps his hands together with finality. "Excellent. You two get some rest. You will be up rather late this evening."

Yolo and Stellen hurry off to the apartment, while Silas continues my training. I don't bother to tell him that teenagers don't require "rest" to stay up past midnight. Let him think what he will.

"I'm afraid this hinges quite heavily on you, Mizithra. You must lead the séance, and you must coax the ghost girl out into the open. She may have a great deal of control over the dog's spirit. It will be up to you to sever that control."

"How am I supposed to do that? She's been a ghost for decades. She's the strongest ghost I've ever encountered."

"Perhaps. Perhaps not. You must remain calm and focused during the séance. Use all of your senses to ascertain what ties her to this plane. You must undo that connection by whatever means necessary."

"Whatever means necessary?" My eyes widen and my stomach churns. "Are you saying I'm gonna try to exterminate a ghost?"

"I'm saying no such thing. I merely propose that you pay careful attention to the messages you receive. You must act on them. Stellen and the girl will be responsible for rescuing the animal. Your mission is to help Irene Tir cross over. Once and for all."

A strange chill twists up my spine like an icy snake constricting my vertebrae. "Understood. Now, how do I run a séance?"

CHAPTER 11

The empty high school looms in the silver light of the quarter moon. If you ever imagined that it would be an exciting adventure to poke around a high school after hours, let me disabuse you of that notion. As we approach the back entrance next to the rows of dumpsters, I can't stop the montage of images from *Buffy the Vampire Slayer*. Nothing good ever happens in a high school after dark.

Stellen opens the door and holds it for Yolo and me. He leads us through the glow of exit signs and emergency lights toward the echoes of the empty gymnasium.

Yolo checks her phone. "Ten minutes 'til midnight. What do we do?"

As official director of the séance, it's time for me to take over. "Stellen, open the compass app on your phone and set up the candles. We need one at each of the cardinal directions. Do you know what that means?"

"North, South, East, West. Got it."

"Yolo, take the canister of salt and pour out a circle inside the candles. But don't complete it. Leave at least a one-foot gap between the start and end points."

She gives me a salute and clicks the heels of her purple brogue boots together.

I carefully remove the camera from my backpack and double-check the settings Silas made me memorize. Everything looks good. Nothing got bumped during transport.

"Do I light the candles yet?" Stellen asks.

"Not yet. We have to wait until midnight."

Yolo completes her partial circle and turns to me. "What do I do with the canister?"

"Place it right next to the opening. I'll sit there. When the dog appears, Stellen takes the picture, you put the collar on, and I close the circle. Everyone clear?"

Yolo tilts her head, and her lavender bangs shimmer silver-pink in the light of the gymnasium's red exit signs. "Don't we have to hold hands during the séance?"

"Apparently that's a myth. Silas says that the candles and the need to reach the spirit are more powerful than any of the other pomp and circumstance."

Stellen steps closer and whispers, "What about Irene?"

"That's the most unpredictable part—and the riskiest. You guys need to grab Bricklin and get out of the circle, before I can pour the rest of the salt and close it. But I have to pour the salt before Irene can follow you out. The timing will be critical." The hairs on the back of my neck tingle at the same time as the mood ring on my left hand forms an icy circle. "She knows we're here."

Yolo shivers, and Stellen clears his throat.

"Let's all step into the circle and take our positions."

"Who's gonna light the candles?" Yolo grips Bricklin's collar with two hands and my psychic senses feel the ripples of fear floating off the young girl.

"You two take your places. Make sure you have the camera ready and the collar. I'll light the candles, take my place, and call the ghosts. Are you guys ready?"

Stellen swallows audibly and nods.

Yolo bobs her head and whispers, "Thank you."

"Don't thank me yet. There's a lot that could go wrong. Let's just stick to the plan and hope for the best. All right?"

They both nod and take their places inside the almost-circle of salt.

I light the candles, beginning with the north and ending with the west, as I was instructed, and take my place inside the circle next to the break in the ring of salt. "We three request access to the spirit world.

One among us has lost a friend. Taken too soon. Taken before his time. One among us bears a message. Irene Tir, come forth. Be here now."

The silence is suffocating. I push my fears away and continue the call. "Bricklin Olson, Yolo needs you. Your spirit is not meant to cross over. She needs you to join her here and now, in the circle. We call upon all helpful spirits and guides to share your positive energy to bring these entities into our circle. The circle is safe. The circle is sacred. The circle is here, now."

My mood ring chills with a fresh set of frosty messages, and I glance down to see an image of the dog's collar. "They're coming. Get ready."

Stellen positions the camera and places his finger on the shutter button.

Yolo rubs the collar like a good luck charm.

"Think of Bricklin with all your heart, Yolo. Think how much you miss him. Think how much he means to you and how much you want him back. Call him with your heart. Love is stronger than fear."

She nods, and I can sense the shift in her energy. I can almost see the waves of love emanating from her little purple being.

The fresh-faced girl in the poodle skirt is not pleased with our intrusion. The angry and potent ghost of Irene Tir appears in the doorway of the gymnasium. She's calling to the dog, but using the name of her own dearly departed pet. Bark Hudson.

Stellen whispers. "Bricklin's coming. He's running toward Yolo."

Grabbing the canister of salt, I steel myself for the confrontation. "Get ready. Irene is right behind him. There won't be much time."

Thankfully, Irene is stubborn. She maintains her position in the doorway and continues to call to the dog. I can't see the animal's ghost, but the increased panic in her tone indicates he's not responding to her commands.

The camera flashes.

The dog flickers between this plane and the other in the center of our circle.

Yolo lunges forward and slips the collar over the dog's head and onto his solidifying neck.

Irene races toward us, screaming in fury.

She flies into the circle, bent on destruction.

"Now. Phase 2! Now!" I shout to my cohorts, and tilt the salt can.

Yolo scoops up the barely corporeal dog.

Stellen grabs the camera, and together they leap out of the circle.

I instantly complete the ring of salt and face a furious, trapped apparition.

"Where are you taking my dog? Bring that dog back to me immediately!"

Reaching out with all of my senses, I come up sadly lacking on intel. The fear of otherworldly retribution is severely limiting my abilities.

Her wrathful gaze falls on me. "You can't take my dog. I sacrificed everything to save Bark Hudson. You better bring him back—or else."

Without the aid of extrasensory solutions, I'm going to have to spitball my way out of this ghostly disaster. "Irene, I'm here to help you reunite with Bark Hudson. Tell me what you did for him, tell me how you tried to help him, so I can help you."

Her boiling fury cools a couple of degrees. "I gave that gypsy woman all the bread I earned from babysitting jobs I worked since I was ten years old. And I stole my mother's favorite amber necklace and gave it to her as the rest of the payment. She promised me the camera would save Bark Hudson. She said it would help him cross over before the illness ravaged his little body. She said he'd be here waiting for me."

"But you didn't plan on dying in the hospital from the poisoning, did you?"

Her ghostly image flickers with shock, and a little more of her fury seeps away. "I didn't die from poisoning. I've had my ears bashed with that story for seventy years, and I'd love to give every one of those gossips a knuckle sandwich! Ethol Olufsen gave me the royal shaft, and that's the truth. That hateful paper shaker stole the camera from me at the dance. She wouldn't tell me where it was, and I just— I just couldn't take it. I went up to the catwalk in the theater and I threw myself off." She scoffs loudly. "That whole baby chicks, salmonella malarkey was a story my parents cooked up to make sure their good Catholic girl wouldn't end up in purgatory. Sadly, I landed in this can. Much worse, if you ask me."

"I'm sorry, Irene. That's terrible."

Her self-pity vanishes, and her eyes turn to living flame. "Now gimme back my dog or I'll flip my lid and show you what I've learned."

All I can do is cross my fingers and hope that Stellen is on the same page.

At last! Phantom flames begin to consume the ghost of Irene Tir. He must've gotten the camera to burn.

"Irene. Your time on this side of the veil has come to an end. You're no longer trapped. Bark Hudson is waiting for you on the other side. He died just a few days after you, back in 1956. He's buried next to you in the cemetery. You can cross over. You're free. You can be reunited with him, like you always wanted."

As her resistance and anger turn to acceptance, the flames of energy shift to a golden glow. A beautiful smile transforms Irene's face into the innocent girl from *Nikdäg* night.

And as the last sparkles of her spirit fade from this reality, I swear I can hear the yodeling of her beloved basenji, Bark Hudson.

No matter how many times I witness it, the experience of helping, or forcing, a ghost to cross over never ceases to amaze.

Lying back on the highly polished gymnasium floor, I stare at the ceiling in the flicker of candlelight. What a wild ride!

Some days I'm so caught up in the comfort and familiarity of my new life, I forget where I came from. Tonight was more than a gentle reminder of how far I've come. My family, my growing powers, and the chance to help people/ghosts give me more satisfaction than I could've imagined.

Back in Arizona, party-girl Mitzy kept busy fighting to survive. There was always a knot of fear in my stomach—waiting for the other shoe to drop. The first shoe dropped when I lost my mother, and after that everything else felt like a prelude to more disasters.

I think tonight, here inside the circle of salt, surrounded by candles, I'm letting that go. I might actually be able to embrace the idea that I deserve to have good things happen to me.

Mind. Blown.

"Mitzy! Mitzy, are you okay?"

Stellen skitters to a stop in the doorway of the gymnasium and gasps when he sees my prostrate form.

"Oh my gosh! She's dead!" He sprints forward as I sit up to reassure him. "I'm fine. Sorry, I'm exhausted, and I was a little lost in my own head. But I'm all right."

He breaks through the circle of salt, and a piece of me feels that release. He hits his knees beside me and hugs me so tight I can't breathe.

"Hey, buddy, I need air."

Stellen flops to the floor and supports himself with one hand. "Sorry. When I thought you— It was just—"

Placing a hand on his shoulder, I stare deep into his tender green eyes. "I get it. You can't lose anyone else."

He nods and swipes the tears from his cheeks.

Yolo appears in the doorway, hugging her basenji and glowing with pure joy. "I can never repay you, Mitzy."

"Don't even think about it. We all played our part. If you guys hadn't executed Phase 2 so effectively, we might not be having this conversation."

Stellen drags his fingers through the salt. "Yeah, let me grab a broom and dustpan. We need to clean this up and get out of here."

"Copy that."

We tidy up the gymnasium and collect our things. When I open the back door to toss the leavings in the trash, I'm met with the sight of a literal dumpster fire. "Wow, that thing is still burning?"

Stellen chuckles. "I used the whole bottle of lighter fluid. I panicked. I just wanted to make sure the camera burned, you know?"

"We better get out of here. There's a real good chance that those flames drew some unwanted attention."

Yolo nods, and her purple eyes shine wide in the moonlight. "Yeah. Me and Bricklin waited over there." She gestures to a snowbank fifty feet away. "The flames were like fifteen or twenty feet in the air!"

A lone siren pierces the crisp night air. "That's our cue. Load up!"

We dive into the Jeep, and I fishtail it out of the icy parking lot.

"Turn left. Turn left, right now!" Stellen shouts out instructions.

I've never driven in a rally race, but I know a good idea when I hear one. I dive down the side street, pull into a driveway—that is not mine—shut off the engine and headlights.

The three of us wait in tense silence as the siren grows near.

Flashing red and blue lights zip past the end of the street and continue on toward the high school.

"Do we wait? Or do we make a break for it?" I whisper to my co-conspirators.

Stellen breathes heavily. "I think we better get out of here. You can take this street down to Maple, and then if you cut across on Jefferson, you'll end up connecting to Gunnison."

I start the Jeep and back out of *someone's* driveway with the lights off. Creeping along the street in the moonlight, I wait until we're a few houses down before I pull the lights on. "Do I even want to know why you're so familiar with the secret back route to the high school?"

He shrugs. "I created a map of Pin Cherry for my sixth-grade project. I just kind of know all the streets, you know?"

I choke on my own laughter. "I absolutely do not know. I can barely manage finding my way to the diner and the patisserie! You know you're kind of amazing, right?"

In the darkness I can't see the blush on his cheeks, but my psychic senses pick up on the embarrassed pride in his energy.

Before I can respond, Yolo pipes up from the back seat. "He really is. I meant to tell you that earlier, Stellen. I'm, like, so glad you came to the convention and helped me set up my booth. I was wondering—"

Stellen clears his throat, and I recognize the nervous signal that means he has something important to say.

"Hold on a minute, Yolo. Were you gonna say something, Stellen?"

He grins and looks at me from the corner of his eye. "Yolo, I was wondering if I could take you to Angelo and Vinci's for Valentine's?"

She giggles in the back seat, and Bricklin yodels supportively. "For sure. That would be, like, so lit."

The buzz of young love warms the inside of the

vehicle faster than my sad little heater ever could. The idea of a Valentine's date with a special someone intrigues. Should I wait and see if Erick has something planned, or should I make a grand gesture of my own?

Decisions, decisions.

CHAPTER 12

Whatever energy reserves I drew upon to hold the séance and help Irene crossover are severely depleted. When we pull up in front of Yolo's house, I'm barely able to keep my eyes open.

"Hey, after you walk her to the door, will you drive us home?"

Stellen nods. "Sure. Yeah, right."

Lucky for him, I gave him the idea to walk her to the door. I don't think it had actually occurred to the sweet, innocent kid.

He hops out and opens the door for her, and she struggles to climb out of the back seat without releasing her hold on Bricklin. I have a feeling she won't be putting that dog down for a couple of days, at least. If Stellen doesn't watch out, that little pupper might be a third-wheel on their Valentine's date.

He steadies her on the icy sidewalk and helps her

up the cement stairs in front of the simple wooden door on the small white ranch-style home.

Before he can muster the courage to kiss her good night, the porch light flips on and a worried mother, followed by an angry father, spill out of the home.

Heated and distressed voices swirl to an increasing volume. I hop out of the Jeep and rush to my brother's aid.

Possibly because of my exhaustion, or more likely due to my unshakable clumsiness, I slip on the ice and go down hard on my backside. Thankfully, I've got plenty of padding.

The upside of my accident is that it silences all parties.

From my vantage point on the ground, I chuckle and call out to the parents. "Please excuse my fantastic entrance. I'm Mitzy Moon, owner of the Bell, Book & Candle Bookshop downtown. We were helping Yolo look for her lost dog, and I'm afraid time got away from us. But the good news is, we found the dog!"

Both concerned parents ask their daughter several questions, and she happily confirms my clever lie while I get to my feet.

As I approach the tense scene on the crowded front stoop, an odd thought pops into my head. In all honesty, it seems a claircognizant message. "Adopted." As I glance back and forth from Yolo's mother to her father, I find no traits in common with their elfin daughter. These are both solid, broad humans of some Nordic or possibly Germanic descent. Their hair is a similar shade of mousy brown, and their eyes are the plain sheen of weak coffee. As I examine the visible effects of their DNA, I can't find a single chromosome appearing on the small lavender-topped human in our midst.

I offer my hand to the father, and he hesitantly reciprocates. "Mitzy Moon, you say?"

"That's right, sir. I'm well acquainted with Sheriff Harper, if you need to check my references. Let me start by apologizing for losing track of time. And I wish I'd thought to have Yolo give you a call or text. That's definitely on me. I hope you won't hold it against the kids." Look at me, being all grown up and taking responsibility.

Yolo pipes up with eager praise. "Honestly, Dad, I never would've found Bricklin without Mitzy. She's literally the best. I mean, things were a straight-up disaster. I wouldn't have had a *ghost* of a chance." Violet eyes dart my way and her lovely lashes offer a secret wink.

Stellen clears his throat and struggles to find his voice. "My name— I'm Stellen Jablonski. We go to school together."

It doesn't take extrasensory perception to see the instant recognition on the parents' faces. Possibly they read the name in the paper, or maybe heard the ever-present small-town rumors. Either way, they are more than familiar with the story that made Stellen an orphan. In unison, both adults tilt their heads to the side and nod. The mother offers her condolences.

"Well, Stellen and I better be getting home. I'm sure glad we could help find this little guy." I scratch Bricklin's head roughly, and he nips at me playfully. Was there a little glow in his eyes? I must've imagined it. I really am sleep deprived.

Stellen offers me his arm and helps me back to the Jeep, sans catastrophe.

Boy, do I have a story to tell Grams and Silas, late, late tomorrow morning, after a sleep-in and a massive breakfast.

CHAPTER 13

There's something you should know about me: I'm not a patient person. Despite the exhaustion that threatens to steal my consciousness, sleep can wait a few minutes more.

I should be more shocked that Silas answers his phone on the first ring, at 2:00 in the morning, but I knew he would. I call it psychic privilege, and I'm a huge fan—when it works.

"Good morning, Mr. Willoughby, thank you for taking my call."

"Indeed. I found myself unable to slumber while a trio of inexperienced youths tampered with powers far beyond their comprehension."

"I'd like to say I'm offended, but your assumptions are accurate."

He harrumphs. "And how did you fare?"

Taking a deep breath, I launch into my tale. "So, to summarize, the good news is we got the dog back.

The bad news is the Sheriff's Department is going to be looking into an unexplained dumpster fire behind the high school."

The late hour has made my mentor punchy, and a deep belly laugh spills from the speakerphone. "I shall rest easy now. I'm pleased the operation was successful. However, I'm unable to join you for your celebratory brunch. The enchantment placed upon that antique camera requires further examination. I must review my notes and discover what I can of its origins. I offer you my congratulations and bid you a pleasant night's sleep."

"Thanks. That shouldn't be a problem. I'm totally wiped." I drop the phone on the nightstand and collapse into bed.

"I'm so glad you were successful, dear."

A huge yawn stretches my jaw to capacity. "Thanks, Grams. Glad you slipped in at the tail end of the story, to save me having to tell it again. When I get back after brunch, I'll make sure everything's in order before Twiggy strolls in to dress me down for bookshop operation infractions."

Ghost-ma giggles and vanishes through the wall.

Pyewacket exercises his superiority by stepping over me as though I don't exist. He circles three times and flops onto the thick down comforter.

Despite my penchant for running a bit late, I'm the first to arrive at Myrtle's. Before I finish my first cup of java, Stellen and Yolo arrive together. Today, she's a vision in blue. Midnight blue jodhpurs slip into black riding boots, and her pale-blue shirt peeks out from beneath a bright-blue pseudo-military jacket, complete with red and gold epaulettes. My adopted brother shadows her with a love-struck grin plastered on his sweet face. They slide onto the bench seat opposite me and sit adorably close together.

"Is everything all right with your folks?"

Yolo nods, and the two lavender knots on the top of her head resemble bouncing hot cross buns. They appear messy and casual, just a couple of twisted knots held in place by mother-of-pearl inlaid chopsticks, but they hold secure. "Yeah, my dad called Sheriff Harper first thing this morning. But lucky for us the sheriff said a bunch of nice things about you, and my dad said to tell you thanks for helping me find my dog."

Stellen flashes me a crooked smile, and I hang my head and sigh. "Well, looks like I know where I'll be going after breakfast."

They laugh, and she lifts her mug to make room for the plates Odell slides across the silver-flecked white Formica.

Stellen and I eagerly look at Yolo's plate to see what Odell thought she would enjoy. Her lovely purple eyes gaze up at the cook with admiration. "Toad in the hole! I love it! You even brought me, like, extra butter. How did you know?"

Odell winks, raps his knuckles on the table twice, and returns to the kitchen, leaving a gruff chuckle in his wake.

Conversation comes to a standstill as we power through the tempting fare.

When I come up for air, an odd thought pops up. "Hey, don't you guys have to go to school?"

"My mom wrote me a fake doctor's note." Yolo grins and guzzles down some cocoa.

I nearly choke on my home fries. "Wow. What did you do to earn that sweet deal?"

She shrugs her tiny shoulders and smiles. "My grades crush, I help around the house without being hassled, and she knows I'm putting, like, way more into school than I'm getting out of it. So when I need a mental health 'late-start,' it doesn't take much to convince her."

"Nice. What's your story, bro?"

"Um, I pretty much plagiarized your entire 'save the dog' story and re-published it to the praise of Jacob and Amaryllis. She had no problem calling the school this morning to let them know I'd be running late due to family issues."

Shaking my head, I take a long satisfying sip of my go-go juice. "Things sure are different than when I was in school. Of course, I was a complete juvenile delinquent who barely got passing grades, so that might've been part of the problem."

We share an extended laugh at my expense, and

they head off to school while I bus the dishes and prepare for a scolding from Sheriff Harper.

The deputy I nicknamed "Furious Monkeys" is hard at work trying to level up on her favorite game.

"What level are you?"

"242." She risks removing her hand from her phone for a brief moment to gesture me through.

"Congrats." You have to admire her dedication, I guess.

The bullpen is empty, and I must admit I'm happy to avoid running into Deputy Candy.

"Boy, am I glad you showed up." Sheriff Harper looks up from the stack of reports on his desk, and a broad smile spreads across his face, all the way to his enticing, blue-grey eyes.

"Well, that's not the greeting I was expecting." I drop onto one of the well-used wooden chairs opposite his desk and return his gorgeous smile. "Were you really looking for me?" A little blush touches my cheeks, and I feel my tummy flip-flop with anticipation.

He leans forward and nods suggestively. "Oh yeah, I figured if I wanted to get to the bottom of the incident at the high school, I should talk directly to the ringleader." His voice takes a decidedly business-y turn, and his eyes no longer hold me in their thrall.

Attempting a surreptitious swallow, I cross my arms over my middle to prepare for the worst. "Should I know what you're talking about?"

He leans back and laces his fingers behind his head.

I recognize a trap when I see one and struggle to keep my eyes focused straight ahead.

"Maybe, maybe not. But I'd love for you to explain to me why Verna Wilson called dispatch last night at 1:46 a.m. to report a 1990s model Jeep Cherokee parked in her driveway for approximately one minute. And while you're at it, maybe you can give me some indication why I had to alibi the story you told Mr. and Mrs. Olson when they called me this morning."

Gulp. Time to battle my own conscience. This would be one of those moments when the truth could get me into more trouble than a lie, but lies are exactly the sort of thing Erick is tired of hearing out of my mouth.

"If you're struggling to fabricate a story, Moon, I don't want to hear it."

"Understood. Would you be willing to meet me halfway?"

He places his hands on the desk and drums his fingers as he weighs his options. "I don't think I like the sound of that."

"I don't mean halfway to the truth, I mean there are certain things I'm not ready to share. So I'll tell you as much as I can, and let you decide what to do with it. I'd love for you to bury it all under a giant mountain of paperwork—" I teasingly gesture toward his desk "—which is not in short supply."

He chuckles lightly and nods. “Let’s give it a whirl. I’m not making any promises, and I’m not granting anyone immunity, but I’ll keep an open mind.”

“Thank you. That’s more than fair.” I uncross my arms and try to remember everything I learned from *Lie to Me,* and NOT do any of those things. “Stellen and I felt confident we could communicate with Bricklin’s ghost. That’s Yolo’s dog.”

Erick holds up his hand. “That’s the little purple girl?”

“Exactly. We figured the best time to do that would be when no one else was at the school. So we headed over there around midnight.”

“And how did you get in?”

This is where it gets tricky for me. If I tell him about Stellen’s key, I could be getting my brother and the janitor into some serious hot water. Better for me to stretch the truth and take the hit. “I picked the lock. You know I can do that.”

He nods but doesn’t respond.

“Once we were inside, we tried to have a séance. We just used stuff we’ve learned from TV shows and cobbled it all together.” I’m not about to throw Silas under the bus.

“And did you talk to the dog’s ghost?” He leans away and tilts his head.

“This is going to sound crazy, I know, but we did. We convinced him to come back. Once Yolo slipped the collar over his head, he was back on this side. Do you know what I mean?"

He shakes his head. "Let's say I believe this wild story. To be clear, I'm not saying I do, it's a hypothetical. What does any of this have to do with the fire in the dumpster?"

"Well, like I said, we based our plan on TV shows. So we figured we better destroy the photocathode if we wanted to keep Bricklin on this side of the veil."

Erick drags his thumb along his jawline, and I can see the muscles flex. "I watch TV too. If I remember my *Supernatural*, burning items is usually part of releasing a spirit's connection to this world. So what is it you're leaving out, Moon?"

Oops. I had no idea his filmography was so current. "True. The next part is going to sound even stranger, but if you really want to hear it, I guess I can risk it."

He leans forward and narrows his gaze. His eyes say, "I'm the law, do what I say," but his energy is desperate for me to simply trust him with the truth.

"All right, here goes." I tell him the sad tale of Irene Tir and the secret about her suicide.

He leans back and exhales. "These details will be easy enough to confirm. The police report would've included the truth, even if it were suppressed for the family's sake. So you burned the camera to release Irene?"

I open my mouth to question how he knew it was

a camera, but the strange shift in his energy stops me in my tracks. Something in his psyche just clicked into place like tumblers in a lock. My mood ring burns, and I glance down in time to see a pile of crumpled twenties on a counter. There's no time to disguise the guilt lingering in my eyes.

Erick's eyes lock onto me like a tractor beam. "The owner of Ania's Emporium called this morning to report a strange theft. She said a vintage camera had been stolen, but the thief left a stack of bills by the register—at least twice what the camera was worth. Do you know anything about that?" There's a layer of accusation under the question, and I know we've come to the place where the rubber meets the road. If I deny this, I can probably kiss my relationship with the handsome Erick Harper goodbye forever.

"Can I possibly get a little immunity on this one?"

He shakes his head. "Depends. What's your side of the story?"

"It's not as bad as you think."

He leans back and crosses his arms over his chest, but there's no joy for me.

Time to face the music. I spill the beans about the tinker, the break-in, the camera, and leaving the money on the counter. I don't mention that Stellen was along for the ride, but I do attempt to toot my own horn by mentioning I locked the door behind me.

Sheriff Harper lets out a long, slow exhale and his hands fall to his lap. "Thanks for that, Moon. You know how important honesty is to me. The owner didn't want to press charges. She just wanted to know who broke into her store; although, it sounded like she already had a good idea. When she called, she was cursing your grandmother's name pretty heavily throughout her complaint."

My shoulders fall and I shake my head. "Yeah, I'm sure this didn't do anything to help their feud."

He taps his thumb on the arm of his chair and stands. "I'll let her know the perpetrator has been issued a warning. And ask her if she wishes to pursue a restraining order."

I look up in shock. "A restraining order? I didn't damage anything or threaten anyone."

He leans forward and places his hands on the desk. "I'm sure you can see why Mrs. Nowak would want you to stay away from her property."

"Copy that."

Scraping myself off the chair, I sulk toward the door.

Erick strides around the desk and catches my elbow.

I turn toward him like a scolded child. Eyes down, shoulders stooped.

He inhales sharply. "The timing on this is gonna suck, but I don't want to be a jerk and wait till the last minute. Do you have any plans for Valentine's Day?"

Gazing up at his inviting grin, I burst with the

happiness of Tiny Tim gazing upon the Christmas goose. "No. No plans. I was hoping my boyfriend might consider an outreach date."

Erick chuckles and tilts his head. "Outreach date?"

"Yeah, it's where upstanding citizens try to reach the downtrodden and delinquent, with generous pay-it-forward style gestures."

He laughs and scoops me into his arms. "I'd hardly call it slumming, Moon. If anyone's dating on the wrong side of the tracks, it's the wealthy heiress offering charity to the civil servant."

I stretch up and kiss his soft, full lips. "I'd say we both won the lottery, Sheriff."

"Oh, I didn't mean to interrupt." Deputy Candy doesn't dart away or avert his gaze. Instead, he stares directly at me as he delivers his message to the sheriff. "I finished alphabetizing the witness statements from the convention, Sheriff."

The benefit of my extrasensory perception reveals a disconcerting hunger lurking beneath the young deputy's boyish exterior. Rather than pull away from Erick in embarrassment, I cuddle closer and glare defiantly at the unnerving deputy.

Oblivious to the nonverbal exchange, Erick attempts to extricate himself from our embrace. "Good work, Deputy. Take over for Baird at the front desk. She's due for a break."

"10-4." Deputy Candy smirks at me as he turns and strolls toward the front of the station.

Erick finally disengages and looks down at me. "What was that all about? Normally you're not about the public displays of affection."

"I'm telling you, he gives me the creeps. He's very flirtatious. Didn't you see it?"

He raises his eyebrows and shakes his head. "I'm not saying you're wrong, but could you possibly be reading too much into his friendly nature?"

"Whatever. I'm still suffering from sleep deprivation. I better get back to the bookshop and straighten up before Twiggy gets home."

"Where'd Twiggy head off to?"

Great! Open mouth, insert foot. I can't tell him she's been scouring the seedy underbelly of the black market bookselling industry to uncover a stolen volume of dark magic. "She was on a book trip."

Erick shakes his head. "If you say so. I'll pick you up at seven on Friday."

"Sounds good. Is there a dress code?"

The flames that lick at the corners of his eyes send a swirl of heat through my body. "Additional details will be forthcoming, but you should pack an overnight bag."

Oh dear. There goes my heart.

CHAPTER 14

Grams is going to flip! I can hardly get back to the bookshop fast enough. When I tell her that Erick is taking me for an overnight Valentine's getaway . . . I mean, her ghost-head might explode.

Even though I slipped out the side door this morning, the heavy brass key around my neck is begging to be used. I stop in front of the intricately carved wooden door and smile fondly at the detailed vignettes.

Someone's car alarm is going off. I can't believe my ears. I thought we got over those in the 90s.

Pulling the chained key out from under my shirt, I turn over the unique triangle barrel in my hand. The sheer heft of it never ceases to bring a twinkle to my naturally curious eyes.

Inserting the one-of-a-kind key into the lock, I twist it three times—ignore the distracting automobile alarm—and listen to the various sets of tumblers fall into place. A satisfying and heartwarming sound.

As soon as I push the door open a crack, piercing sirens hit my eardrums full force and a nauseous swirl stabs me in the gut like a knife.

Not a car alarm.

"Grams! Grams, where are you?"

No response.

"Pyewacket! Pye, what happened?"

No reply.

The stress sends my heart racing, and my breathing comes in shallow gasps. I have to get a hold of myself. I have to calm down and shut off this stupid alarm.

Rushing to the back room, I type in the code. The ensuing silence nearly breaks my heart.

Slipping the key back around my neck, I press both hands to my chest, take slow, deep breaths, and reach out with all my psychic senses.

A montage of unsavory images steals my breath and slaps me across the face like a scorned Victorian woman in *Jane Eyre*.

Steadying myself on the railing, I swallow hard and race up the circular staircase.

There, on the floor beneath the candle handle and my copy of *Saducismus Triumphatus*, lies the motionless Pyewacket.

I surge forward and drop to my knees next to him. He's breathing, but barely. His front paws are covered in blood, and there's something clenched in his jaw.

"Pyewacket, sweetie. Are you in there?"

His eyelids crack open, and his large golden eyes seek out my face. The weakest sound I've ever heard whispers from his mouth. "Reow." Can confirm.

My first instinct is to call Stellen, but he's at school and the best thing for me to do is get Pye to the animal hospital. Stat. "I'm gonna get a towel, Mr. Cuddlekins. I need to take you to see Doc Ledo."

Pyewacket groans, in a decidedly argumentative way.

"Look, I have to take you to the hospital. What could possibly be more important than your life?"

Before he can find the strength to answer, the mood ring on my left hand burns like fire.

I pull the ring into view as an image of the lost red book shimmers in and out of existence. "*Loca Sine Lumine, Loca Sine Lege.*"

The furry mess whines.

"Someone was here? The person who stole the book?"

Pye opens his mouth, but he's too weak to respond. I carefully extricate the tattered shred of fabric from his mouth. And as I rub it between my fingers, the gypsy's name tastes like vinegar on my tongue.

Ania Karina Nowak!

"I knew it." I carefully stroke his head. "Can you

wait just another minute while I make sure Grams is all right?"

He groans a second time. This one holds the sorrow of loss. All the pain of the banshee's cry, but none of its malice.

I push away the messages struggling to get through. But in the end it's all too much, and I collapse onto the floor in a pile of tears. My hands shake as I pull my phone into view.

Four missed calls from Twiggy? She's probably on her way to the bookshop to wring my neck.

Great day to forget to turn your ringer on, Mitzy! I hang my head in shame as I hit speakerphone and call my mentor.

"Good morning, Mitzy. I have discovered some alarming details in the layered enchantment used on that old camera."

I open my mouth to share the terrible news, but the only thing that comes out is a horror-filled sob.

"Mizithra, what has occurred? I'm making haste to my car now. What do you need?"

I gasp a ragged breath and choke out the news. "The gypsy— Grams— Pyewacket's hurt."

The terrifying silence on the other end of the phone does nothing to boost my confidence. "You must take Pyewacket to see Doc Ledo at once. I'm on my way to the bookshop, and I will ascertain what Ania Karina Nowak has done with your grandmother."

Attempting to mumble my thanks only brings a

fresh set of tears. I slip the phone in my pocket and run into the apartment for a towel.

Carefully wrapping the limp form of my favorite fiendish feline, I shamble to the Jeep like a zombie.

Speed limits are exceeded. Stop signs barely acknowledged.

Fortunately, Doc Ledo is at the front desk when I burst through the door of the animal hospital. He glances at my face and the bundle in my arms and wheels toward me. "Breathing or not breathing?"

"Breathing, but I think he's unconscious. There's so much blood."

"Follow me." He spins in his wheelchair and zooms toward one of the surgical suites.

I place Pyewacket on the table, and Doc Ledo immediately begins his examination.

"Nothing is broken, at least no compound fractures. We'll run a set of x-rays to make sure there are no hairline fractures."

"That seems good, right?"

"That is absolutely good. I'm also not finding any open wounds. Is it possible this isn't his blood?"

The moment Ledo says "blood" I know beyond a shadow of a doubt that Pyewacket got his claws into that gypsy. "It's probably the attacker's. Can you take some samples for DNA testing? I need to pass it on to the sheriff when I report the break-in."

The doctor nods affirmatively and grabs his supplies. He takes careful swabs from each of Pyewacket's front paws and removes some additional fibers, which appear to be human hairs. He packages and labels each piece of evidence with meticulous notations.

"You wait here, Mitzy. I'm going to grab a technician to assist with the x-rays and then we'll get an IV started. My initial examination confirms that there are no physical injuries. He may have been knocked unconscious, as you guessed, and that would explain his grogginess."

Doc Ledo rolls out of the room, and I lean close to Pyewacket. "I know it was the gypsy. Did she hurt you with some kind of magic?"

A fraction of his strength has returned, but his response is not as cavalier as I'd like. "Reow." Can confirm.

"And Grams? Did she do something to Isadora?"

If caracals can cry, then those have to be tears leaking from Pyewacket's eyes.

It's the only response I need. That horrible gypsy woman has done something to my grandmother, and I'm not going to rest until she pays. Dearly.

Ledo insists that I leave Pyewacket at the clinic for observation. It pains me to be away from him so soon after his injury, but I have to get back to the bookshop and see what Silas has uncovered.

"Silas? Silas, are you in the loft?"

"Indeed." He offers no further information or invitation.

Stumbling up the stairs, I collapse into a chair and let my head drop onto one of the reading tables. "How bad is it?"

He walks to my side and rubs my back with gentle reassurance. "I have never kept things from you, Mizithra. I will tell you everything I know."

My heart sinks and my gut twists in turmoil.

The comfort ceases, and he draws a chair up next to me. "Your grandmother's ghost is gone."

An aching sob rips from my dry throat.

He leans forward and touches my arm. "From what I have deduced, the gypsy has placed your grandmother's ghost in a soul trap. That correlates with the disconcerting information I uncovered as I examined the layers of enchantments placed upon that old camera. Where Ania Karina's mother chose to use her gifts for good, it seems the daughter has been driven to a darker side of the magical arts. If she uncovered her mother's grimoire and, as I suspect, is the individual responsible for the disappearance of *Loca Sine Lumine, Loca Sine Lege*, then she would've had more than enough information to create such a trap."

It takes all of my strength to peel my head away from the desk and wipe my tears. "Is Grams still on this side of the veil?"

"I believe she is. I believe the gypsy trapped her in some type of gemstone or amulet. My forensic magic skills are not as strong as they once were, but I can assure you there was a great battle. Your grandmother did not go without a fight, and her fearless feline protector nearly sacrificed another of his own lives to protect her."

"That blood on his paws has to be the gypsy's. And the piece of fabric in his mouth must be from whatever she was wearing. Doc Ledo collected all the samples, and I can take them to Erick and file a complaint. Kidnapping is a felony, right?"

Silas smooths his bushy mustache with his thumb and forefinger. "I regret to inform you the Penal Code does not carry a punishment for ghost-napping."

Leaning back in my chair, I let my head fall backward as I moan. "Breaking and entering? Animal cruelty? She did something awful to Pyewacket. Something unnatural. The doc said he didn't have any broken bones or open wounds, but he's completely listless and weak."

As I sit up, Silas nods. "You may pursue the punishable offenses with your sheriff. The return of your grandmother's ghost must be left up to me."

The hairs on my arms lift as a chilling wave of power rolls off the alchemist.

"I'm going with you."

Silas rises to his full height, and I shudder in the shadow of his strength. "You shall not. You must remain here and do exactly as I say. I will return to my home, complete my research, and keep you abreast of my plans. Under no circumstances will you accompany me to my confrontation with Ania Karina."

"All right." I choke on my breath a little and feel a wave of weeping clutching at my throat.

"Don't waste your energy on despair. Love is the strongest magic of all. You must stay here, speak your grandmother's name, and keep her memory alive. It is the loss of those who remember us that strips our souls of their connection. If there is any hope of reaching your grandmother's heart, we must not let the darkness win."

Slowly getting to my feet, I step forward and throw my arms around his neck. "I'll do anything you say. You just bring her back to me, all right?"

I can feel his jowls bounce against my shoulder as he nods his head. "I can assure you that I will do everything within my power."

Time to pull myself together and launch Phase 1 of the attack. Hustling into the bathroom, I splash cold water on my face to reduce the sob-related eye puffiness, and scrape a comb through my hair.

A little mascara to detract from the redness and some lip tint will hopefully draw the eye away from the hot mess above.

I grab the bag of samples Doc Ledo collected for me and head toward the sliding bookcase door.

"Hold something back."

The clairaudient message drifts to me from the ether and I stop stark still.

Rummaging through the bag, I select one of the blood samples and one of the fiber samples and approach the hidden compartment. Below the bookcase, a large piece of raised paneling décor pops open when pressed firmly. I drop the two samples into the drawer and close it.

My eyes move to the rolling corkboard that normally contains all the 3 x 5 cards from the current investigation, and another wave of grief hits me. There's no need for a murder wall. I know exactly who stole my grandmother, and I'm going to get her back alive and well. And by *alive* I mean in her ghost form, and by *well* I mean exactly as she was before.

The chilly breeze gusting up from the great lake is a welcome touch on my hot, puffy face. I slow my pace and take several deep breaths as I stroll toward the sheriff's station.

The front desk is unmanned, and I'm grateful I don't have to speak to Furious Monkeys or creepy Deputy Candy. I hurry through the bullpen and make a sharp left turn into Erick's office.

Where I slam directly into the exiting Deputy Candy.

He scoops his unwelcome arms around me. "Well, hello there. Let me help you out, Miss Moon. Are you okay? What's in the bag?"

Yanking my arm away from him, I step back. "I'm fine. And I think you were just leaving."

He raises his eyebrows and regards me as though I'm the one who's crossed a line before walking out of Erick's office.

I close the door behind him.

"Geez, Moon. He was only trying to keep you from falling over."

"Look, I don't have time to debate the underlying motives of dodgy Deputy Candy. My grandmother has been kidnapped and Pyewacket was attacked."

Erick's first instinct is to grab his notepad and pen, but as my words roll around in his mind, a look of confusion twists his expression. "Hold on. You said your grandmother? You mean Isadora, the one who is a ghost?"

I collapse onto a sturdy but uncomfortable chair and sigh. "I know. Silas already told me there's no Penal Code for ghost-napping. But that crazy gypsy woman broke into my bookshop, injured Pyewacket, and literally stole my grandmother!"

Erick rubs a hand across his brow and scrapes back a loose chunk of sexy blond bangs. "Start from the beginning and try to remember you're talking to a guy who barely believes ghosts are real."

My eyes widen, and I gasp.

He waves his hands in surrender. "Wait, I believe you. I'm just saying it's a lot for me to take in. So explain it to me like I'm a kid. A kid who doesn't believe in ghosts."

Exhaling loudly, I blink back the tears already threatening to spill from my eyes and tell the tale as slowly as I can. However, I continue to indict the wicked gypsy and insist on retribution.

Erick leans back in his chair and nods slowly. "So

the evidence you're talking about is in that bag?" He gestures to the small paper sack on my lap.

"Oh, right." I dump the contents of the bag onto his desk, and he examines the individually packaged specimens. "Doc Ledo did a great job collecting this evidence. We certainly have enough here to press charges on the breaking and entering and possibly animal cruelty. But you know there's nothing I can do about the ghost stuff."

"Yeah, I guess." My heart cracks a little more and a traitorous tear leaks from the corner of my eye.

Erick is up in a flash and at my side. "If it was up to boyfriend me, I'd toss her in a cell and throw away the key. But I uphold the law, and that law applies equally to all citizens. I think you better sleep on this. The evidence you brought me definitely places her at your bookshop—if that's her blood and her clothing. But she just agreed to drop similar charges against you. And I hate to be the one to tell you this next part, but the blood evidence collected from Pyewacket's paws is a double-edged sword."

I lay my head on his shoulder, snuffle, and suck in a quick breath. "What do you mean, double-edged sword?"

"It would be very easy for her to say that a vicious wildcat attacked her. She could force you to put Pyewacket to sleep."

I bolt upright and look down at him in shock. "She wouldn't dare."

Erick gets to his feet and pulls me close. "Like I

said, it's a double-edged sword. After what she did today, I don't think it's a good idea to make guesses about what she may or may not do next. Sleep on it. Talk to Silas. I know how your little supercomputer brain works. You'll come up with a viable plan by tomorrow."

I want to argue. I want to beat my fists against his chest like every romantic drama I have ever watched on the silver screen, but he's right. My eagerness to punish the gypsy could backfire. I have to weigh my options carefully and also admit I'm too emotional to make this massive decision today.

He pulls me close, and I lay my head on his chest and trace my finger along the outline of his badge. His woodsy-citrus scent comforts me as I listen to the steady thrumming of his heart.

He kisses the top of my head. "I'm not sure what I can do to help, but we'll get your grandmother back. If it's within my power, I will get it done."

"Thank you. That's what I needed to hear."

He tucks his finger under my chin and lifts my mouth to meet his.

The power of this kiss is everything. He's on my side. He's got my back.

CHAPTER 15

The short walk back to the bookstore feels hollow and pointless. There's nothing there. No interfering ghost waiting to scare the bejeezus out of me, and no entitled feline to boss me around. When I reach the ornate wooden door, I crouch and run my fingers over the carving of the wildcat that bears a striking resemblance to Pyewacket. "I'll make things right, Mr. Cuddlekins. I promise."

Wandering between the stacks, I drag my fingers across the spines of the volumes my grandmother left me. In her absence, it's painfully obvious to me that the bookshop and its contents hold very little value without Isadora.

A noise from the back room stands my hairs on end. I hunker down and creep along the aisle. "I have a gun, and I know how to use it."

The responding cackle sends a wave of relief

down my spine. "I doubt either of those things is true, kid." Twiggy saunters out of the back room, stomping her biker boots along the floor. "I'm back."

"No kidding. A text would've been nice." My heartbeat slowly returns to normal.

"Oh, a text, eh? I called you four times and you couldn't be bothered, but a text would've been the ticket. Why the heck are you so jumpy? Where's the spoiled cat?"

My defenses crumble, and Twiggy is forced to endure a flood of my tears before I find the strength to tell her my sad story.

Her hands ball into fists, and she narrows her gaze. "What are we waitin' for? Let's march over to that gypsy's hovel and set her straight."

"Silas is concerned about the new powers she's displaying since her acquisition of *Loca Sine Lumine, Loca Sine Lege.*"

Twiggy shakes her head and pretends to spit. "I can't believe she snuck into this place to steal that book during a wedding! The woman has no manners whatsoever."

"Agreed. Silas told me to take care of Pye and leave the gypsy to him."

She chuckles and nods her head. "Yeah, I wouldn't want to land on the wrong side of that guy."

A heavy sigh escapes. "I don't know what to do without Grams."

Twiggy tramps toward me and pats me roughly

on the back. "Don't fret, kid. If death couldn't keep Isadora down, I doubt very much some two-bit gypsy will succeed."

Every fiber of my being desperately wants to believe Twiggy and share her optimism, but my psychic senses refuse to get on board. Everything trickling in from the great beyond is laden with doubt and dread.

"I'm going to head upstairs and do a little research before I have to pick up Pyewacket."

She nods and returns to the back room without another word.

When I walk into the apartment and catch sight of the murder wall/lost dog investigation, I lose it. Ripping all the cards from the tacks, I tear them and throw them to the ground. I kick the rolling corkboard to teach it a lesson, but only succeed in sending a sharp pain shooting from my big toe up my leg.

"Stupid. Stupid. Stupid. How could I have let this happen? I'm supposed to be some kind of psychic. Why didn't any of my super-special superpowers warn me that Grams was in danger?"

Maybe they did. Maybe my preoccupation with the missing dog and the 1950s ghost got my signals crossed or messages misinterpreted. The bottom line is that it's up to me to get her back.

I march into the closet and run my fingers over the sacred couture. "What would you want me to wear, Grams?"

Silence.

Picking up a pair of dangerously high Jimmy Choos, I hold them above my head like the baby Simba in *The Lion King*. "If you come back to me, I promise I'll wear any shoes that you want any day of the week!"

Nothing.

My arms drop to my sides, and the shoes tumble onto the thickly carpeted floor. An instant pang of guilt stabs my heart. "Sorry. Sorry. I'll put them back on the shelf right now." I retrieve the shoes and carefully arrange them in the footwear Hall of Fame.

There's no response from the ether, and no otherworldly tingling in my mood ring. Desperation takes my bargaining to a new level.

Yanking open one of the built-in drawers, I grab a sexy negligée and wave it in the air. "If you come back to me, I'll wear this for Erick!"

Nada. Bupkus.

The flush that tinges my cheeks is part embarrassment and part frustration. This is beneath me. I'm a doer, not a beggar. I'm not going to sit here and feel sorry for myself, and bargain with invisible forces. I'm going to *do* something.

As I shove the negligée back in the drawer, my hand bumps the cold steel of my handgun.

My throat tightens and my conscience hits me with a thousand warnings.

Slipping the gun out of the drawer, I turn it over in my hand and grimace. "I hope it doesn't come to this." I place the weapon back in the drawer and slowly push it closed.

I honestly hope it doesn't come to that, but if it does . . .

Time to end this pity party and get crackin' like the super-sleuth heiress that I am!

Without bothering to wait for permission, I push through the swinging gate at the sheriff's station and coldly ignore the overreaching welcome from Deputy Candy.

Stopping in the doorway to Erick's office, I lean against the doorjamb, kick out a hip, and attempt a seductive grin.

He looks up from the reports on his desk and his surprise rapidly shifts to anticipation. "You look like a lady with something on her mind."

So far, so good. "I have several things on my mind, Sheriff Harper, not the least of which is our overnight Valentine's Day getaway." I flash my eyebrows, in case there is any confusion about my meaning.

Erick's pupils dilate, and he strides toward me with a naked hunger percolating in his eyes. "Go on." He scoops me into his office and closes the door.

I'm struggling with my options. Should I kiss him first and then ask the favor, or ask the favor and offer the smooch as the reward?

"I recognize that look, Moon."

Oops. I hesitated too long and lost my advantage. "I need a small favor."

He loosens his hold and sighs. "I should have known your performance was too good to be true."

"Rude."

He shrugs. "What do you need?"

"I was wondering if you could bring Mrs. Nowak in for questioning?"

He sits on the edge of his desk and scrunches up his face in confusion. "What for? I recommended you not press charges, because of how it could endanger Pyewacket."

"Sure. I get that part, but she doesn't know that, right? Couldn't you just bring her in and, you know, shake her up a little?"

He laughs out loud. "Shake her up a little? The woman is in her late sixties! Not that I advocate police violence with suspects of any age, but I'm certainly not going to threaten a woman of her age in such ill health."

My psychic antennae perk up and take notice of this newsflash. "Ill health? What do you mean?"

"When she came in to file the complaint about the break-in, she did not look well. Her skin was sallow, the bones in her face were too visible, and even the subtlest movements seemed to cause her pain."

I might actually be able to use this little tidbit. "So, is that a no?"

He narrows his gaze and tilts his head. "It's a hard pass on harassing Mrs. Nowak."

"Fair enough. It was worth a shot." I turn to leave, but he catches my hand and pulls me tight.

"Now that the favor topic has been shelved, I'd like to revisit the discussion of our getaway."

Beads of sweat pop out along my hairline, and my knees go wobbly. "What about it?"

"Am I making a reservation for one room or two?"

Dear Lord, baby Jesus! This can't be happening. I need more time. I need a distraction. "Do I have to decide today?"

"Valentine's is less than three days from now. I'm sure the inn would like to finalize my reservation."

His phrasing seems to indicate he's already reserved two rooms, so the worst thing that could happen as a result of my delay tactics would be that I don't have to face this "blue pill or red pill" choice today. "I have too much on my mind. Once Grams is back safe and sound—"

He presses a finger to my lips. "No more excuses, Moon. One room or two?"

My chest constricts.

The door to his office bursts open, and Deputy Candy marches in.

Hallelujah! It's actually the first time I've been happy to see this guy. "I better get going, Erick. Talk to you later."

Sheriff Harper exhales with force and shakes his head. "Yes, you will."

I push past Candy and hustle out of the station.

Normally I'd stick around to eavesdrop, but I can't take that kind of risk today. Especially not in the middle of such a delicate negotiation with a lawman.

I'm going to start by saying this isn't the best idea I've ever had. But there's literally no one to stop me. I tug on a mousy-brown, shoulder-length wig and bobby pin it into place just like Ghost-ma taught me. Next, I wipe the tears that are streaming down my cheek and apply a little lip tint.

My usual skinny jeans, high tops, and a T-shirt that says "Challenge Accepted" below a traffic signal with the yellow light on, will work perfectly for this undercover mission.

Oh, did I mention the wad of cash in my pocket? That's right, I'm not above bribery, should it be necessary.

Driving toward the hospital, I'm plagued by second thoughts. I push through and convince myself that it's a good idea.

My colorful résumé will serve me well tonight. I've cleaned more than my share of office buildings and restaurants, and I know for a fact that employees are always calling in sick or sometimes not showing up at all, and not bothering to make any excuse.

Luck is on my side. Someone from the custodial staff comes out the rear entrance of the hospital and unloads several bags of waste from his cart into a large dumpster.

Casually walking toward the door, I drop my keys and fiddle around retrieving them while he turns his cart to head back inside.

He taps his ID card against the keypad and pulls open the door. I silently scoot up behind him as he pushes through and grab the handle just before the door closes.

A quick ten-count ensures that he'll be down the hall when I slip in.

And . . . I'm in. So far, my plan is flawless.

Hastily putting distance between me and the door, I look for an orderly or a candy striper. Bingo. Candy striper it is.

"Hey, can you help me?"

The young redhead turns, and I'm not sure which one of us is more shocked.

"Mitzy?"

"Tatum?" Leave it to me to find the one person in the hospital that knows me on sight, despite the wig—Tally's daughter.

"Of course I can help you, Mitzy. Sorry, it just threw me to see you in that wig and in this part of the hospital. It's normally employees only. What do you need?"

Decisions, decisions. I decide to roll the dice and hope she buys what I'm selling. "I'm kind of doing one of those *Undercover Boss* things. The Duncan-Moon Foundation is getting ready to make a donation to the hospital, but I wanted to do some first-hand investigating. My plan was to work a shift on the custodial staff and see how things really run. Would you mind taking me to the supervisor's office and going along with my story?"

She smiles and claps me on the shoulder. "My

mom was right about you. You really are the best. Of course I'll help you. Follow me."

Great. I've bamboozled a perfectly innocent and generous young girl. Instead of the thrill of victory, I'm feeling the sickening swirl of compromised values. Too late to turn back now. Looks like I'll be making an actual donation to the hospital to do proper penance.

Tatum walks me into the Environmental Services office and introduces me to the manager. "Mr. Osborne, I found this poor girl wandering around the floor. She's—" Her eyes widen and she freezes.

Thrusting my hand forward, I jump in. "Darcy Brown. The temp agency sent me over to fill in for someone who called in sick. Just give me a cart and tell me which floor to start on."

The baffled Mr. Osborne stares at me and chews his lower lip. "Someone called in sick? What agency?" Before he can think of any additional questions, his phone rings. "Mr. Osborne here. I see. Well, I'm sorry to hear that. You take care." He gently places the receiver back in the cradle and looks up at me in awe. "That was my first-floor guy. He just called in sick."

I smile and nod. "Like I said, just give me a cart and tell me where to start."

My accidental rhyme hits a positive note with the confused Mr. Osborne, and he grabs a spare key card from his top right drawer. "Thank you, Tatum. I'll take it from here."

She smiles at me, winks unnecessarily, and departs.

"Follow me, Miss Brown."

Fortunately, I've used this fake identity enough times that I actually remember to respond. "You bet."

He leads me to a large storage room filled with janitorial carts, cleaning supplies, and racks of toilet paper and paper towel refills.

"You can grab that cart there, and here's your key." He hooks it through a metal ring on the side of the cart. "Your shift doesn't start for half an hour, but if you want to clock in early, that's fine by me. It'll give you a chance to get acquainted with the layout on the first floor."

He rattles off a list of departments and shares several special requests that I will certainly forget, but there is one thing he mentions that brings a warm inner glow to my heart: medical records is also on the first floor.

Medical records is the only reason I'm here. "Copy that, Mr. Osborne. Is there a night supervisor, or anyone I should check in with if I have a question?"

"Nah. Everyone mostly keeps to their floor, but if you get confused, or forget something, you can come in here and use one of those radios to reach the night security. They'll be roaming the floors, but I'll let them know you've been cleared for first floor."

"Great. Thanks very much."

He leaves, mumbling under his breath about my

uncanny timing, and I stand in the janitorial closet bursting with anticipation.

One thing I learned from my extensive movie and television education is that if there is a radio, it must be tucked under a towel in one's cart. Later, when I help myself to a peek at the records, I'll need to keep tabs on those roving security guards.

CHAPTER 16

My natural dislike of hospitals has lessened during my time in Pin Cherry. To be fair, this particular institution has saved the lives and mended the injuries of a number of my closest friends. I'm pleased that the first floor is rapidly emptying as the administrative offices close for the day and employees scurry from their cubicles.

A somewhat colorful history, on several cleaning crews, prepared me perfectly for this ruse. I'm emptying waste bins, cleaning windows, and dusting desks and countertops. Deep down, I'm hoping that the coast will clear for operation Sneak a Peek, long before I have to do any serious work.

One of the security officers makes a pass through the first floor and offers me a friendly head nod and a finger gun.

I smile and throw him a harmless coworker wink.

He struts off toward the elevator, and I slip into an empty supervisor's office to catch the radio traffic.

Crackling and static. "That new girl on the first floor is a hottie. You wanna take the next pass in an hour and check her out?"

Security guard number two quickly replies, "10-4. Maybe she's supply-closet worthy."

Gross. I cross my fingers in hopes that my mission is complete long before security guard number two comes a leering.

Turning down the volume and slipping the radio back into its hiding place, I reenter the main hallway and check for any stragglers.

Ladies and gentlemen, the coast is clear.

Trundling toward the records office, I swipe at a couple of countertops and clear three windowless rooms that could be concealing dedicated employees.

The records office beckons me like a shining beacon. The brown plastic sign with its thick, white sans serif letters draws me as a moth to the flame. I swipe my key card and pull my cart inside behind me. No point in leaving a calling card in the hallway, should security guard number two make an early pass.

My janitorial history includes libraries, restaurants, and office buildings. No hospitals. However, taking into consideration my television education, I know that records are not stored in alphabetical order. Patients are given numbers, and those numbers are stored—in a tech-less town like Pin Cherry—on microfilm.

The hospital's machine is not the same as the one at the Pin Cherry Library. Rather than spools, here we have 4 x 6 sheets of film that lie on a glass plate and are moved around under the reader which projects the image onto a screen.

It takes some finagling to figure out the correct direction to move the piece of film in order to see what I want, but after a couple minute's practice with a random sheet, I'm a pro. I search through the card-catalog style drawers and locate the piece of film containing names starting with the letters "N-o-w."

Laying the film on the plate, I slide it into position and grab the six-digit code for Ania Karina Nowak's medical records.

A moment of temptation bubbles up as I spy the drawer marked "Ha - Ho."

Nope. Bending the law is one thing, secretly perusing my boyfriend's medical records is quite another. I'm not gonna cross that line.

However . . .

My hands move to the "Do - Du" drawer and I quickly locate the code for Isadora Duncan. There's no harm in checking a dead woman's records.

My breath catches in my throat. *I miss you, Grams.*

Carefully replacing every item in the exact place I found it, I move to the physical files. They are six shelves high, with the top shelf above my head, and I hope I don't need a stepstool. The last thing I want is to fall in the records room, knock myself unconscious, and get busted by security.

Hooray! Mrs. Nowak's name falls in a section of the shelf just below eye level. I pull out the file and search for recent entries.

Bingo. She's suffering from severe aortic stenosis and peripheral arterial disease.

The moment I identify her illness and read the doctor's projection of her remaining months to live, my moody mood ring flares to life.

The image reveals a powerful Silas Willoughby transmuting time and space as he dishes out retribution.

She wants Silas angry and vengeful. Why? The words flow through the ether like a dangerous whisper. "To die."

What? She wants to die? I snap a picture of the pertinent information on my phone, replace the file, and search for my grandmother's folder.

Holy moly! Isadora's file is over an inch thick. No time to view that now. I wedge the hefty manila folder under my shirt and tuck it into the back of my waistband. Once I replace my coat, the bulge is barely noticeable.

Time to hightail it out of the records room, and the hospital.

Barely thirty seconds elapse before the elevator pings and security guard number two, I'm assuming, struts onto the floor.

He strides toward me purposefully. His swagger sends a wave of nausea through my gut.

"What's cookin' good lookin'?"

He can't be serious. Time for Mitzy Moon to make a grand exit and end this charade.

He winks and licks his lips.

Going where the material leads me, I hunch over and grab my stomach. "Oh no! Morning sickness!" Using all of my acting skills to fake gag, I struggle to hold back imaginary regurgitation as I run toward the back door.

"Hold on, gorgeous. I can hold your hair back for ya."

Get a load of this guy! I might actually spew.

Busting out the back door, I pull my coat tight to keep the file from escaping and hustle to the Jeep. Hopping inside, I floor it and fishtail out of the parking lot. The great thing about winter is that ice really lends itself to dramatic getaways.

It's probably too late to call Silas, even with information this juicy. Plus, I want to rifle through Isadora's file guilt-free. Once I admit what I've done, he's sure to arrive on my doorstep with a heaping helping of condemnation.

The site of the animal hospital on my right hits me like a slap across the face. Shoot! Pyewacket! How could I forget my poor little fur baby? I turn into the parking lot and check my phone. It's after 8:00 p.m.

Running to the doors, I'm unsurprised to find

them locked. Standing in front of the entrance, I weigh my options. I could call the emergency number to see if—

My phone dings with a text notification.

"hi frgt 2 text. i got pye"

Wow. Stepbrothers can come in real handy. Especially ones with after-school jobs at veterinary clinics. I definitely caught a lucky break on that one. Pyewacket would never have forgiven me for leaving him at the clinic overnight.

The glowing marquee of our local Italian restaurant catches my eye, and I turn in to grab some takeout lasagna for dinner.

Whether it's an extrasensory thing or big sister thing, I can't be sure, but a wonderful idea pops to mind. "Do you have a reservation for Stellen Jablonski on Valentine's Day?"

The owner's son runs his finger down the list of names in the book and smiles. "I do. Reservation for two at 7:00 p.m. on the fourteenth. Did you need to make a change?"

"No, not at all. I was wondering if I could pre-pay for his dinner?"

He looks up and smiles. "Of course. That's so generous. How much did you want to put on account?"

"No idea. What's a good amount? Dinner for two, appetizers, desserts . . ."

"Did you want to include a tip?"

"Absolutely. Would a hundred be enough?"

His eyes widen. "More than enough."

My to-go order comes out, and we complete our transactions.

There. I have a few surprises of my own, Stellen.

After suffering the slings and arrows of an ungrateful wildcat, I abandon Pyewacket to his impromptu sleepover at the penthouse. Stellen created a small feline infirmary in my dad's living room, complete with a saucer of cream, a bowl of Fruity Puffs, and pizza cut into cat-sized bites.

I mean, I'm sure Pye is uneasy about returning to the scene of the attack at the bookshop, but clearly his refusal to accompany me back to the apartment was caused by more than trepidation.

The loudest sound in the Bell, Book & Candle is the beat of my heart as I make my way upstairs with the aid of the light on my phone.

First things first. I change into my reindeer onesie pajamas and drag a space heater over to the settee. It doesn't take long to polish off the lasagna, which leads me to the stolen files.

I'm sure Silas will warn me about the legal ramifications of stealing medical records, but Isadora Duncan has passed away, and, if I can't bask in the glory of her designer ghost, at least I can learn something about her past in these documents.

The recent entries all pertain to the terminal illness that took her life months before I arrived in town. As she's always indicated, the doctors blamed a history of alcoholism as the catalyst for her multiple organ failures.

As I delve deeper into the reports from years before, it's evident there were several asymptomatic incidents, seemingly unrelated to her cause of death, which landed her in the hospital. Reading between the lines, and leaning into my extrasensory perceptions, I can see where her hunger for magical knowledge and tendency to drive her explorations beyond the limits of her physical body could easily have led to her untimely demise.

Regardless of the parade of last names that dance through the paperwork, the Duncan surname seems to have served as the constant in her file.

The waxing moon peeking through the large 6 x 6 windows that face the great lake draws my gaze from the page, and a quick check of my phone confirms it's time to turn in.

My curiosity delays me a moment longer, and I flip to the oldest entries in the file.

The hairs on the back of my neck tingle the moment my eyes discover the word "miscarriage."

I run my fingers down the sheet, check the dates, and note the name at the top of the sheet. Myrtle Isadora Johnson.

My hands go weak and the file drops into my lap.

Odell and Grams had a child. Perhaps it was the loss of her baby rather than the feud between Odell and Cal that pushed her so deep into the bottle.

Closing the file, I lay it tenderly on the coffee table and stumble to bed.

As I lie in the large, four-poster slice of heaven, I stare at the ceiling and flick through the images and ideas bouncing around my consciousness.

Odell never remarried. Maybe the loss of my grandmother isn't the only hurt he's nursing.

No wonder Isadora doted so extravagantly on my father. I don't have any kids, and I'm not sure I ever will, but it doesn't take an empath to imagine the depth of pain and suffering that losing one's child would cause.

A wave of guilt rushes over me, and my eyelids refuse to close. I never expected to find something like this. I guess that's why it's not a good idea to stick your nose where it doesn't belong. I'm sure Silas will have a long prepared speech to dump all over me once he finds out what I've done.

All I can do now is pray that we find a way to get Isadora's ghost back, and that I have a chance to confess my sin directly to her.

The emotional exhaustion of the last couple of days finally drags me under. My dreams are filled with hope, and my nightmares are fraught with deadly confrontations with the gypsy and sinister images of the grim reaper, plague doctors, and, for some reason, the flaming eye of Sauron.

Morning finds me exhausted and highly agitated. Time to pull my mentor into my web and hope that he'll find it in his heart to forgive my transgressions.

CHAPTER 17

THE COFFEE IS BREWING, and my eyes are barely open. There's a distinctive scratching on the metal door leading to the alleyway.

Opening the door, I glance down at my fiendish feline. "Welcome home, traitor."

Pyewacket saunters past me and allows his tail to thwack me on the leg. He proceeds directly to the cabinet holding his favorite sugary children's cereal and plops expectantly onto his haunches.

"Oh, I see how this works. You run off and spend the night wherever you want and the second you come home, I'm supposed to drop everything."

"Reow." Can confirm.

I crouch and scratch him roughly between his black-tufted ears. "You have to stop scaring the living daylights out of me, Pye. I know you were trying to protect Grams, and I do appreciate that. But I'd be lost without you. Do you understand?"

He places his front paw on my knee, rises up and licks my cheek.

The gesture brings tears to my eyes. "What's your deal, son? You're so flippin' smart!"

"RE-OW!" Game on!

"I know, right? We're gonna get Grams back and teach this gypsy a lesson she'll never forget."

His only response is a casual shoulder nudge to the cabinet holding his Fruity Puffs.

I pour him a large bowl, gulp down a few swigs of java, and call my alchemist.

Once I spill the beans about my undercover operation, the voice emanating from my speakerphone pulls no punches.

"Mizithra Achelois Moon! Not only was that a dangerous plan, but highly illegal. Medical records are protected by a number of state and federal laws, and breaking into a hospital records office is certain to carry punishments that even I could not erase."

I'm pleased he can't see the smirk on my face. "I wore a disguise. The only person that even knew I was there is Tatum. And she thinks I was doing some undercover work for the foundation."

Silas harrumphs. "So where will I be making the donation?"

"How about something to pediatrics? That's always good for PR, right?"

Shockingly, my comment brings a chuckle. "Why don't I pick up some pastries and two large coffees at

Bless Choux and join you at the bookshop presently?"

"That would be divine." Where did that come from? Must be the weight of the guilt wreaking havoc on my vocab. "By the way, Pyewacket is home safe, and I don't think that mishap should count as one of his lives. Do you?"

A true belly laugh echoes from my mobile before Silas manages an answer. "I agree. I believe the count remains at five. Is that correct, Robin Pyewacket Goodfellow?"

"Reow." Can confirm.

By the time Silas arrives with the blessed sustenance, I've changed out of my pajamas and even managed to brush my hair like a big girl.

The chocolate croissant never ceases to tantalize my pallet, and the subtle hazelnut undertone in the secret Bless Choux coffee blend offers a magical combination.

Silas moves the pink pastry box, catches sight of the thick medical file on the coffee table, and stares at me in horror. "You stole the entire file? I thought you simply took a picture of the pertinent information."

Uh oh. Looks like it's time for true confessions, round two. "That's not Mrs. Nowak's file."

Silas reclines into the scalloped-back and interlaces his fingers expectantly.

After a difficult swallow and a deep breath to steady myself, I come clean. "That's Isadora's file."

"Mizithra!"

"I know. I know. It was wrong, but I miss her so much. I thought maybe I could learn something that would help us get her back." I stare at him pleadingly and rub the back of my hand.

Silas eyes me suspiciously. "Your body language is at odds with your words, my dear."

I flop onto the settee, and all the air rushes out of my lungs. "All right. I was curious. She's dead and gone, and her ghost is rather tightlipped. Did you know that—?"

Silas raises his hand, and I'm not sure whether it's the gesture or an alchemical transmutation that freezes the words on my tongue. "It is not your place to share your grandmother's secrets. I cannot undo what you have done. However, when Isadora is returned to us, I shall expect a full confession of your deeds. I will leave your punishment to her, as it is her protected world that you have invaded."

Well, now I feel like a giant pile of— "Understood. That's more than fair." Leaning forward, I attempt to redeem a small portion of my compromised morals. "I resisted the urge to look at Erick's file. I didn't even pull the microfilm to get the digits." My smile is a tad triumphant, but my timid gaze longs for understanding.

"I should think not! The very idea." He nods vigorously, and his jowls bounce beneath his red cheeks. "Indeed. Now, what is this information you obtained, so unethically, regarding Mrs. Nowak?"

"She's dying." I share the diagnosis and the prognosis and wait for his reply.

"And you're sure the message you heard was 'to die'?"

"Yeah, I'm sure. Why?"

"If you connect all the data points, I'm not sure your conclusion is the only one we may reach."

"Silas, you're talking in riddles. If you don't think she's trying to incite you to end her life before the ravages of the disease take her, what other conclusion is there?"

He leans back, steeples his fingers, and bounces his chin on the tip of his pointer.

Oh boy! Here comes a lesson.

"Close your eyes and review the events that have occurred since the young girl's dog went missing."

"You think Yolo is connected to the gypsy?"

"Close your eyes and review."

I do as I'm told. Letting my eyelids fall, I take several deep, cleansing breaths, try not to chuckle or think of Sedona gurus, and let my mind pull up the images.

Yolo—a vision in purple.

The dog—friendly, obedient, innocent.

The tunnel—mysterious, otherworldly.

The repair—a gesture of love.

The tinker—harmless, clueless, eager to make a buck.

The disappearance—shocking, inexplicable, terrifying.

The camera— My eyes pop open. “Maybe she was planning on using the camera on herself! Maybe she wants to cross over and we ruined her plan!”

Silas nods and smooths his mustache with his thumb and forefinger. “As you can see, there are subtleties. Her kidnapping of your grandmother’s ghost may not be malicious. Perhaps she intends to use Isadora as a bargaining chip.”

The color drains from my face, and a sickening swirl grips my stomach. “But we destroyed the camera. We don’t have anything to bargain with.”

Silas nods solemnly and stares out the windows. “Perhaps, perhaps not.”

“What do you mean?” My heart thumps in my chest, and the chill of knowing grips me.

He takes a moment to savor a sip of coffee. “Mrs. Nowak has been seeking arcane knowledge for some time. She delves too quickly and with little regard for her personal health. At some juncture she must have realized the cost of her relentless pursuit. Based on her prognosis, her condition is beyond the point of reversal.”

“That’s why she wants to die?” The idea fights with the otherworldly messages wrestling for my attention.

“She correctly ascertained the existence of Isadora’s ghost. You may be correct in assuming that she intended to experiment with the camera. However, the gypsy is a devout Catholic—”

“But she’s a witch!”

"The two may coexist. Magic, philosophy, religion, alchemy—there is a cord that binds them all."

My shoulders slump under the weight of this idea. "But isn't suicide a mortal sin in Catholicism?"

He sighs and brushes pastry crumbs from his bushy mustache. "Indeed. I believe you must request a parley with the gypsy. We may have nothing to offer, at least nothing discernible. However, it will behoove us to gather additional information if we are to have any chance of recovering Isadora."

Collecting my phone from the sofa, I pace across the thick Persian rug as I place the call to Mrs. Nowak. It's safe to say my penance has officially begun. Tapping the speakerphone on gives me the advantage of any ideas that may occur to my mentor.

"Hallo, Ania's Emporium."

"Good morning, Mrs. Nowak, it's Mitzy Moon."

A brief silence hangs between us. "I've been expecting your call, little thief." Her thick Polish accent hides none of her gloating.

Silas shakes his head in a clear warning against snarky retorts and frowns.

So much for returning her insult with one of my own. Apparently, I have to take the high road and put the "more flies with honey" theory to the test. "I never should have broken into your shop, and I'm genuinely sorry about that. Would you agree to meet with me?"

"Why? Why this meeting?" Her breathing is labored.

"I need my grandmother back. I must have something I can offer you in exchange."

Soft muttering and a cross between a scoff and possibly a spit is my only reply.

"Mrs. Nowak, I know why you wanted the camera. I'm willing to help you if I can."

A gasp followed by a tiny squeak, and then she must've dropped the phone. Glancing toward Silas, I lift a hand and shrug.

He gestures for me to simmer down and wait.

"Come to my shop. One hour. Bring the wizard."

Before I can correct her error, Silas nods and waves it away with a flick of his wrist.

"I'll be there—we'll be there, Mrs. Nowak. Thank you."

"Pshaw." The line goes dead.

Looking from the blank screen of my phone to my mentor, I scrunch up my face and ask, "Do you think it's a trap?"

Silas works his mouth back and forth as he seems to literally chew on my question. "It may be a trap, or you may have something that she wants. The question you must ask yourself before we proceed is: Will you be willing to meet her demand?"

Dropping my phone on the coffee table, I wring my hands and choke back a sob. "I would do anything to get Grams back."

Silas slowly rises from the chair and strides toward me. "Would you give Mrs. Nowak your mood ring?"

I clutch my left hand to my chest and cover it with my right. "Why my mood ring? She doesn't even know what it does, does she?"

Silas harrumphs. "Before you enter into a negotiation, you must be clear about what you are willing to lose. You are not willing to do *anything* to facilitate Isadora's return. Perhaps you can spend the next forty-five minutes weighing your options. Decide what it is you are truly willing to risk and see that you bend the negotiation in the direction you wish to take. If you enter into this parley without a goal or an exit strategy, you will either fail miserably or sacrifice far more than you can afford. And I'm sure you realize I'm not speaking in terms of finances."

Struggling to swallow, I loosen my hold on the mood ring and glance around the apartment. Maybe I'm not willing to do anything? "I see your point. I'll think things over and try to come up with a strategy. But what if she wants something from you?"

Silas exhales and clasps my shoulder firmly. "I have erected a clear set of boundaries in my life, Mitzy. I know myself, and I am all too familiar with my limits. I shall support you to the very edge of them, but not beyond."

"Copy that."

He slips out of the apartment and busies himself in the Rare Books Loft.

I step into the closet and drop onto the padded mahogany bench. For some reason, this is where I feel closest to her. This is where I can best "weigh my options" and come up with a workable strategy for the negotiations.

As I ponder my next move, a blur of tan races into the closet and leaps onto the bench.

Scratching the softer fur under his chin, I share my dilemma. "I have to decide what I'm willing to sacrifice, Pye. It's a lot harder than I imagined. I thought I would give up anything to get her back, but that's not true."

"Ree-oow." Conspiratorial agreement.

My eyes travel over the nearly endless content of my walk-in wardrobe. The elegant blue dress I wore to Kitty Zimmerman-Duncan's ladies lunch, the adorable black dress with its red cherries that Grams insisted I wear to the Pin Cherry Festival, the sexy black boots that put my undercover disguise over the top as an anthropology student at Birch County Community College . . . Isadora was always there for me. Always supporting my crazy plans and helping me pull myself together to complete the missions required to solve cases and help people. What will I do without her?

Pye rubs his head against my shoulder, as though he's reading my mind.

I suppose the real question is, what will I do to get her back?

CHAPTER 18

Silas appears in the doorway with a look that combines empathy and warning. "It is time."

Time is up. We have to go and meet the gypsy and hope we can find a way to save my grandmother. To be honest, I don't think I used my time very wisely. I mostly reminisced, and, when I wasn't doing that, I was feeling sorry for myself. I didn't really come up with any boundaries. I probably confused myself more than I already was.

Rising from the bench, I stroke Pyewacket's head and smile down at him. "You watch the shop while we're gone, all right?"

"Reow." Can confirm.

"But don't risk your life! If things get dicey, run."

He blinks his eyes slowly. It's a tolerant gesture that I've come to interpret as subtle disagreement.

Silas seems to have taken the same interpretation, and his soft chuckle lightens the mood. "Come,

Mizithra. One mustn't be late to such an important engagement."

We load into my vehicle, and I drive at a surprisingly reasonable speed. This does not escape the notice of my mentor.

"It would appear that you are in no great hurry to face Mrs. Nowak."

"You're not wrong. I definitely want Grams back, and the sooner the better, but I didn't really come to any shattering decisions during my interminable forty-five-minute wait."

He harrumphs and adjusts his seatbelt. "I should like to do most of the talking, in light of your undefined boundaries. To be clear, the goal of this negotiation is to understand what the gypsy will accept in exchange for the safe return of Isadora."

Taking my eyes off the road for a moment, I flash Silas a look of disdain. "What are you saying? I thought we were going there to get Grams back?"

"Then you would be sadly mistaken. This is the first step of the process. If Mrs. Nowak required something as simple as the coat off your back or a yet to be determined sum of money, she would not have escalated things to this height. The knowledge and energy required to kidnap your grandmother's ghost is substantial. A woman looking for an easy payout would not have gone to such lengths. You must prepare yourself for the magnitude of what may be required. I shall, of course, protect you from overstepping, but that is not to say the pound of flesh will be taken painlessly."

A heaviness settles over me, and I feel the subtle pressure of suffocation on my chest and throat. I'm not ready. My film-based education and my cursory knowledge of alchemy have not prepared me for such a dangerous game. Silas calmly places his hand on the steering wheel, and, as my focus returns to the road in front of me, I can see why. "Holy space cadet! I totally forgot I was driving."

"Indeed."

How the man can remain so calm and unruffled, I will never know. If I could mimic a fraction of that steadiness, I may be able to make it through this confrontation without promising her my firstborn child, or possibly my soul. The emporium looms into view, and a sickening chill flutters through my body when I turn off the engine.

Silas takes my hand and mumbles something almost under his breath.

As I open my mouth to ask what he said, a calming warmth flows up my arm, across my shoulders, to the top of my head, and then cascades all the way down to my toes.

"Thank you."

He smiles and pats my hand. "Follow me."

We approach the front door, and he politely holds it open for me. Once inside, the now-familiar mixture of herbs, incense, and scented soaps fills my nostrils. My throat tightens and I cough to clear the airway. "Mrs. Nowak? Mrs. Nowak, are you here?"

The response that greets me nearly knocks me off my feet.

"Mitzy! Mitzy! I knew you'd come for me!"

My body curls in on itself as though I've been shot, and my eyes fill with unshed tears.

Silas grips my arm and gazes at me questioningly.

Ghost-ma sweetens the deal. "She can't hear me! Trust me, I've called her every name in the book and she's done nothing. Our secret is safe!"

The corner of my mouth turns up, and I lean on Silas for support. "Grams is all right. She's talking to me."

His thick eyebrows arch, and he nods. "How useful."

Hoping against hope that, despite her kidnapping, she's retained her powers, I press my lips together and fire off a thought message. *I miss you so much! We're absolutely going to get you out of here!*

"I never doubted you for a minute, sweetie."

Mrs. Nowak clatters through the bead curtain, and I whisper a hasty secret to Silas. "Grams can still hear my thoughts."

He smiles and nods as though I've simply told him the time.

"No tricks." The gypsy dangles a beautiful glowing amulet in one hand and brandishes a large steel hammer in the other.

I gasp in horror as my brain struggles to comprehend the unspoken threat.

Silas steps forward and raises both of his hands in a gesture of surrender. "We have not come to hoodwink you, Mrs. Nowak. We come in peace and hope for an amicable resolution. Please, begin."

She lays the amber pendant on a stocky wooden table displaying decks of tarot cards, and I hold my breath while I wait to see what she has planned for the hammer. Thankfully, she places it next to the pendant and claps her hands twice.

As I wait for a Clapper-activated light to switch on, Silas stiffens. "What? What did she do?"

The gypsy grins, and the gold-cap over her eyetooth glistens. "The trap is set."

I don't know about you, but I'm still a little hung up on the gold tooth. That's definitely new.

Silas asks the question I should have. "Why did you call this meeting?"

I wish I could say that I hear the gypsy's reply, but Grams is blurting out information faster than I can process it.

"She has a death wish! Or maybe I should say a ghost wish. The nerve of this woman. She thought she could manipulate Silas by holding me for ransom. Don't listen to her, Mitzy. She's as phony as a two-dollar bill!"

I think you mean a three-dollar bill, Grams. We actually have two-dollar bills. Not that you'd waste your time with anything less than a Benjamin.

"Oh Mitzy! You're such a hoot!"

A movement beside me interrupts my spirit chat. Silas strides forward, and his spine straightens as he rises into his full power. "Ania, your mother would not want her precious grimoire abused in this way. We know that your time on this plane is coming to an end. Stealing *Loca Sine Lumine, Loca Sine Lege,* and trapping Isadora in that pendant, cannot change your fate. Give us what we came for and we shall never bother you again."

She takes a step forward and energy crackles around her like the snaps of static electricity on a blanket in the darkness. "You take nothing. I give nothing. I want to be like her." Her finger points dramatically at the amulet encasing my grandmother's ghost.

I can't comprehend why she wants this. "You want to be a ghost? Why would you want to be a ghost? If you only have a few months to live, don't you want to be with your family? Don't your children want to see you one more time?"

My psychic senses pick up on a tidal wave of sorrow that nearly consumes Mrs. Nowak.

"Ania, what's wrong? Where are your children?"

Her rheumy eyes are rimmed by red lids, which fail to contain her tears. "They leave me. I am embarrassment. Evil witch. They couldn't escape fast enough."

Walking closer, in spite of my dislike for this woman, my heart hurts with her pain. "I know what it's like to live without family. I lost my mother when I was eleven. I thought I'd be alone for the rest of my life. Opening your heart is a risk, but every time I've taken that risk since I came to Pin Cherry, my life has been richer for it. I found my father, I have a stepmom, and a stepbrother." I have to pause and draw an emotion-laden breath. "My grandmother is the most important thing in the world to me. If I help you—" My tears are flowing unabated now. "If I help you mend fences with your children, will you please give me back my grandmother?"

Her thin shell of hatred cracks, and the pain of loss seeps from the fractures like yolk from a broken egg.

"Ania, you and I have no quarrel. Whatever stood between you and my grandmother died with her. Let me help you make things right with your children."

Regret and relief wash over her wrinkled visage, but she stands her ground. "I don't want pain. The pain is too much." She rubs her right hand along her left arm and winces.

In addition to the pain of her terminal illness, I'd be willing to bet that arm bears the marks of the indefatigable Pyewacket.

Silas moves closer to her and offers her a small blue vial. "Place two grains in a cup of elderflower tea each morning. The pain will subside and you may focus on healing your family, before it's too late."

Her natural suspiciousness flares up, and she pulls her hand back for a moment. "No tricks?"

Silas wags his jowls. "Absolutely none."

She snatches the vial from his hand and slips it into her cleavage. "If this works"—she pats her bosom—"tomorrow this one helps me with the children. Then I return the ghost." She gestures to the amulet on the table.

Every fiber of my being wants to scream, "No!" I want to lunge toward the table and take whatever punishment her trap has to offer, so long as I get my hands on that amber pendant.

"Don't do anything stupid, sweetie. I heard her reading the spells out loud. I think there's a very good chance that you could lose your entire hand."

Right! Grams can hear everything I'm thinking. *Copy that. I'll keep my hands to myself.*

"Good girl."

Silas bows slightly and nods his head. "We have an accord, Mrs. Nowak. Mitzy will return tomorrow morning to assist in contacting your family. We appreciate this opportunity to start anew."

Her sadness and vulnerability vanish in the blink of an eye. She steps behind the table and retrieves the hammer. "You go now."

Without another word, Silas grips my elbow and steers me, quite against my will, out of the emporium.

A heavy silence consumes the drive back to the bookshop. It fills every corner of the vehicle and seems to make speech impossible.

My swanky apartment feels like a cheap hotel.

The façade of elegance is meaningless without its creator.

"Why did you let her keep Grams?"

Silas drops into the scalloped-back chair and exhales as he rests his hands on his round belly. "Your grandmother is in no immediate danger—"

"How can you say that? That crazy gypsy was waving a hammer around over the amulet!"

"I should think your gifts would have shown you the lack of intent in her actions. What we saw was playacting, posturing. Would you not agree?"

There is nothing to prevent me from rolling my eyes and scoffing. "What I would say is that she is suffering physically and emotionally. My special *gifts* lead me to believe the ache in her heart is more uncomfortable than the pain in her body."

"Agreed. We shall reclaim Isadora in due time. I suggest you spend the remainder of the day gathering what information you can of Mrs. Nowak's descendants. If her claim that they abandoned her due to an aversion to the dark arts is true, that is a simple fix. If, however, there are deeper wounds at play, you must be prepared. Your success is all that stands between us and your grandmother."

"Great. No pressure, Silas."

He chuckles and flicks his wrist halfheartedly, as though my success is a foregone conclusion.

"Hey, what about the book? You didn't say anything about getting the book back as part of our negotiation."

He smooths his mustache and nods. "She will return the book. Focus your energies on the family matters and the rest will follow."

Sadly, the phrase *Family Matters* immediately brings Urkel to mind, and I can't keep the voice in my head from asking, "Did I do that?"

Silas tilts his head. "Did I say something to amuse you?"

Shaking my head, I smile. "Trust me, it's not worth explaining. I'm going to head over to City Hall and see what I can find in the birth records. Unless you happen to know the names of her children?" I raise my eyebrows hopefully.

"I do not. I have some research to complete, and then I must return home to check on my experiments. Give Pyewacket my best when you see him."

"I think you mean 'if' I see him. He's been spending a lot of time with Stellen."

My mentor nods as though my complaint makes perfect sense. "The boy suffered a great loss with the recent death of his father. Pye is simply offering him comfort."

Crossing my arms over my chest like a spoiled child, I mumble, "I could use some comfort, too."

A mischievous twinkle lights the alchemist's eyes. "You could always confide in Sheriff Harper."

My jaw drops. My cheeks redden, and I scoot out of the apartment without another word.

CHAPTER 19

The outside temperature is slowly pushing the mercury up, but it's still not warm enough to walk to City Hall.

My previous trips to the clerk's office have trained me to be patient, vague, and never ask for copies of anything. That way lies madness. More forms, fees, and waiting periods. All I need is a believable story, and a moment or two of privacy for snapping pics with my phone.

There's a plethora of parking in the central square of the historic district, which, if you ask me, describes the entire town.

Since Pin Cherry Harbor is also the county seat of Birch County, our city hall contains county records too. The impressive structure is picture perfect, reminding me of the courthouse from *To Kill A Mockingbird*. Three stories of solid granite with copper parapet walls, beautiful terrazzo floors, ornamental plaster cornices, and marble walls in the elevator lobby. Everyone considers it the height of architectural design in the region.

The clerk looks as old as the building and takes a millennium to close her magazine and creep toward me at a sloth's pace.

"Good afternoon, ma'am. I'm working on a genealogy project for submission to the historical society, and I need to examine some birth certificates. Would you be able to help me with that?"

She slips her bifocals from the top of her head to her nose and pushes a notepad across the well-worn wooden counter. "Write the names here, and if they were born in Birch County, I'll find them. Did you want to pick up copies next week?"

Much like a Boy Scout, I'm prepared. "Oh no, I don't need copies. I'm trying to get this project in before the deadline, so I'll just wait while you pull what you have and then I'll make some notes."

"How many records did you need?" Her eyes blink rapidly behind the glasses, and I feel her concern deepen.

"I'm not sure. I only have the mother's name, and I was hoping you could search by that."

Her demeanor shifts, and I sense a kernel of suspicion looking to sprout.

Better head that off at the pass. "I'm sure it couldn't be more than two or three. I know with your expertise that should be no problem."

Unbelievable. Flattery does the trick. "Well, I do have a knack for remembering things."

"I thought so." Gratuitous wink. "Here's the name." I write Ania Karina Nowak on the notepad and push it across the countertop to the clerk.

She gazes at the name and recognition flashes across her face. At first, I assume it's simply because she's worked in City Hall for so long, and has a vague familiarity with likely every resident of Pin Cherry, but my extrasensory perception picks up another thread. She's dealt with this woman. Perhaps even purchased something from this woman. I'd love to pull that thread and unravel the secrets of the seemingly straight-laced County Clerk, but I have a far more pressing quest.

She clears her throat and rips the top sheet off the notepad. "Have a seat in the waiting chairs, dear. This will take a few minutes."

I'm dying to run down the street and grab a pastry and hot coffee, but I don't want to give her any excuse to interrupt her search. Sitting in the chair, I stare at the rack of forms and the plain, uninviting atmosphere.

Erick! I can't explain the connection, other than maybe this drab wasteland makes me long for something far more inviting.

As I begin tapping out a text, but before I press send, my conscience assures me this is something I should handle face-to-face, or, at the very least, voice-to-voice. I dial the sheriff's station and ask to be put through. "Hey, I have some bad news." Classic me. Tact? Who needs it? I can picture him in a track stance with one hand on his gun as he asks if I need to be rescued.

"Sorry for the abrupt start. But you know how fond I am of getting to the point. I'm not in any danger. Buuuut, things have gotten rather complicated with the gypsy and getting my grandmother back. I don't think I'm going to be available for a Valentine's getaway."

The silence on the other end of the phone nearly breaks my heart. I wish I could explain the life-threatening details of why I can't leave town in the middle of such a delicate negotiation, but that's not an option.

His mumbled reply is barely audible.

"Why don't you come by the apartment tonight? I could use the company and I can explain it better when I'm not sitting in a chair in the clerk's office at City Hall."

He reluctantly agrees and ends the call before I can offer any overzealous promises.

It's official. I'm the world's worst girlfriend. I have an amazing boyfriend who went out of his way to plan a romantic Valentine's getaway, and my ridiculous personal dramas have derailed our relationship—once again.

Maybe he would be better off without me. I'm kind of *a lot*. He needs someone less complicated. Someone more traditional. Someone who wants a big fancy wedding and a brood of little rugrats. A girl with a checkered past and a psychically unpredictable future probably isn't the best match for our hometown American hero.

Hold on. Am I talking myself into breaking up with Erick Harper on Valentine's Day?

Now I'm not just the world's worst girlfriend, I'm the world's worst—everything.

The clerk returns with two documents. She peers at me over the top of her reading glasses, and her gaze is not friendly. "These are the only birth certificates I was able to locate in the mother's married name."

"Great. Thank you." I shuffle the papers and wait for inspiration to strike. "Can you see if you have the mother's birth certificate? It says here the maiden name is Jankowski."

She continues to eye me over the rim of her tortoise-shell glasses. She's waiting expectantly for something.

It takes a moment to sink in, but I finally grab the pen and write Ania Jankowski on the notepad and push it toward her.

As soon as she walks out of sight, I snap pictures of the two birth certificates and slip my phone back in my pocket. Two children. Sons. Rajmund and Tadjo. The boys shouldn't be too hard to find, because their names will have remained the same. Fortunately there weren't any daughters. Tracking down marriage-related name changes would muddy the waters.

The clerk returns with another document and

slides it across the counter. She pushes the note pad toward me. "In case you wanted to write down the names, dear."

Oh right. I'm supposed to pretend that I didn't take those pictures. Of course, that would mean I need notes. "Thank you. I will."

I write the names of the two Nowak children and add Ania Karina's birth date at the bottom of the list. "Do you know if any of the children remained in the area?"

She points toward the boys' certificates. "I think they all moved away. Right out of high school, if I remember correctly. Just disappeared one by one, you know?"

"Yes, I'm sure you're right." I take the two Nowak sons' birth certificates and push them toward her. "I'm finished with these, if you want to refile them."

She looks up, and for a moment I think she might have winked at me. She collects the two documents and returns to the back room.

I snap a quick photo of Ania Karina Jankowski's birth certificate, in case I need that info later, and hastily stow my phone.

When the clerk returns, I push the final birth certificate toward her. "Thank you very much for your help today."

She nods. "Good luck with your *project*, Miss Moon."

The way she says the word project shows she's probably on to my ruse. But as long as she's a willing participant, I won't complain. "Thank you," I call as I hustle out of City Hall.

Before my luck turns, I hurry back to the bookshop, hoping to catch Silas before he leaves.

No such luck. The bookstore is as empty as empty can be.

Grams, a hostage.

Twiggy, gone for the day.

Silas, heading home to his experiments, and Robin Pyewacket Goodfellow curled up in the lap of luxury in my father's penthouse across the alley.

Seems like the perfect time to have an extended pity party, but before I can throw myself into the role of wronged orphan a text pings on my phone. It's from Erick.

"Should I bring dinner?"

"Sure. You pick. About an hour?"

"K."

Yeesh! Never has one letter held so much information. If I'm going to have any hope of dragging this relationship back onto the rails, I better work a little harder in the "girlfriend" department.

Cut to—

Freshly showered Mitzy Moon, desperately seeking an appropriate outfit without the help of her fashion-diva Ghost-ma.

I grab the black skinny jeans and my super-cozy striped cashmere boyfriend sweater. It's an oldie, but a goodie. Now to create something hairstyle-adjacent, and go the extra mile with a slathering of makeup.

The eerie silence in the apartment is unnerving. I search for a party playlist on my phone and crank up the volume to drive away the *lack* of ghosts.

When all is said and done, even I have to admit I've made a solid effort.

Dancing my way out of the bathroom, I'm determined to boogie away my blues and make the best of my night with Erick.

BING. BONG. BING.

"He's here!" The missing echo of Grams' ethereal voice casts a shadow over my positive vibes.

Pausing beside the alleyway door, I catch my breath and paste on a disarming smile. "Good evening, Sheriff. Won't you come in?"

His worn-in-all-the-right-places jeans and casual button-down shirt show an effort that deserves to be acknowledged. "You look nice. I like that shirt."

He smiles, but the expression doesn't reach his eyes. "Thanks. You look nice too."

Oh boy! This is turning into a terrible first-date facsimile. "Why don't you head upstairs. I'll grab plates and stuff."

"K."

There it is again. That single letter doing the job of an entire soliloquy of disappointment. Come on, Moon. You got this.

Adding a couple cans of pop to the tower, I carefully make my way to the wrought-iron staircase. As you might've predicted, one of the cans rolls off when

I attempt to climb over the "No Admittance" chain, and it bounces to the floor.

Embarrassment floods over me, and I snatch up the can and rush upstairs.

Of course, by the time I reach the apartment I'm not entirely sure which can is which.

Erick sets out the boxes from Myrtle's Diner, and, despite my happiness at the sight of the golden french fries, the thought of my grandmother releases a cascade of tears.

He halts the setup and takes a seat next to me, but offers no comfort. "What's wrong now?"

"I deserve that. You have every right to be tired of the drama in my life. In fact, you have every right to a *way* better girlfriend. Someone who—"

His lips are on mine before I can finish my sentence.

The surge of love and tenderness that flows from that simple kiss erases all my excuses and nightmares.

He scoops me closer and tightens his arms around me.

The passionate kiss touches my heart and releases a fresh flood of tears. He tips my head back and wipes my tears with his thumb. "Don't ever say anything that foolish again. Okay?"

I nod and sniffle.

"And I think it's only fair to warn you, I'm not leaving this apartment until you tell me exactly what is going on with you, your grandmother's ghost, and this gypsy."

Dabbing my nose with the back of my hand, I nod. "That's fair. Let me clean myself up, and I'll tell you everything you want to know."

He slowly slides his hand from my side as I stand.

Before I make it two steps from the settee, a husky voice pierces the silence behind me. "I love you."

And there it is. The three little words that change everything.

This is absolutely one of the tropes that all the Rom-Coms get right. Time stands still.

In this case, though, I'm not sure if it's because the quicksand is sucking me under or because little cherubs in diapers are bearing me aloft.

I have to say something. Too much time is passing, and with each additional second of silence the impact of my reply increases exponentially.

I'm halfway through my achingly slow turnaround when Erick slides his arms around my waist. "Hey, you don't have to say anything. I'm not one of those guys with an ego made out of papier-mâché."

I nod and struggle to pull a small amount of air into my constricted chest.

He brushes a strand of hair from the side of my face and smiles that crooked smile that melts my heart and turns my legs to jelly. "I know my timing isn't great. But with the life I've lived and the things I saw on the battlefield, I think it's important to say what I feel when I feel it."

For some reason, his use of the word "battlefield" makes me giggle. I bite my lip to force the inappropriate silliness back into hiding.

His eyes widen. "Quick update: my ego is also not made out of titanium."

I wave my hands in surrender. "I'm sorry. I'm not laughing at you directly. It's just how my stupid brain works. When you said 'on the battlefield,' it brought up images of Civil War love stories in the Deep South, and it made me giggle."

He hugs me tight and kisses the tip of my nose. "And that's one of your many irresistible traits."

My head is filled with possible replies and a montage of "shoulds," but if my goal is to err on the side of honesty, there's only one thing I can say. "I'm in a weird place right now. I have way too much on my mind and way too many variables in getting my grandmother back safely."

He listens, and slowly slides his hand down my arm until he grips my fingers. "Go grab some tissues, and then you can fill me in on the details that were too top-secret for the telephone."

Nodding, I ease my hand from his, step into the bathroom, and wipe the smeared mascara from under my eyes. Bringing the tissue box back to the settee is probably a good idea.

"Let's dig into our food before it gets cold. My story's not going to get any better or worse because of a ten-minute delay."

He laughs out loud. "Ten minutes? Are you slowing down on me, Moon?"

"Rude."

We dig into our burgers and fries, and a scant five minutes later I'm wiping my mouth and preparing to spin my yarn.

He reaches for a soda, and, as he wiggles his finger under the tab, my accident on the circular staircase flashes to mind. "Wait!"

Too late. He chose poorly.

Soda sprays out of the can and all over his shirt. To his credit, his reflexes are remarkable, and he gets his mouth over the opening and shotguns the entire soft drink before a single drop hits my floor or the chair.

"Dude! That was impressive. I don't even want to know where you got those skills."

His eyes are watering and he waves a hand toward me as he chokes out the word, "Napkin."

I grab a handful and press them into his outstretched fingers. He wipes his face, dabs at his eyes, and makes a paltry attempt to soak some of the fizzy corn syrup from his shirt.

"Here, give me that shirt and I'll rinse it out in the sink. I can turn the heater on in the bathroom, and it should dry quickly."

It's not until he stands up and starts unbuttoning his shirt that the full effect of my offer dawns on me. Holy six pack! Erick is going to be shirtless in my apartment—for quite some time! For a split second,

I'm almost grateful Grams isn't here to witness my serendipitous catastrophe.

He hands me the shirt, and his crooked grin is everything. "No rush."

My cheeks redden, and I hurry into the bathroom, shirt in hand, before I say anything I'll regret.

CHAPTER 20

I'M A GENUINE EXPERT at washing clothes in a bathroom sink. I shudder to think of the number of times I found myself without the requisite stacks of quarters required to use the sketchy pay-to-play laundry facilities in my rundown apartment.

Scrub, rinse, wring, shake out the wrinkles, and hang in front of the heater.

Closing the door behind me on my way out, I struggle to maintain my cool when I catch another glimpse of the shirtless sheriff. "It's not a very big room. It should heat up in there quick enough."

He walks toward me with the confidence of a jungle cat. "Like I said, no rush. Are you gonna tell me about this gypsy, or did you have something else planned?"

Oh brother! The way those jeans ride low on his hips . . . I'm not sure how much more weak in the knees I can get without collapsing onto the floor. "I'd like to— When we— You sit."

Erick chuckles, clearly enjoying the power his semi-nakedness wields over me. He settles onto the couch and pats the cushion next to him.

With great effort, I attempt to ignore the rush of tingles bouncing around my body like a marble in a pinball machine and give him the highlights of my meeting with Mrs. Nowak and her terms of release.

"Did you have any luck tracking down the kids?"

"I know their names. Not sure how much that will help me, because the clerk said she thought they had all moved away. But I have a starting point with the two sons."

"What were the sons' names?"

"The oldest was Rajmund and the youngest Tadjo."

A flicker of recognition flashes across Erick's face. "What's the oldest boy's middle name?"

I flick to the image of the birth certificate on my phone and zoom in. "The birth record says, Rajmund Osburn Nowak."

Erick leans back and rubs his thumb along his jawline.

I'm mesmerized by the rise and fall of his broad chest.

"Moon, my eyes are up here." He points to his devilish blue-grey peepers.

Giggling with embarrassment, I playfully push

him. The firm planes of his chest seem to trap my hand and I'm unable to withdraw.

He places his hand on top of mine and strokes his thumb along the back of my hand as he replies. "Have you considered the possibility that it's Ray Osborne at the hospital? He came into town about three years ago, if I remember correctly. No one seemed to know him, but he knew everything about the town. Isn't Nowak's husband named Osburn?"

There's no need to consult the images. As soon as Erick suggests the connection, my mood ring sizzles on my left hand. A casual glance reveals the face of Environmental Services manager Ray Osborne. I can instantly see the family resemblance. Now I'll have to cross my fingers and hope that he has a very poor memory for faces. Grams would know exactly what to wear to distract him from drawing any connection between the philanthropic Mizithra Moon and the temporary replacement janitor Darcy Brown.

Erick leans toward me and whispers hotly in my ear. "Where'd you go? How can I get you back?"

Oh, I'm back. I'm back and rapidly running out of oxygen. "Nothing. No one. I mean, I think I know Ray." I lean back and attempt a subtle gasp for air, and a quick subject change. "What are the odds he'd be open to a family reunion?"

"I've only had a couple conversations with him. We had to request 'no access' to a suspect's room last year and he coordinated with the cleaning crew. He seems like a decent guy. It can't hurt to ask."

"I'll take any slim chance of success I can get."

He smiles and looks deep into my eyes. "If we can get your grandmother back by Valentine's Day, will you promise to join me on the getaway?"

THUD. THUD. THUD. My heart feels as though it could beat straight out of my chest. "Um. Well . . ."

"It's a yes or no question, Moon." His smile is playful, but his eyes are pools of vulnerability.

"Yes. If Grams is back safe, then I'll feel better about taking off for the weekend."

He leans toward me and whispers a single word, "Deal." And then he seals that deal with a kiss.

As he slips his arms around me and the kiss continues, all I can picture is a high-stakes poker game where someone just pushed all their chips to the middle, and I have to either raise or fold.

I raise.

The time for all-night chat sessions or canoodling until the wee hours has passed. I'm going to take the risk.

I'm pushing in all my chips.

Leaning in to Erick's embrace, I allow my kiss to express my deepest feelings.

He leans back, and I follow, as though our hearts are bound together by an invisible thread. I feel the heat of his body through my sweater.

The sensation of cashmere slowly sliding upward fills me with anticipation.

CRASH!

In the blink of an eye, Erick is off the couch and pushing me protectively behind him. "Stay here." He reaches in the pocket of his coat and pulls out a small handgun.

Good to know. Even when he's sporting civilian clothes, my guy is still strapped up. And for those of you not addicted to real-crime TV, that means he's packing heat, or carrying a loaded weapon.

He presses the medallion by the secret door and waits for it to slide open, before slipping out and moving across the Rare Books Loft with the stealth of a—

"Don't shoot!" My extra senses deliver a shocking newsflash. "It's Pyewacket. It's only Pye! He must've accidentally knocked something over."

Erick flicks the safety on his gun and turns with a wry half grin. "Accidentally?"

I paint my features in a portrait of innocence and shrug. "What else could it be?"

He hooks his thumb in the waistband of his jeans and shakes his head. "I couldn't say, but I have my suspicions about that beast."

Pyewacket saunters across the mezzanine, and I swear that fiendish feline is wearing a smirk under his whiskers.

"Well, well, well. If it isn't Mr. Cuddlekins returning to subjugate yet another human."

Erick chuckles and puts his weapon back into the pocket of his coat.

I kneel and run my fingers along Pyewacket's spine. "Let's go see what mess you've made for me."

My half-naked boyfriend jogs into the bathroom and returns, buttoning up his shirt with a click of his tongue and a sigh that's more than mild disappointment. "I'll take the hint and head home for the night, Moon. But I think we made some real progress here."

He chuckles, and I blush beet red. "I'll let you know how things go with Ray tomorrow. Would it be all right if I drop your name, Sheriff?"

He zips his jacket, offers me a hand, and pulls me close for a goodnight kiss. "You can say anything you like as long as we get your grandmother home safe and sound."

It doesn't take a psychic to read the subtext of that message. "Copy that."

We walk hand-in-hand to the alleyway door, and I offer him one last kiss before he disappears into the frosty February night.

Flipping on the lights, I peruse the first floor in search of Pyewacket's intrusive message.

Sure enough, he's knocked a book from the shelves. I stoop and retrieve it. "*Navigating the Healthcare System*, eh?"

"Ree-ooow!" His back arches in an unfriendly pose.

"Thanks, Pye. I definitely have to navigate something tomorrow. I'm not sure what drove Ray and his mother apart, but hopefully it's something that begging and/or money can fix."

I drop to the floor and sit cross-legged.

Pyewacket crawls into my lap and pushes his black-tufted ears against me.

"I miss her too. I miss her so much, it feels like there's a hole in my heart. I'm not sure how much longer I can be patient."

He nods his head as if he agrees.

"If this angle with the long-lost kids doesn't work, I'm afraid I'm gonna have to go rogue."

"REE-ow!" The sound of imminent retribution.

"I agree. We definitely can't tell Silas about our Plan B."

CHAPTER 21

Without the guiding fashion wisdom of my grandmother, I'm left to my own devices in a confusing closet of couture.

In the end, I select a low-cut top, in the hopes that my cleavage will distract Mr. Osborne from taking notice of my face. Even though I take the easy way out by pairing it with skinny jeans, I force myself to choose a boot with a four-inch heel in honor of Grams.

"I'm off to save the day, Pyewacket. Are you going to wish me luck?"

He barely lifts his head from his perch amidst the depths of the down comforter. A soft growl is his only reply before he returns to kitty-cat dreamland.

Since today's visit is on the up and up, when I reach the Birch County Regional Medical Facility, I enter through the front door and head straight to reception.

"Good morning. Mitzy Moon with the Duncan-Moon Philanthropic Foundation, here to see Mr. Osborne."

Might as well throw the cash around right out of the gate.

The receptionist obviously recognizes the name and quickly picks up the phone to call Ray.

Smiling pleasantly, I glance around the waiting room and ask myself why so many hospitals think pale-green is an attractive color.

"Mr. Osborne said to send you right down. Do you need a map?"

"I'm sure I can find it. Just point me in the direction I need to go."

She places a map of the facility on the counter. "Reception is here, and Environmental Services is back here. If you head down that hallway—"

"Thank you so much." A little too sing-songy, but pretending I don't know where I'm going is already boring me to death. I strut down the corridor and rehearse my speech as I go.

Having lost my mother at such a young age, I would do anything to have her back. It's a little hard for me to understand what could drive a child away from a parent so completely. But I'm not here to pass judgment on Ray. I'm here to see if there is anything, in all of Christendom, I can do to bring him into the same room with his dying mother.

Fingers crossed. Accepting any and all help from the universe.

Before entering the Environmental Services manager's office, for the second time, I take a deep breath and paste on an enormous fake smile.

"Good morning, Mr. Osborne." The false jubilant tone rings hollow in my ears, but seems to do the trick with my mark.

Ray Osborne, a.k.a. Rajmund Osburn Nowak, looks away from his computer screen and barely manages a smile. "How can I help you, Miss Moon?"

I carefully drop into one of the dusty-rose vinyl-covered chairs in front of his desk and cross my arms under my bosom in hopes of enhancing my assets.

He continues to stare directly at my face—unblinkingly. He has zero interest in my wares.

Here goes nothing. "Mr. Osborne, I am actually not here on behalf of the foundation. However, if there is anything that we can do for your department, I hope you'll let me know. My visit this morning is of a personal nature."

His energy shifts immediately. My clairsentience picks up on a hint of fear with a side of irritation. "As I'm sure you can imagine, Miss Moon, running a medical facility this size requires my complete focus. I'm afraid I don't know you, and I'm certain we don't have any personal business to discuss."

Well, he asked for it. No more beating around the bush. "Mr. *Nowak*, I'm here to discuss your mother."

His eyes widen, and he pushes back from his desk. His arms cross over his chest and my clairaudience distinctly hears the word "run."

"I know you came back to town about three years ago with a new name and no intention of letting your parents know you'd returned. I'm not here to out you or cause you any personal problems. Your mother has something of mine, and her condition to return it to me is that I facilitate a meeting with her children."

Rather than reducing his defiant posture and uncooperative energy, my statement seems to cause his resistance to deepen.

"Ray . . . May I call you Ray?"

He does not respond.

"Your mother is dying. I have no idea what happened to you and your brother to cause such a rift between you and your parents—"

"Just her."

Interesting. "I'm sorry, between you and your mother, but I'm desperate to get back what she took from me."

His arms loosen slightly, and his jaw flinches. "Aren't they all."

"What do you mean?"

"You want to know what happened, growing up with that witch for a mother? I'll tell you. Every person in this town had something against us. Her quack potions or her spells gone wrong. My brother and I were the butt of endless Polack jokes at school, not to mention every possible form of witch hunt. I can't even begin to count the number of times there were dead animals or bowls of pig's blood in my locker."

A sick feeling twists in my gut. "I'm so sorry. Why dead animals?"

He leans forward and looks at me as though I'm an idiot. "Don't you know anything about witchcraft? People always think it's Satan worship and animal sacrifice. It's none of those things. My brother and I had no interest in the craft, and we certainly didn't have any interest in educating a backward population." The anger and vehemence in his words are as fresh as if the wounds were inflicted yesterday.

"Ray, I'm truly sorry. I know how cruel children can be. I grew up in the foster system, and there may not be as many Orphan Annie jokes as there are witch trials, but it was no picnic."

His energy softens, and his hands fall to his lap.

We're not friends, but at least there's a faint thread of connection. Nothing like childhood trauma to create a bond. "I'm going to go out on a limb and tell you the truth. Your mother stole my grandmother's ghost. My grandmother has been trapped on this side of the veil since she crossed over, and she and I have been building a posthumous relationship that we never had the opportunity to forge when she was alive. She's practically the most important thing in the world to me, and your mother took her, to force me—"

He exhales loudly and hangs his head. "Say no more. The truth is, I know all about her illness. It's the reason I came back. My father told me about episodes she'd been having and her refusal to get any treatment, because of the cost." He takes a deep breath and rubs a hand along his receding hairline. "I changed my name years ago, right after I left home. So it was easy to come back here with my résumé and pretend I had no connection to the community. I was overqualified for this job, and they gave it to me in a heartbeat. I set up a shell company to pay a portion of her medical bills without her knowing. I don't want a relationship with her, Miss Moon. But I also didn't want my father to have to watch her suffer or drown under a mountain of bills."

"Ray, I don't have anything to offer you beyond money, and you don't seem like the kind of guy who is open to bribery. But I need you to call your brother and promise me that you'll meet with her. I have to get my grandmother back. Please, please help me."

The tense muscles along his jaw relax and the lines around his eyes fade as I feel his energy shift toward cooperation. "My brother is a tough nut to crack."

"I'm happy to call him with you right now. Maybe if he understands how desperate I am, he'll take the chance."

Ray chews his bottom lip and shakes his head. "I don't know. He chose a lifestyle she wouldn't approve of."

"What do you mean?"

He rubs his hands together and rests them on his desk. "I'm not sure if it's my place to say." There's an uncomfortable pause and his eyes dart left and right.

"He's in the theater. She wanted him to be a lawyer. Said he always had the smarts for it, and he got top marks. Probably could've gotten a scholarship anywhere. But the second he graduated, he loaded everything in a car and headed for New York. He eked out a living on the boards for years, before he found his path as a director."

For the first time since I walked through the door, a tinge of happiness filters through Ray's aura.

"He's doing all right for himself."

Leaning forward, I take a chance and place my hand on top of Ray's. "My grandmother means everything to me. Will you please call him?"

He pulls out his cell phone, taps a number on his speed dial, and places it on speaker. "Tadjo, do you have a minute?"

"Always for you, big brother."

Ray looks at me and shrugs. "Full disclosure, I'm here on speakerphone and there's a woman in my office named Mitzy Moon."

Tadjo's light laughter filters through the phone. "Are you finally going to tie the knot, bro?"

Ray shakes his head and chuckles. "Confirmed bachelor. One divorce is enough for me. She's actually—" Ray looks at me helplessly.

"Hi Tadjo. I'm gonna jump into this headfirst and I hope you'll forgive me later. I've been living with the ghost of my grandmother for more than a year. A couple of days ago your mother ghost-napped my grandma, and as ransom she's demanding a meeting with you and your brother."

Bitter laughter, followed by whooping and hollering, surprises me. "Some things never change, eh, Ray? Look, miss, I left that town thirty years ago, and I've never looked back. What makes you think I'd drag myself back there for some woman I've never met with a story as ludicrous as yours?"

Two things I know about Broadway: it's very expensive to put on a show; and you're only as good as your last review. Advantage Moon. "I tell you what, Tadjo, you come back here and do me this favor, and I'll make sure your next production is fully funded before the script is finished."

Silence.

My extrasensory perception picks up on the fact that it's an awestruck moment of quiet, rather than non-responsiveness. "I must've failed to mention, my grandmother was Isadora Duncan."

Tadjo gasps. "My, my, my! So that funding promise is no joke?"

"I don't joke about money, Mr. Nowak."

Ray and I exchange a glance and sit in silence, waiting for Tadjo's reply.

"As it happens, I'm in between shows right now. I can be on a plane this afternoon. But I'm booking my return flight for tomorrow. Set up the meeting for tonight, and be sure to let Ania know this is a one-time thing, and I have no plans to stay in town."

"Acceptable terms. I'll set up the meeting for

7:00 p.m." I glance at Ray and raise my eyebrows questioningly.

"Works for me. I'll pick you up at the airport, Tadjo. Text me when your plane lands."

The Broadway director clears his throat and sings his next line. "Hold on to your cherries kids, Broadway's coming to town."

Visions of "jazz hands" dance in my head.

CHAPTER 22

THE MEETING IS SET. Ray and Tadjo are going to meet us in the parking lot outside the emporium. Silas is coming with me in case Grams needs some type of alchemical triage after we make the exchange.

The day's half-frozen sleet left a coating of treacherous ice on the roads. Even if the roads were clear, I think I'd still be driving slowly. The weight of the handgun tucked in my jeans and pressing against my spine has me on edge.

Don't worry, I'm not planning to kill anyone. But I promised Pyewacket I'd have a Plan B, and if this gypsy doesn't hold up her end of the bargain, I will do whatever it takes to get my grandmother back.

Despite my slow rate of travel, we're the first to arrive. I leave the engine running to keep warm as long as possible.

"I shall require you to pass me the gun, at once."

"How did you— I mean, what gun?"

Silas ignores my attempt at a cover-up and calmly holds his open palm in front of me.

Exhaling in frustration, I lean forward and slide the gun out of my waistband. "Here. But don't blame me if things go sideways in there and we're left without a back-up plan."

He chuckles to himself as he checks the gun's safety catch and places the firearm in the glove box.

"What do we do if she reneges on the deal?"

"Are you concerned the boys were engaged in subterfuge? Do you feel they will not arrive?"

"No. I got the feeling they were legit. I just don't think it's going to be some sappy holiday-movie reunion. Neither of them wants anything to do with their mother. If she's expecting an otherworldly mending of hearts, I'm worried she'll be disappointed."

Silas smooths his mustache and nods. "And you fear this disappointment will lead to further blackmail?"

"Exactly. The gun was my insurance policy. Shoot some stuff up, cause a distraction, and grab the amulet."

"The situation is not like one of your movies, Mizithra. Shooting things up to cause a distraction could end badly. Far worse than you imagine. If Mrs. Nowak does not honor our bargain, I am prepared to take extreme measures."

An odd chill ripples from the top of my skull,

across my shoulders. I'm not sure I want to find out what it's like to disappoint Mr. Willoughby in such important matters. "Copy that."

Another vehicle pulls into the parking lot and two men step out.

Silas and I exit the Jeep and walk toward them.

Waving hesitantly at Ray, I'm both shocked and pleased when I take in all that is Tadjo. He's everything I'd imagined. Sophistication ensconced in a luxuriously long scarf, his head tucked snugly into a slouchy beanie, and his designer coat screaming New York. In a word—fabulous! I offer my hand. "I'm Mitzy Moon."

He grips my outstretched hand, and the buttery leather of his kidskin gloves caresses my fingers. "Well, aren't you a dream! I can't promise you this tête-à-tête is going to give you the results you want, darling, but I'm here to give the performance of a lifetime." He drops my hand and flourishes his arm as he strikes a pose.

Perhaps Ray's statement about Tadjo being "in theater" was a code phrase for his brother's obviously flamboyant lifestyle. No judgment. But there could be more at play between the younger brother and the matriarch than a failure to attend law school.

Silas and I enter the emporium first. When I see Mrs. Nowak in an old chair with a hand-knitted afghan covering her legs, I almost fall prey to her deception.

Silas whispers softly in my right ear. "Perhaps

Tadjo is not the only one giving the performance of a lifetime."

I bite my tongue sharply to prevent an outburst of laughter, but Silas is not wrong.

"Mrs. Nowak, your sons have agreed to meet with you as a one-time-only favor to me. Now, I'd like to collect my grandmother and leave."

A flash of amber in her lap catches the light. "Not so fast, girly. Where are my boys?"

Turning to take in the empty space behind me, I hustle back to the door and motion for them to come in. Neither of them is in any hurry.

The moment they enter, she gasps and clutches her chest. Tears spring to her eyes as she stares wordlessly at her sons.

Tadjo is the first to find his voice. "Good evening, mother. I'm catching a plane home tomorrow, so you should know that whatever nonsense you have planned with this one-woman show, it won't be getting an encore." He swishes his scarf over his shoulder and places his hands on his hips defiantly.

Ray is less dramatic and more direct. "The only reason we're here, Mrs. Nowak, is to prevent you from ruining yet another life. You don't get to control us anymore, and this is not a reconciliation. You stole something from Miss Moon. We're here to see that you give it back. That is all."

Her tears vanish, and the invalid's throw falls to the shabby carpet as she gets to her feet. "Thankless children. After everything I did for you."

Oh dear! This is headed south rapidly.

A voice drifts through the ether. "I hope you and Silas have an exit strategy, dear. She's been lining up spells all day to try and trap her sons here and bind them to her somehow. You've got to get that book away from her! She's a dangerous woman, with horrible plans."

Understood, Grams.

I whisper the SparkNotes version to Silas and feel power swirl around him.

He steps forward. "Mrs. Nowak, we will be taking the amulet and *Loca Sine Lumine, Loca Sine Lege*. Delving into powers not meant for you is what has led to your severe illness—"

Tadjo pushes past Silas and strides closer to his mother. "Illness? No one said anything about an illness. Are you dying? Has your obsession with dark magicks finally robbed you of your life?"

His words are grandiose, but my heart feels the pain of a young son who may lose his mother far sooner than he imagined.

Ray slips past me, places a hand on his brother's arm, and attempts to pull him toward the exit. "Come on, T. The illness was bound to happen someday."

Tadjo shakes his brother's hand off his arm and stands toe to toe with his mother. "All these years, trying to wield power you had no business with, and now this? You've taken this poor girl's grandmother?" He weeps openly.

My extra senses confirm that his performance is

only ten percent authentic. She reaches for him, and he steps back in horror. "You can't rebuild a relationship with your own family by destroying someone else's." He turns with a flourish and crosses his arms.

"Mitzy, can you hear me?"

Quick thought message to Grams. *Loud and clear.*

"The book is behind the counter. There's a secret panel in the kick plate, near the register."

I send a mental picture of the book to Silas, and he nods once.

Stepping behind the counter, I drop to all fours and let my psychic senses guide me to the panel.

"What is happening? Where did she go?" The concern and panic in the gypsy's voice are not an act.

Silas replies without hesitation. "You made a bargain. And we are here to collect."

My fingers tingle and I press the panel. It pops open and I grab the book. "Got it!"

As my head surfaces above the counter, several things happen simultaneously.

Silas reaches his hand forward, and the amulet struggles to answer the call.

The gypsy holds the chain and fights the commanding force of my mentor.

Tadjo steps between his mother and the alchemist, and yanks the amulet from his mother's hands. He drops it into Silas's outstretched palm. "This is your last chance, mother. Let these people leave in peace, or you will never see me again. You will die alone and unloved. No less than you deserve."

I hustle toward the door, and Silas turns to join me.

Ray nods to us, and I mouth a "thank you" in his direction.

Energy snaps and crackles inside the emporium, and I glance over my shoulder in time to see the wooden table with the display of tarot cards explode into pieces.

Rajmund shields his brother from the debris, and Mrs. Nowak sobs as her sons turn to leave.

Silas grips my elbow and moves me purposefully across the icy parking lot. The slick surface seems to melt beneath our feet, and I wonder what transmutation creates this safe passage.

Risking one more glance as we exit the parking lot, I note the boys are still inside. Perhaps they will find a way to call a truce with their mother, but, in all honesty, I don't care.

I got my grandmother back, and, right now, nothing else in the world matters.

Well, possibly one thing . . .

Successful grandmother recovery = Valentine's overnight getaway with Erick.

Gulp!

CHAPTER 23

Silas promises to return first thing in the morning and use his wealth of arcane knowledge to release Grams from the amulet and put everything right in our world.

Meanwhile, I have a phone call to make. Laying the amulet on the four-poster bed next to Pye, I promise to return as soon as I update Erick.

"Be careful with Ghost-ma while I'm gone, Pyewacket." Addressing the amulet, I add, "I'll be back in a flash."

Out to the mezzanine, with a thin veil of privacy, I blurt out my exciting news the second Erick answers the phone.

A soft groan wasn't the response I was expecting.

"What's wrong? I thought that was our deal? I get Grams back and off we go."

He explains how the fates have sabotaged our Valentine's getaway. His mother slipped on a dangerous patch of ice in the driveway, returning from the mailbox, and broke her wrist. He's currently in the emergency room and will be spending his Valentine's weekend playing nursemaid to his injured mother.

I have to chuckle. Not about his mother's injury, but definitely in regard to my love life. "It really wasn't meant to be. You take care of your mom, and I'll try to bring Isadora up to speed on everything she missed. We'll have another opportunity for a getaway." My tummy tingles and my heart pitter-patters, when he promises to make good on our "deal."

"All right, Grams, I'm all yours."

"No Valentine's plans with your yummy sheriff?"

"Um, no, and I'm not sure I like you referring to him as yummy." I scoop the pendant from the bed, carry it into the closet, and hang Grams on a hook. Over the next several hours, I take her through a wardrobe recap of everything she missed.

My attempt to skip over the details of my evening with Erick, and the cashmere boyfriend sweater, fails miserably. I'm forced to tell her every sordid detail about the splattered soda and the shirtless sheriff.

When the thin grey light of morning interrupts my update, my body finally admits defeat. "Grams, I've gotta catch a little shuteye. Where would you like me to leave you?"

"Just leave me in here, dear. Next to you, these are the things I love the most."

After an intense three-hour power nap, the voice of Silas Willoughby crackles over the intercom.

"Good morning, Mizithra. I hope you are decent. I must speak with you."

Sleep deprived and more than a little punchy, I roll out of bed with a case of the giggles. "Did you hear that, Grams?"

She adds her tinkling laughter to mine. "That man could make a dessert menu sound like an end-of-days catastrophe!"

Searching the floor, I find my robe and make my-self *decent*.

The bookcase door slides open, and my regular and extra senses take a simultaneous shot to the gut. "What's wrong? It's bad, isn't it?"

He shuffles toward the scalloped-back chair, and his jowls seem to sag more than normal. Silas col-lapses into the chair and adjusts his tattered tweed coat. His entire being emanates defeat.

"Silas? What's going on?"

"Mitzy! Don't leave me hanging." Ghost-ma calls from the closet.

Grams and I burst out laughing at her clever pun.

Silas moans and shakes his head. While he fishes something out of his fusty old coat, I step into the closet and retrieve my grandma-in-a-stone.

Placing the pendant on the coffee table, I take a seat. "Are you ready to break her out of this amber prison?"

Silas moans a second time, and this one sounds like a wounded animal.

"He needs to get over himself, Mitzy. If he has bad news, tell him to spill it."

Taking a quick stint as an afterlife interpreter, I share her message.

The weary alchemist smooths his mustache and draws a slow breath. "I have delved into every tome I possess on the topic. I fear we find ourselves in the very worst of a Catch 22."

"How's that now?"

"When the gypsy trapped your grandmother in the amulet, she wielded powers beyond her understanding. She successfully severed the tie that bound Isadora to this bookshop. Hence the ability to trap her ghost in the stone and remove her from the property."

Grams snickers. "Tell us something we don't know."

I chew the inside of my cheek and stifle any bubbling silliness. "All right. That seems obvious. What about the spe— transmutation, to release Ghost-ma from this stupid necklace?"

He clicks his tongue and exhales. "And that is where we reach the impasse. I have already been to the emporium this morning. On that front, I do have a bit of good news. Tadjo canceled his return flight to New York and has chosen to stay with his mother during her last days. Your efforts were not wasted. Healing has begun."

"That's good, right?"

"Indeed. Mrs. Nowak was in a fine mood, and allowed me to persuade her to give me a peek at her mother's grimoire. Sadly, the notes provided no solution of which I was not already aware."

Smiling hopefully, I lean toward my mentor. "Solution seems like a positive word."

"Forgive me. I misspoke. Possible solution. The issue I cannot solve is the one that cuts the deepest. I have found at least three possible ways to release Isadora's ghost from imprisonment. The issue—"

"That's great!" Grams and I shout in unison.

"The issue becomes the event that transpires immediately following the release."

"What's he talking about? Ask him what he's talking about, dear."

"She wants to know what you mean?"

A dark cloud seems to pass over him and his gaze drops to the floor. "The tether we implanted before her death has been broken. If I release Isadora from the amulet, I have uncovered no way to keep her from crossing over."

A dreadful silence floods the apartment.

Staring at the pendant as though it's a coiled rattlesnake ready to strike, I've never felt more helpless. "So what do we do? How do we get her out of *there* but keep her in *here*?"

Silas shakes his head and wipes a small tear from the wrinkled corner of his eye. "We cannot. If you choose to release her, we will lose her forever. For now, we must keep her in the amber while I continue my research. There are a few trusted souls I may contact for help, but you and your grandmother must face the truth. She may never be free to roam this bookstore again."

Grams started crying several sentences ago, but I caged my emotions in hopes that there would be a happy ending to his story. Now my tears flow freely, and Pyewacket hurries over to comfort me.

"I don't want to lose you, Grams. It's not fair for me to make the decision, though. Staying, just to be trapped in that stupid necklace—it's too much to ask. What do you want?"

She's sobbing and sniffling, and I can picture the sparkling tears streaming down her ethereal face. "Of course I choose to stay with you, sweetie. I'd rather be trapped in a piece of amber than on the other side of the veil without you. Have faith. Silas will find a way. For now, nothing has changed. We can still talk, and laugh, and I can tell you what to wear."

Smiling through my tears, I share her decision with Silas.

"Very well. I must return home and rest. I was at the books all night. I will not give up the search, but I shall not make empty promises. If at any point you change your mind, Isadora, I will be here to release you."

I pass along her thanks, and Silas takes his leave.

My grumbling stomach echoes in the silence. "I need to grab some breakfast at the diner. I'll be back before you know it." I stumble toward the closet to grab jeans and a sweater.

"Take me with you!"

"Isadora, you know you're tethered—" Wait! She's not tethered. She's free as a bird. As long as her ghost is trapped in that amulet, she can go anywhere she likes. I mean, I can take her anywhere she likes.

"I can't wait to see Odell!"

"Look, just because your circumstances have changed, doesn't mean our rules have. No thought-dropping!" My attempt at a stern warning fails miserably as my excitement builds.

She giggles when I secure the pendant's chain around my neck.

The warmth of the diner is more welcoming today than it has ever been. I stomp the dirty slush off my shoes and walk across the black-and-white checkered floor with a spring in my step.

Tally places a cup of coffee on the table and winks. The diner is bustling, and she doesn't have time for chitchat.

"My goodness, that woman looks younger now than last time I saw her. Hard work does a body good."

I bite my lower lip to prevent myself from blurting my reply out loud. *Easy, Grams. I don't want to mess up in public. All right?*

"10-4. And I'm saluting. Since you can't see me, I thought I'd give you the play-by-play."

Please, spare me.

Odell approaches the table, and his eyes immediately fall on the pendant. "That's a beautiful necklace, Mitzy. Seems like it sparkles from the inside."

I can hear Grams crying softly and force myself to ignore it. "Thanks. It's really special. Glad you like it. Maybe I'll wear it more often."

He pushes my breakfast toward me, raps his knuckles twice on the table, and returns to the kitchen.

"Oh Mitzy, I miss him terribly."

Her passion for her first husband reminds me of the pilfered medical files. Fast as lightning, I force myself to think of anything else. Stellen and Yolo enjoying their Valentine's dinner. Pyewacket pushing a book off the shelf.

"What's going on? What medical records?"

My guilt flashes like a neon sign in my consciousness, and she easily reads the message. The inappropriate review of her private medical records is now public knowledge—at least between the two of us. *I'm sorry. I wanted to tell you. I mean, I didn't plan to tell you right now, over breakfast, but I was going to tell you. I'm sorry that I invaded your privacy. I'm also really sorry about the baby you lost. That must've been hard for you and Odell. You love my dad so much, and you're a wonderful mother—but you're an even better grandmother. Can you forgive me?*

Sniffling is interrupted by a ragged sigh. "It was all too much for me. The fights between Odell and Cal, losing the baby. I had to run away. Then I made a lot of bad choices with my second husband. I loved Max, in my own way, but I never got over Odell. Don't get me wrong, my years with Cal and raising your father are still some of the happiest memories I have, but Odell was my first love. True love never leaves you. Do you know what I mean?"

The door opens and a gust of brisk air blows in a handsome sheriff in civilian clothes.

Tally walks toward him with a perfectly packaged to-go order.

He hands her some cash and catches sight of me just in time. Striding to my booth, he leans down, and, right as he's about to kiss me, the amulet stops him in his tracks. "Is that your grandmother?" he whispers.

"Shhhh. I'm having enough trouble keeping her in line. I don't need you jumping on her bandwagon."

"Kiss him, Mitzy. Be in the moment! Don't miss an opportunity like this."

Not sure whether my actions are under my own control, I lean forward and firmly kiss Erick Harper's pouty mouth. "I'm sorry we had to cancel our plans. I hope your mother's feeling better. You'll give her my best, won't you?"

His warm smile sends a flash of heat through my body. "I will." The next kiss lingers longer than appropriate in public, and I sense a distraction. When he finally pulls away, there's a mischievous grin on his face, and he winks as he turns to leave.

Don't get me wrong, I could watch this man walk

away all day long. However, as the door closes behind him and my attention returns to the table, I'm greeted by the charming homemade Valentine that he slipped under the edge of my plate while his luscious lips distracted me.

Grams is crying again. "He's the sweetest man! What is it they say? Lock that down? You need to lock that down, Mitzy."

I chuckle into my napkin and beg her to be quiet while I read the card's sentiment:

> Dear Mitzy,
>
> Fate only counts if you let it. You and I are destined to be.
>
> No rush. No worries. Our future is forever.
>
> Love, Erick.

Grams gasps, and I can picture her clutching her pearls.

It might not be a typical Valentine's Day, but it's definitely the best one I've ever had.

End of Book 12

A NOTE FROM TRIXIE

Should we get Stellen and Yolo their own series? Another case solved! I'll keep writing them if you keep reading . . .

The best part of "living" in Pin Cherry Harbor continues to be feedback from my early readers. Thank you to my alpha readers/cheerleaders, Angel and Michael. HUGE thanks to my fantastic beta readers who continue to give me extremely useful and honest feedback: Veronica McIntyre and Nadine Peterse-Vrijhof. And big "small town" hugs to the world's best ARC Team – Trixie's Mystery ARC Detectives!

All hail my long-suffering editor, Philip Newey. Thank you for continuing to help me understand the power of the comma. I'd also like to give mad props to Brooke for her tireless proofreading! Any errors are my own, as my outdated version of Word insists on showing me only what it likes and when it feels so moved.

Shout out to H. Claire Taylor for an intense story session that helped me refine this adventure and flesh out new characters.

FUN FACT: Once upon a time, I worked as a custodian in a high-rise office building!

My favorite quote from this case: "I wish I could tell you that I was able to stop myself from rolling my eyes, but I can't." ~ Mitzy

I'm currently writing book fourteen in the Mitzy Moon Mysteries series, and I think I may just live in Pin Cherry Harbor forever. Mitzy, Grams, and Pyewacket got into plenty of trouble in book one, *Fries and Alibis*. But I'd have to say that book three, *Wings and Broken Things*, is when most readers say the series becomes unputdownable.

I hope you'll continue to hang out with us.

Trixie Silvertale (February 2021)

SPECIAL INVITATION . . .

Come visit Pin Cherry Harbor!

Get access to the Exclusive Mitzy Moon Mysteries character quiz – free!

Find out which character you are in Pin Cherry Harbor and see if you have what it takes to be part of Mitzy's gang.

This quiz is only available to members of the Paranormal Cozy Club, Trixie Silvertale's reader group.

Click the link below to join the club and get access to the quiz:

Click here: Join Trixie's Club

Once you're in the Club, you'll also be the first to receive

updates from Pin Cherry Harbor and access to giveaways, new release announcements, behind-the-scenes secrets, and much more!

Scan this QR Code with the camera on your phone. You'll be taken right to the page to join the Club!

DAMES AND DEADLY GAMES

Mitzy Moon Mysteries 13

A murder mystery game. A terminal twist. Can this psychic sleuth swap coal for clues?

Mitzy Moon hopes to earn some girlfriend points on a scenic weekend get-away. Steaming off on a historic train with her handsome beau seems like the perfect way to outrun fate. But their 1920s-themed sleuthing party abruptly derails when they discover an actual corpse . . .

Now they're on the wrong side of the tracks, and

Mitzy and her sheriff will have to solve the case before the guilty party disappears at the next depot. With a list of suspects as long as the cast of characters, she'll need to push her powers to the boiling point before more tickets get lethally punched.

Will Mitzy's dangerous excursion end with an arrest, or will the killer claim another life?

Dames and Deadly Games is the thirteenth book in the hilarious paranormal cozy mystery series, Mitzy Moon Mysteries. If you like snarky heroines, supernatural misfits, and a dash of romance, then you'll love Trixie Silvertale's iron horse escapade.

Buy *Dames and Deadly Games* to blow the whistle on a murderer today!

Grab yours here!
readerlinks.com/l/1671623

Scan this QR Code with the camera on your phone. You'll be taken right to the Mitzy Moon Mysteries series page. You can easily grab any mysteries you've missed!

THANK YOU!

Trying out a new book is always a risk and I'm thankful that you rolled the dice with Mitzy Moon. If you loved the book, the sweetest thing you can do (*even sweeter than pin cherry pie à la mode*) is to leave a review so that other readers will take a chance on Mitzy and the gang.

Don't feel you have to write a book report. A brief comment like, "Can't wait to read the next book in this series!" will help potential readers make their choice.

Thank you kindly, and I'll see you in Pin Cherry Harbor!

EXCLUSIVE - SILAS WILLOUGHBY INTERVIEW

"Today we're talking to Silas Willoughby, local attorney, self-taught alchemist, and longtime resident of Pin Cherry Harbor. Welcome and thank you for joining us, Mr. Willoughby. Let's start things off with a simple question. How long have you lived in Pin Cherry Harbor?"

"Well, that's not a terribly simple question." He smooths his mustache with a thumb and forefinger. "I should say it's longer than most but not as long as others."

"Okay, thank you, Mr. Willoughby. It's my understanding that you held the position of a tenured professor at our regional law school and you were actually one of Amaryllis Peterson's professors. I have two questions about that. First, was Amaryllis a good student?"

He harrumphs, uncrosses his legs, and re-crosses them in the opposite direction. "As a professor of law,

I am required to evaluate students' knowledge on a particular subject. I am not the embodiment of St. Nicholas making a list of who's been naughty or nice. If your inquiry is regarding Ms. Peterson's knowledge of the law, I can assure you it was extensive."

The interviewer chuckles. "Boy, you don't plan on making this easy for me, do you, Mr. Willoughby?"

"I fail to understand your question."

"Fair play to you, sir. Did you enjoy your years as a professor?"

His gaze intensifies. "Must one choose a profession for its joy? Or is contributing to the proper education of the next generation of barristers not noble enough?"

"Thank you for clarifying." The interviewer gazes thoughtfully at the wizened man and smiles briefly. "Can you tell me how Pyewacket came to be both Isadora's pet and feature prominently on the intricate carvings displayed on the front door of the Bell, Book & Candle?"

Mr. Willoughby sighs and pulls out his pipe. "The story of Robin Pyewacket Goodfellow is not mine to tell. However, the door I discovered in San Miguel de Allende. The delicate hand of the carver is a mystery I choose not to question." A hint of a grin blossoms beneath his bushy grey mustache and he slips his unlit pipe into the corner of his mouth with a bite of finality.

The interviewer takes a deep breath, scans her

notes, and skips ahead several questions. "Let's jump right into your study of the arcane. Were you always interested in magic— Pardon me, alchemy?"

He exhales loudly, interlaces his fingers, and rests them on his round belly. "I suffered a great loss in my life at a young and impressionable age. I believed the knowledge of the ages could provide me with the means to protect those closest to me in the future."

Leaning forward, the interviewer nods encouragingly. "And have you done so for her?"

His thick eyebrows lift. "To whom do you refer?"

"Well, let's start with Isadora. Did you protect her?"

Mr. Willoughby harrumphs and fidgets in his seat. "You cut me to the quick. While I assisted Isadora in her last wish, I feel I could have prolonged her life if I had refused her."

"But she seems happy with her current arrangement. She's getting to know her granddaughter and her ghostly existence seems to agree with her. Would you not agree?"

His rheumy blue eyes gaze at me. And it feels as though he's peering into the depths of my mind. "Are you some type of witch or alchemist yourself? Where did you learn of these things?"

"I'm an avid reader, Mr. Willoughby."

A brief grin graces his heavily jowled face. Apparently, the vague specificity of my answer pleases him. "Fair play to you, madame."

Taking a deep breath and regrouping, I consult

my list of questions and place them to the side. "Tell me about mentoring Mitzy Moon."

He steeples his fingers and bounces his chin on the tip of his pointers for nearly a minute before he responds. "I must admit, on our first meeting, I had little faith in her ability. However, after working beside her and offering guidance for these few years, I see great potential within her. She is a conundrum. Miss Moon is gifted beyond measure, but lacks focus. She shows the magnanimity of her forebears, but suffers from youthful impulsivity. In truth, I believe she would lie down her life for those she holds dear. An admirable but dangerous trait." He tugs at his worn tweed coat and shakes his jowly face back and forth.

"Dangerous? How?"

Mr. Willoughby harrumphs and exhales loudly. "She is of more use to those who love her on this side of the veil. Miss Moon is too eager for danger and too naïve for death. I trust my guidance and the gentle hands of time will tame her wild spirit."

"I'm afraid I have to disagree, Mr. Willoughby. I think an untamed Mitzy is exactly what almost-Canada needs."

His unexpected guffaws lighten the mood. "Perhaps you are correct, but her impertinence is imprudent."

"I might not know the young Miss Moon as well as you, sir, but her impertinence has saved the day on more than one occasion."

"Indeed. And I remain certain it shall do so many

more times in the future." A proud smile lifts his round cheeks.

"Is there anything I haven't asked that you would like to share?"

"I think not. The world is to be explored, examined, experienced. There are many paths to that end. And for those who read their way through universes to discover the truths that soothe their soul, my hat is off to them."

"An excellent sign off, Mr. Willoughby. Thank you for joining us today."

Pin Cherry Harbor Animal Hospital
Birch County Regional Medical Facility
3rd
Sheriff's Station
2nd
MYRTLE'S
MAIN STREET
Myrtle's Diner
GUNNISON AVENUE
Angelo & Vinci's Ristorante
1st
Bell, Book & Candle
Marina
Hawk Island Casino

gly Wiggly
WIGGLY
Pin Cherry Harbor High School
City Hall
3rd
3rd
Train Depot
TRAIN
ux
PATISSERIE
Pin Cherry Harbor Library
2nd
1st
Final Destination
n Restorative Justice
Pin Cherry Harbor
est. 1894
Chez Osprey
Lighthouse
REN

ALSO BY TRIXIE SILVERTALE

MITZY MOON MYSTERIES

Fries and Alibis: Paranormal Cozy Mystery

Tattoos and Clues: Paranormal Cozy Mystery

Wings and Broken Things: Paranormal Cozy Mystery

Sparks and Landmarks: Paranormal Cozy Mystery

Charms and Firearms: Paranormal Cozy Mystery

Bars and Boxcars: Paranormal Cozy Mystery

Swords and Fallen Lords: Paranormal Cozy Mystery

Wakes and High Stakes: Paranormal Cozy Mystery

Tracks and Flashbacks: Paranormal Cozy Mystery

Lies and Pumpkin Pies: Paranormal Cozy Mystery

Hopes and Slippery Slopes: Paranormal Cozy Mystery

Hearts and Dark Arts: Paranormal Cozy Mystery

Dames and Deadly Games: Paranormal Cozy Mystery

Castaways and Longer Days: Paranormal Cozy Mystery

Schemes and Bad Dreams: Paranormal Cozy Mystery

Carols and Yule Perils: Paranormal Cozy Mystery

Dangers and Empty Mangers: Paranormal Cozy Mystery

More to come!

ABOUT THE AUTHOR

Trixie Silvertale grew up reading an endless supply of Lilian Jackson Braun, Hardy Boys, and Nancy Drew novels. She loves the amateur sleuths in cozy mysteries and obsesses about all things paranormal. Those two passions unite in her Mitzy Moon Mysteries, and she's thrilled to write them and share them with you.

When she's not consumed by writing, she bakes to fuel her creative engine and pulls weeds in her herb garden to clear her head (*and sometimes she pulls out her hair, but mostly weeds*).

Greetings are welcome:
trixie@trixiesilvertale.com

BB bookbub.com/authors/trixie-silvertale

facebook.com/TrixieSilvertale

instagram.com/trixiesilvertale

Printed in Great Britain
by Amazon

26911145R00416